image comics presents

CHEW

created by John Layman & Rob Guillory

BAD APPLES

written & lettered by
John Layman

drawn & colored by
Rob Guillory

Color Assists by Taylor Wells

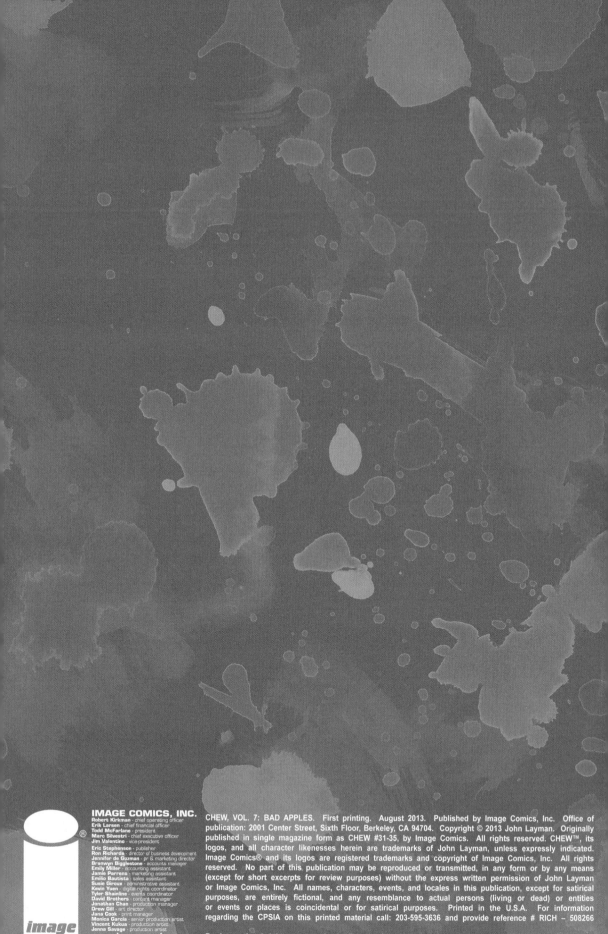

IMAGE COMICS, INC.

Robert Kirkman - chief operating officer
Erik Larsen - chief financial officer
Todd McFarlane - president
Marc Silvestri - chief executive officer
Jim Valentino - vice-president

Eric Stephenson - publisher
Ron Richards - director of business development
Jennifer de Guzman - pr & marketing director
Branwyn Bigglestone - accounts manager
Emily Miller - accounting assistant
Jamie Parreno - marketing assistant
Emilio Bautista - sales assistant
Susie Giroux - administrative assistant
Kevin Yuen - digital rights coordinator
Tyler Shainline - events coordinator
David Brothers - content manager
Jonathan Chan - production manager
Drew Gill - art director
Jana Cook - print manager
Monica Garcia - senior production artist
Vincent Kukua - production artist
Jenna Savage - production artist

www.imagecomics.com

ISBN: 978-1-60706-767-2

Dedications:

JOHN: *To James, James & James*

ROB: *For C.B. Cebulski, who found me amid a sea of MySpace bathroom selfies.*

Thanks:

Taylor Wells, for the coloring assists.
Tom B. Long, for the logo.
Comicbookfonts.com, for the fonts.

And More Thanks:

Rich Amtower, Dan Burgos, Charlie Chu, Brandon Jerwa, Robert Kirkman, Adam Levine, Mike Norton, Allen Passalaqua, Kathryn & Israel Skelton, Fiona Staples, Josh-Josh Williamson, Brian K. Vaughan and Maki Yamane. Plus: The Image gang of Drew, Jennifer, Jonathan, Branwyn, Ron, Tyler and eric. And Kim Peterson and April Hanks.

Chapter 1

ROB!

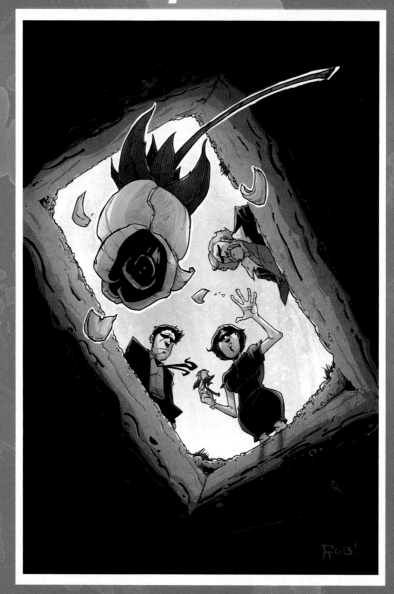

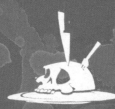

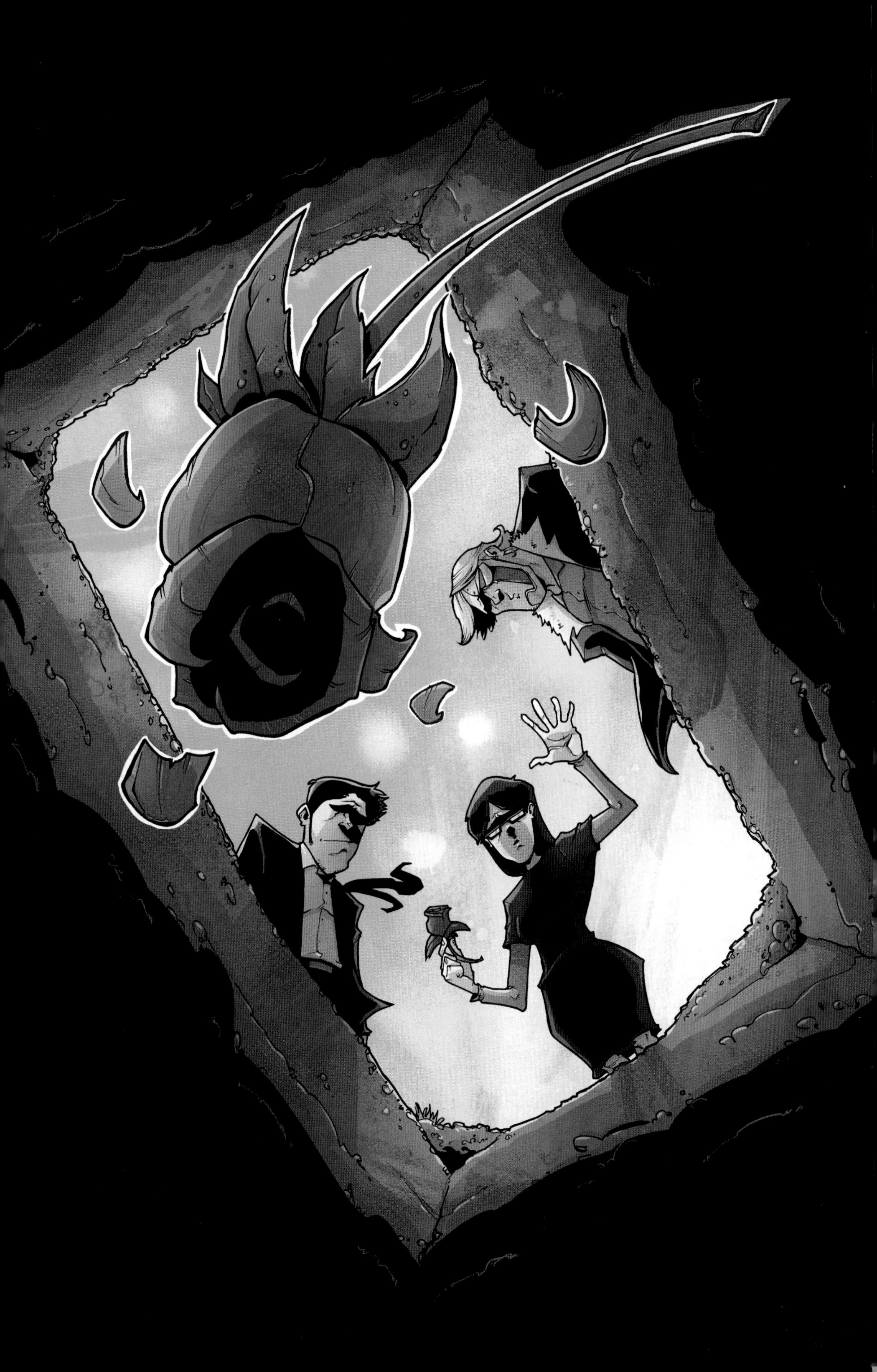

CATCH HIM, TONY. CATCH HIM, THEN FUCKING *KILL* HIM.

SISTER ROSEMARY.

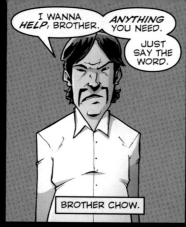

I WANNA *HELP*, BROTHER. *ANYTHING* YOU NEED. JUST SAY THE WORD.

BROTHER CHOW.

FUCK HIM UP *FIRST*, TONY. KILL HIM *SLOW*.

SISTER SAGE.

DO YOUR *JOB*, ANTHONY. MAKE THAT SON OF A BITCH *PAY*.

BROTHER/SISTER HAROLD.

STAGE NAME: MISO HONEY.

HONOR YOUR FAMILY.

MOTHER BAO.

FIND HIM, TONY, AND MURDER THE *SHIT* OUT OF HIM.

COUSIN CHARLIE.

(WORKS FOR ONI PRESS.)

F-F-F-F-... K-K-K-K-

GRANDFATHER ONG.

YOU HAVE MY CONDOLENCES, ANTHONY. AND MY FULL CONFIDENCE YOU CAN BRING THIS MONSTER TO JUSTICE.

BROTHER-IN-LAW TANG.

DAUGHTER OLIVE.

I NEED A MINUTE ALONE.

ANTHONY AND ANTONELLE CHU WERE FRATERNAL TWINS.

TONY AND TONI.

EACH WITH THEIR OWN EXTRAORDINARY, ALBEIT DIAMETRICALLY OPPOSED, ABILITY.

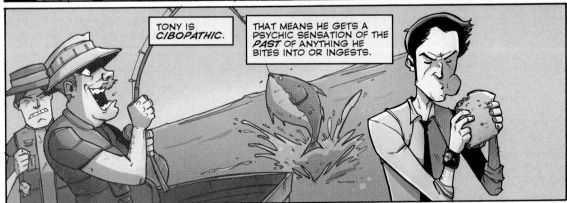

TONY IS *CIBOPATHIC*.

THAT MEANS HE GETS A PSYCHIC SENSATION OF THE *PAST* OF ANYTHING HE BITES INTO OR INGESTS.

TONI WAS *CIBOVOYANT*.

ABLE TO FLASH ONTO A VISION OF THE *FUTURE* OF ANY LIVING THING *SHE* BIT INTO OR INGESTED.

TONI WAS *MURDERED* AT THE HANDS OF *ANOTHER* CIBOPATH, A PSYCHO-PATHIC *COLLECTOR* OF EXTRAORDINARY ABILITIES.

AND THOUGH SHE WAS ABLE TO *SEE* HER UNTIMELY DEMISE--

--SHE WAS UNABLE TO *PREVENT* IT.

AND SO TODAY, TONY MOURNS THE *SECOND* GREAT LOSS OF HIS LIFE.

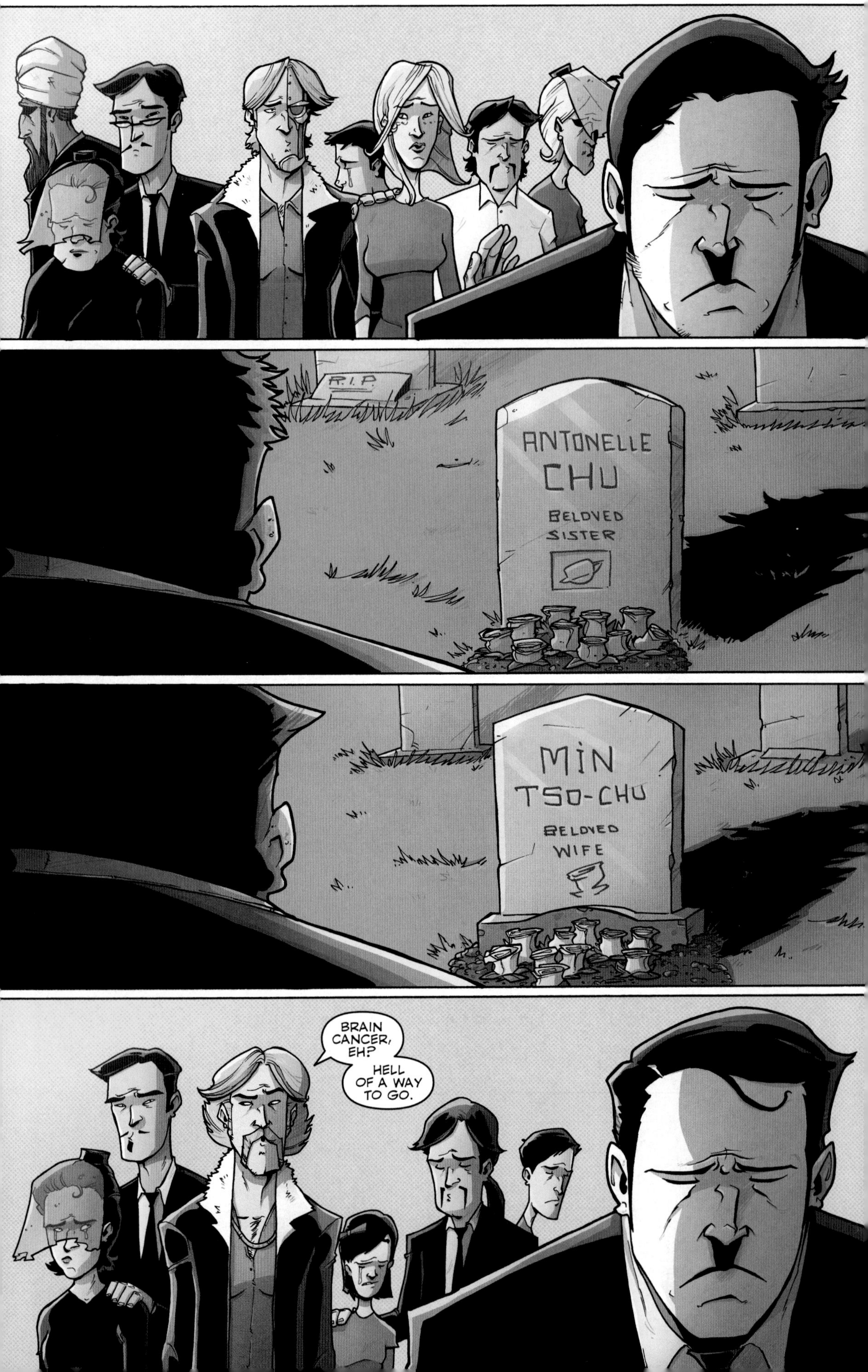
R.I.P.
ANTONELLE CHU
BELOVED SISTER
MIN TSO-CHU
BELOVED WIFE
BRAIN CANCER, EH?
HELL OF A WAY TO GO.

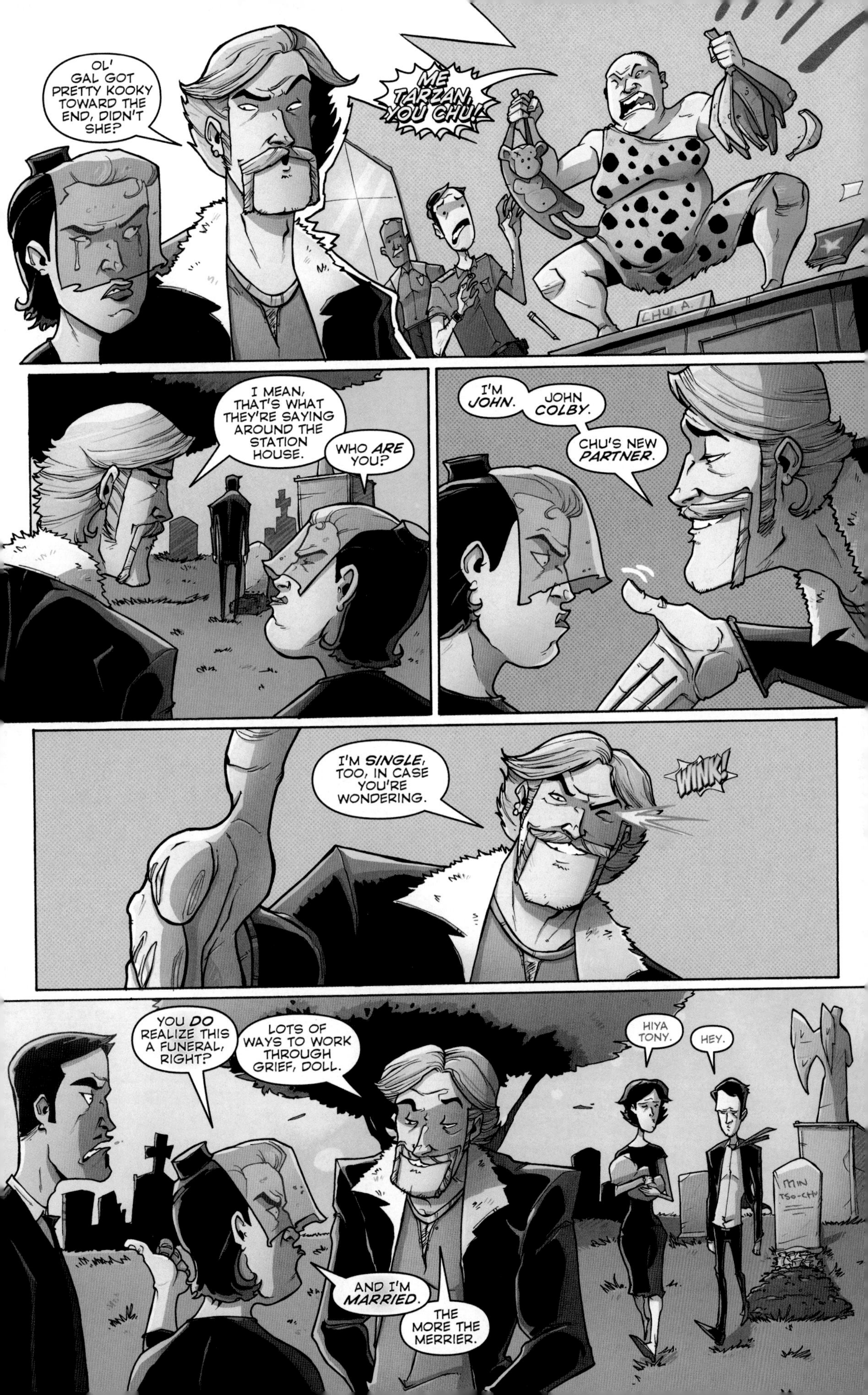
OL' GAL GOT PRETTY KOOKY TOWARD THE END, DIDN'T SHE?
ME TARZAN, YOU CHU!
CHU, A.
I MEAN, THAT'S WHAT THEY'RE SAYING AROUND THE STATION HOUSE.
WHO ARE YOU?
I'M JOHN.
JOHN COLBY.
CHU'S NEW PARTNER.
I'M SINGLE, TOO, IN CASE YOU'RE WONDERING.
WINK!
YOU DO REALIZE THIS A FUNERAL, RIGHT?
LOTS OF WAYS TO WORK THROUGH GRIEF, DOLL.
HIYA TONY.
HEY.
AND I'M MARRIED.
THE MORE THE MERRIER.
MIN TSO-CHU

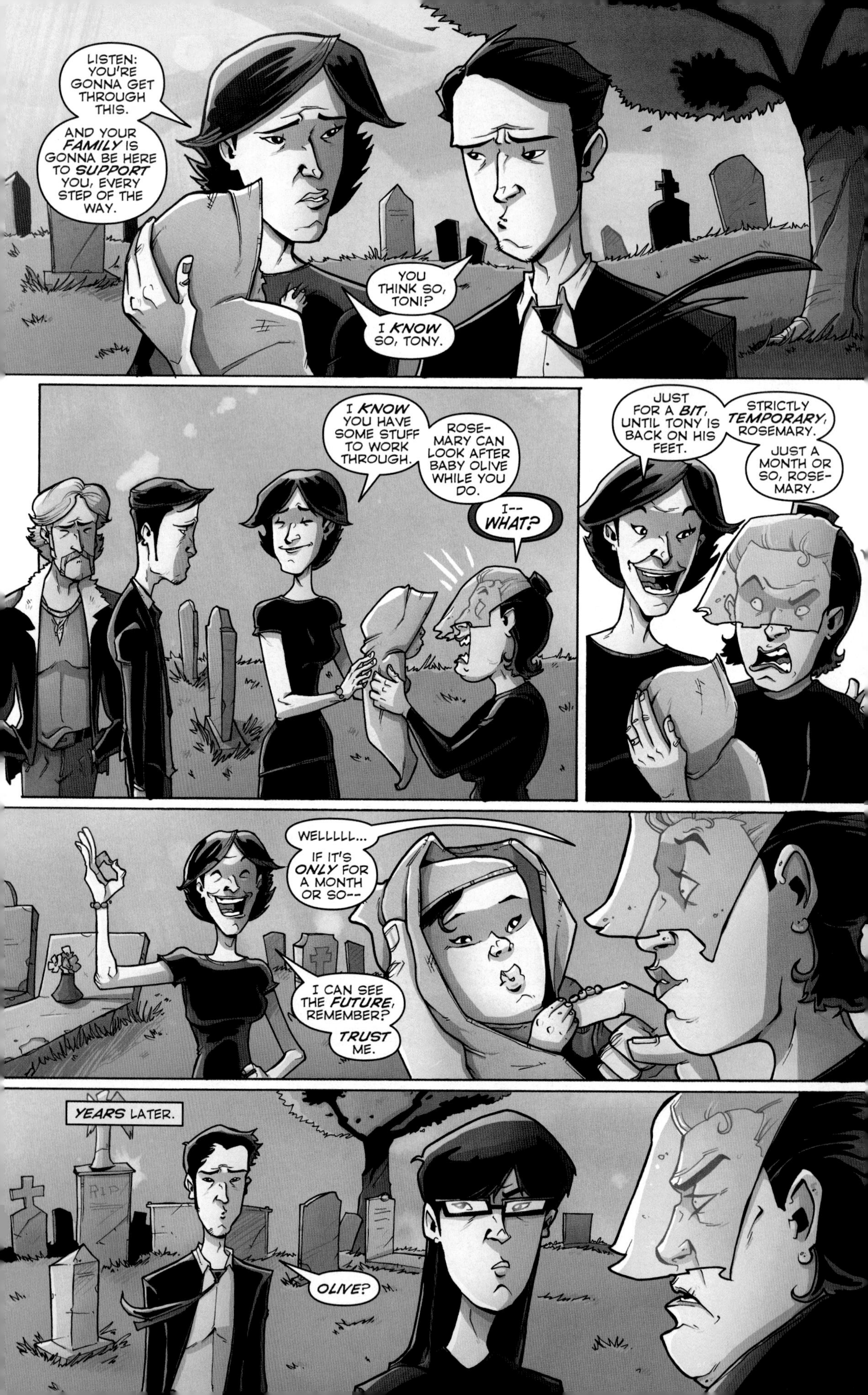
LISTEN: YOU'RE GONNA GET THROUGH THIS.
AND YOUR FAMILY IS GONNA BE HERE TO SUPPORT YOU, EVERY STEP OF THE WAY.
YOU THINK SO, TONI?
I KNOW SO, TONY.
I KNOW YOU HAVE SOME STUFF TO WORK THROUGH.
ROSE-MARY CAN LOOK AFTER BABY OLIVE WHILE YOU DO.
I-- WHAT?
JUST FOR A BIT, UNTIL TONY IS BACK ON HIS FEET.
STRICTLY TEMPORARY, ROSEMARY.
JUST A MONTH OR SO, ROSE-MARY.
WELLLLL... IF IT'S ONLY FOR A MONTH OR SO--
I CAN SEE THE FUTURE, REMEMBER?
TRUST ME.
YEARS LATER.
RIP
OLIVE?

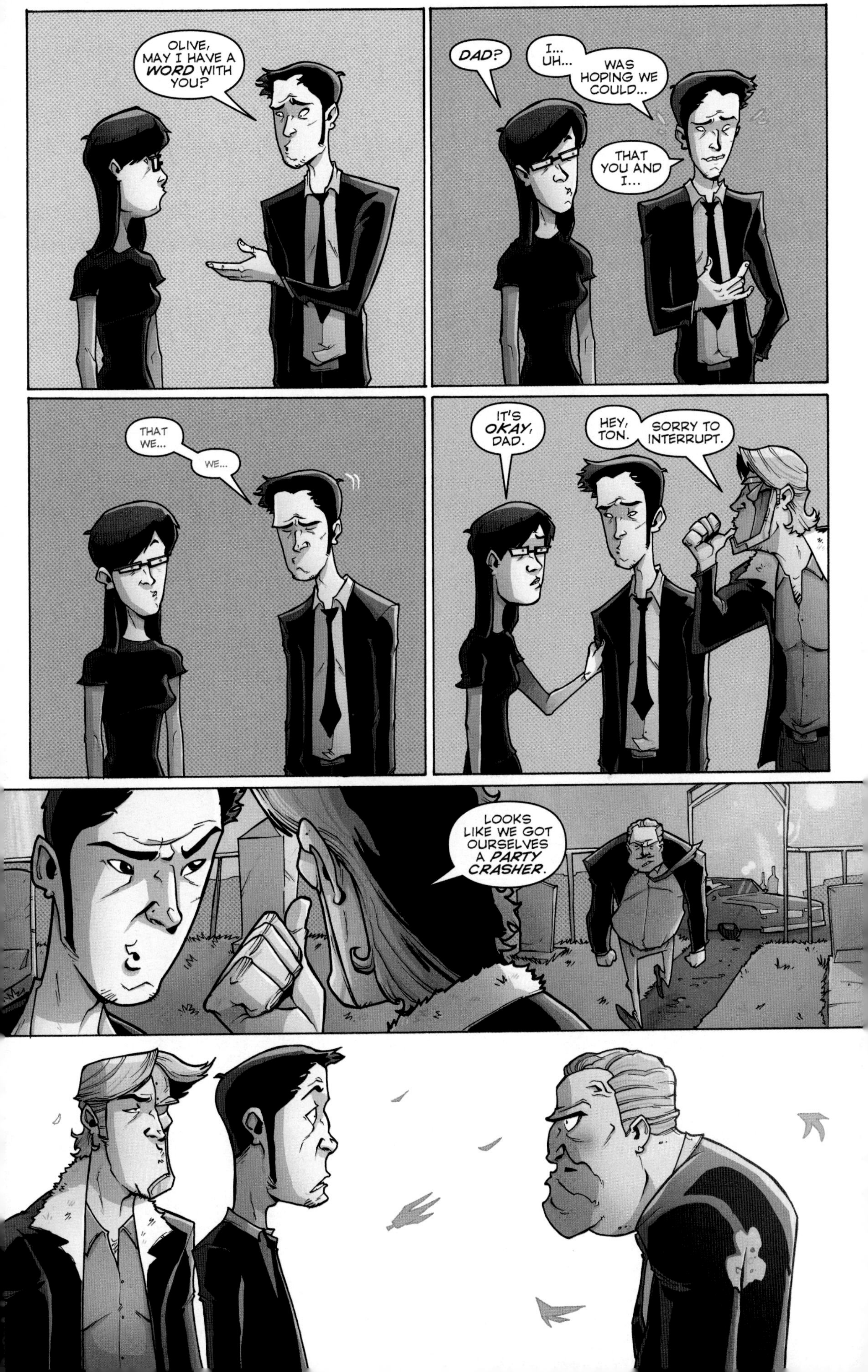
OLIVE, MAY I HAVE A WORD WITH YOU?
DAD?
I... UH...
WAS HOPING WE COULD...
THAT YOU AND I...
THAT WE...
WE...
IT'S OKAY, DAD.
HEY, TON.
SORRY TO INTERRUPT.
LOOKS LIKE WE GOT OURSELVES A PARTY CRASHER.

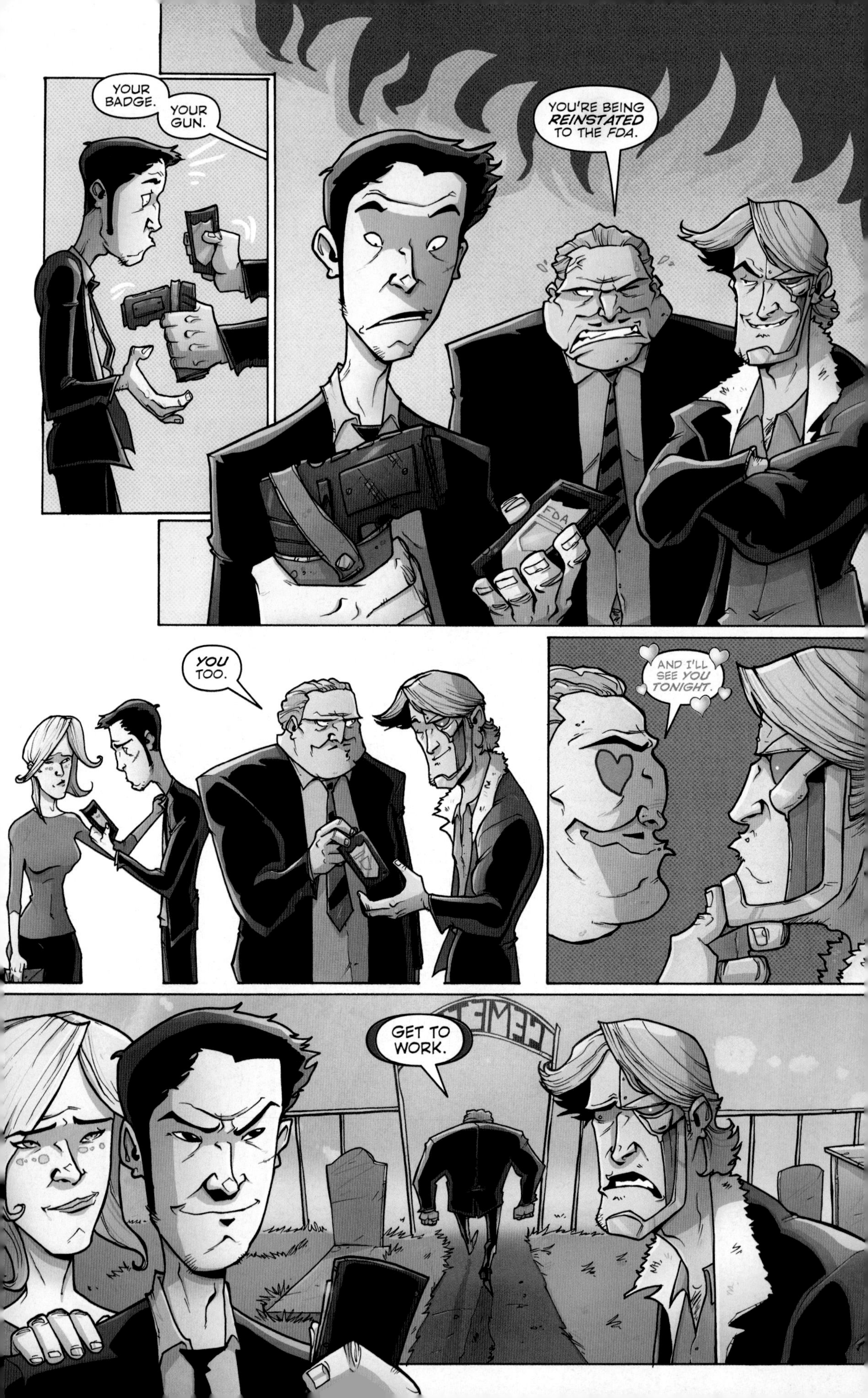
YOUR BADGE.
YOUR GUN.
YOU'RE BEING *REINSTATED* TO THE *FDA*.
FDA
YOU TOO.
AND I'LL SEE *YOU TONIGHT*.
GET TO WORK.

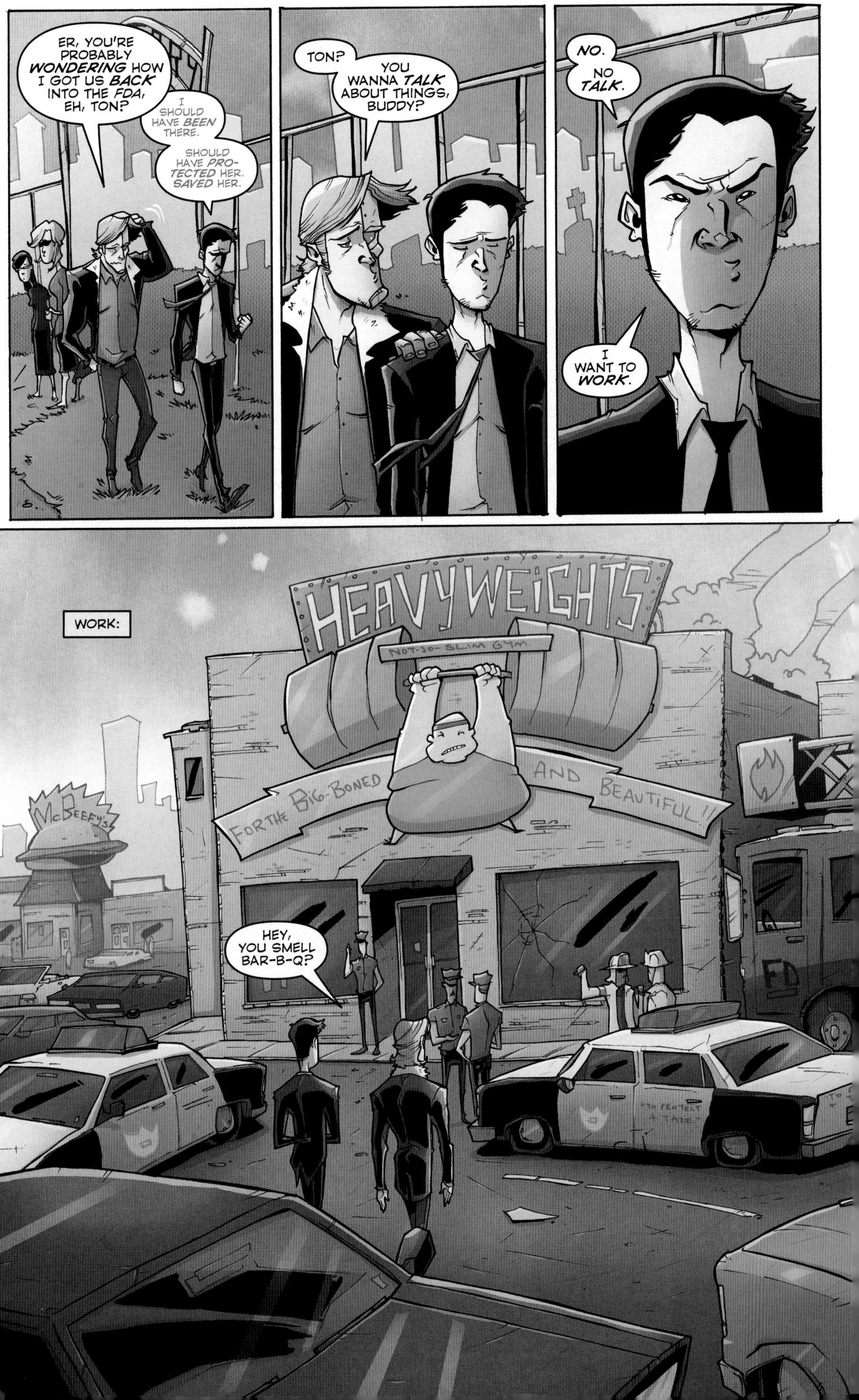
ER, YOU'RE PROBABLY WONDERING HOW I GOT US BACK INTO THE FDA, EH, TON?
I SHOULD HAVE BEEN THERE.
SHOULD HAVE PRO-TECTED HER. SAVED HER.
TON?
YOU WANNA TALK ABOUT THINGS, BUDDY?
NO.
NO TALK.
I WANT TO WORK.
WORK:
HEAVYWEIGHTS
NOT-SO-SLIM GYM
FOR THE BIG-BONED AND BEAUTIFUL!!
McBEEFY's
HEY, YOU SMELL BAR-B-Q?
FD

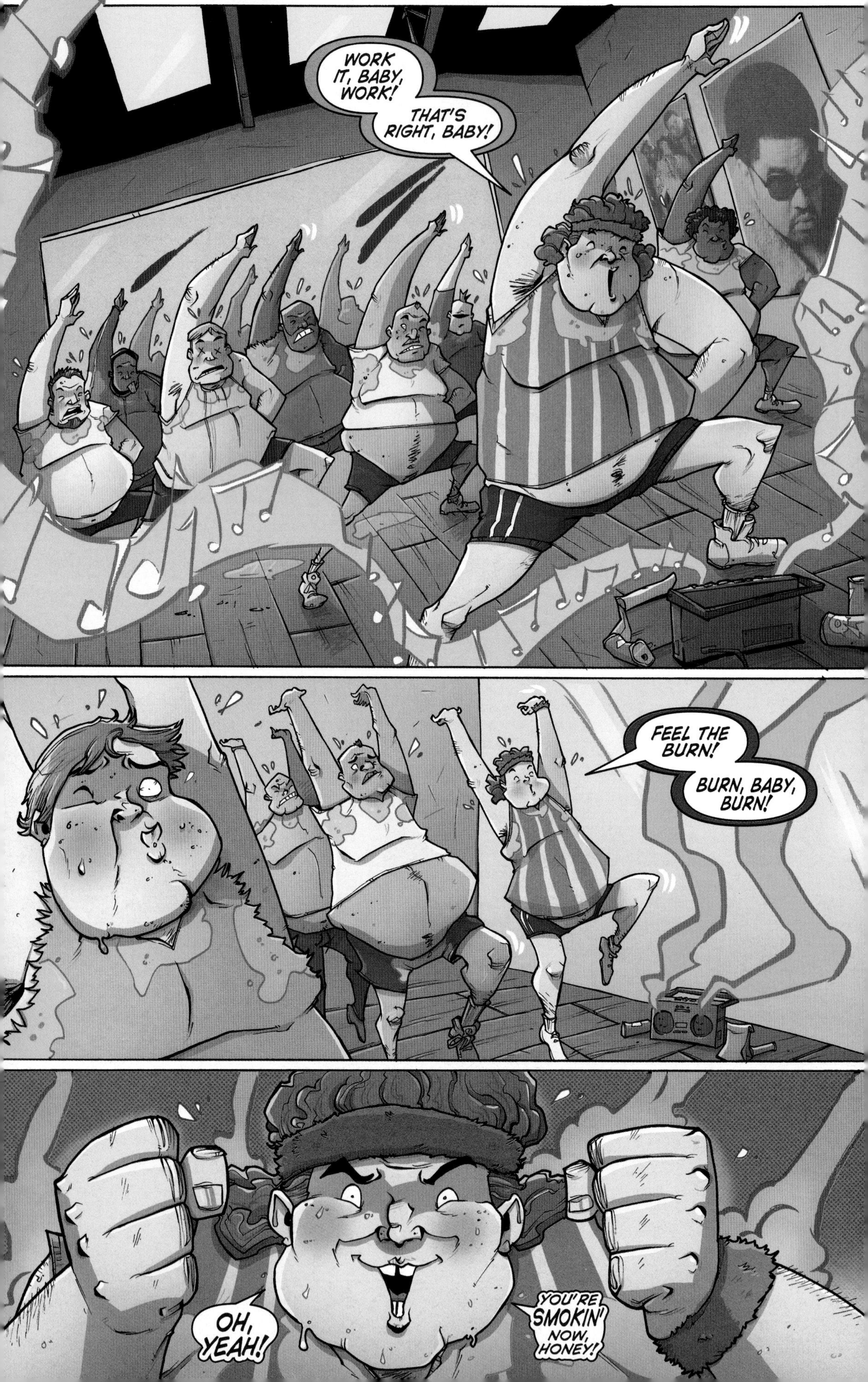
WORK IT, BABY, WORK!
THAT'S RIGHT, BABY!
FEEL THE BURN!
BURN, BABY, BURN!
OH, YEAH!
YOU'RE SMOKIN' NOW, HONEY!

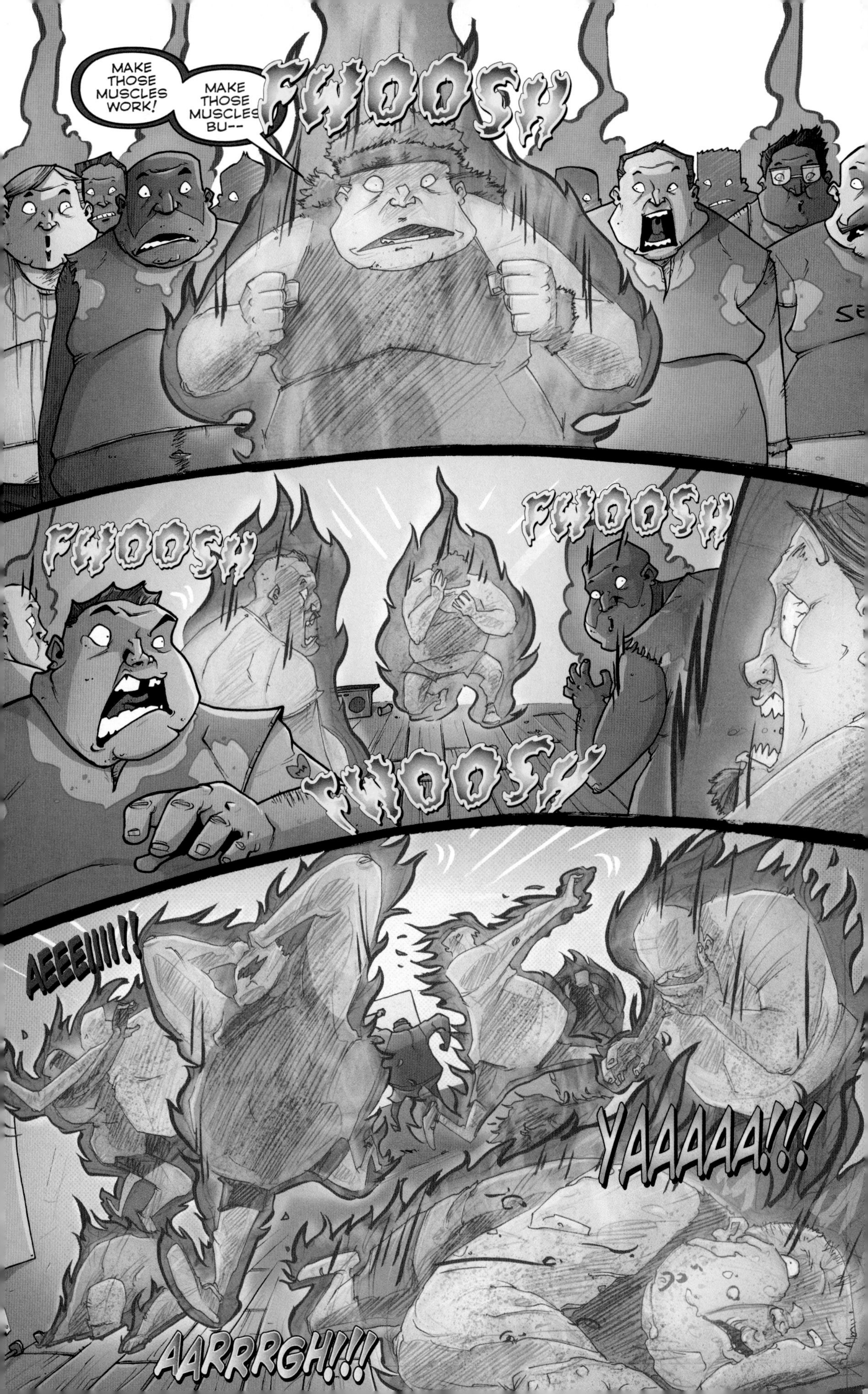
MAKE THOSE MUSCLES WORK!
MAKE THOSE MUSCLES BU--
FWOOSH
FWOOSH
FWOOSH
FWOOSH
AEEEIIIII!!
YAAAAA!!!
AARRRGH!!!

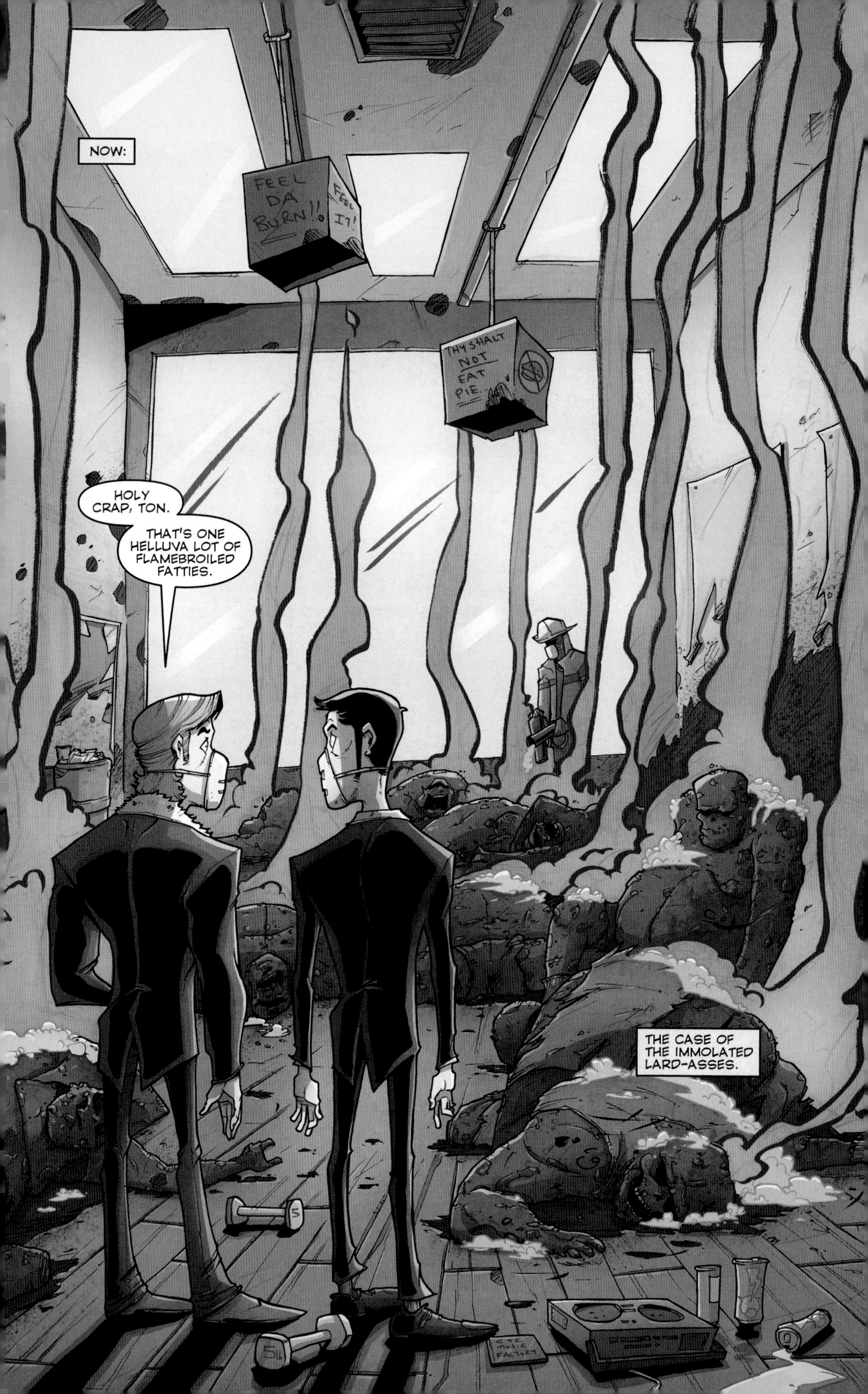
NOW:
FEEL DA BURN!!
FEEL IT!
THY SHALT NOT EAT PIE.
HOLY CRAP, TON.
THAT'S ONE HELLUVA LOT OF FLAMEBROILED FATTIES.
THE CASE OF THE IMMOLATED LARD-ASSES.

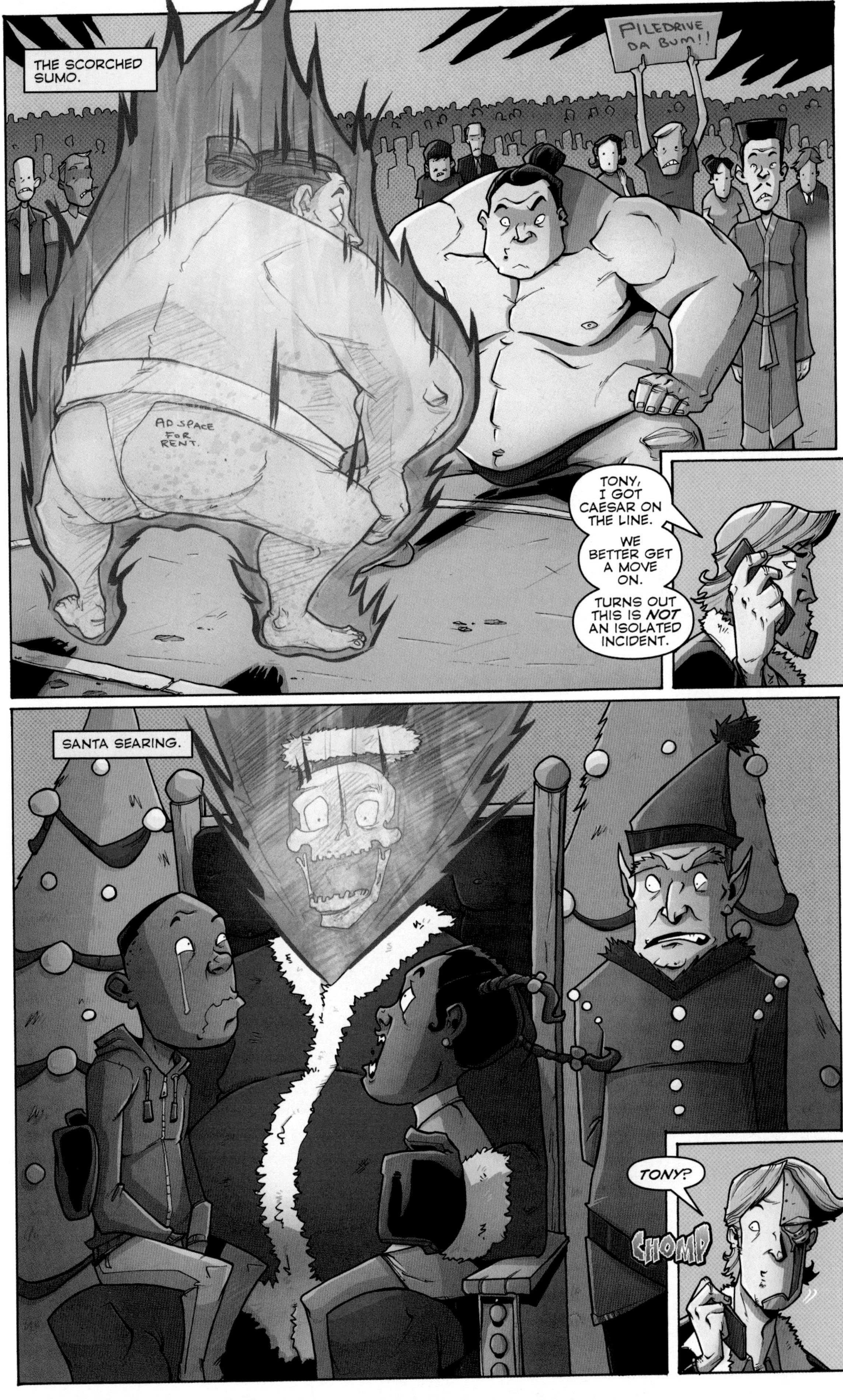
THE SCORCHED SUMO.
PILEDRIVE DA BUM!!
AD SPACE FOR RENT.
TONY, I GOT CAESAR ON THE LINE.
WE BETTER GET A MOVE ON.
TURNS OUT THIS IS *NOT* AN ISOLATED INCIDENT.
SANTA SEARING.
TONY?
CHOMP

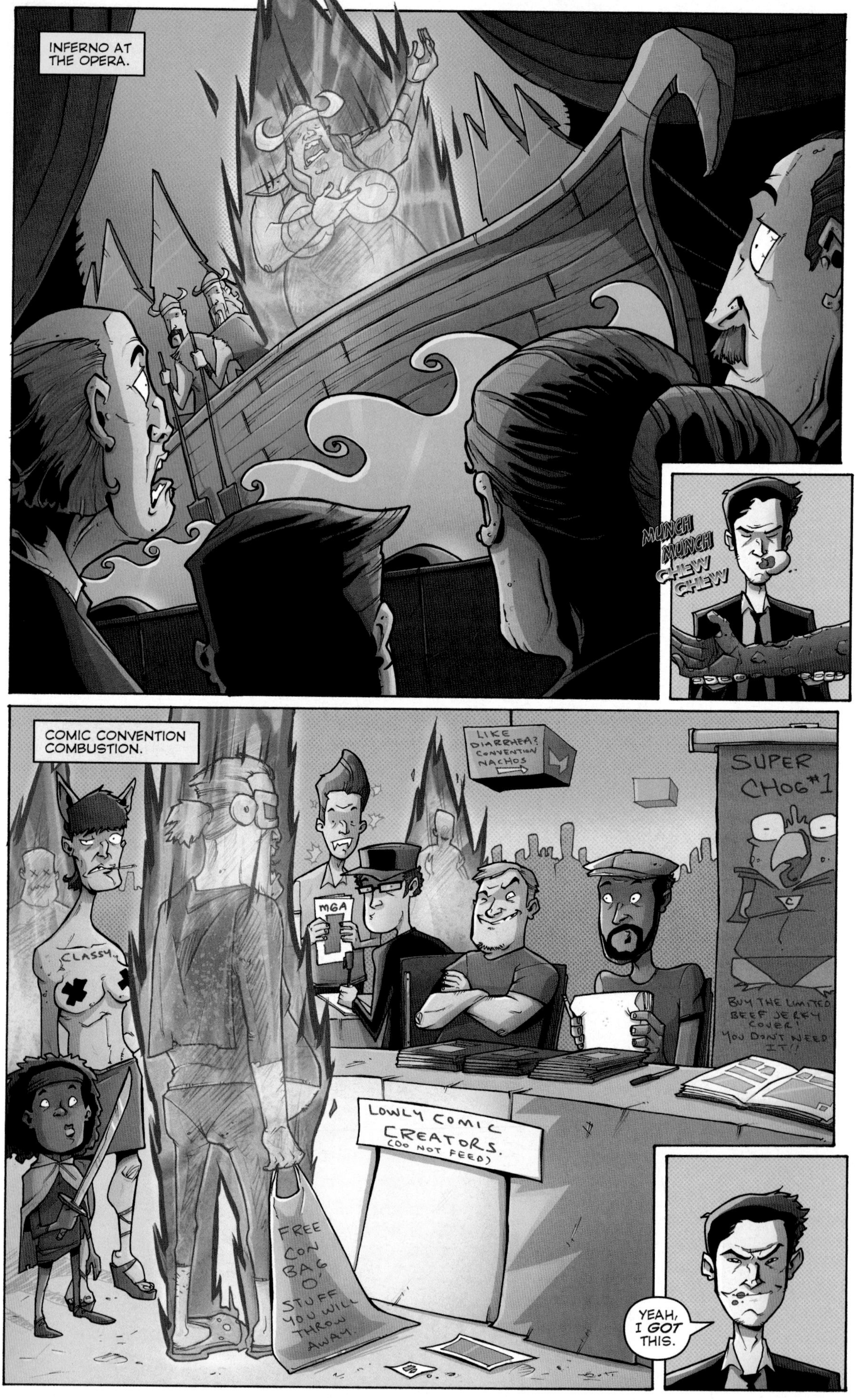

INFERNO AT THE OPERA.
MUNCH MUNCH
CHEW CHEW
COMIC CONVENTION COMBUSTION.
LIKE DIARRHEA? CONVENTION NACHOS
SUPER CHOG #1
BUY THE LIMITED BEEF JERKY COVER! YOU DON'T NEED IT!!
MGA
CLASSY.
LOWLY COMIC CREATORS. (DO NOT FEED)
FREE CON BAG O' STUFF YOU WILL THROW AWAY
YEAH, I GOT THIS.

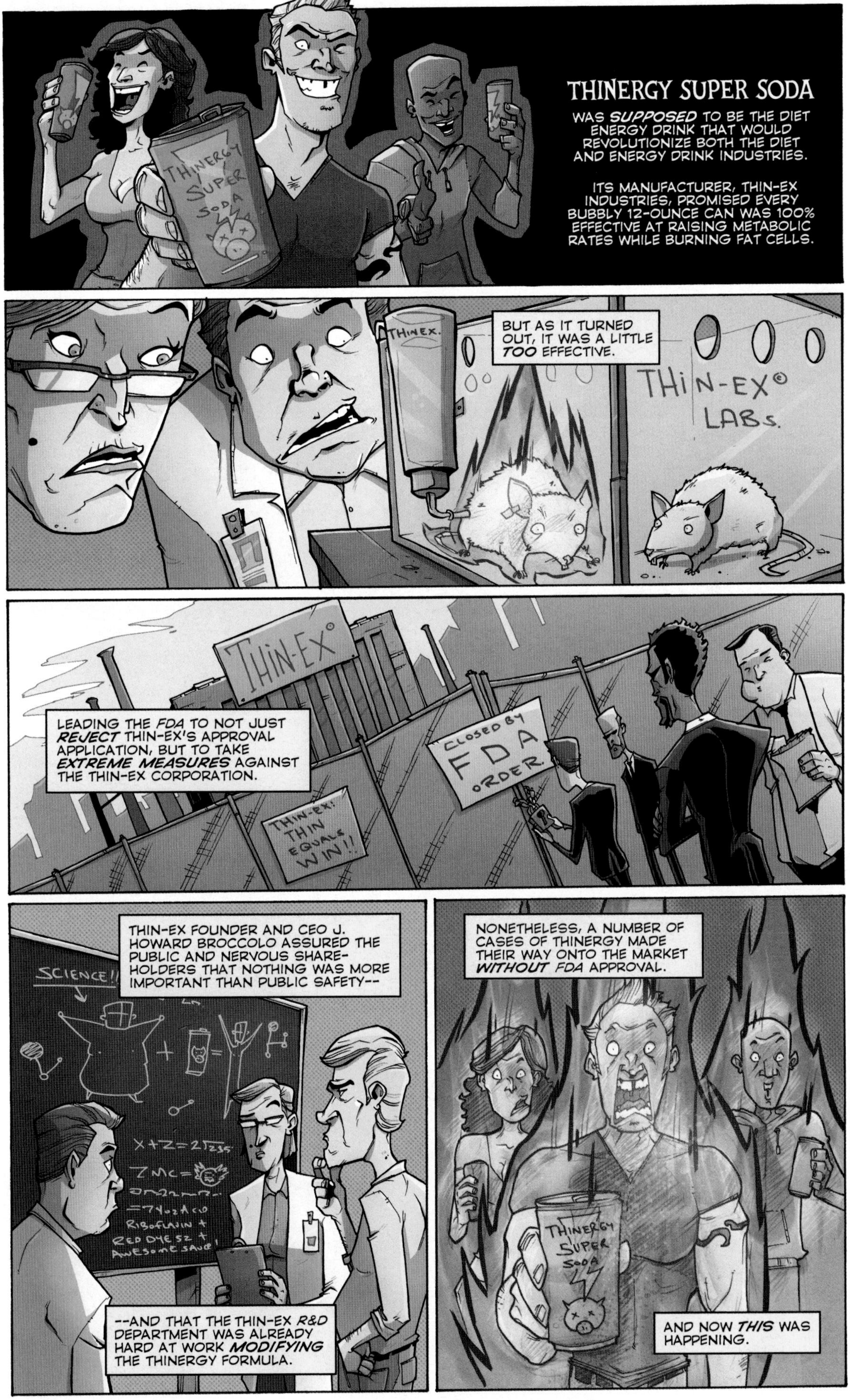
THINERGY SUPER SODA
WAS SUPPOSED TO BE THE DIET ENERGY DRINK THAT WOULD REVOLUTIONIZE BOTH THE DIET AND ENERGY DRINK INDUSTRIES.
ITS MANUFACTURER, THIN-EX INDUSTRIES, PROMISED EVERY BUBBLY 12-OUNCE CAN WAS 100% EFFECTIVE AT RAISING METABOLIC RATES WHILE BURNING FAT CELLS.
THINERGY SUPER SODA
BUT AS IT TURNED OUT, IT WAS A LITTLE TOO EFFECTIVE.
THINEX.
THIN-EX© LABS.
THIN-EX©
LEADING THE FDA TO NOT JUST REJECT THIN-EX'S APPROVAL APPLICATION, BUT TO TAKE EXTREME MEASURES AGAINST THE THIN-EX CORPORATION.
CLOSED BY FDA ORDER
THIN-EX: THIN EQUALS WIN!!
THIN-EX FOUNDER AND CEO J. HOWARD BROCCOLO ASSURED THE PUBLIC AND NERVOUS SHARE-HOLDERS THAT NOTHING WAS MORE IMPORTANT THAN PUBLIC SAFETY--
SCIENCE!!
RIBOFLAVIN + RED DYE 52 + AWESOME SAUCE!
--AND THAT THE THIN-EX R&D DEPARTMENT WAS ALREADY HARD AT WORK MODIFYING THE THINERGY FORMULA.
NONETHELESS, A NUMBER OF CASES OF THINERGY MADE THEIR WAY ONTO THE MARKET WITHOUT FDA APPROVAL.
THINERGY SUPER SODA
AND NOW THIS WAS HAPPENING.

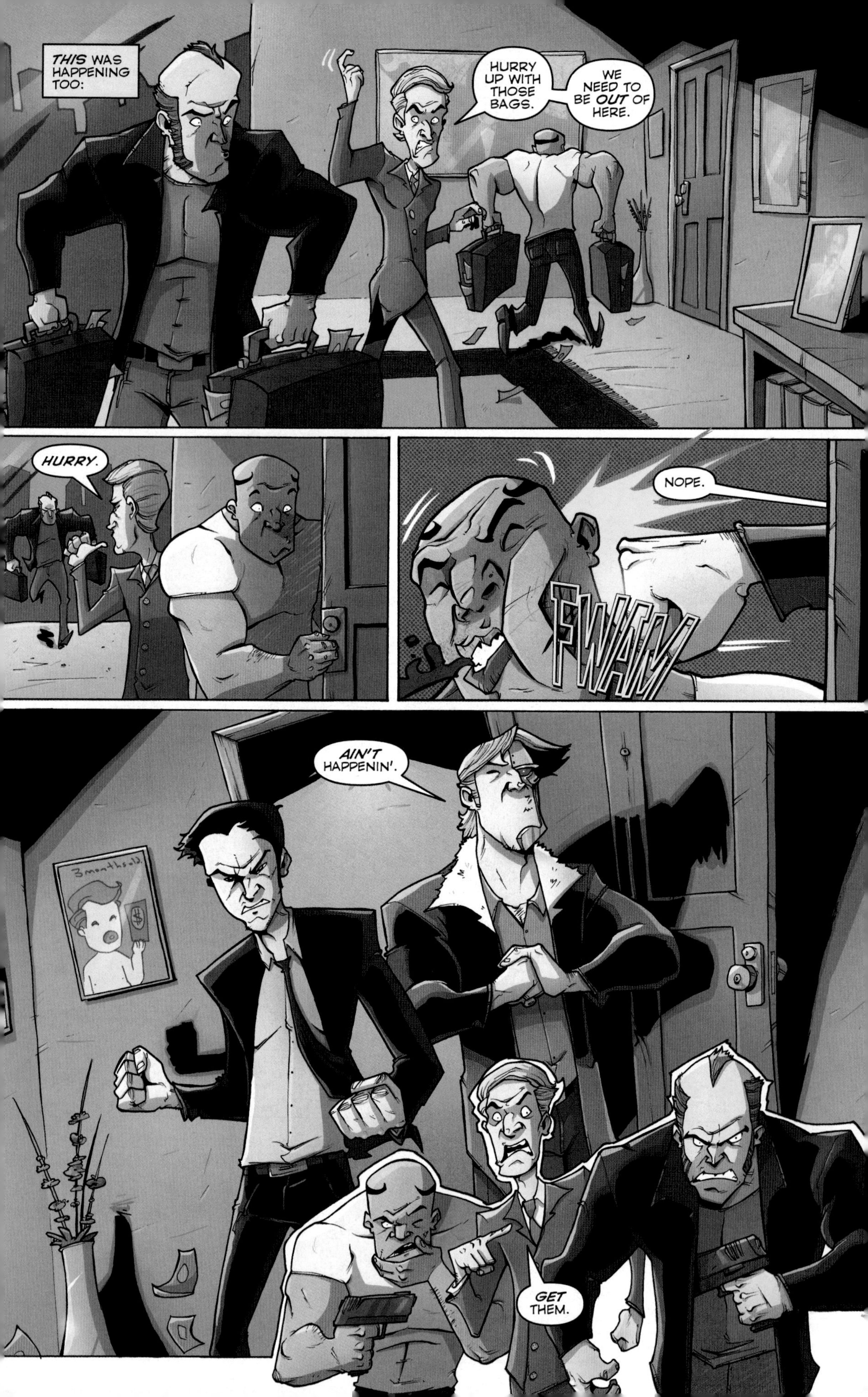

THIS WAS HAPPENING TOO:
HURRY UP WITH THOSE BAGS.
WE NEED TO BE *OUT* OF HERE.
HURRY.
NOPE.
FWAM
AIN'T HAPPENIN'.
GET THEM.

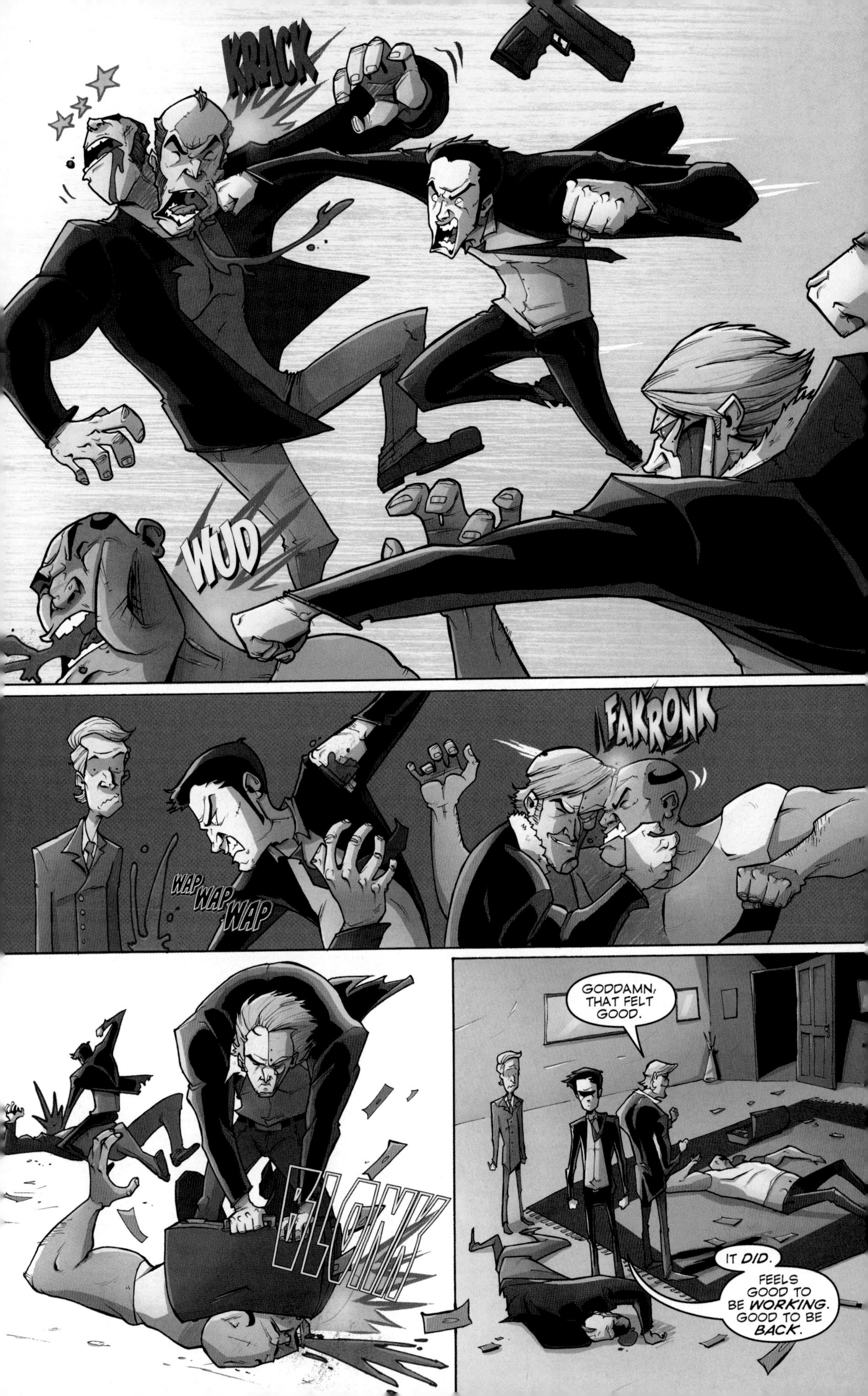
KRACK
WUD
FAKRONK
WAP WAP WAP
GODDAMN, THAT FELT GOOD.
IT DID.
FEELS GOOD TO BE WORKING. GOOD TO BE BACK.

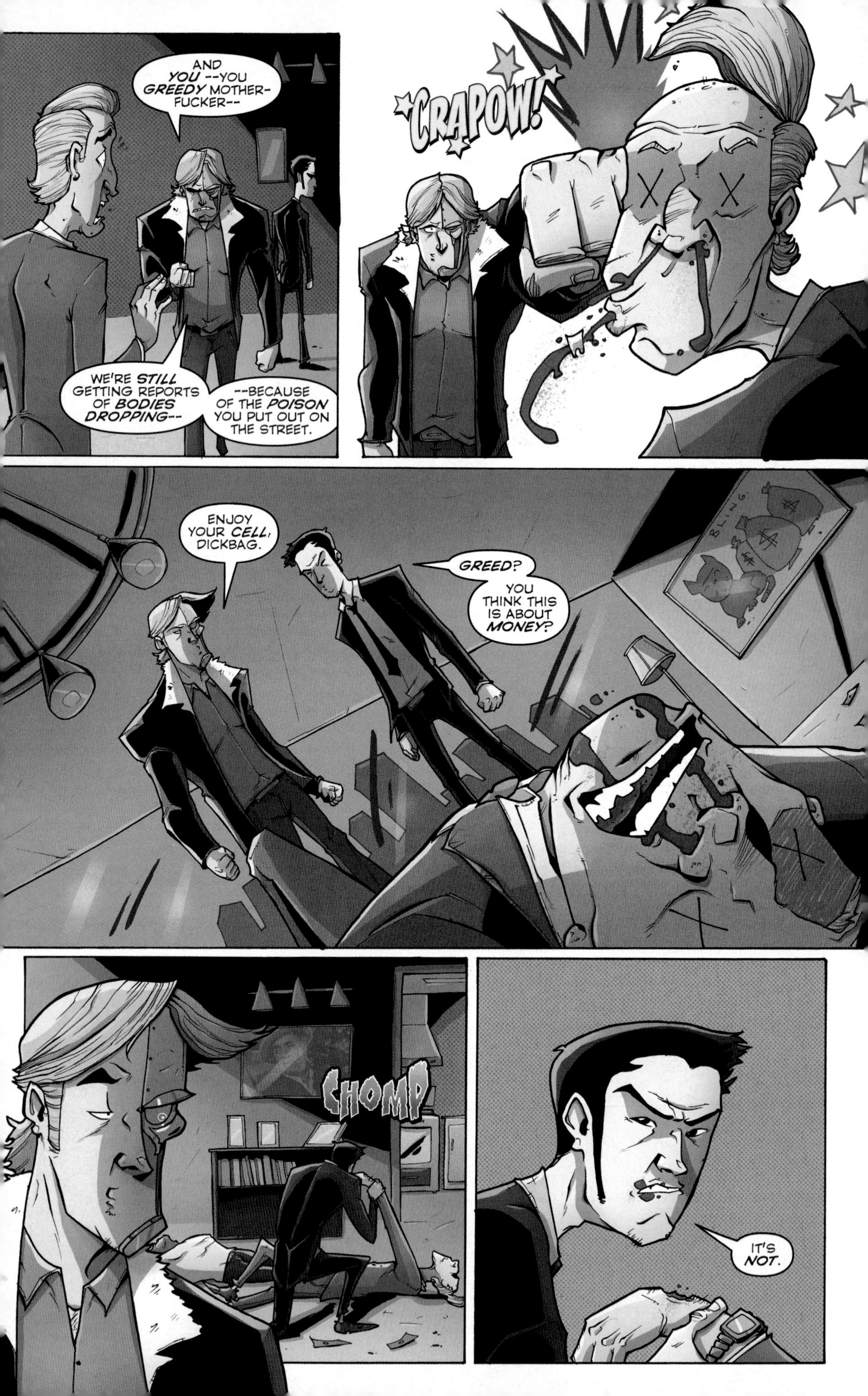

AND YOU --YOU GREEDY MOTHER-FUCKER--
WE'RE STILL GETTING REPORTS OF BODIES DROPPING--
--BECAUSE OF THE POISON YOU PUT OUT ON THE STREET.
CRAPOW!
ENJOY YOUR CELL, DICKBAG.
GREED?
YOU THINK THIS IS ABOUT MONEY?
BLING
CHOMP
IT'S NOT.

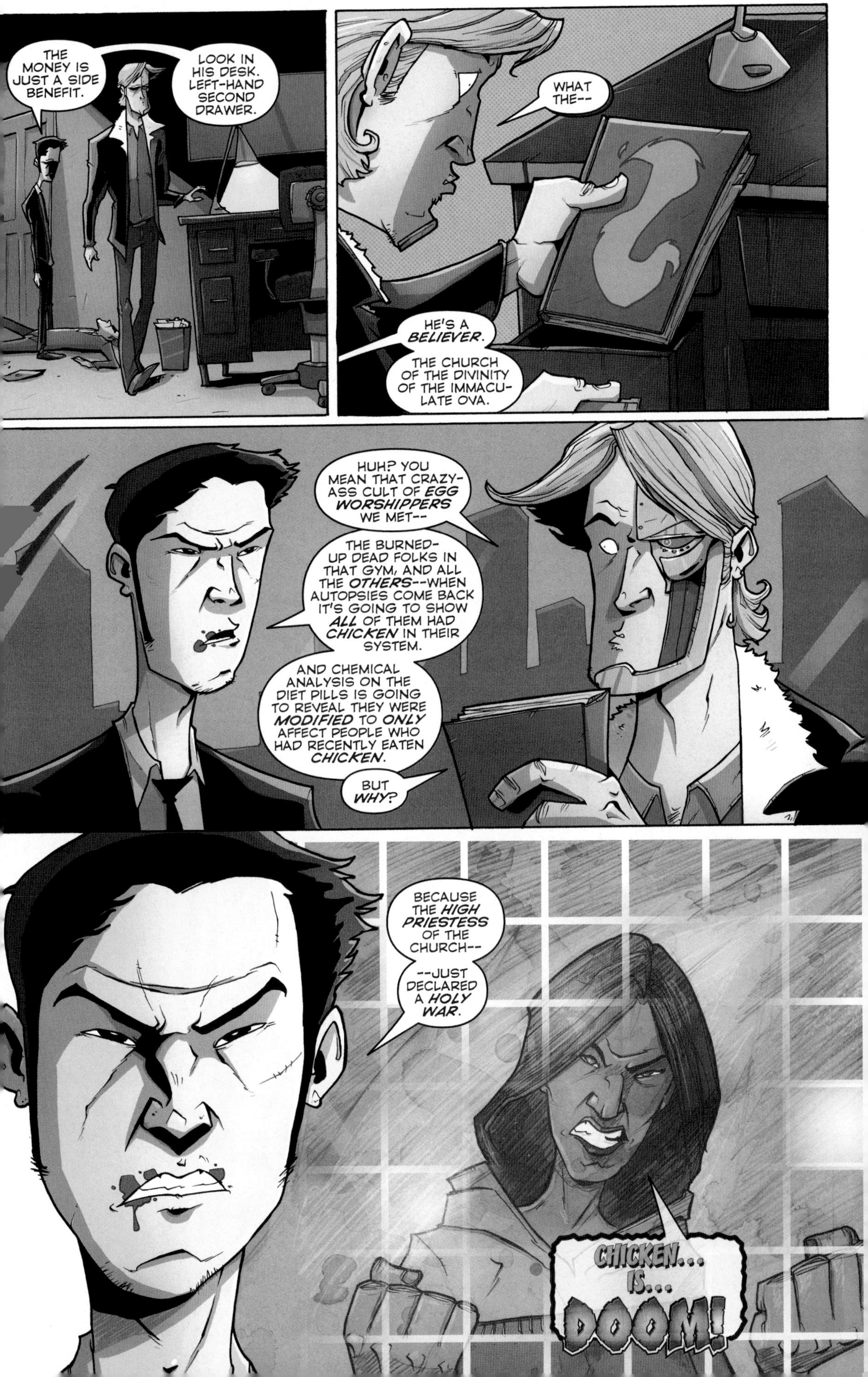
THE MONEY IS JUST A SIDE BENEFIT.
LOOK IN HIS DESK. LEFT-HAND SECOND DRAWER.
WHAT THE--
HE'S A ***BELIEVER***.
THE CHURCH OF THE DIVINITY OF THE IMMACULATE OVA.
HUH? YOU MEAN THAT CRAZY-ASS CULT OF ***EGG WORSHIPPERS*** WE MET--
THE BURNED-UP DEAD FOLKS IN THAT GYM, AND ALL THE ***OTHERS***--WHEN AUTOPSIES COME BACK IT'S GOING TO SHOW ***ALL*** OF THEM HAD ***CHICKEN*** IN THEIR SYSTEM.
AND CHEMICAL ANALYSIS ON THE DIET PILLS IS GOING TO REVEAL THEY WERE ***MODIFIED*** TO ***ONLY*** AFFECT PEOPLE WHO HAD RECENTLY EATEN ***CHICKEN***.
BUT ***WHY?***
BECAUSE THE ***HIGH PRIESTESS*** OF THE CHURCH--
--JUST DECLARED A ***HOLY WAR***.
CHICKEN... IS... DOOM!

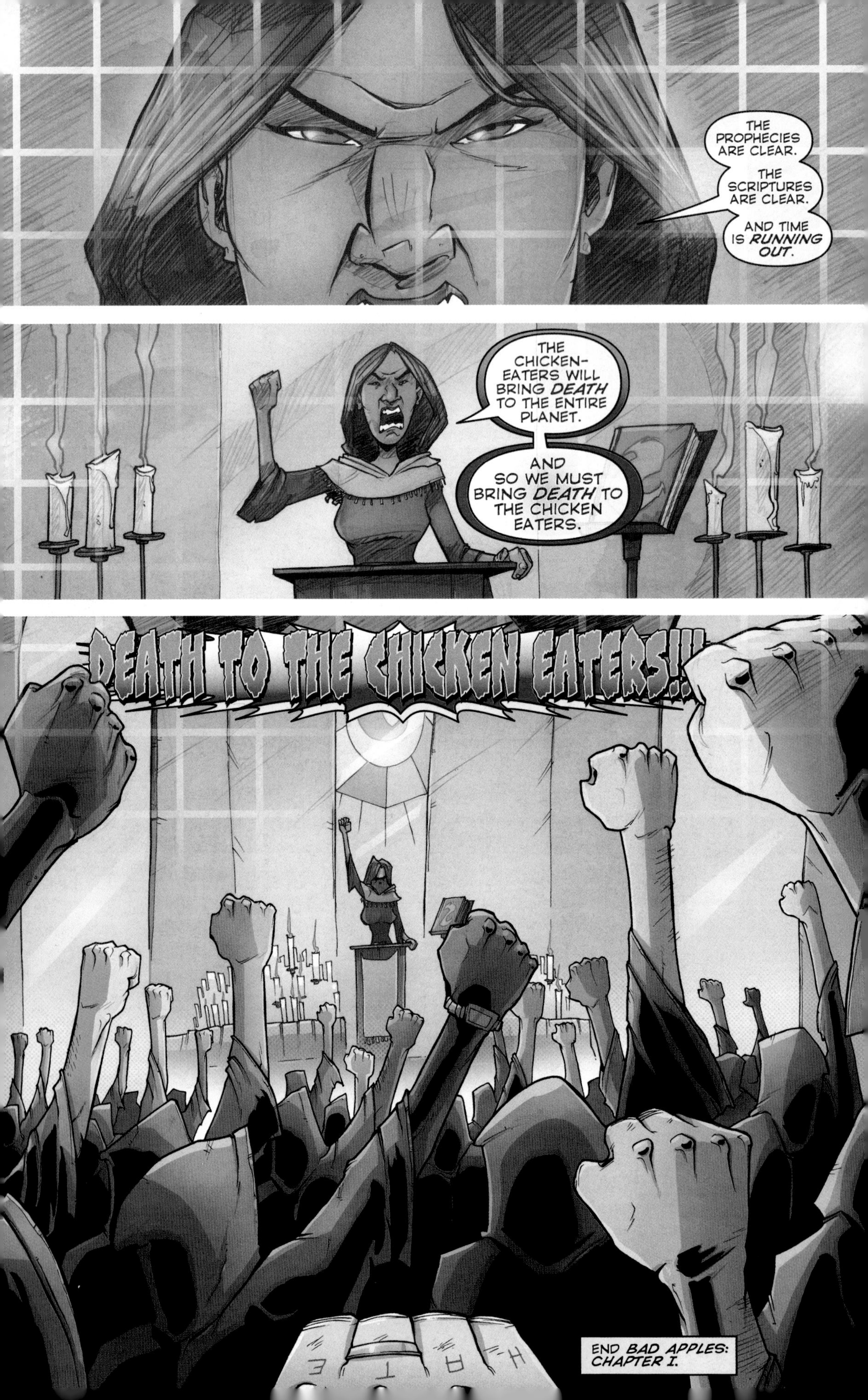
THE PROPHECIES ARE CLEAR.
THE SCRIPTURES ARE CLEAR.
AND TIME IS *RUNNING OUT*.
THE CHICKEN-EATERS WILL BRING *DEATH* TO THE ENTIRE PLANET.
AND SO WE MUST BRING *DEATH* TO THE CHICKEN EATERS.
DEATH TO THE CHICKEN EATERS!!!
END *BAD APPLES: CHAPTER I.*

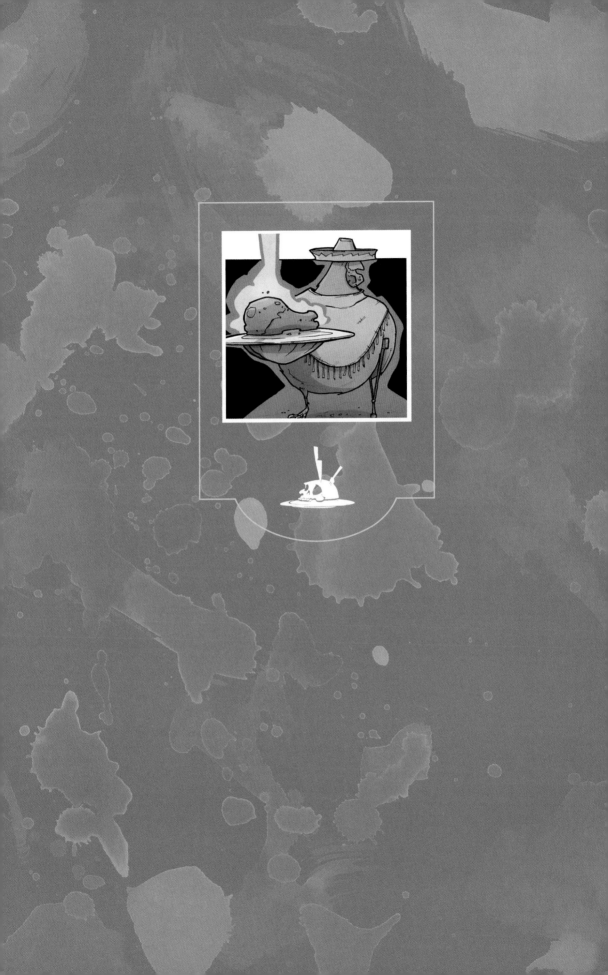

Chapter 2

ROB!
E PLURBUS BLING!

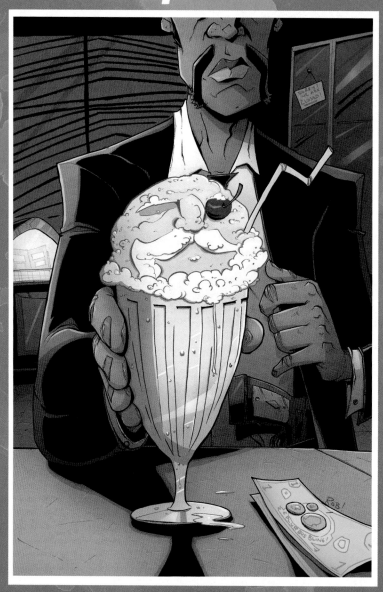

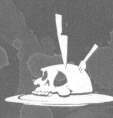

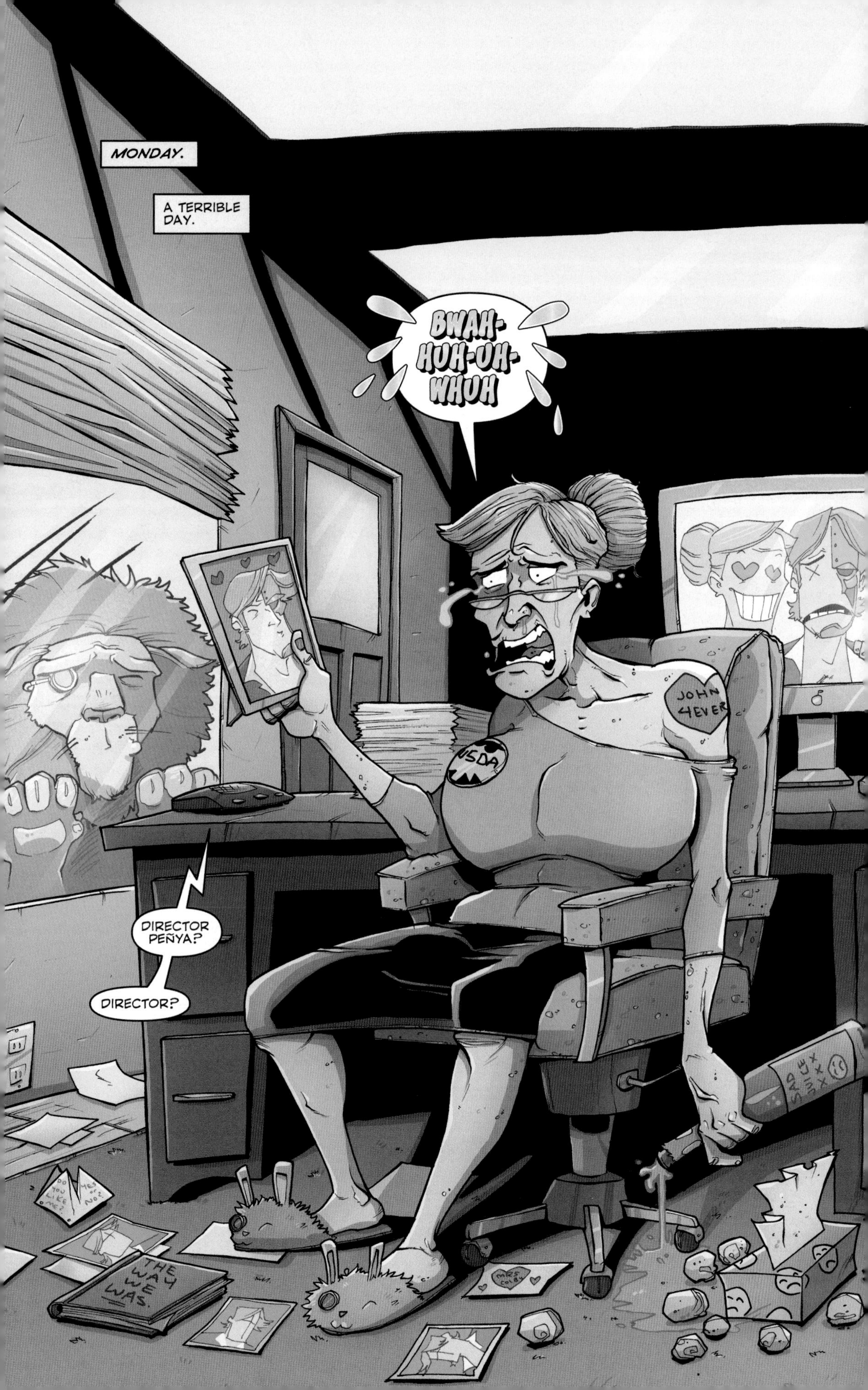
MONDAY.
A TERRIBLE DAY.
BWAH-HUH-UH-WHUH
DIRECTOR PEÑYA?
DIRECTOR?
JOHN 4EVER
USDA
SAD JUICE XXX
THE WAY WE WAS.

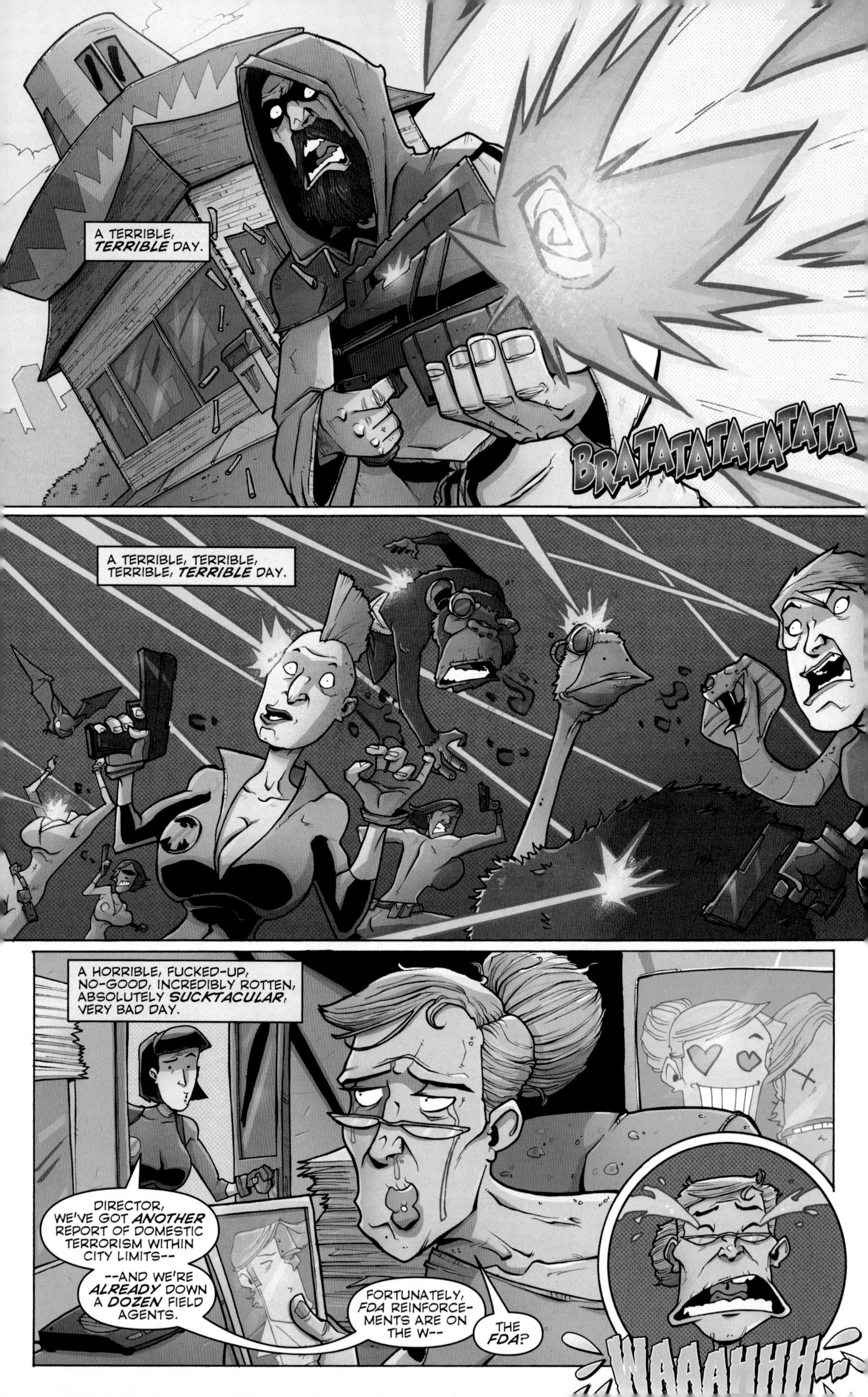
A TERRIBLE, TERRIBLE DAY.
BRATATATATATATA
A TERRIBLE, TERRIBLE, TERRIBLE, TERRIBLE DAY.
A HORRIBLE, FUCKED-UP, NO-GOOD, INCREDIBLY ROTTEN, ABSOLUTELY SUCKTACULAR, VERY BAD DAY.
DIRECTOR, WE'VE GOT ANOTHER REPORT OF DOMESTIC TERRORISM WITHIN CITY LIMITS--
--AND WE'RE ALREADY DOWN A DOZEN FIELD AGENTS.
FORTUNATELY, FDA REINFORCE-MENTS ARE ON THE W--
THE FDA?
WAAAHHH--

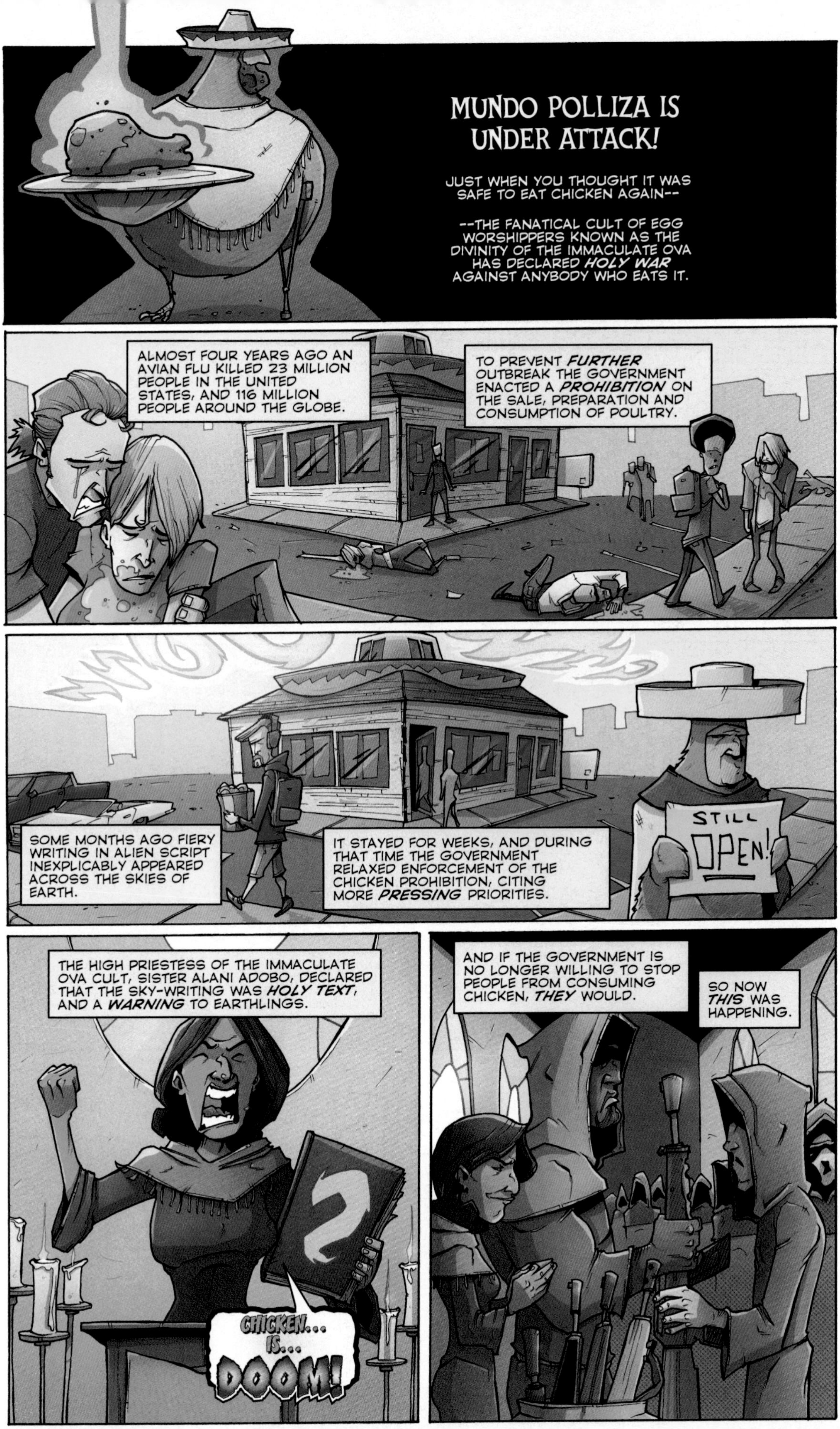
MUNDO POLLIZA IS UNDER ATTACK!
JUST WHEN YOU THOUGHT IT WAS SAFE TO EAT CHICKEN AGAIN--
--THE FANATICAL CULT OF EGG WORSHIPPERS KNOWN AS THE DIVINITY OF THE IMMACULATE OVA HAS DECLARED HOLY WAR AGAINST ANYBODY WHO EATS IT.
ALMOST FOUR YEARS AGO AN AVIAN FLU KILLED 23 MILLION PEOPLE IN THE UNITED STATES, AND 116 MILLION PEOPLE AROUND THE GLOBE.
TO PREVENT FURTHER OUTBREAK THE GOVERNMENT ENACTED A PROHIBITION ON THE SALE, PREPARATION AND CONSUMPTION OF POULTRY.
SOME MONTHS AGO FIERY WRITING IN ALIEN SCRIPT INEXPLICABLY APPEARED ACROSS THE SKIES OF EARTH.
IT STAYED FOR WEEKS, AND DURING THAT TIME THE GOVERNMENT RELAXED ENFORCEMENT OF THE CHICKEN PROHIBITION, CITING MORE PRESSING PRIORITIES.
STILL OPEN!
THE HIGH PRIESTESS OF THE IMMACULATE OVA CULT, SISTER ALANI ADOBO, DECLARED THAT THE SKY-WRITING WAS HOLY TEXT, AND A WARNING TO EARTHLINGS.
CHICKEN... IS... DOOM!
AND IF THE GOVERNMENT IS NO LONGER WILLING TO STOP PEOPLE FROM CONSUMING CHICKEN, THEY WOULD.
SO NOW THIS WAS HAPPENING.

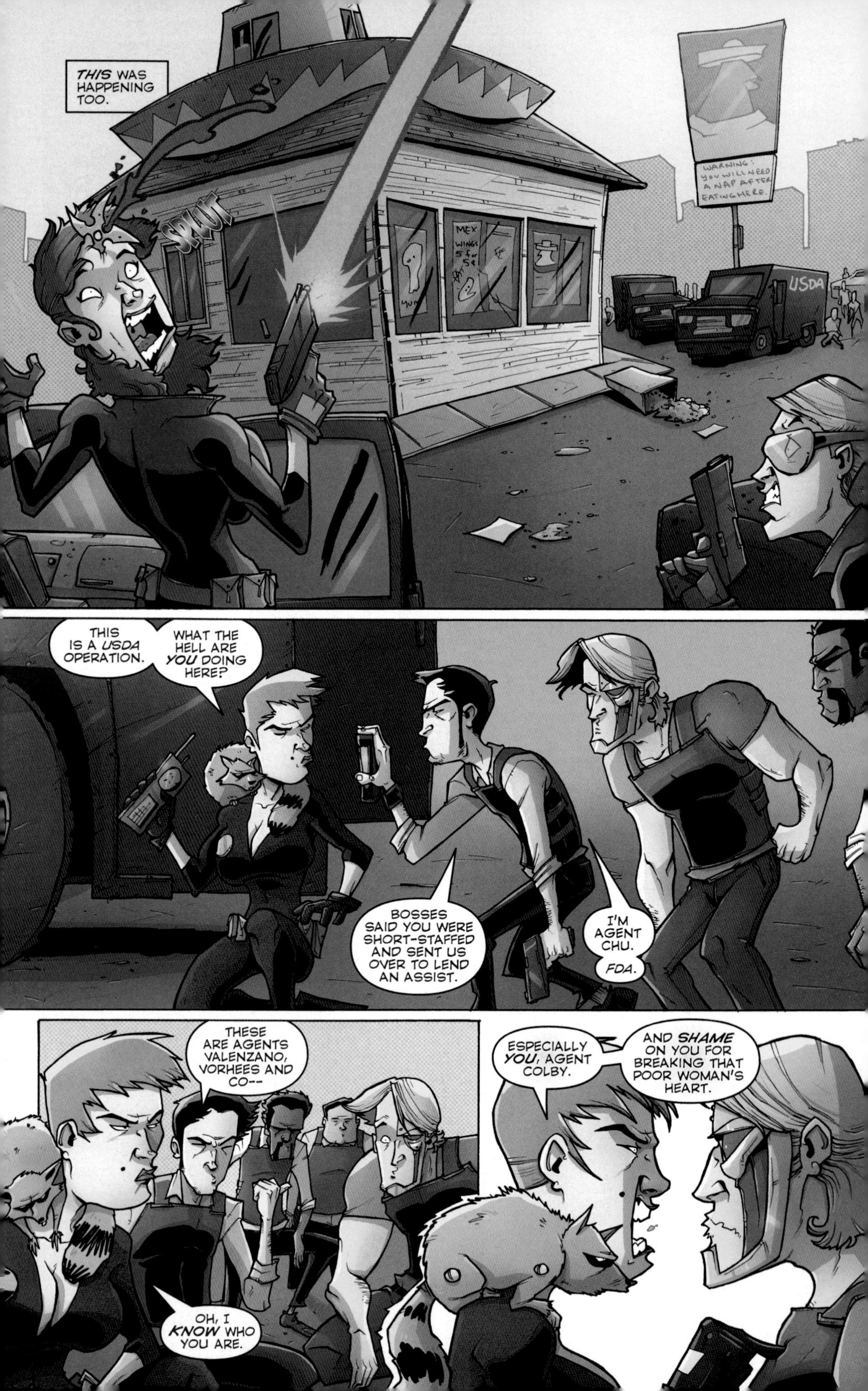
THIS WAS HAPPENING TOO.
SPLUT
WARNING: YOU WILL NEED A NAP AFTER EATING HERE
MEX WINGS 5 for 5$
USDA
THIS IS A USDA OPERATION.
WHAT THE HELL ARE YOU DOING HERE?
BOSSES SAID YOU WERE SHORT-STAFFED AND SENT US OVER TO LEND AN ASSIST.
I'M AGENT CHU.
FDA.
THESE ARE AGENTS VALENZANO, VORHEES AND CO--
OH, I KNOW WHO YOU ARE.
ESPECIALLY YOU, AGENT COLBY.
AND SHAME ON YOU FOR BREAKING THAT POOR WOMAN'S HEART.

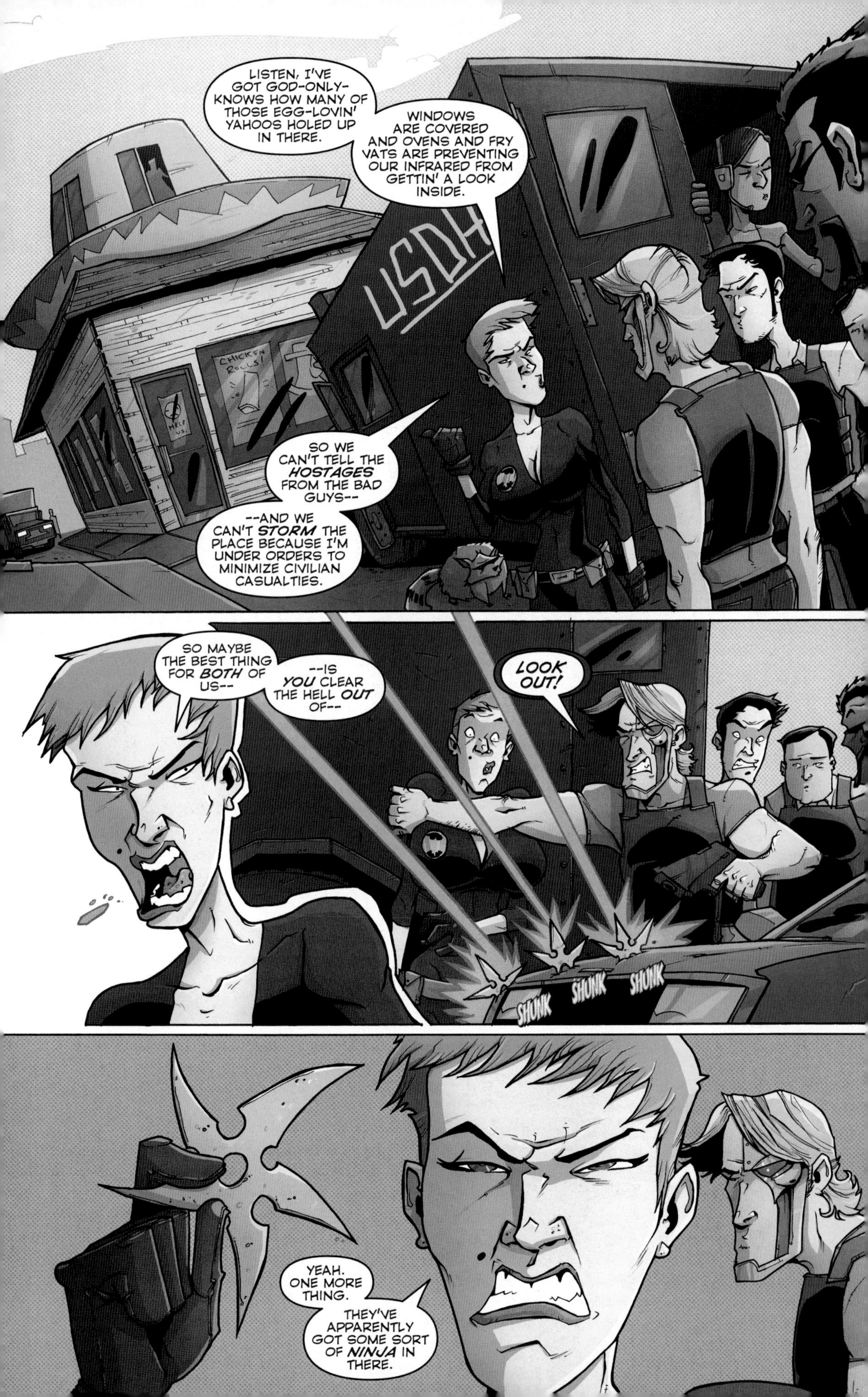
LISTEN, I'VE GOT GOD-ONLY-KNOWS HOW MANY OF THOSE EGG-LOVIN' YAHOOS HOLED UP IN THERE.
WINDOWS ARE COVERED AND OVENS AND FRY VATS ARE PREVENTING OUR INFRARED FROM GETTIN' A LOOK INSIDE.
USDH
CHICKEN ROLLS!
HELP US.
SO WE CAN'T TELL THE *HOSTAGES* FROM THE BAD GUYS--
--AND WE CAN'T *STORM* THE PLACE BECAUSE I'M UNDER ORDERS TO MINIMIZE CIVILIAN CASUALTIES.
SO MAYBE THE BEST THING FOR *BOTH* OF US--
--IS *YOU* CLEAR THE HELL *OUT* OF--
LOOK OUT!
SHUNK
SHUNK
SHUNK
YEAH. ONE MORE THING.
THEY'VE APPARENTLY GOT SOME SORT OF *NINJA* IN THERE.

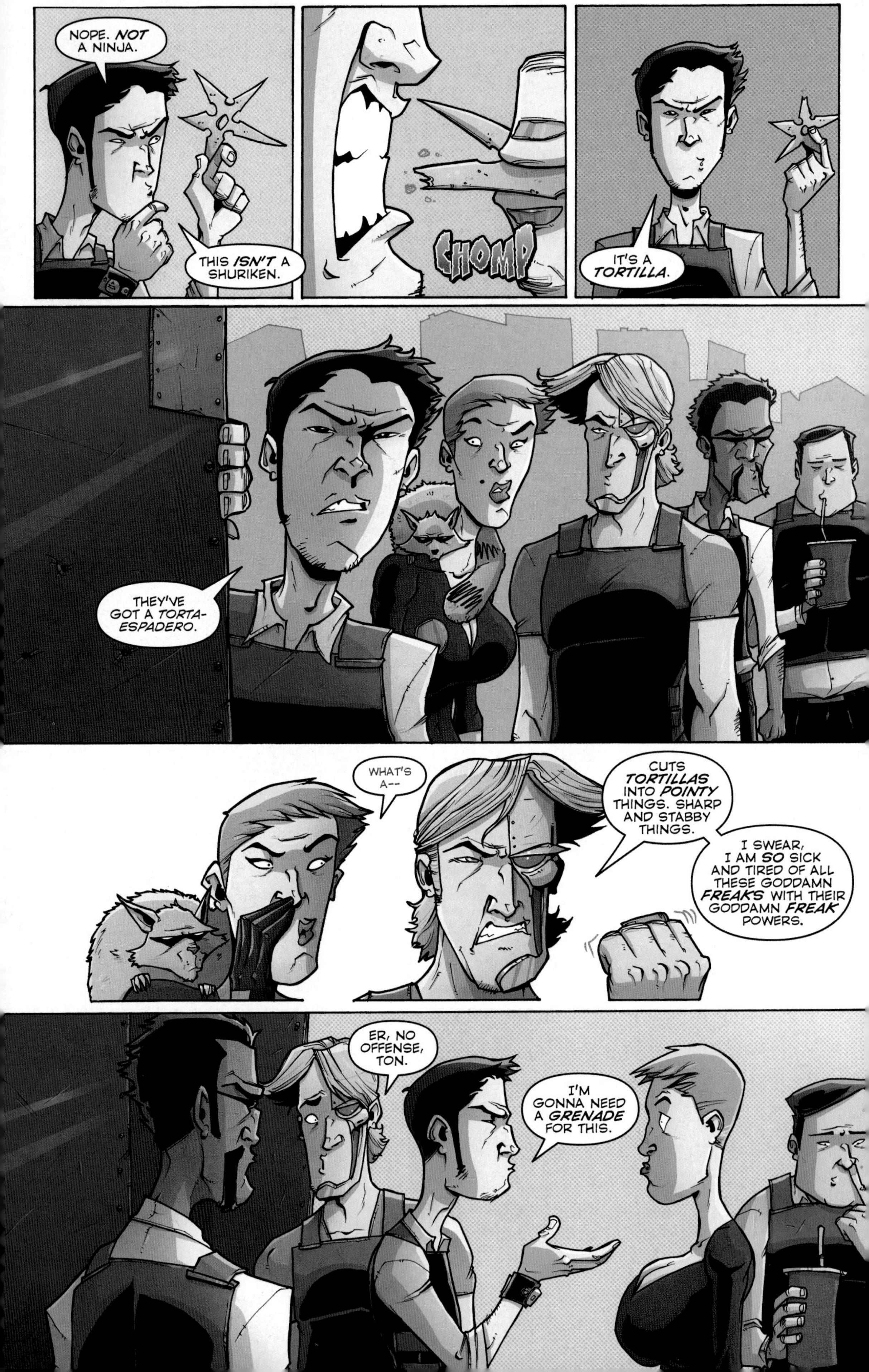
NOPE. NOT A NINJA.
THIS ISN'T A SHURIKEN.
CHOMP
IT'S A TORTILLA.
THEY'VE GOT A TORTA-ESPADERO.
WHAT'S A--
CUTS TORTILLAS INTO POINTY THINGS. SHARP AND STABBY THINGS.
I SWEAR, I AM SO SICK AND TIRED OF ALL THESE GODDAMN FREAKS WITH THEIR GODDAMN FREAK POWERS.
ER, NO OFFENSE, TON.
I'M GONNA NEED A GRENADE FOR THIS.

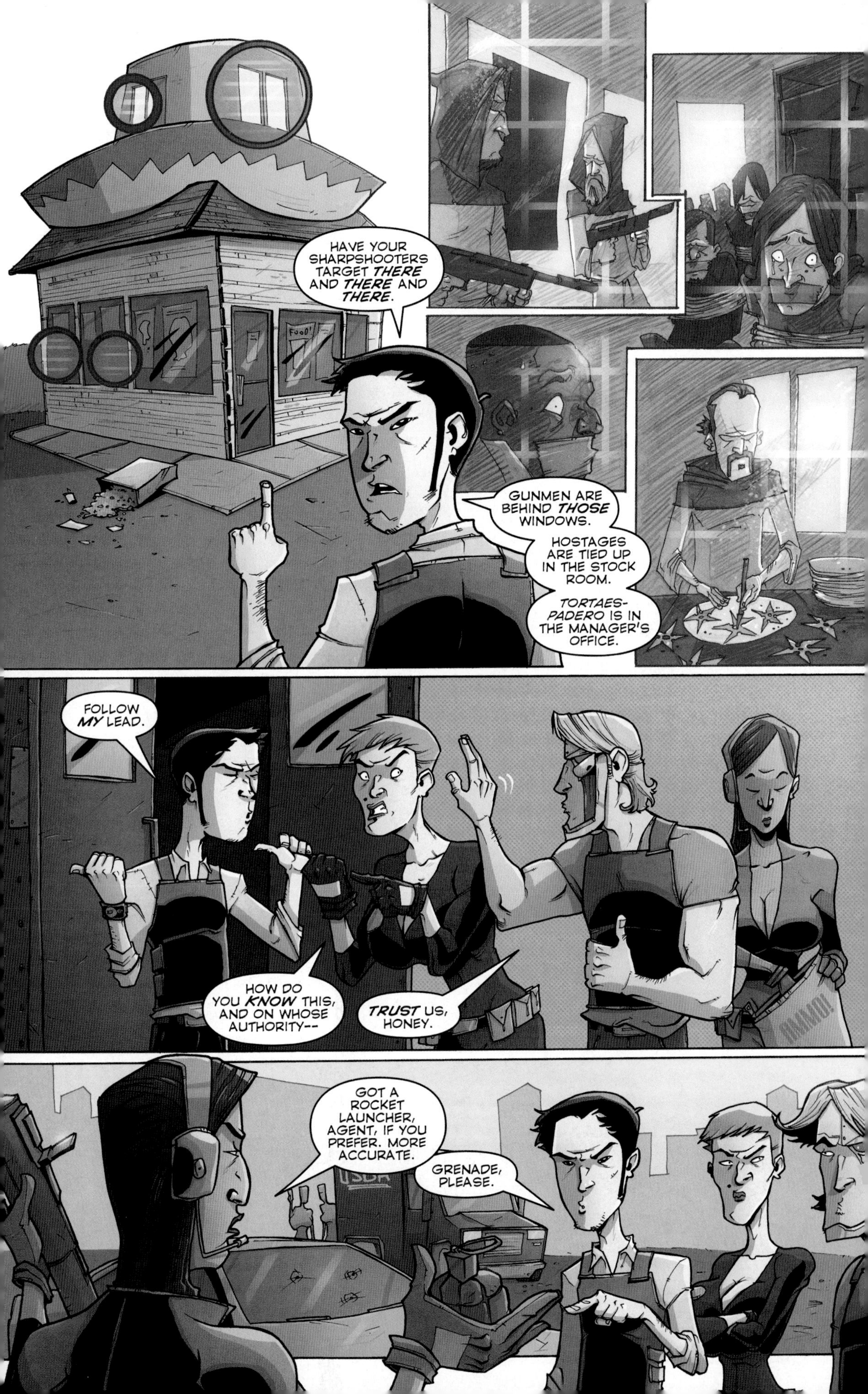
HAVE YOUR SHARPSHOOTERS TARGET THERE AND THERE AND THERE.
FOOD!
GUNMEN ARE BEHIND THOSE WINDOWS.
HOSTAGES ARE TIED UP IN THE STOCK ROOM.
TORTAES-PADERO IS IN THE MANAGER'S OFFICE.
FOLLOW MY LEAD.
HOW DO YOU KNOW THIS, AND ON WHOSE AUTHORITY--
TRUST US, HONEY.
GOT A ROCKET LAUNCHER, AGENT, IF YOU PREFER. MORE ACCURATE.
GRENADE, PLEASE.

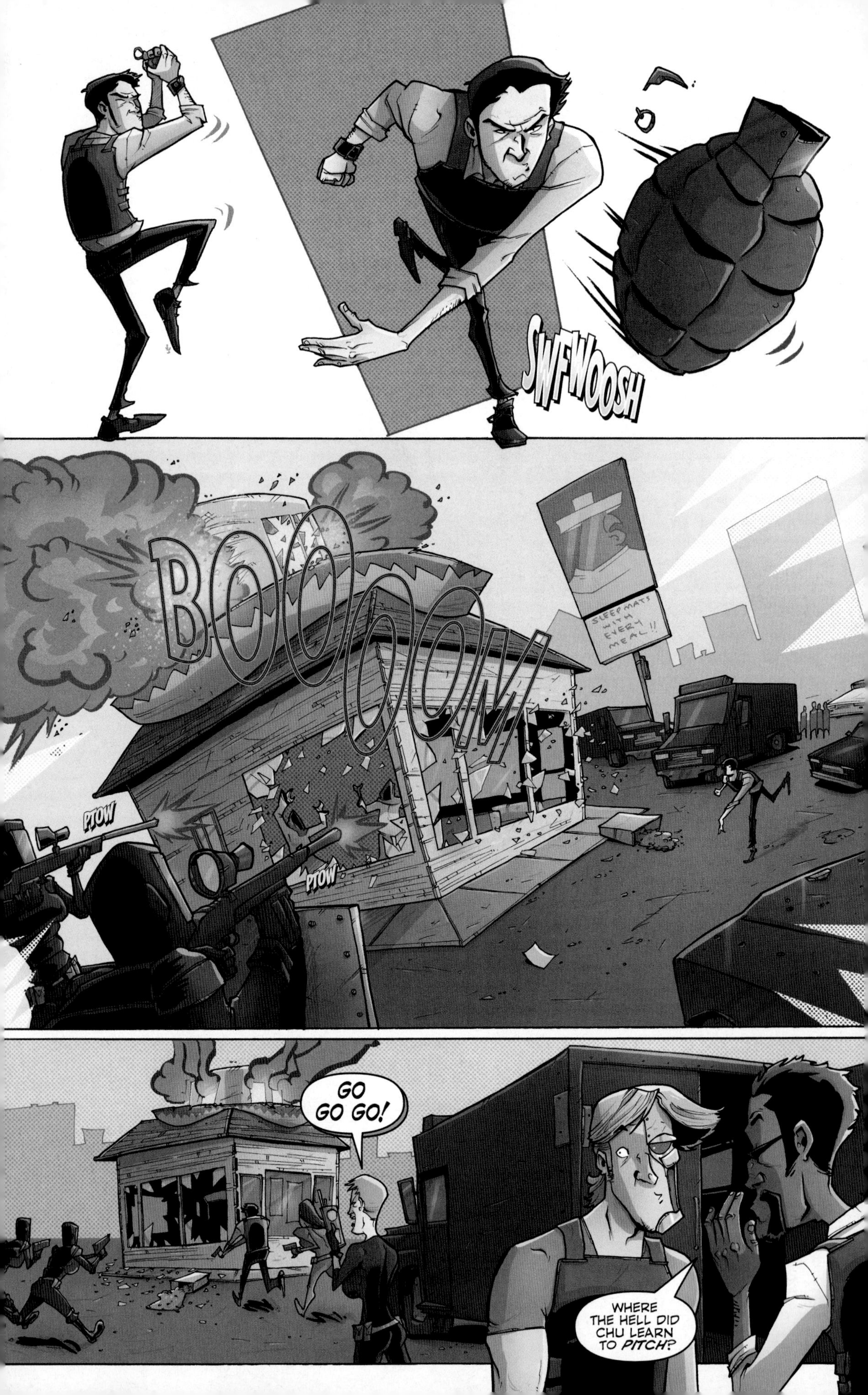
SWFWOOSH
BOOOOOM
SLEEP MATS WITH EVERY MEAL!!
PTOW
PTOW
GO GO GO!
WHERE THE HELL DID CHU LEARN TO *PITCH*?

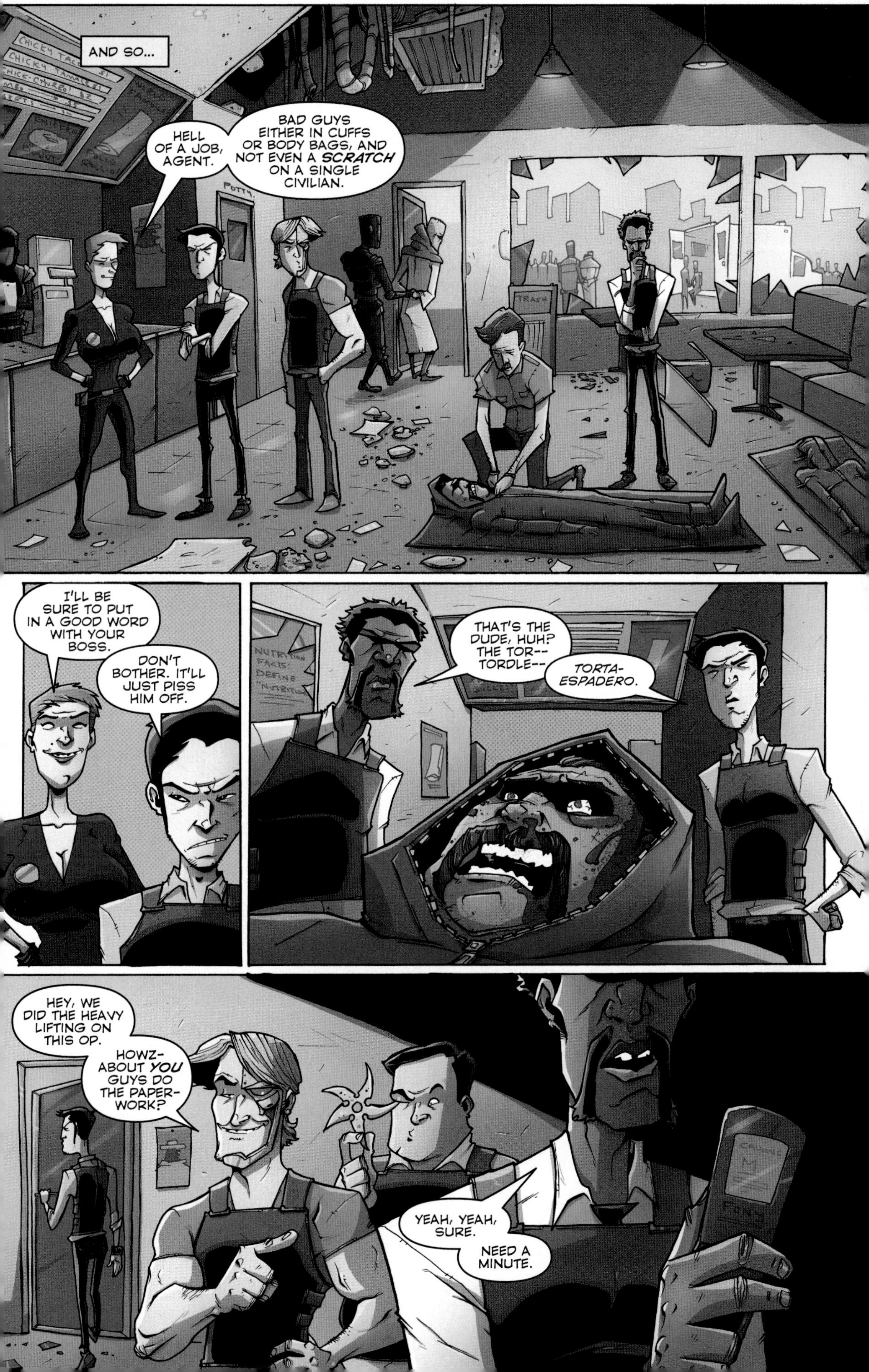
AND SO...
HELL OF A JOB, AGENT.
BAD GUYS EITHER IN CUFFS OR BODY BAGS, AND NOT EVEN A SCRATCH ON A SINGLE CIVILIAN.
I'LL BE SURE TO PUT IN A GOOD WORD WITH YOUR BOSS.
DON'T BOTHER. IT'LL JUST PISS HIM OFF.
THAT'S THE DUDE, HUH? THE TOR-TORDLE--
TORTA-ESPADERO.
HEY, WE DID THE HEAVY LIFTING ON THIS OP.
HOWZ-ABOUT YOU GUYS DO THE PAPER-WORK?
YEAH, YEAH, SURE.
NEED A MINUTE.

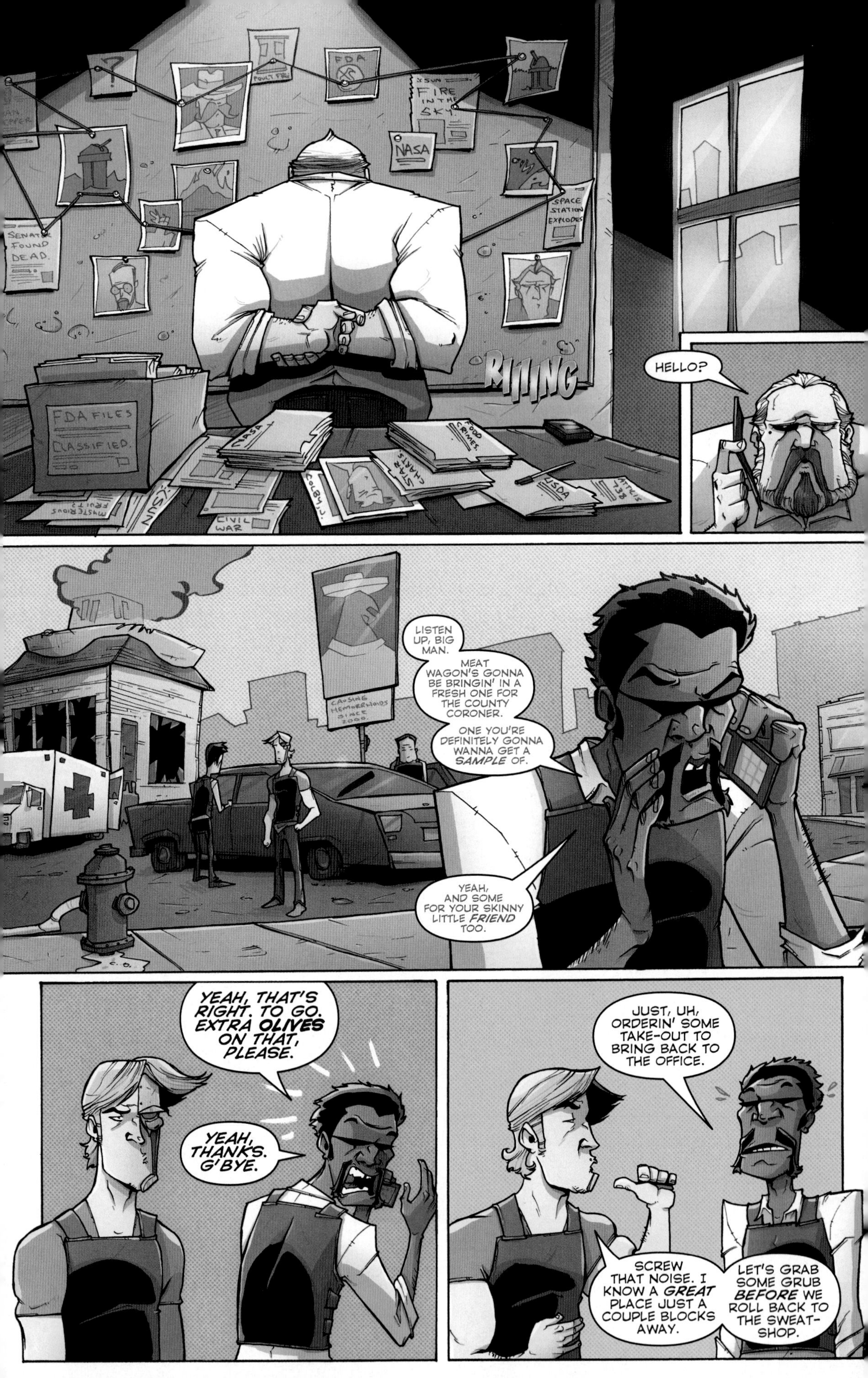
FDA FILES
CLASSIFIED
SENATOR FOUND DEAD.
FIRE IN THE SKY
NASA
SPACE STATION EXPLODES
RIIIING
HELLO?
LISTEN UP, BIG MAN.
MEAT WAGON'S GONNA BE BRINGIN' IN A FRESH ONE FOR THE COUNTY CORONER.
ONE YOU'RE DEFINITELY GONNA WANNA GET A SAMPLE OF.
YEAH, AND SOME FOR YOUR SKINNY LITTLE FRIEND TOO.
YEAH, THAT'S RIGHT. TO GO. EXTRA OLIVES ON THAT, PLEASE.
YEAH, THANKS. G'BYE.
JUST, UH, ORDERIN' SOME TAKE-OUT TO BRING BACK TO THE OFFICE.
LET'S GRAB SOME GRUB BEFORE WE ROLL BACK TO THE SWEAT-SHOP.
SCREW THAT NOISE. I KNOW A GREAT PLACE JUST A COUPLE BLOCKS AWAY.

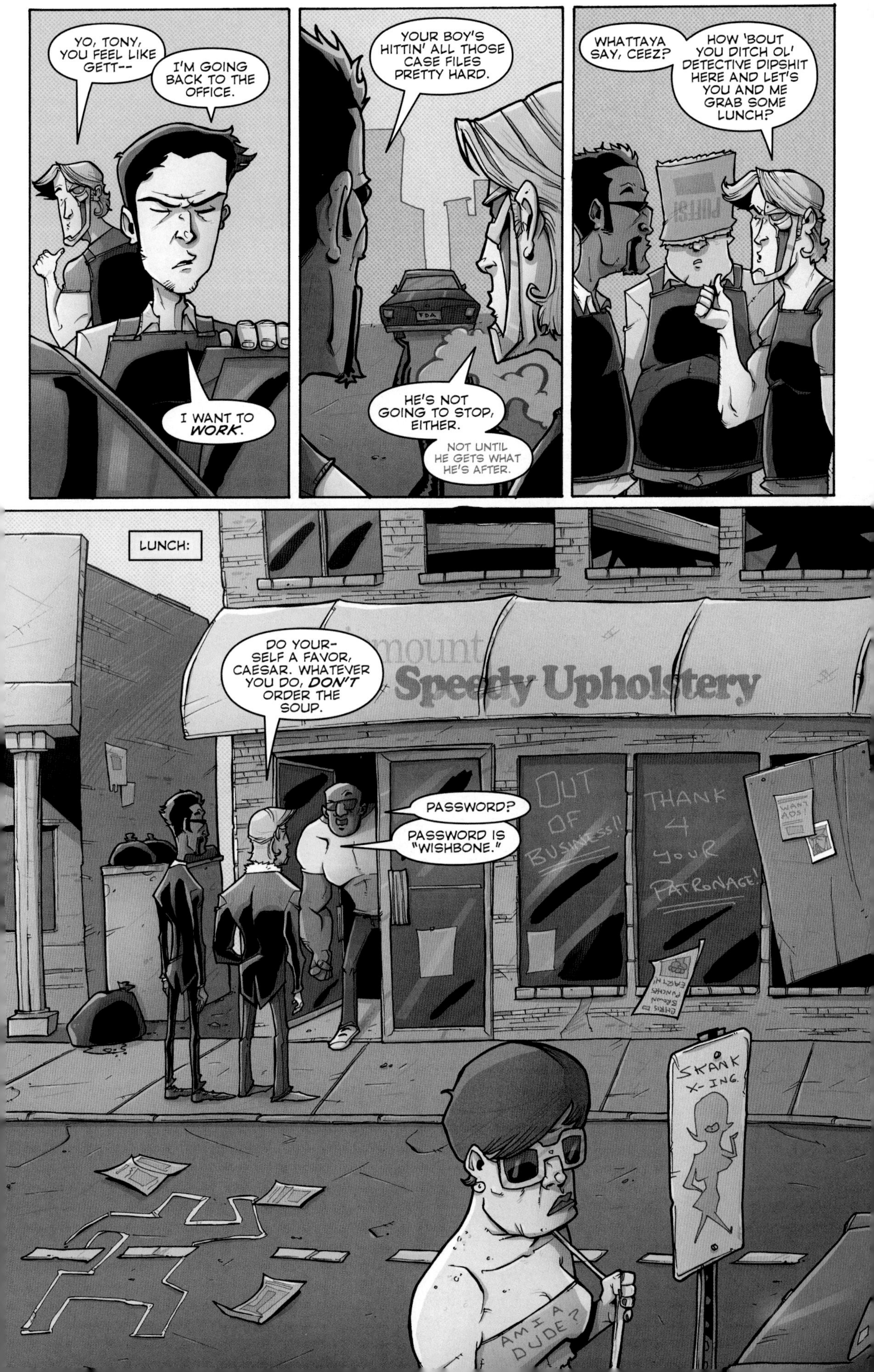
YO, TONY, YOU FEEL LIKE GETT--
I'M GOING BACK TO THE OFFICE.
I WANT TO *WORK*.
YOUR BOY'S HITTIN' ALL THOSE CASE FILES PRETTY HARD.
HE'S NOT GOING TO STOP, EITHER.
NOT UNTIL HE GETS WHAT HE'S AFTER.
WHATTAYA SAY, CEEZ?
HOW 'BOUT YOU DITCH OL' DETECTIVE DIPSHIT HERE AND LET'S YOU AND ME GRAB SOME LUNCH?
LUNCH:
Speedy Upholstery
DO YOURSELF A FAVOR, CAESAR. WHATEVER YOU DO, ***DON'T*** ORDER THE SOUP.
PASSWORD?
PASSWORD IS "WISHBONE."
OUT OF BUSINESS!!
THANK 4 YOUR PATRONAGE!
WANT ADS!
SKANK X-ING.
AM I A DUDE?

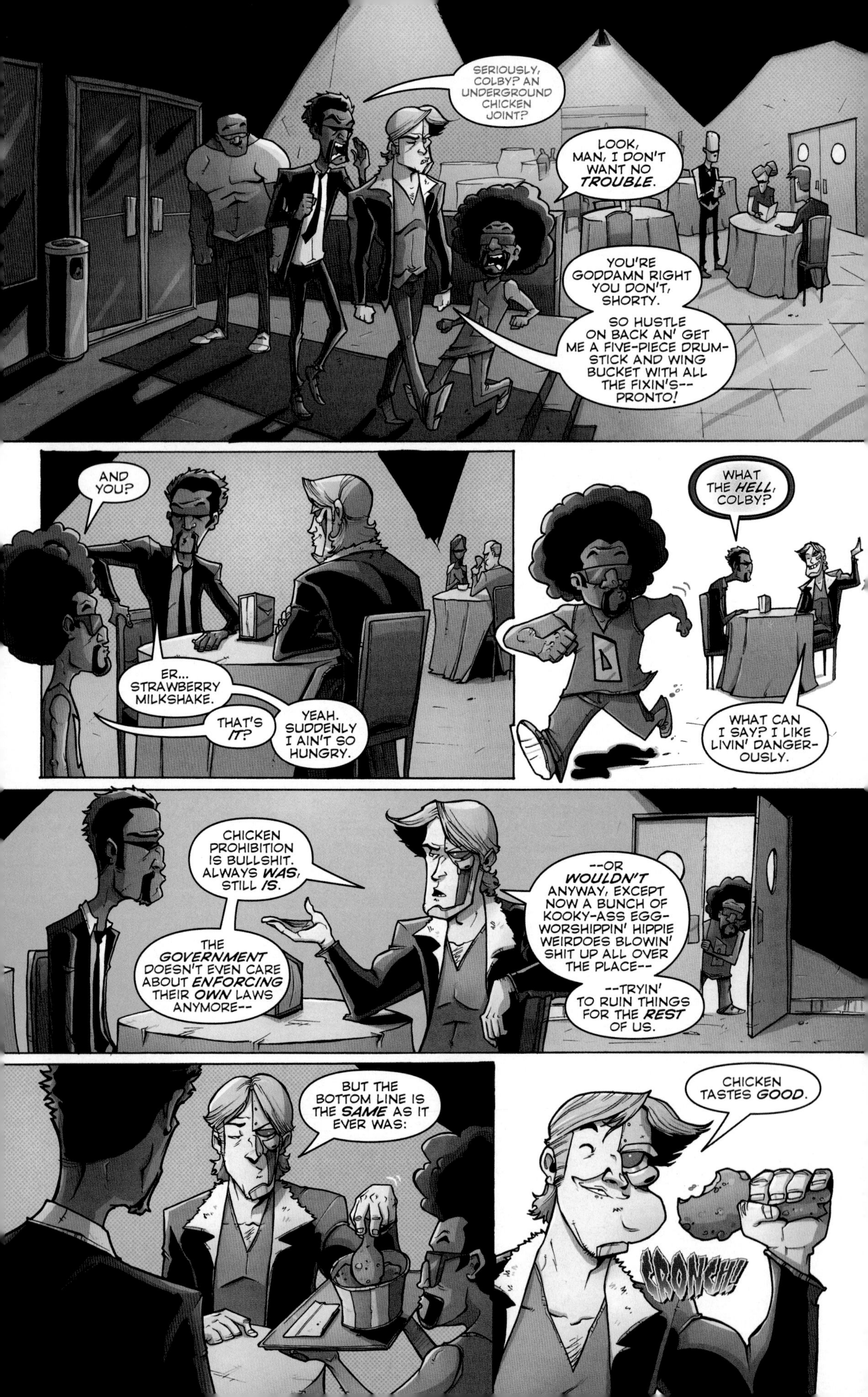
SERIOUSLY, COLBY? AN UNDERGROUND CHICKEN JOINT?
LOOK, MAN, I DON'T WANT NO TROUBLE.
YOU'RE GODDAMN RIGHT YOU DON'T, SHORTY.
SO HUSTLE ON BACK AN' GET ME A FIVE-PIECE DRUM-STICK AND WING BUCKET WITH ALL THE FIXIN'S-- PRONTO!
AND YOU?
ER... STRAWBERRY MILKSHAKE.
THAT'S IT?
YEAH. SUDDENLY I AIN'T SO HUNGRY.
WHAT THE HELL, COLBY?
WHAT CAN I SAY? I LIKE LIVIN' DANGER-OUSLY.
CHICKEN PROHIBITION IS BULLSHIT. ALWAYS WAS, STILL IS.
THE GOVERNMENT DOESN'T EVEN CARE ABOUT ENFORCING THEIR OWN LAWS ANYMORE--
--OR WOULDN'T ANYWAY, EXCEPT NOW A BUNCH OF KOOKY-ASS EGG-WORSHIPPIN' HIPPIE WEIRDOES BLOWIN' SHIT UP ALL OVER THE PLACE--
--TRYIN' TO RUIN THINGS FOR THE REST OF US.
BUT THE BOTTOM LINE IS THE SAME AS IT EVER WAS:
CHICKEN TASTES GOOD.
CRONCH!!

IF YOU DON'T WANT TO ENFORCE THE CHICKEN LAWS, WHY'D YOU COME *BACK* TO THE FDA?

I *KNOW* WHAT IT'S COSTIN' YA.

YEAH, WELL... FOR *TONY.*

TONI TOO, OBVIOUSLY, BUT I'M NOT GONNA LET MY *PARTNER* DOWN.

OH YEAH, I HEAR YA. GOTTA BE LOYAL TO THE PARTNER.

I KNOW HOW *THAT* GOES.

FRIEND OF MINE GAVE ME THE IDEA.

whisper, whisper.

SAVOY AND ME BEEN ON HIM NOW FOR MORE YEARS THAN I CAN COUNT.

EXTRACTED SOME BLOOD AND MIXED IT IN.

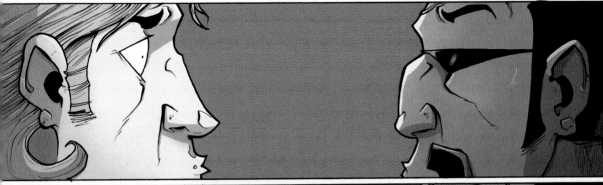

WHAT?

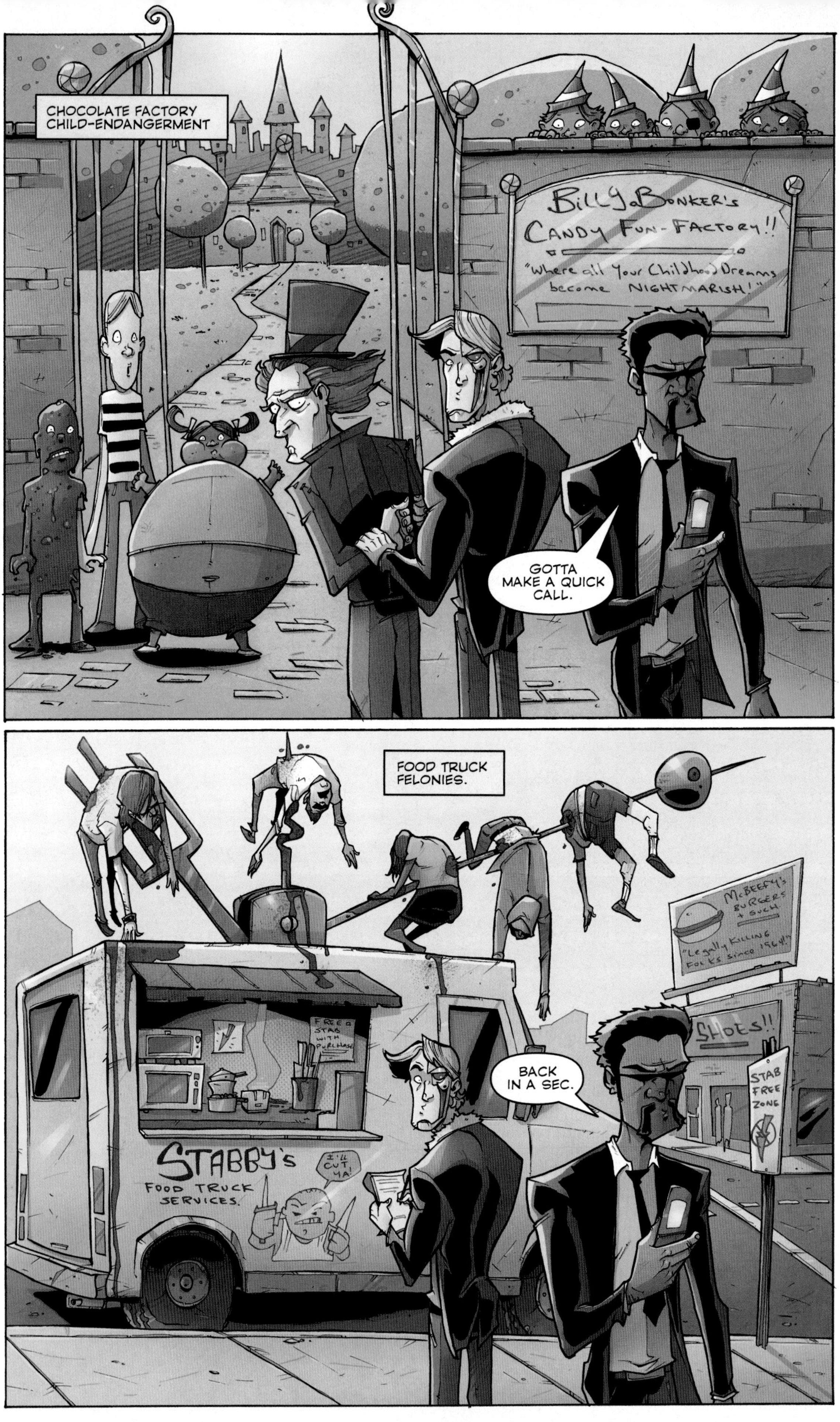
CHOCOLATE FACTORY CHILD-ENDANGERMENT
Billy Bonker's
Candy Fun-Factory!!
"Where all Your Childhood Dreams become NIGHTMARISH!"
GOTTA MAKE A QUICK CALL.
FOOD TRUCK FELONIES.
McBeefy's Burgers + Such
"Legally Killing Folks since 1964!"
FREE STAB WITH PURCHASE
SHOTS!!
BACK IN A SEC.
STAB FREE ZONE
STABBY's
FOOD TRUCK SERVICES.
I'LL CUT YA!

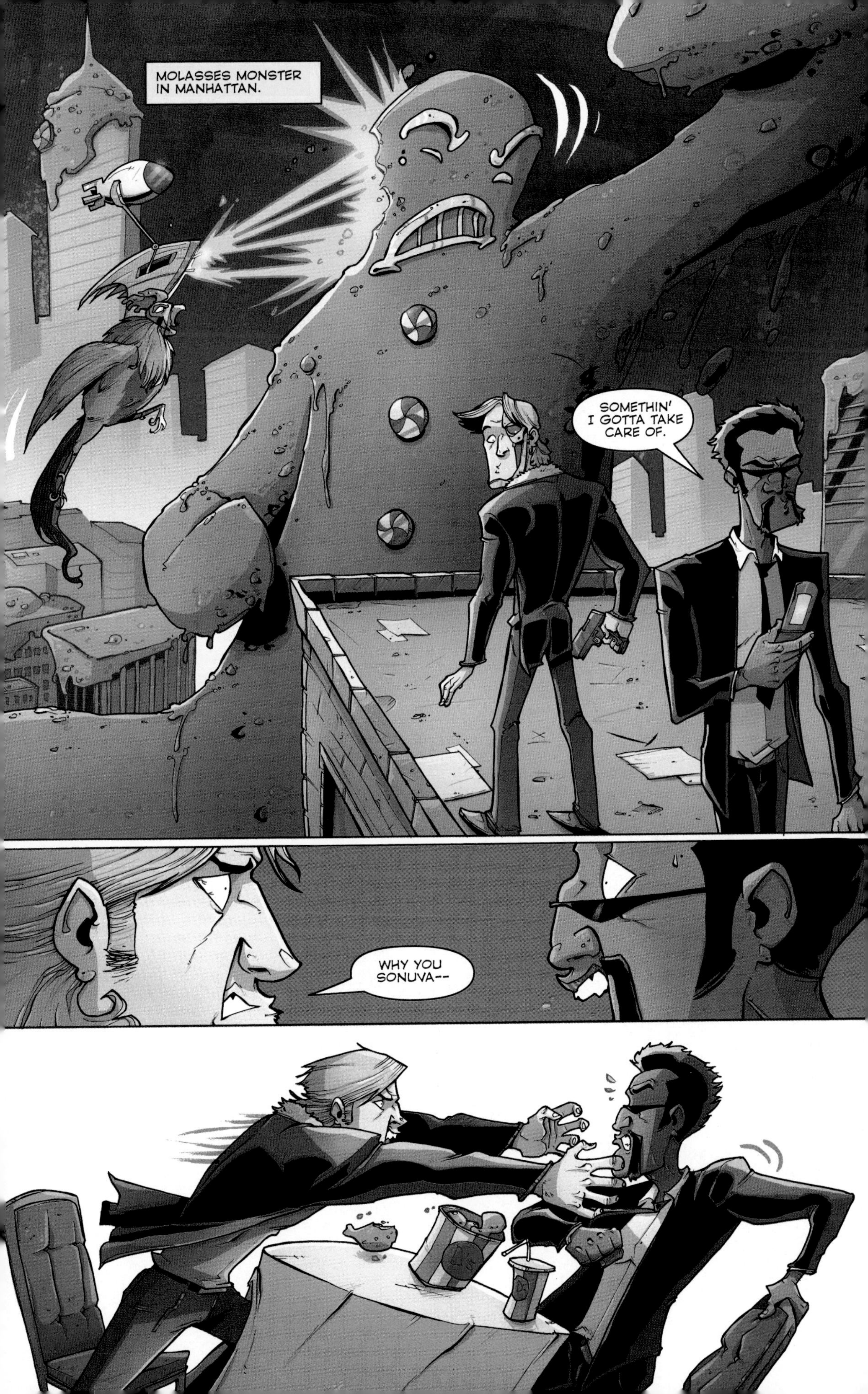
MOLASSES MONSTER IN MANHATTAN.
SOMETHIN' I GOTTA TAKE CARE OF.
WHY YOU SONUVA--

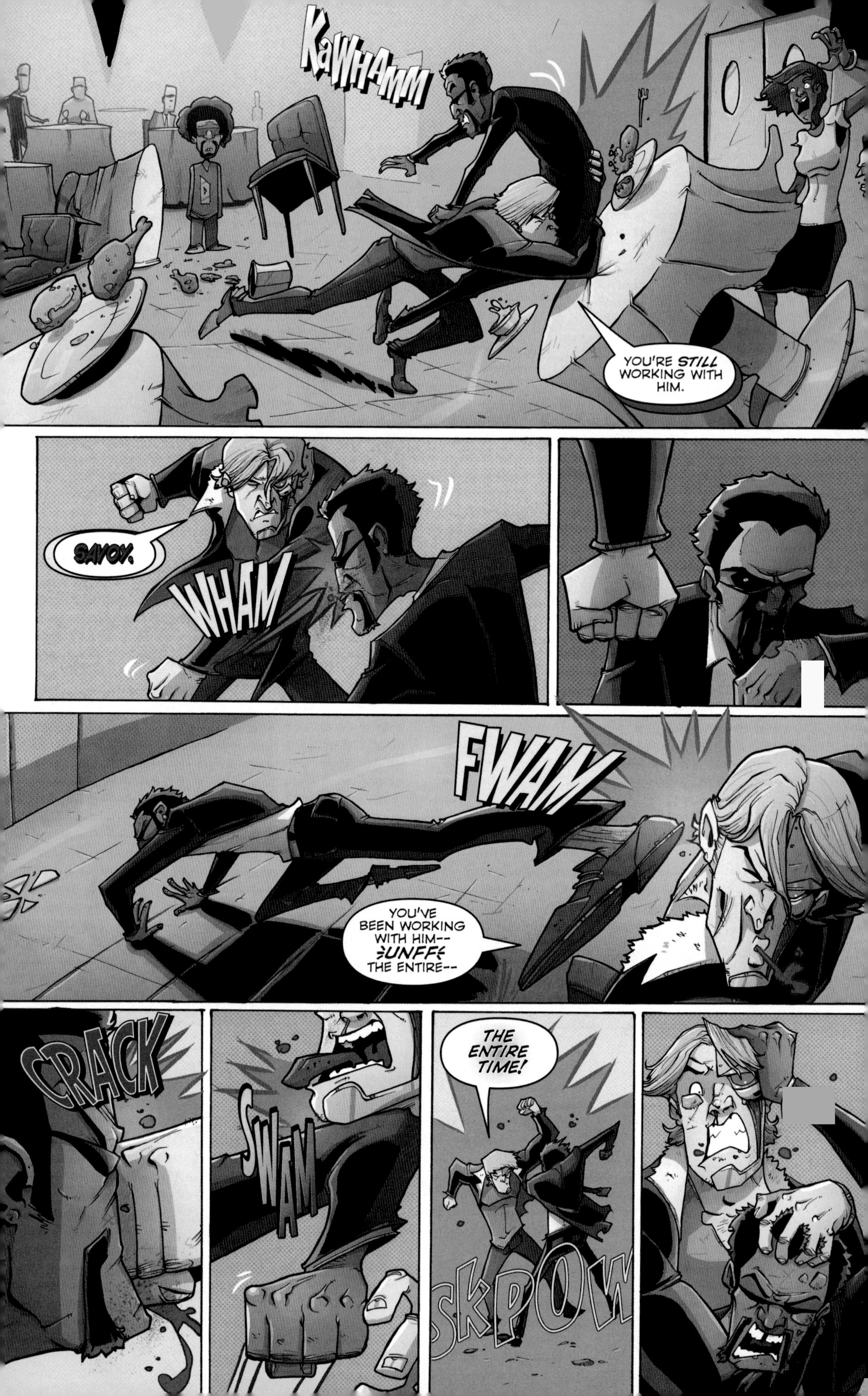
KaWHAMM
YOU'RE STILL WORKING WITH HIM.
SAVOY.
WHAM
FWAM
YOU'VE BEEN WORKING WITH HIM-- UNFF THE ENTIRE--
CRACK
SWAM
THE ENTIRE TIME!
SKPOW

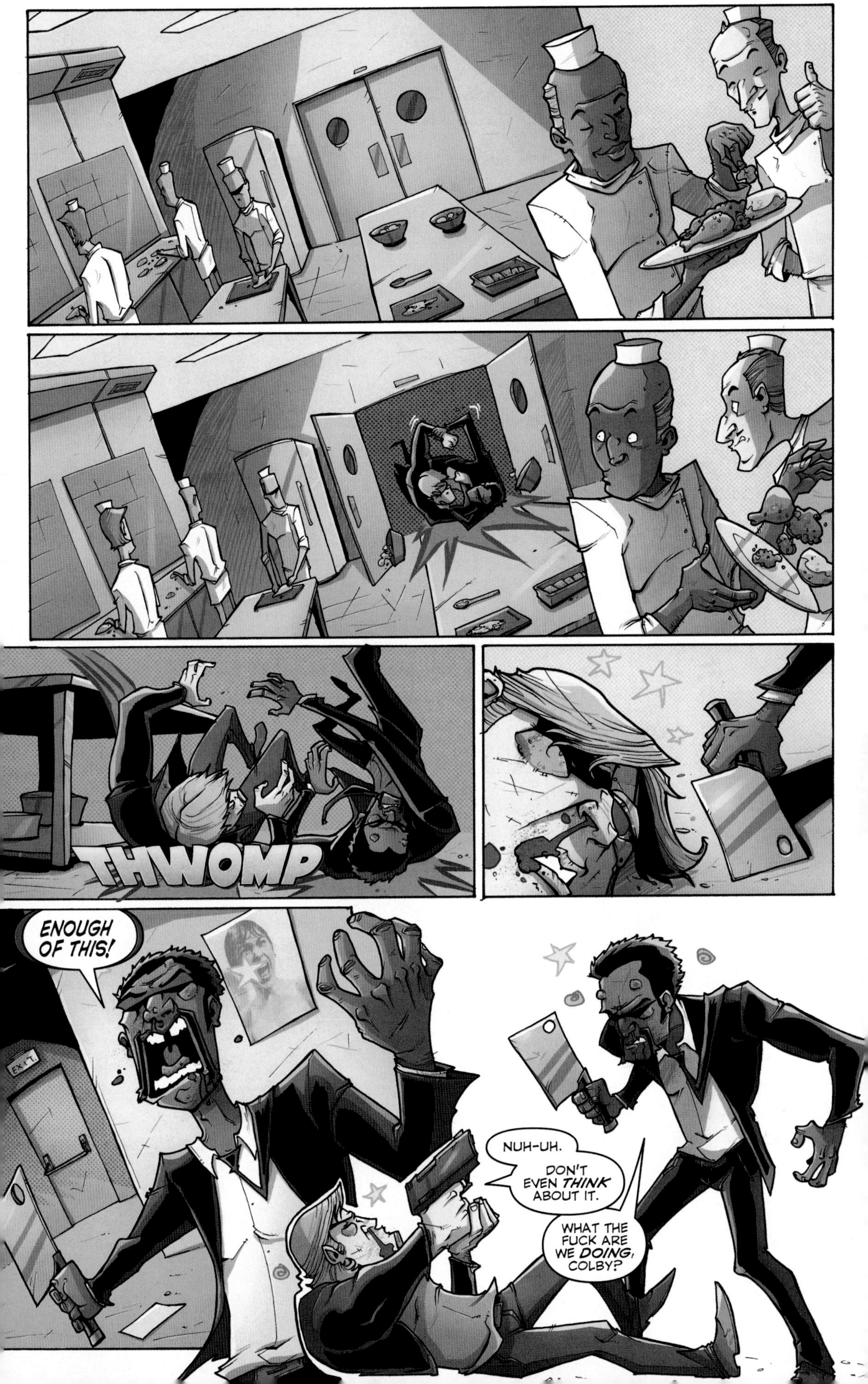
THWOMP
ENOUGH OF THIS!
NUH-UH.
DON'T EVEN *THINK* ABOUT IT.
WHAT THE FUCK ARE WE *DOING*, COLBY?

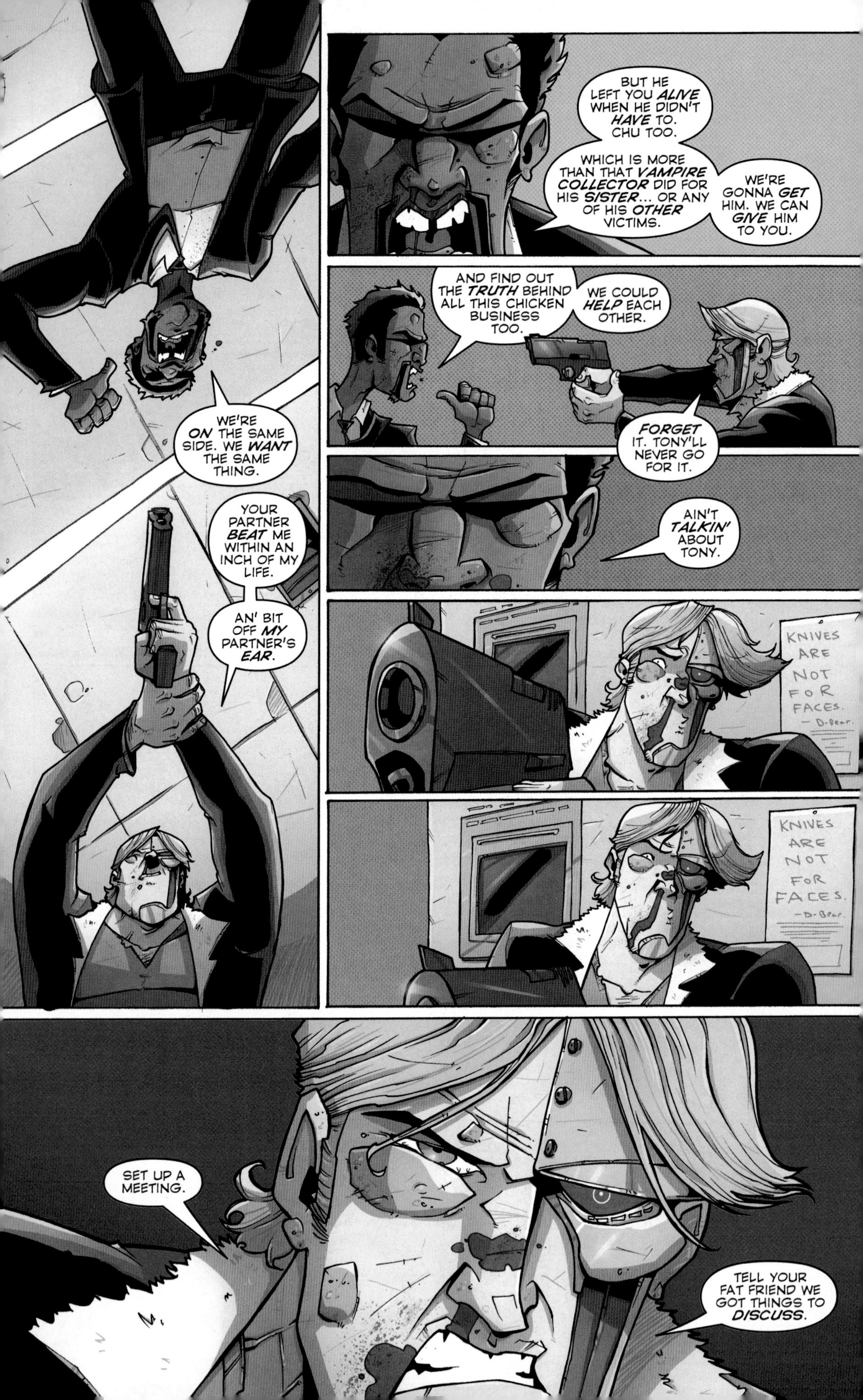
WE'RE ON THE SAME SIDE. WE WANT THE SAME THING.
YOUR PARTNER BEAT ME WITHIN AN INCH OF MY LIFE.
AN' BIT OFF MY PARTNER'S EAR.
BUT HE LEFT YOU ALIVE WHEN HE DIDN'T HAVE TO. CHU TOO.
WHICH IS MORE THAN THAT VAMPIRE COLLECTOR DID FOR HIS SISTER... OR ANY OF HIS OTHER VICTIMS.
WE'RE GONNA GET HIM. WE CAN GIVE HIM TO YOU.
AND FIND OUT THE TRUTH BEHIND ALL THIS CHICKEN BUSINESS TOO.
WE COULD HELP EACH OTHER.
FORGET IT. TONY'LL NEVER GO FOR IT.
AIN'T TALKIN' ABOUT TONY.
KNIVES ARE NOT FOR FACES. —D-Bear.
KNIVES ARE NOT FOR FACES. —D-Bear.
SET UP A MEETING.
TELL YOUR FAT FRIEND WE GOT THINGS TO DISCUSS.

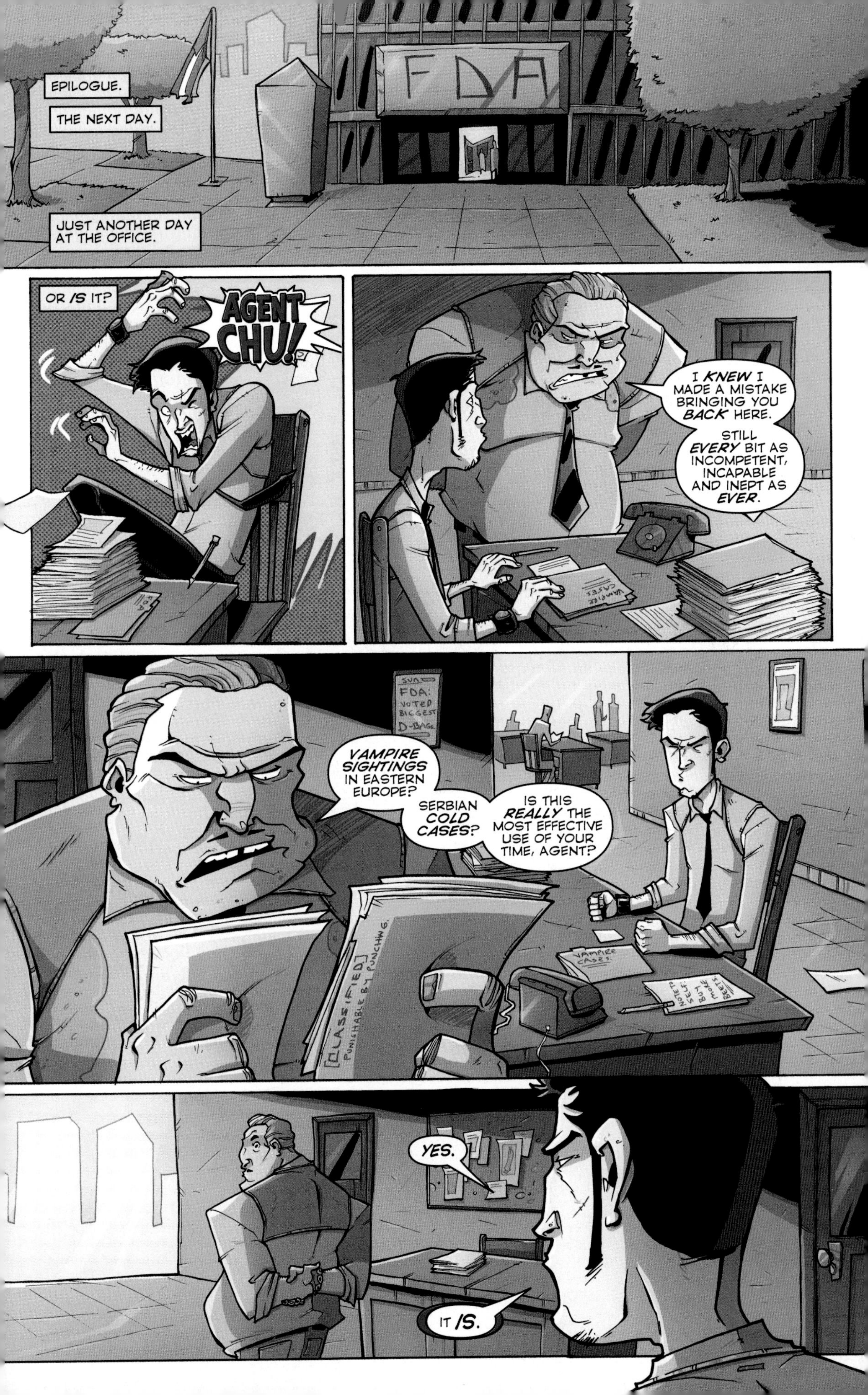
EPILOGUE.
THE NEXT DAY.
FDA
JUST ANOTHER DAY AT THE OFFICE.
OR IS IT?
AGENT CHU!
I KNEW I MADE A MISTAKE BRINGING YOU BACK HERE.
STILL EVERY BIT AS INCOMPETENT, INCAPABLE AND INEPT AS EVER.
VAMPIRE CASES
SVA FDA: VOTED BIGGEST D-BAG
VAMPIRE SIGHTINGS IN EASTERN EUROPE?
SERBIAN COLD CASES?
IS THIS REALLY THE MOST EFFECTIVE USE OF YOUR TIME, AGENT?
[CLASSIFIED] PUNISHABLE BY PUNCHING.
VAMPIRE CASES.
NOTE TO SELF: BUY MORE BEETS
YES.
IT IS.

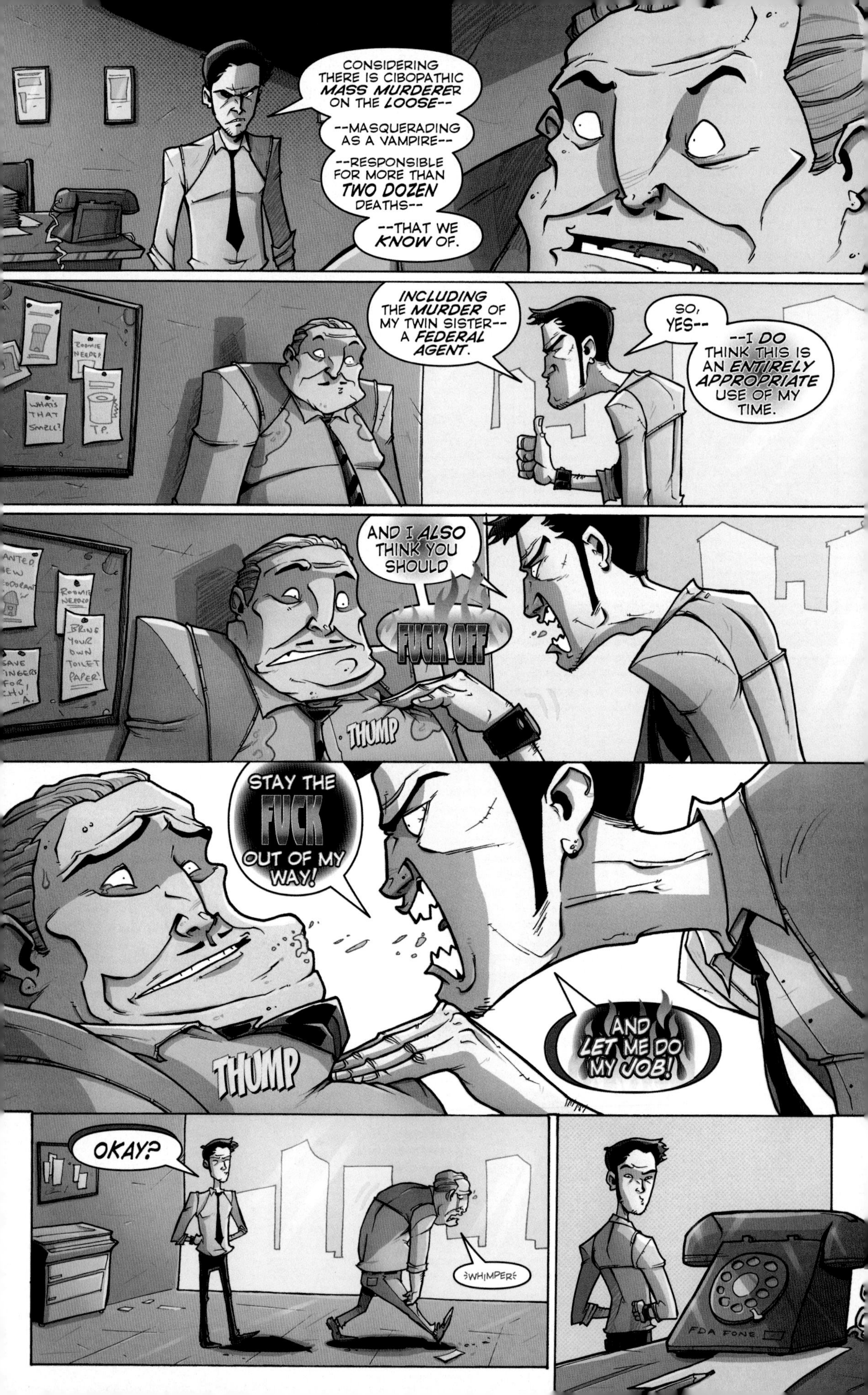
CONSIDERING THERE IS CIBOPATHIC MASS MURDERER ON THE LOOSE--
--MASQUERADING AS A VAMPIRE--
--RESPONSIBLE FOR MORE THAN TWO DOZEN DEATHS--
--THAT WE KNOW OF.
INCLUDING THE MURDER OF MY TWIN SISTER-- A FEDERAL AGENT.
SO, YES--
--I DO THINK THIS IS AN ENTIRELY APPROPRIATE USE OF MY TIME.
ROOMIE NEEDED
WHAT'S THAT SMELL?
T.P.
AND I ALSO THINK YOU SHOULD
FUCK OFF
ROOMIE NEEDED
BRING YOUR OWN TOILET PAPER!
THUMP
STAY THE FUCK OUT OF MY WAY!
AND LET ME DO MY JOB!
THUMP
OKAY?
WHIMPER
FDA FONE

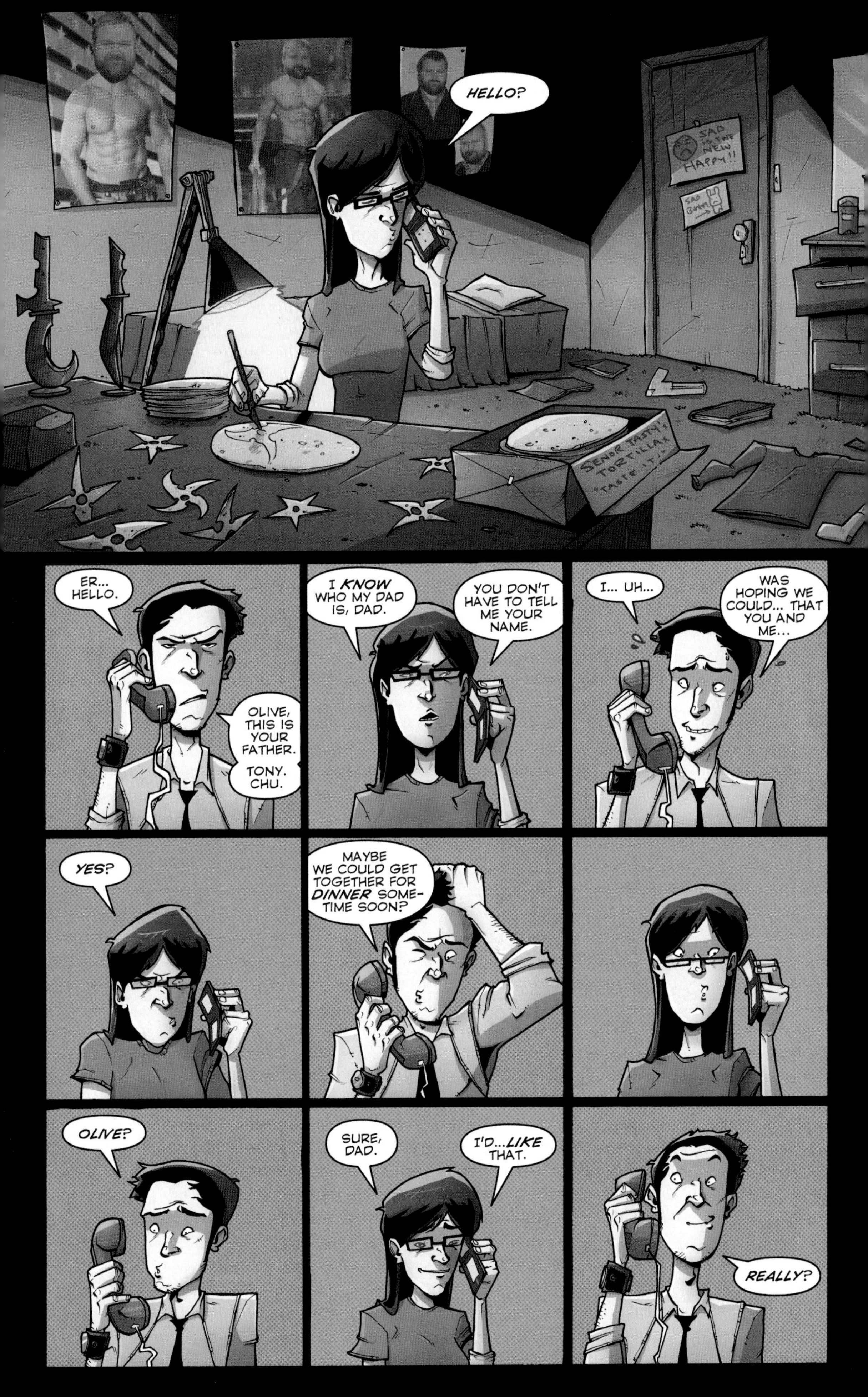

HELLO?
SAD IS THE NEW HAPPY!!
SAD BUNNY
SENOR TASTY'S TORTILLAS "TASTE IT."
ER... HELLO.
OLIVE, THIS IS YOUR FATHER.
TONY. CHU.
I KNOW WHO MY DAD IS, DAD.
YOU DON'T HAVE TO TELL ME YOUR NAME.
I... UH...
WAS HOPING WE COULD... THAT YOU AND ME...
YES?
MAYBE WE COULD GET TOGETHER FOR DINNER SOME-TIME SOON?
OLIVE?
SURE, DAD.
I'D...LIKE THAT.
REALLY?

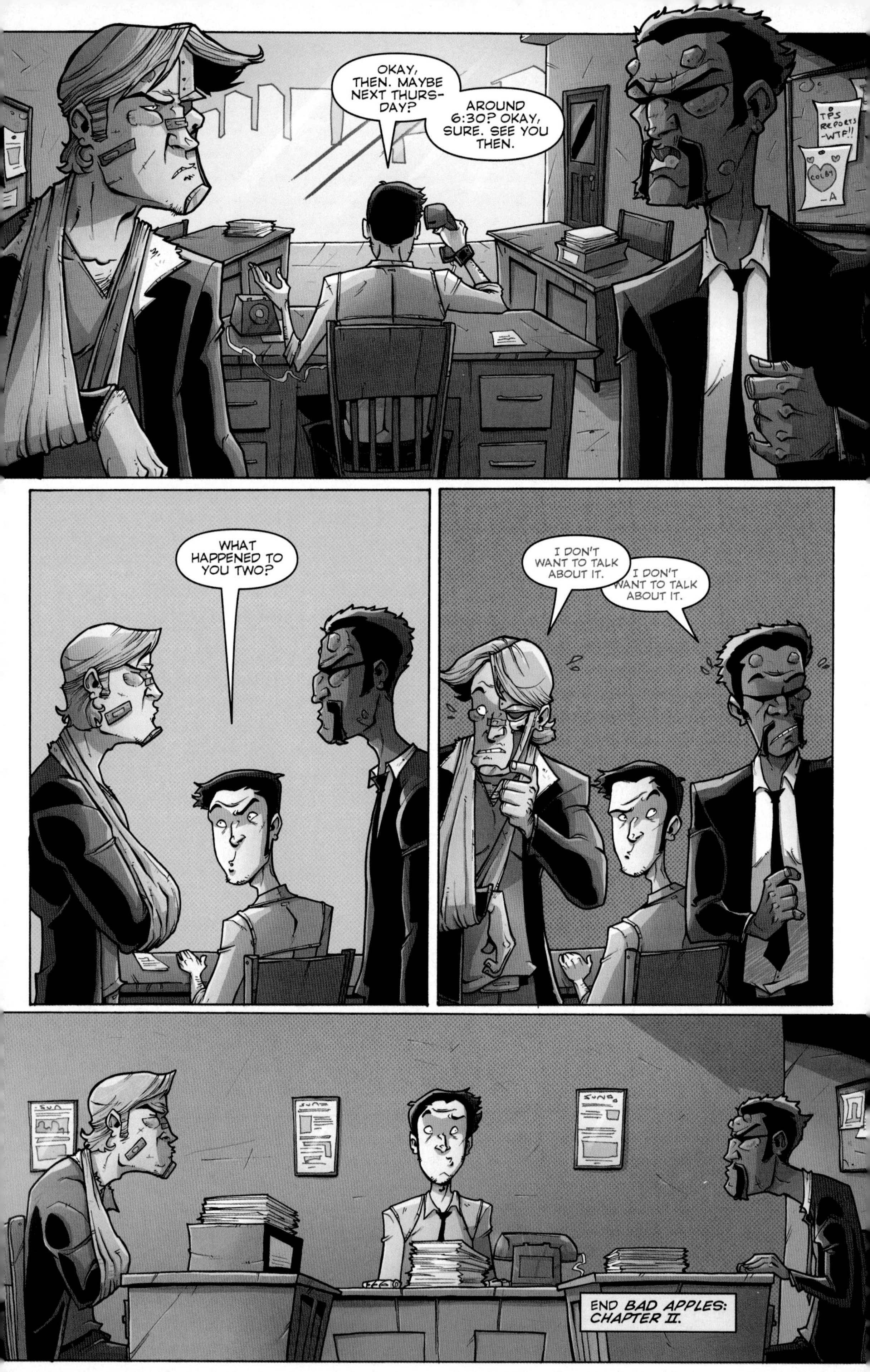
TPS REPORTS -WTF!!
COLBY -A
OKAY, THEN. MAYBE NEXT THURS-DAY?
AROUND 6:30? OKAY, SURE. SEE YOU THEN.
WHAT HAPPENED TO YOU TWO?
I DON'T WANT TO TALK ABOUT IT.
I DON'T WANT TO TALK ABOUT IT.
END *BAD APPLES: CHAPTER II.*

HAZARD

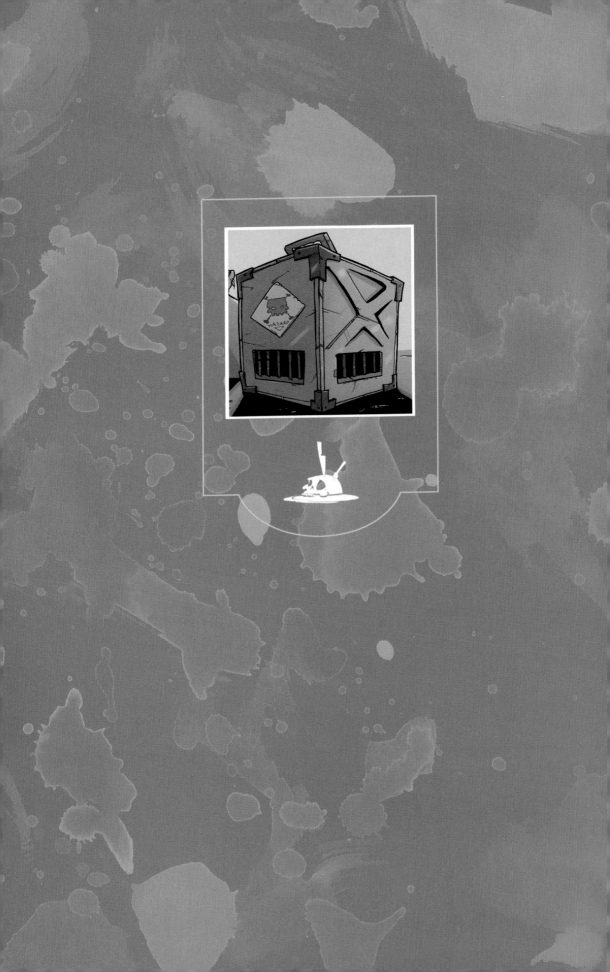

Chapter 3

NAVY
FDA
Rob!

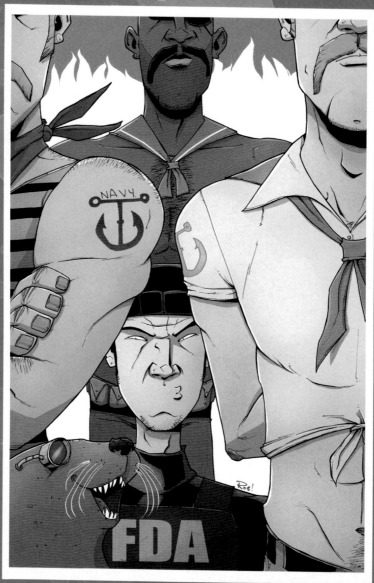

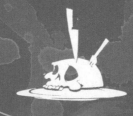

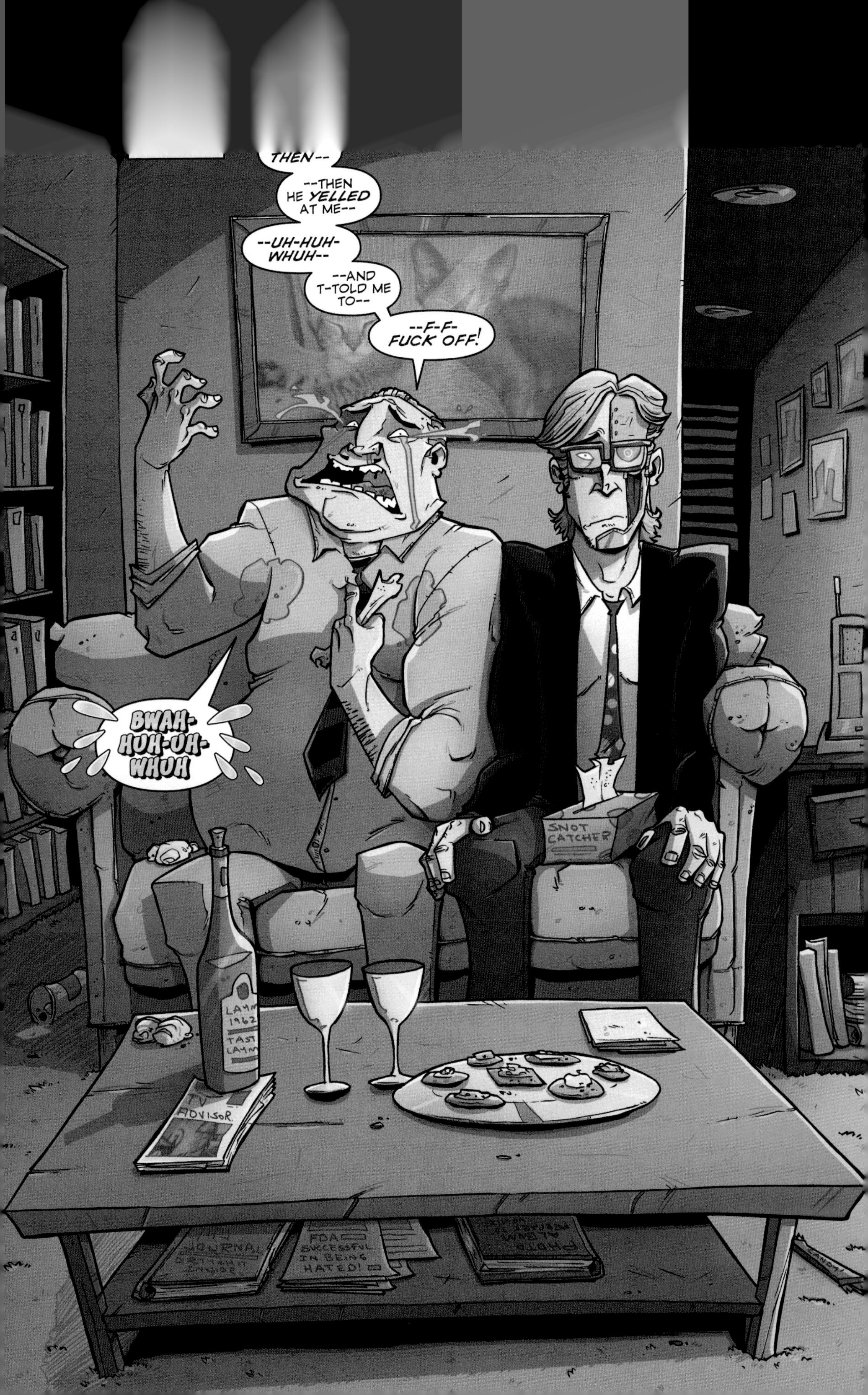
THEN--
--THEN HE YELLED AT ME--
--UH-HUH-WHUH--
--AND T-TOLD ME TO--
--F-F-FUCK OFF!
BWAH-HUH-UH-WHUH
SNOT CATCHER
TV ADVISOR.
FBA SUCCESSFUL IN BEING HATED!

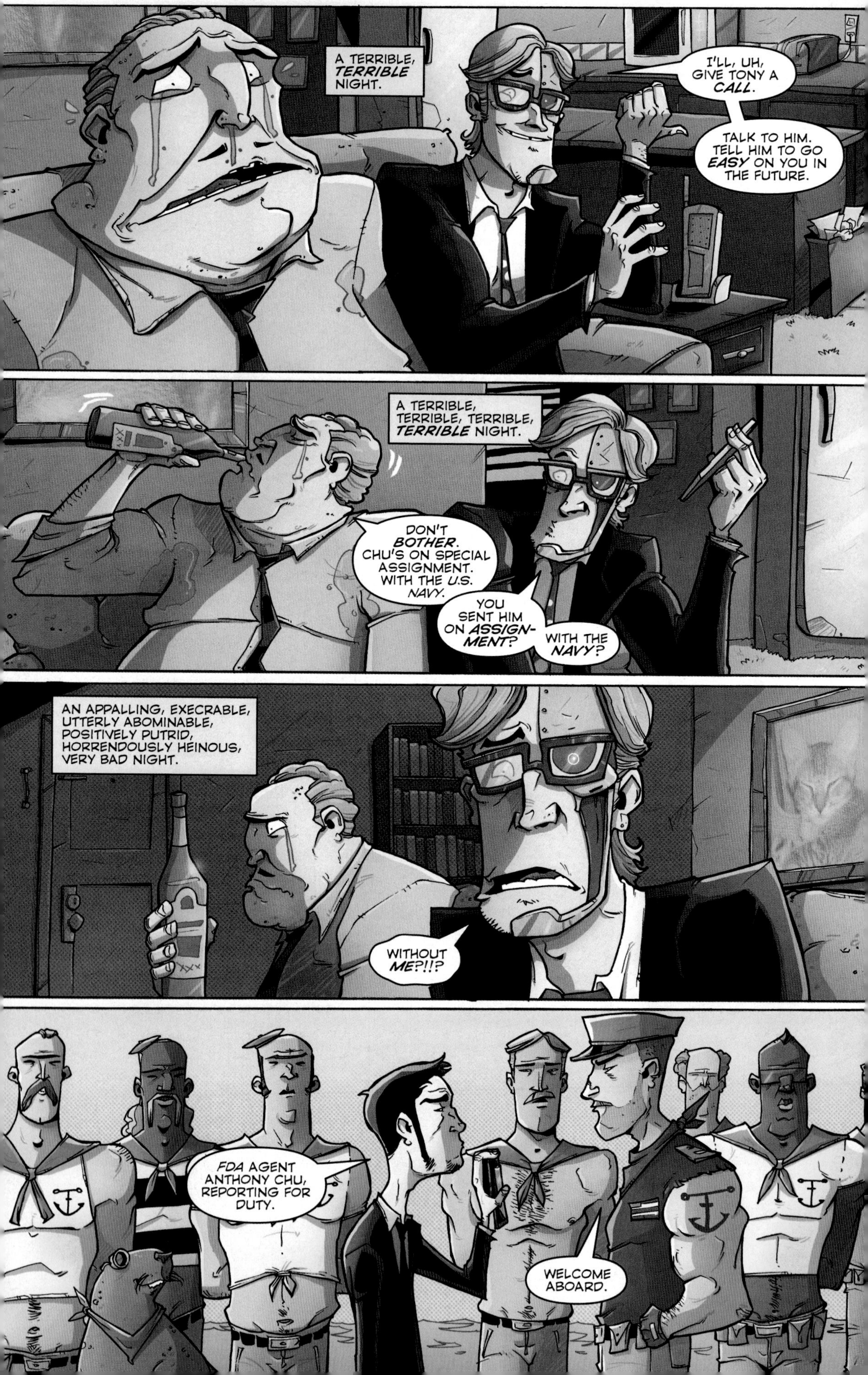
A TERRIBLE, TERRIBLE NIGHT.
I'LL, UH, GIVE TONY A CALL.
TALK TO HIM. TELL HIM TO GO EASY ON YOU IN THE FUTURE.
A TERRIBLE, TERRIBLE, TERRIBLE, TERRIBLE NIGHT.
DON'T BOTHER. CHU'S ON SPECIAL ASSIGNMENT. WITH THE U.S. NAVY.
YOU SENT HIM ON ASSIGNMENT?
WITH THE NAVY?
AN APPALLING, EXECRABLE, UTTERLY ABOMINABLE, POSITIVELY PUTRID, HORRENDOUSLY HEINOUS, VERY BAD NIGHT.
WITHOUT ME?!!?
FDA AGENT ANTHONY CHU, REPORTING FOR DUTY.
WELCOME ABOARD.

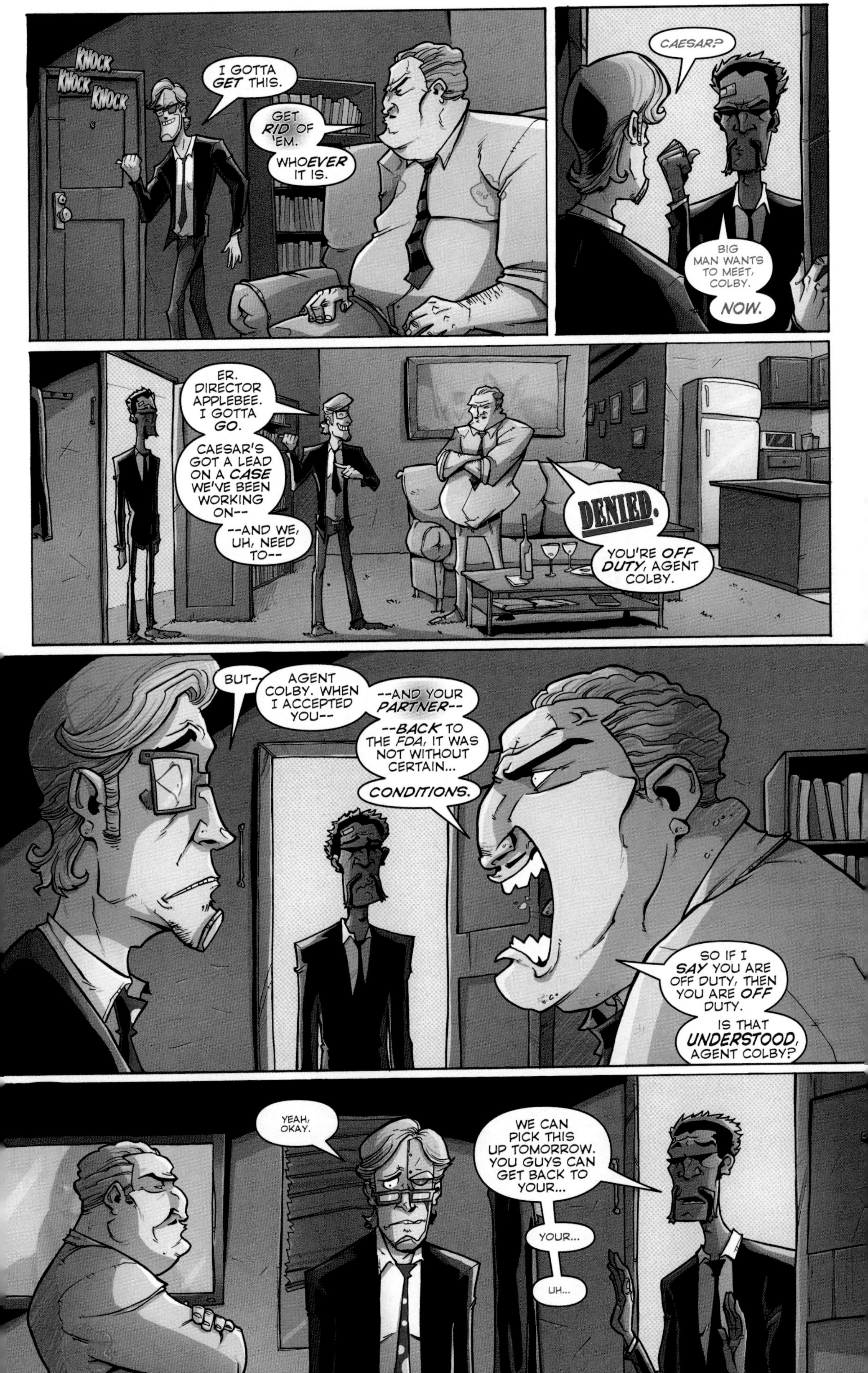
KNOCK KNOCK KNOCK
I GOTTA GET THIS.
GET RID OF 'EM.
WHOEVER IT IS.
CAESAR?
BIG MAN WANTS TO MEET, COLBY.
NOW.
ER. DIRECTOR APPLEBEE. I GOTTA GO.
CAESAR'S GOT A LEAD ON A CASE WE'VE BEEN WORKING ON--
--AND WE, UH, NEED TO--
DENIED.
YOU'RE OFF DUTY, AGENT COLBY.
BUT--
AGENT COLBY. WHEN I ACCEPTED YOU--
--AND YOUR PARTNER--
--BACK TO THE FDA, IT WAS NOT WITHOUT CERTAIN...
CONDITIONS.
SO IF I SAY YOU ARE OFF DUTY, THEN YOU ARE OFF DUTY.
IS THAT UNDERSTOOD, AGENT COLBY?
YEAH, OKAY.
WE CAN PICK THIS UP TOMORROW. YOU GUYS CAN GET BACK TO YOUR...
YOUR...
UH...

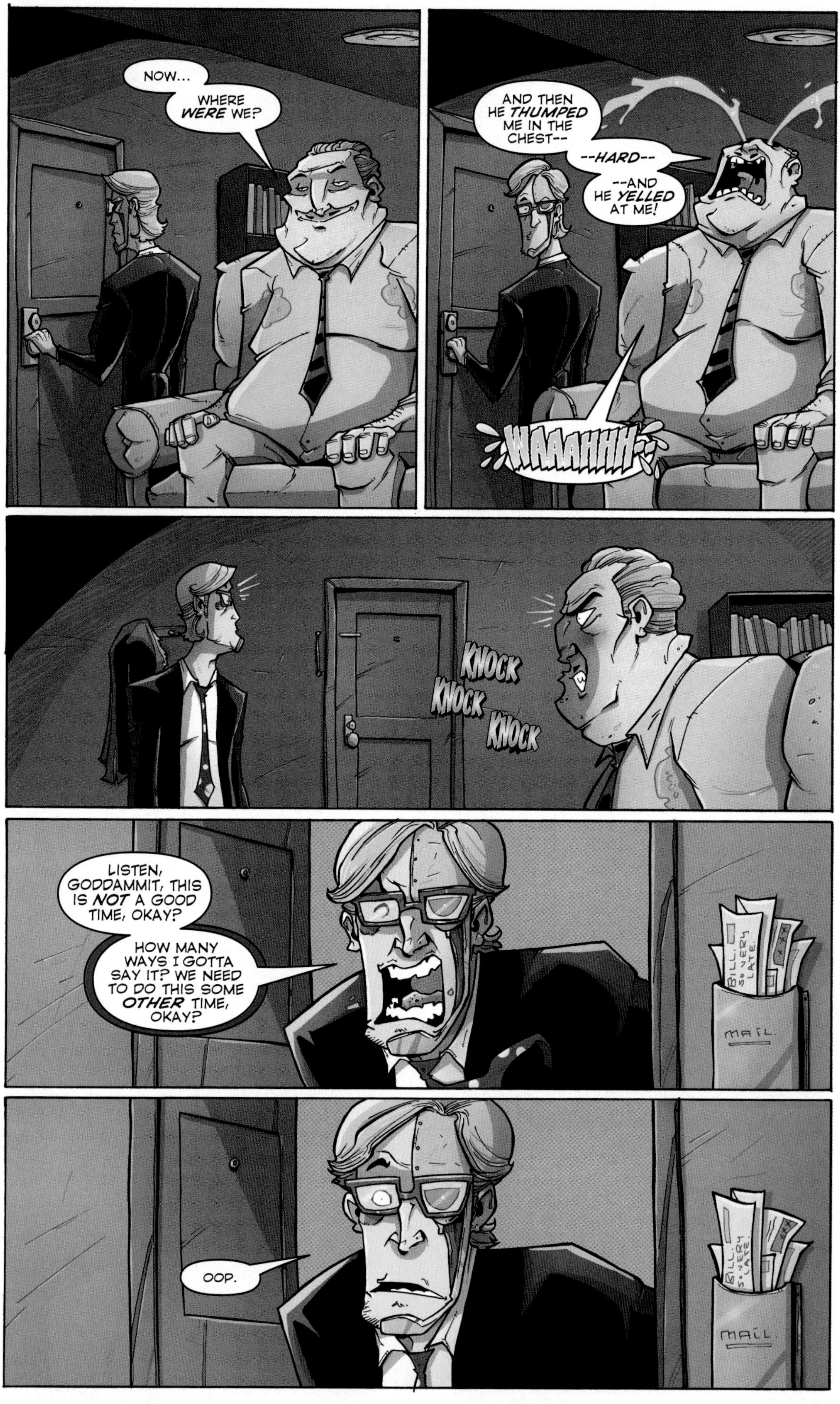
NOW...
WHERE WERE WE?
AND THEN HE THUMPED ME IN THE CHEST--
--HARD--
--AND HE YELLED AT ME!
WAAAHHH
KNOCK KNOCK KNOCK
LISTEN, GODDAMMIT, THIS IS NOT A GOOD TIME, OKAY?
HOW MANY WAYS I GOTTA SAY IT? WE NEED TO DO THIS SOME OTHER TIME, OKAY?
BILL. SO VERY LATE.
MAIL.
OOP.
BILL. SO VERY LATE.
MAIL.

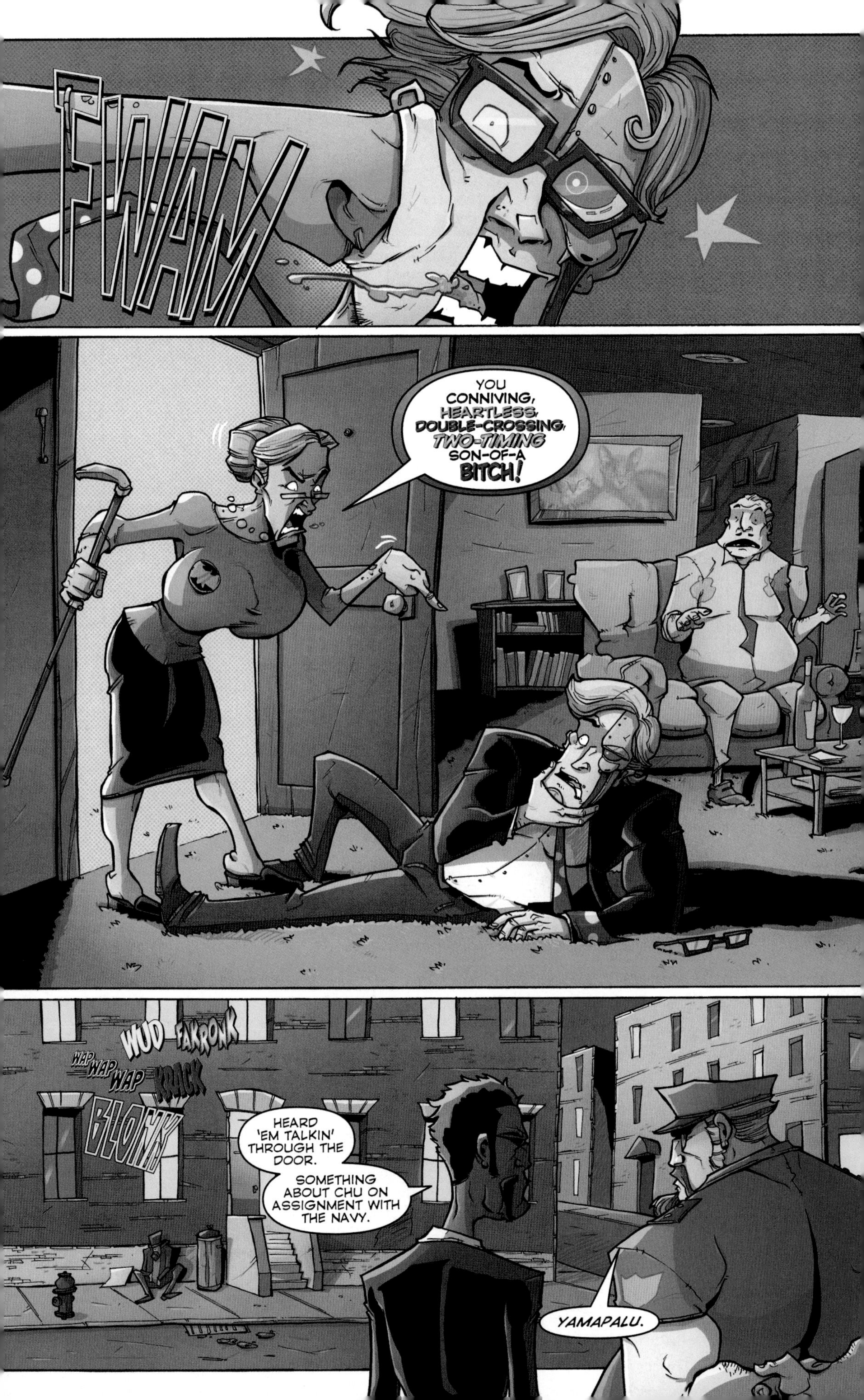
FWAM
YOU CONNIVING, HEARTLESS, DOUBLE-CROSSING, TWO-TIMING SON-OF-A BITCH!
WUD
FAKRONK
WAP WAP WAP
KRACK
BLOMK
HEARD 'EM TALKIN' THROUGH THE DOOR.
SOMETHING ABOUT CHU ON ASSIGNMENT WITH THE NAVY.
YAMAPALU.

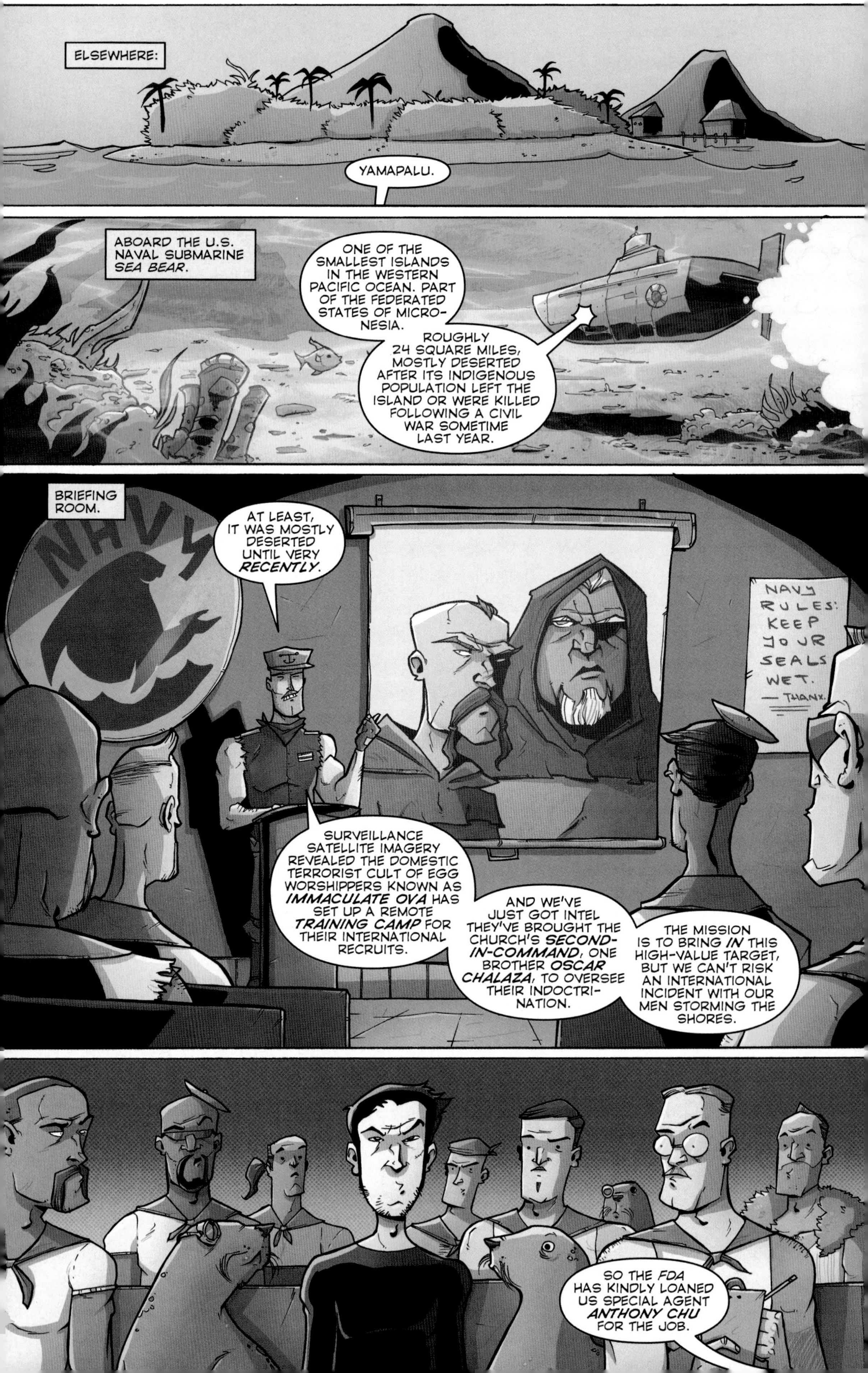
ELSEWHERE:
YAMAPALU.
ABOARD THE U.S. NAVAL SUBMARINE *SEA BEAR*.
ONE OF THE SMALLEST ISLANDS IN THE WESTERN PACIFIC OCEAN. PART OF THE FEDERATED STATES OF MICRO-NESIA.
ROUGHLY 24 SQUARE MILES, MOSTLY DESERTED AFTER ITS INDIGENOUS POPULATION LEFT THE ISLAND OR WERE KILLED FOLLOWING A CIVIL WAR SOMETIME LAST YEAR.
BRIEFING ROOM.
AT LEAST, IT WAS MOSTLY DESERTED UNTIL VERY *RECENTLY*.
NAVY
NAVY RULES: KEEP YOUR SEALS WET. —THANX.
SURVEILLANCE SATELLITE IMAGERY REVEALED THE DOMESTIC TERRORIST CULT OF EGG WORSHIPPERS KNOWN AS *IMMACULATE OVA* HAS SET UP A REMOTE *TRAINING CAMP* FOR THEIR INTERNATIONAL RECRUITS.
AND WE'VE JUST GOT INTEL THEY'VE BROUGHT THE CHURCH'S *SECOND-IN-COMMAND*, ONE BROTHER *OSCAR CHALAZA*, TO OVERSEE THEIR INDOCTRI-NATION.
THE MISSION IS TO BRING *IN* THIS HIGH-VALUE TARGET, BUT WE CAN'T RISK AN INTERNATIONAL INCIDENT WITH OUR MEN STORMING THE SHORES.
SO THE *FDA* HAS KINDLY LOANED US SPECIAL AGENT *ANTHONY CHU* FOR THE JOB.

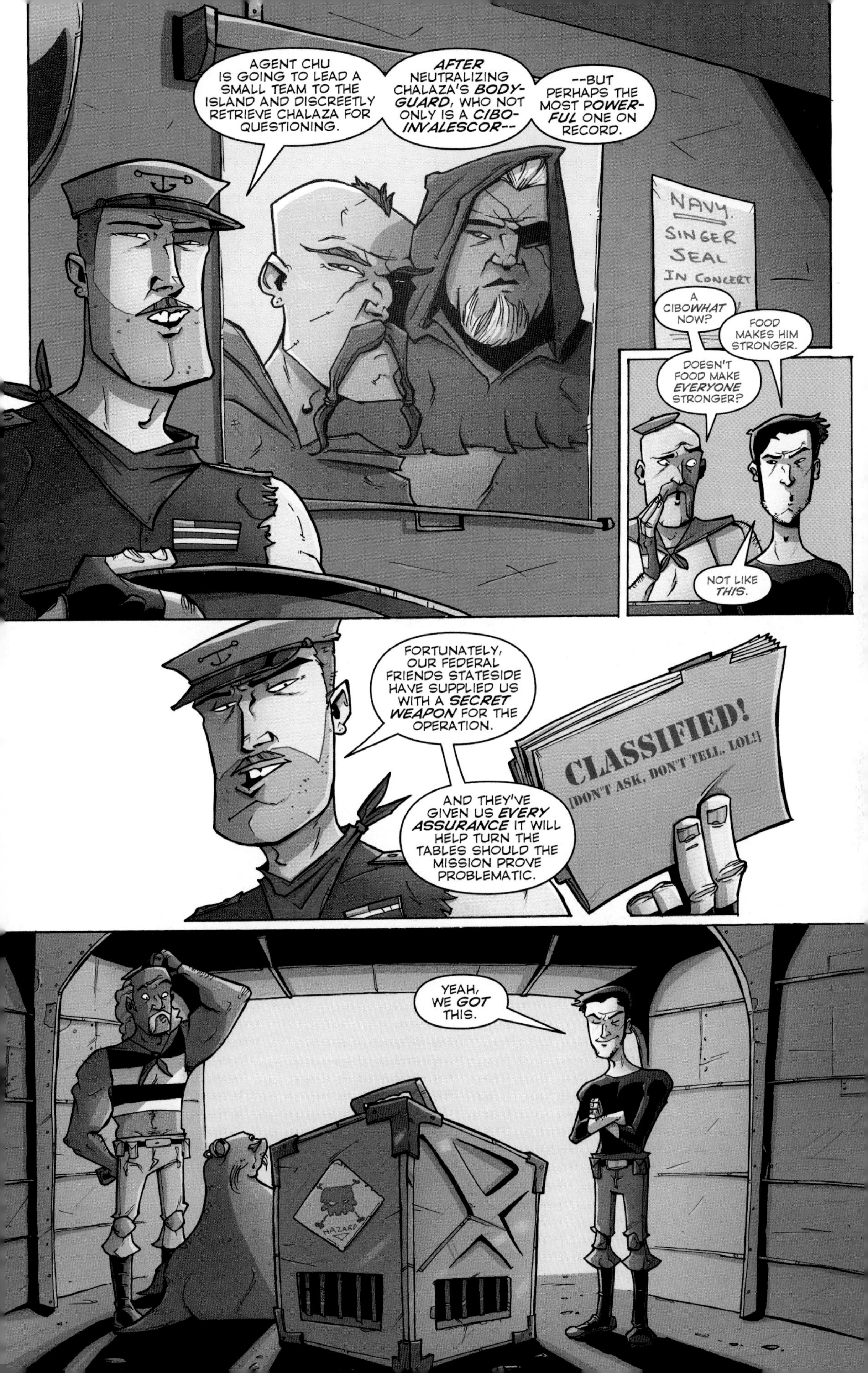
AGENT CHU IS GOING TO LEAD A SMALL TEAM TO THE ISLAND AND DISCREETLY RETRIEVE CHALAZA FOR QUESTIONING.
AFTER NEUTRALIZING CHALAZA'S BODYGUARD, WHO NOT ONLY IS A CIBO-INVALESCOR--
--BUT PERHAPS THE MOST POWERFUL ONE ON RECORD.
NAVY. SINGER SEAL IN CONCERT
A CIBOWHAT NOW?
FOOD MAKES HIM STRONGER.
DOESN'T FOOD MAKE EVERYONE STRONGER?
NOT LIKE THIS.
FORTUNATELY, OUR FEDERAL FRIENDS STATESIDE HAVE SUPPLIED US WITH A SECRET WEAPON FOR THE OPERATION.
AND THEY'VE GIVEN US EVERY ASSURANCE IT WILL HELP TURN THE TABLES SHOULD THE MISSION PROVE PROBLEMATIC.
CLASSIFIED!
[DON'T ASK, DON'T TELL. LOL!]
YEAH, WE GOT THIS.
HAZARD

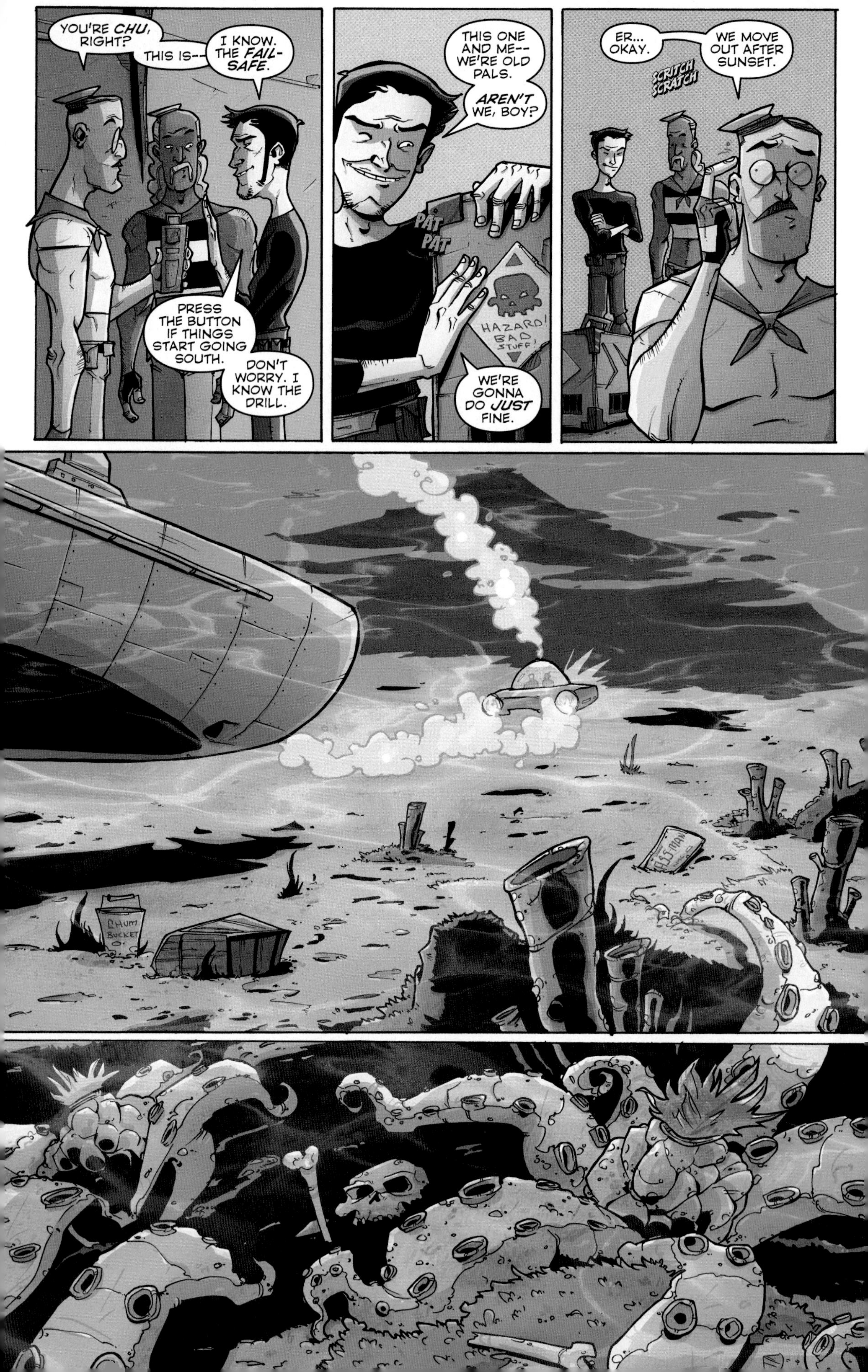
YOU'RE CHU, RIGHT?
THIS IS--
I KNOW. THE FAIL-SAFE.
PRESS THE BUTTON IF THINGS START GOING SOUTH.
DON'T WORRY. I KNOW THE DRILL.
THIS ONE AND ME-- WE'RE OLD PALS.
AREN'T WE, BOY?
PAT PAT
HAZARD! BAD STUFF!
WE'RE GONNA DO JUST FINE.
ER... OKAY.
WE MOVE OUT AFTER SUNSET.
SCRITCH SCRATCH
CHUM BUCKET

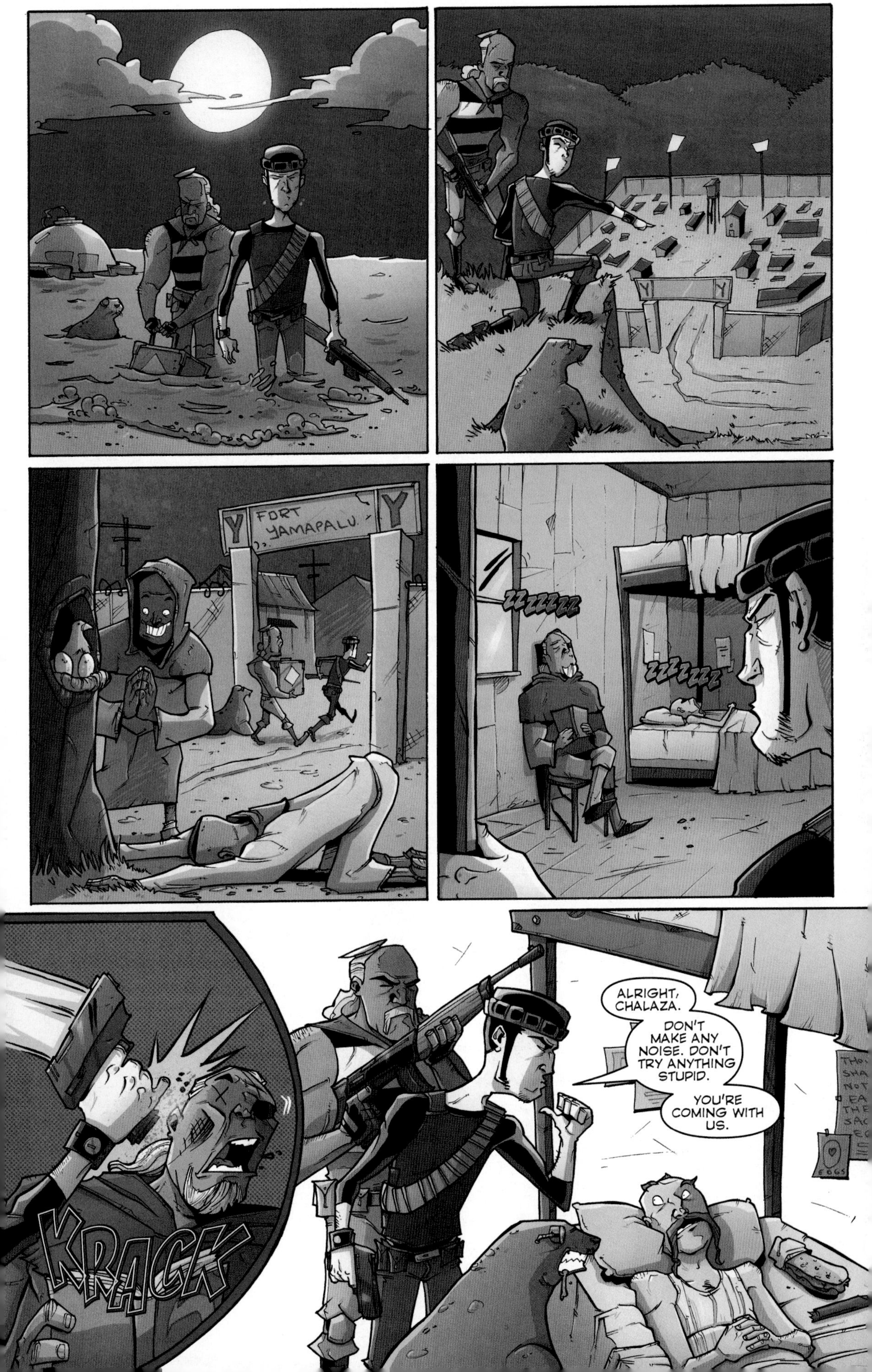
FORT YAMAPALU
KRACK
ALRIGHT, CHALAZA.
DON'T MAKE ANY NOISE. DON'T TRY ANYTHING STUPID.
YOU'RE COMING WITH US.

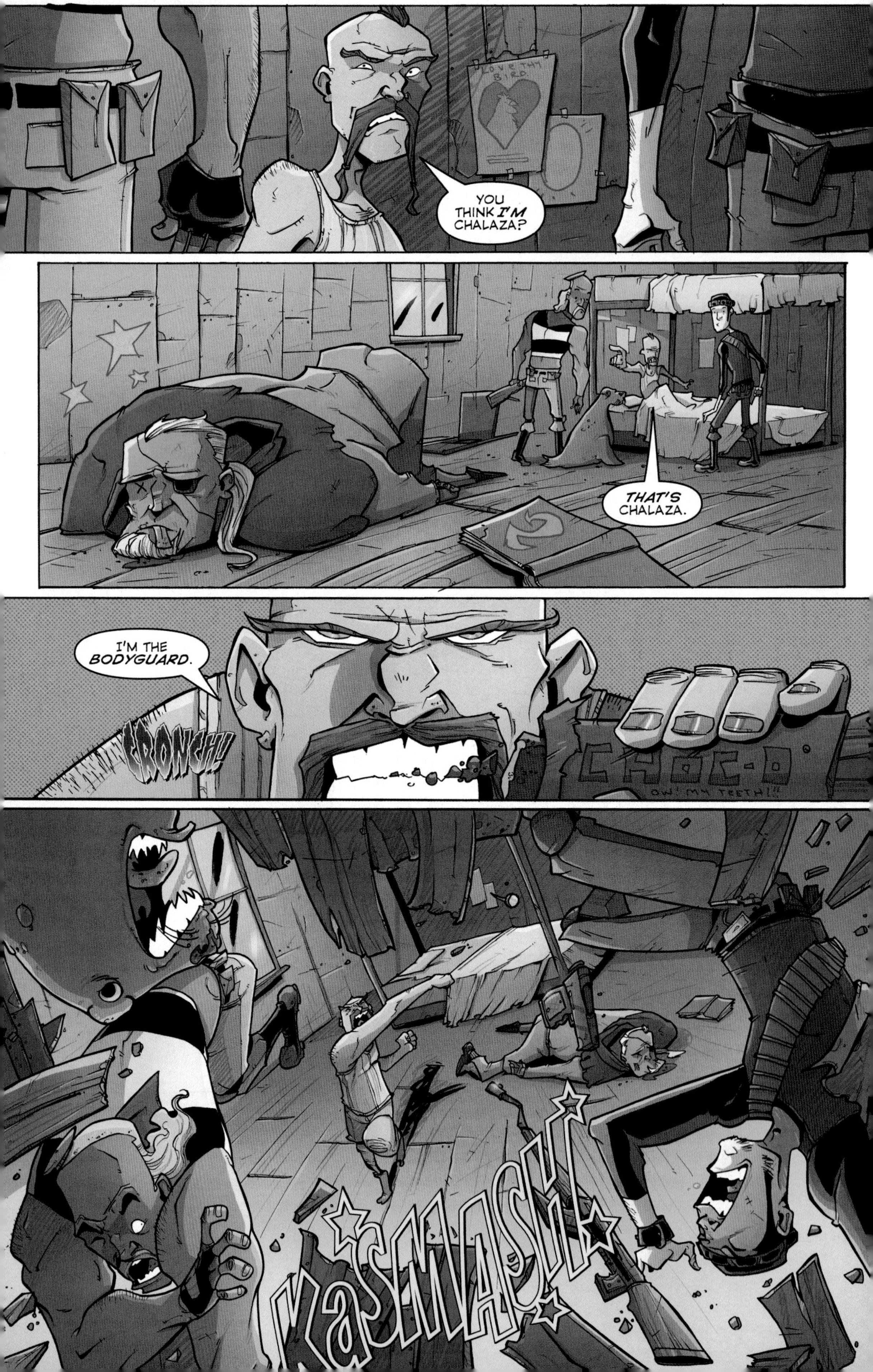
LOVE THY BIRD
YOU THINK I'M CHALAZA?
THAT'S CHALAZA.
I'M THE BODYGUARD.
CRONCH!
CHOC-O
OW! MY TEETH!!
KASMASH!

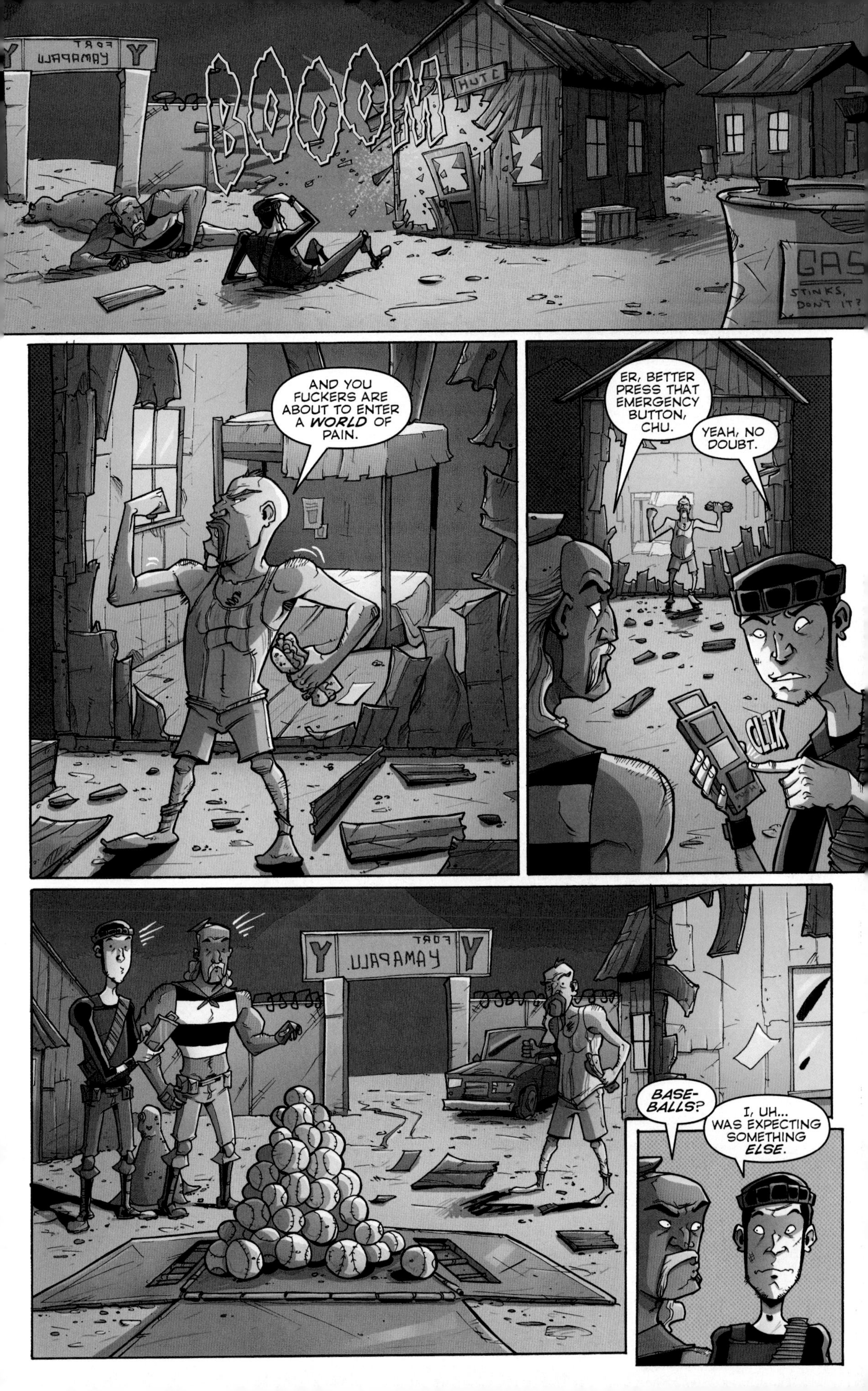

FORT YAMAPALU
BOOOOM
HUT C
GAS
STINKS, DON'T IT?
AND YOU FUCKERS ARE ABOUT TO ENTER A *WORLD* OF PAIN.
ER, BETTER PRESS THAT EMERGENCY BUTTON, CHU.
YEAH, NO DOUBT.
CLIK
FORT YAMAPALU
BASE-BALLS?
I, UH... WAS EXPECTING SOMETHING *ELSE*.

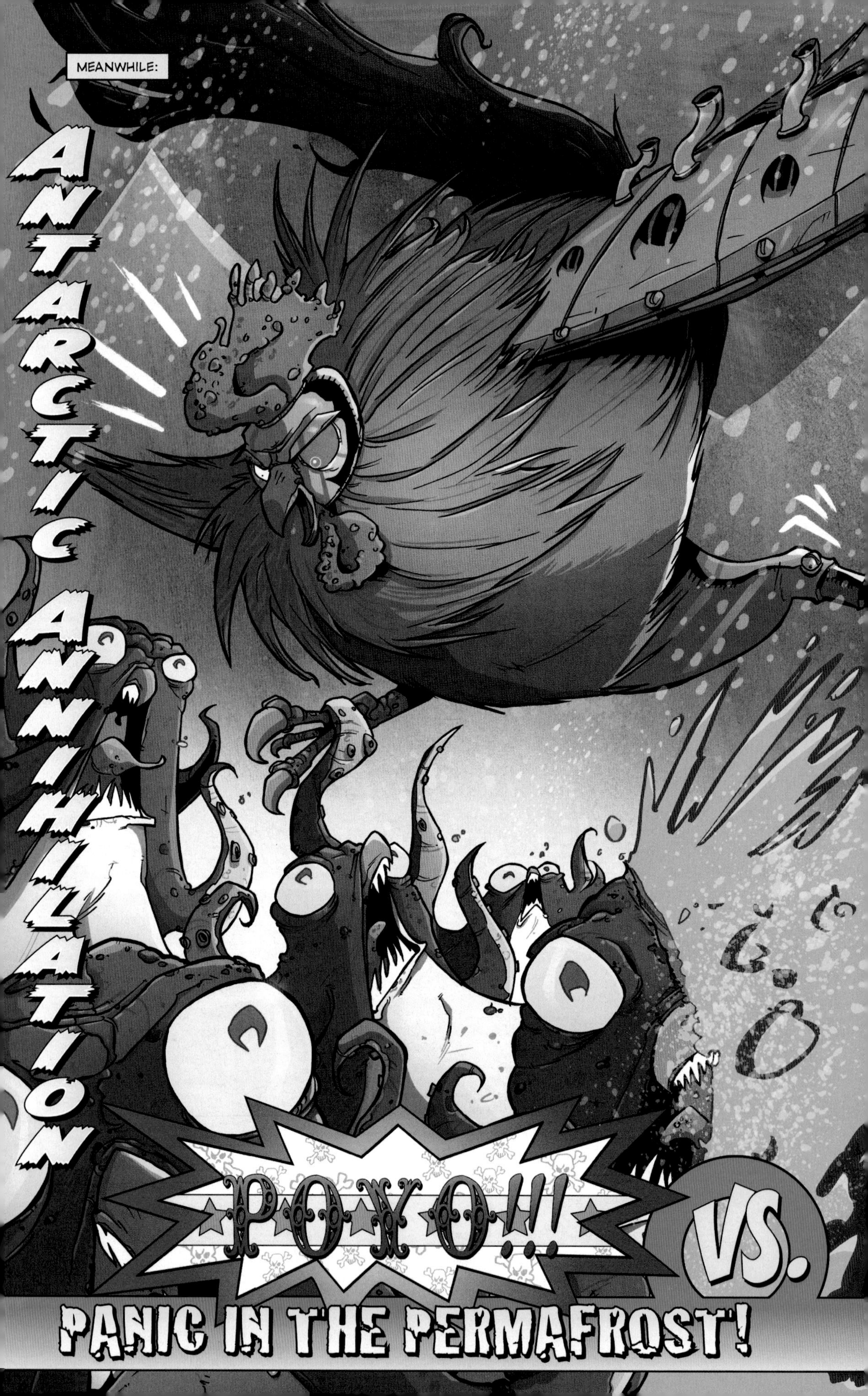
MEANWHILE:
ANTARCTIC ANNIHILATION
POYO!!!
VS.
PANIC IN THE PERMAFROST!

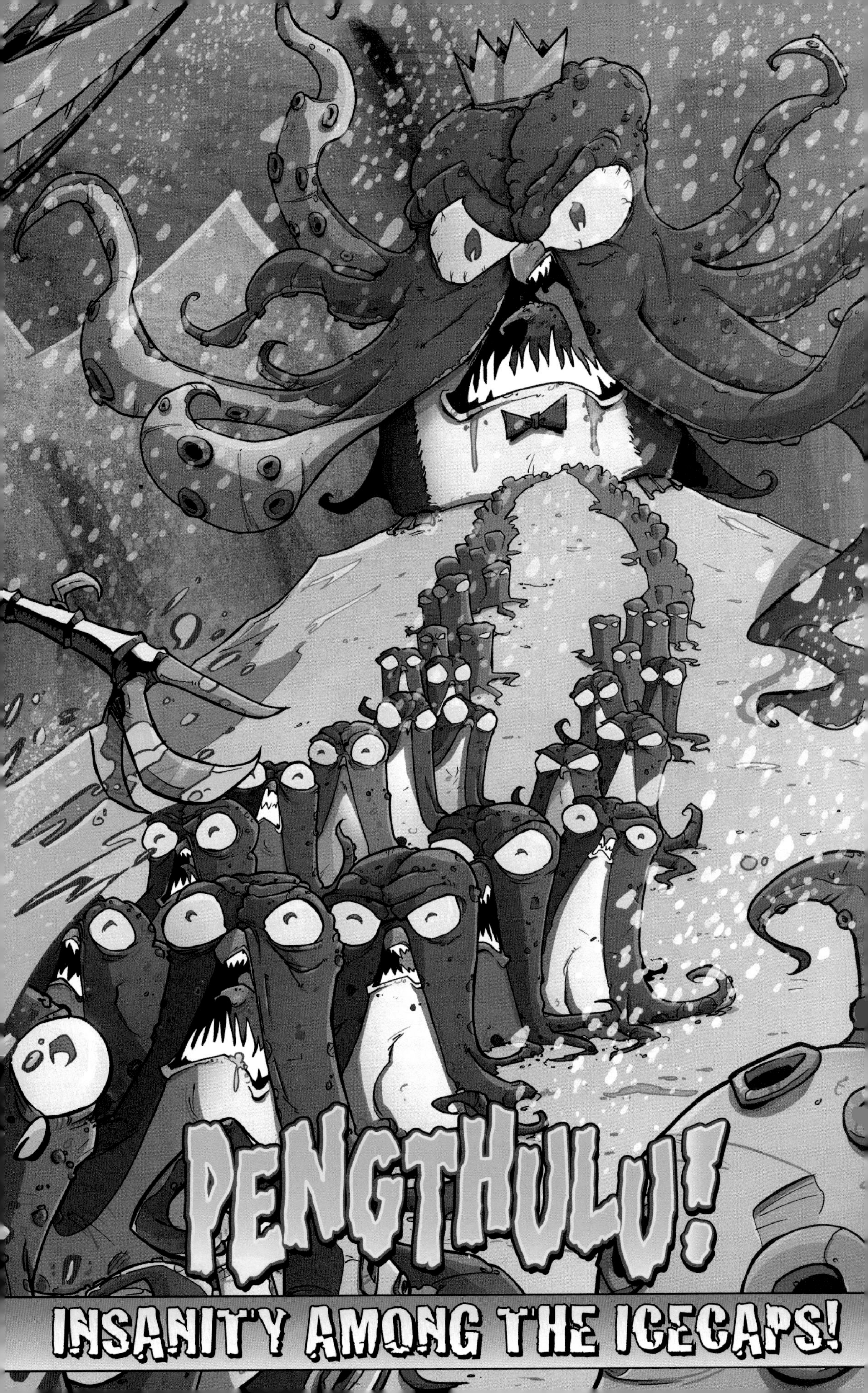
PENGTHULU!
INSANITY AMONG THE ICECAPS!

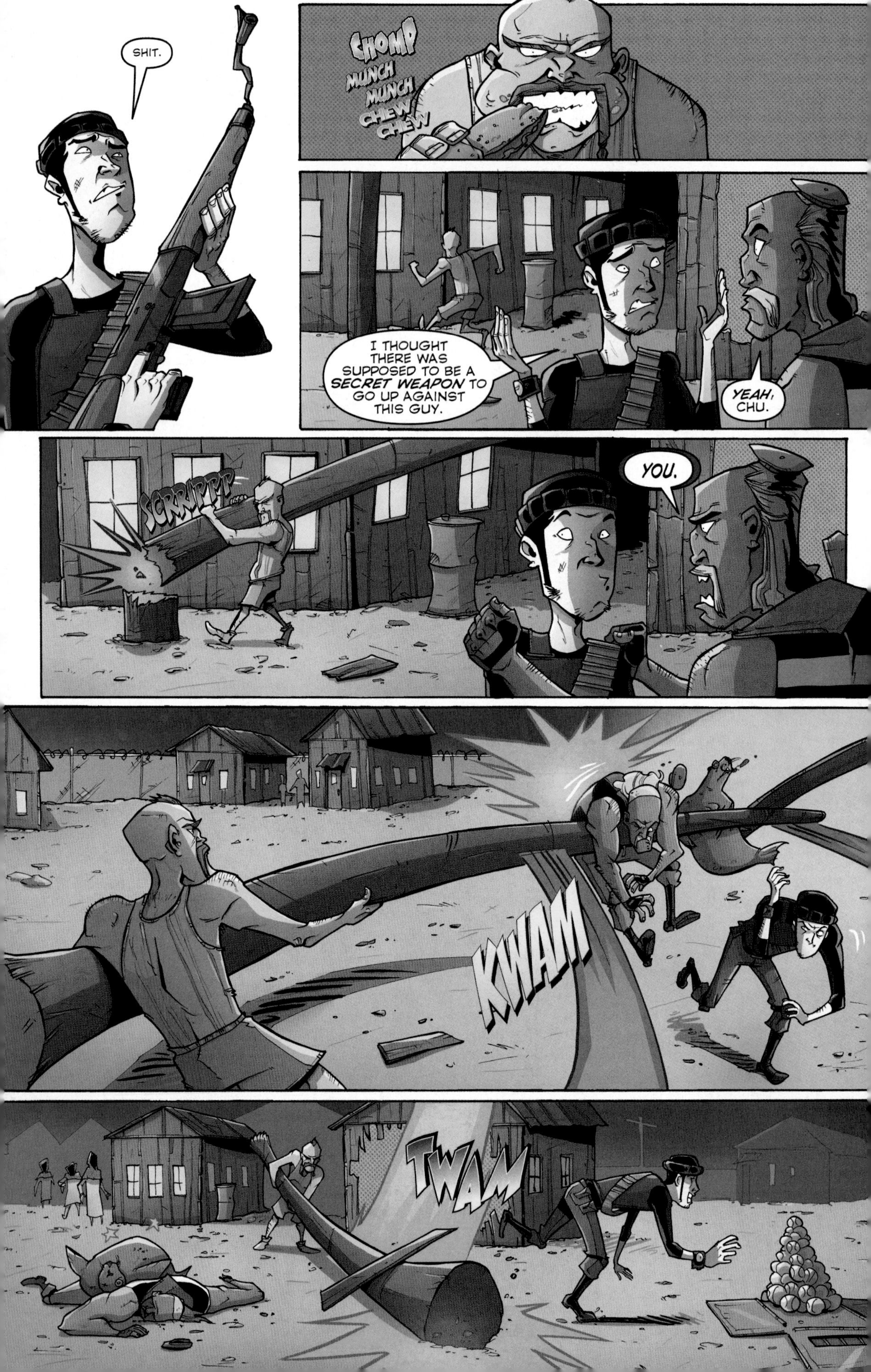
SHIT.
CHOMP
MUNCH
MUNCH
CHEW
CHEW
I THOUGHT THERE WAS SUPPOSED TO BE A SECRET WEAPON TO GO UP AGAINST THIS GUY.
YEAH, CHU.
SCRIPPP
YOU.
KWAM
TWAM

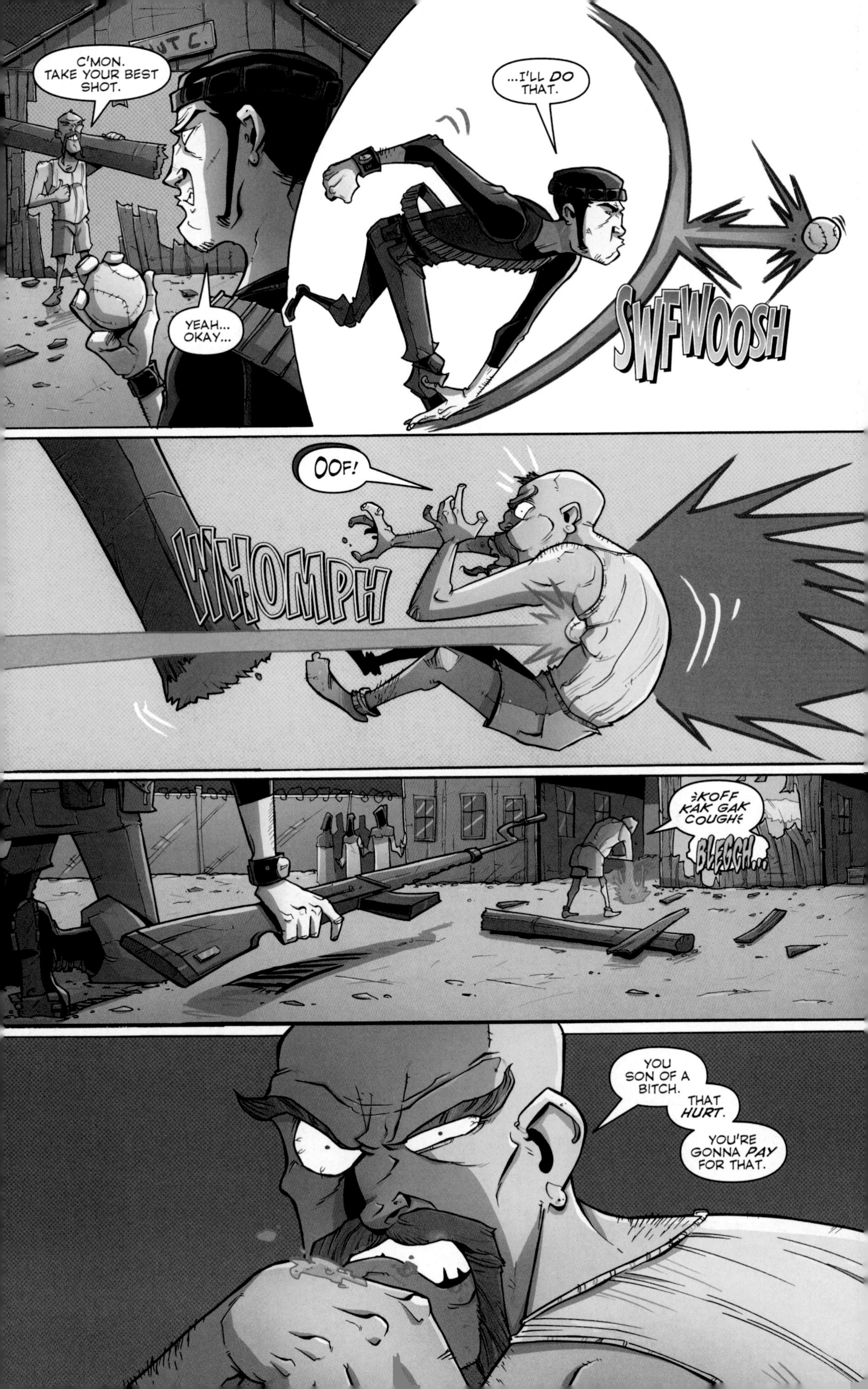
C'MON. TAKE YOUR BEST SHOT.
YEAH... OKAY...
...I'LL DO THAT.
SWFWOOSH
OOF!
WHOMPH
KOFF KAK GAK COUGH
BLEGCH...
YOU SON OF A BITCH.
THAT HURT.
YOU'RE GONNA PAY FOR THAT.

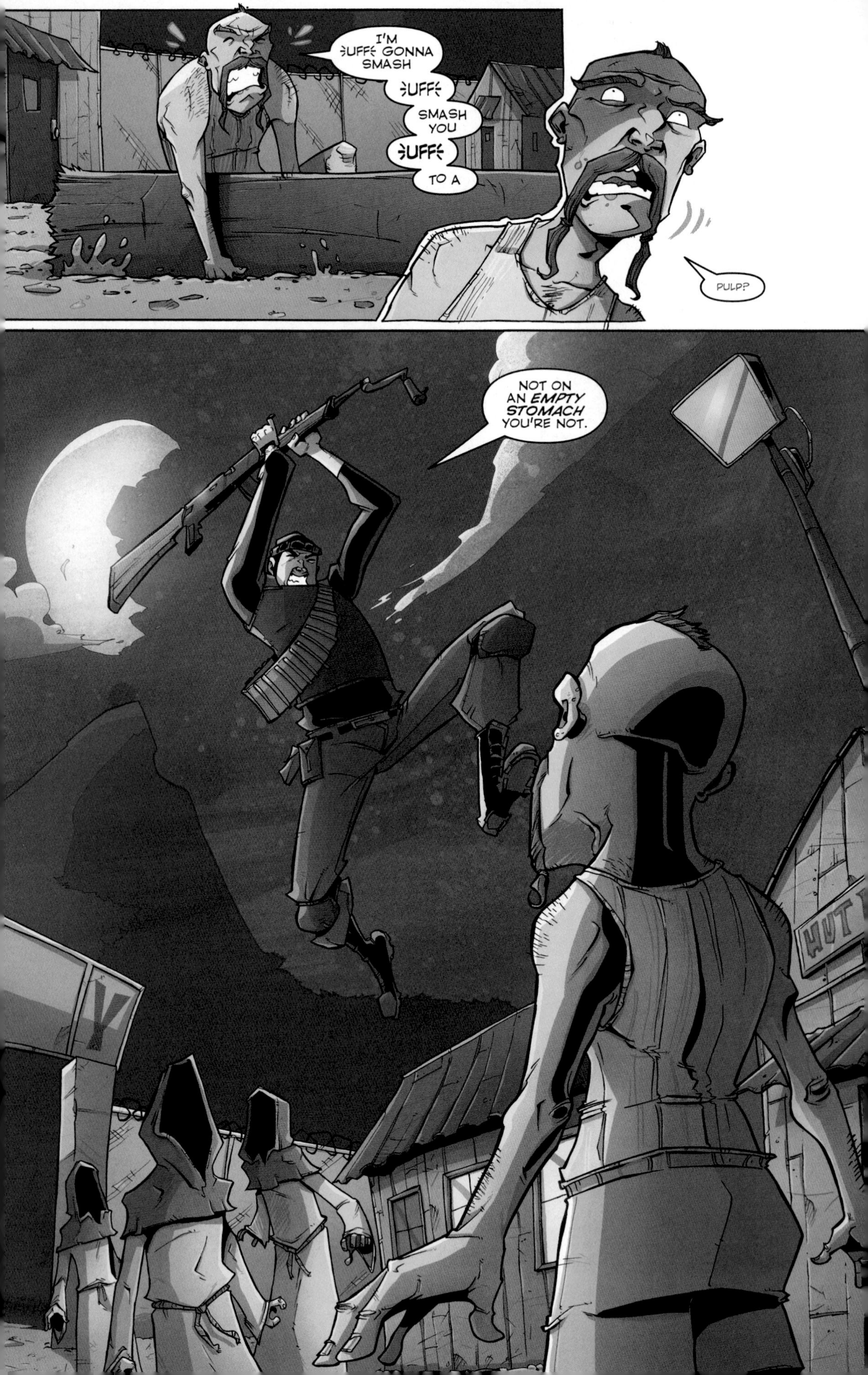
I'M
UFF GONNA
SMASH
UFF
SMASH
YOU
UFF
TO A
PULP?
NOT ON AN *EMPTY STOMACH* YOU'RE NOT.
HUT

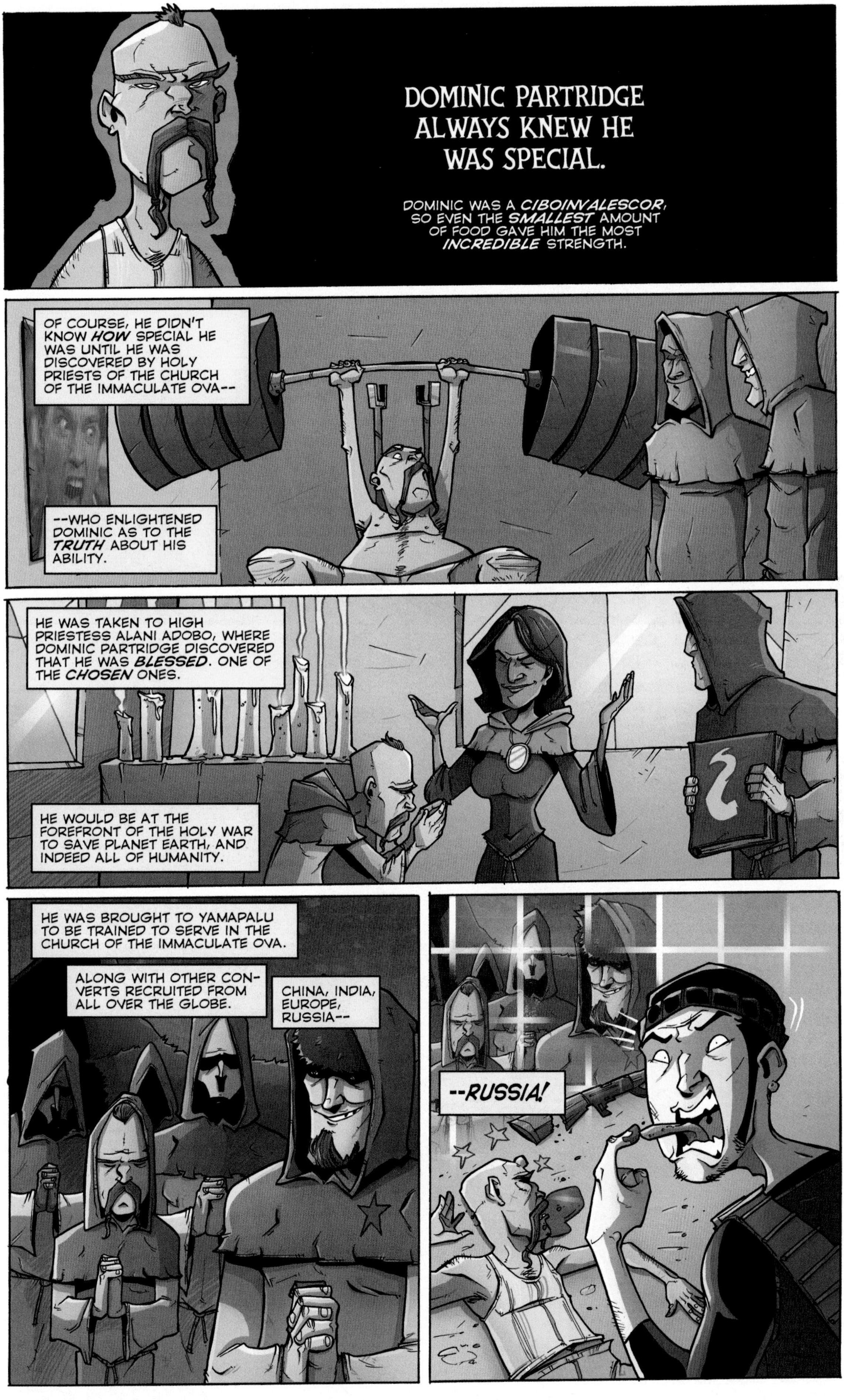
DOMINIC PARTRIDGE ALWAYS KNEW HE WAS SPECIAL.
DOMINIC WAS A CIBOINVALESCOR, SO EVEN THE SMALLEST AMOUNT OF FOOD GAVE HIM THE MOST INCREDIBLE STRENGTH.
OF COURSE, HE DIDN'T KNOW HOW SPECIAL HE WAS UNTIL HE WAS DISCOVERED BY HOLY PRIESTS OF THE CHURCH OF THE IMMACULATE OVA--
--WHO ENLIGHTENED DOMINIC AS TO THE TRUTH ABOUT HIS ABILITY.
HE WAS TAKEN TO HIGH PRIESTESS ALANI ADOBO, WHERE DOMINIC PARTRIDGE DISCOVERED THAT HE WAS BLESSED. ONE OF THE CHOSEN ONES.
HE WOULD BE AT THE FOREFRONT OF THE HOLY WAR TO SAVE PLANET EARTH, AND INDEED ALL OF HUMANITY.
HE WAS BROUGHT TO YAMAPALU TO BE TRAINED TO SERVE IN THE CHURCH OF THE IMMACULATE OVA.
ALONG WITH OTHER CONVERTS RECRUITED FROM ALL OVER THE GLOBE.
CHINA, INDIA, EUROPE, RUSSIA--
--RUSSIA!

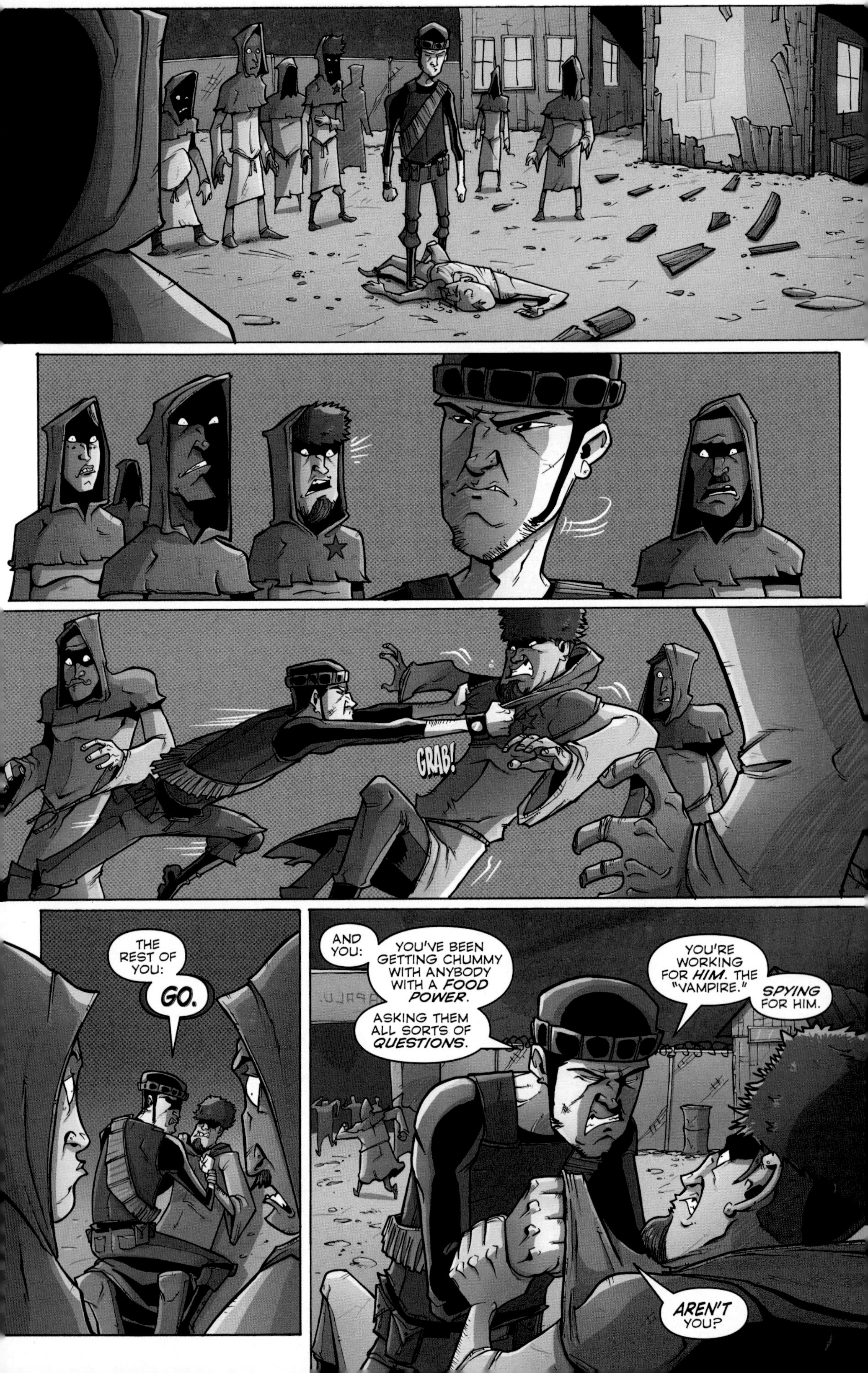
GRAB!
THE REST OF YOU:
GO.
AND YOU:
YOU'VE BEEN GETTING CHUMMY WITH ANYBODY WITH A FOOD POWER.
ASKING THEM ALL SORTS OF QUESTIONS.
YOU'RE WORKING FOR HIM. THE "VAMPIRE."
SPYING FOR HIM.
AREN'T YOU?

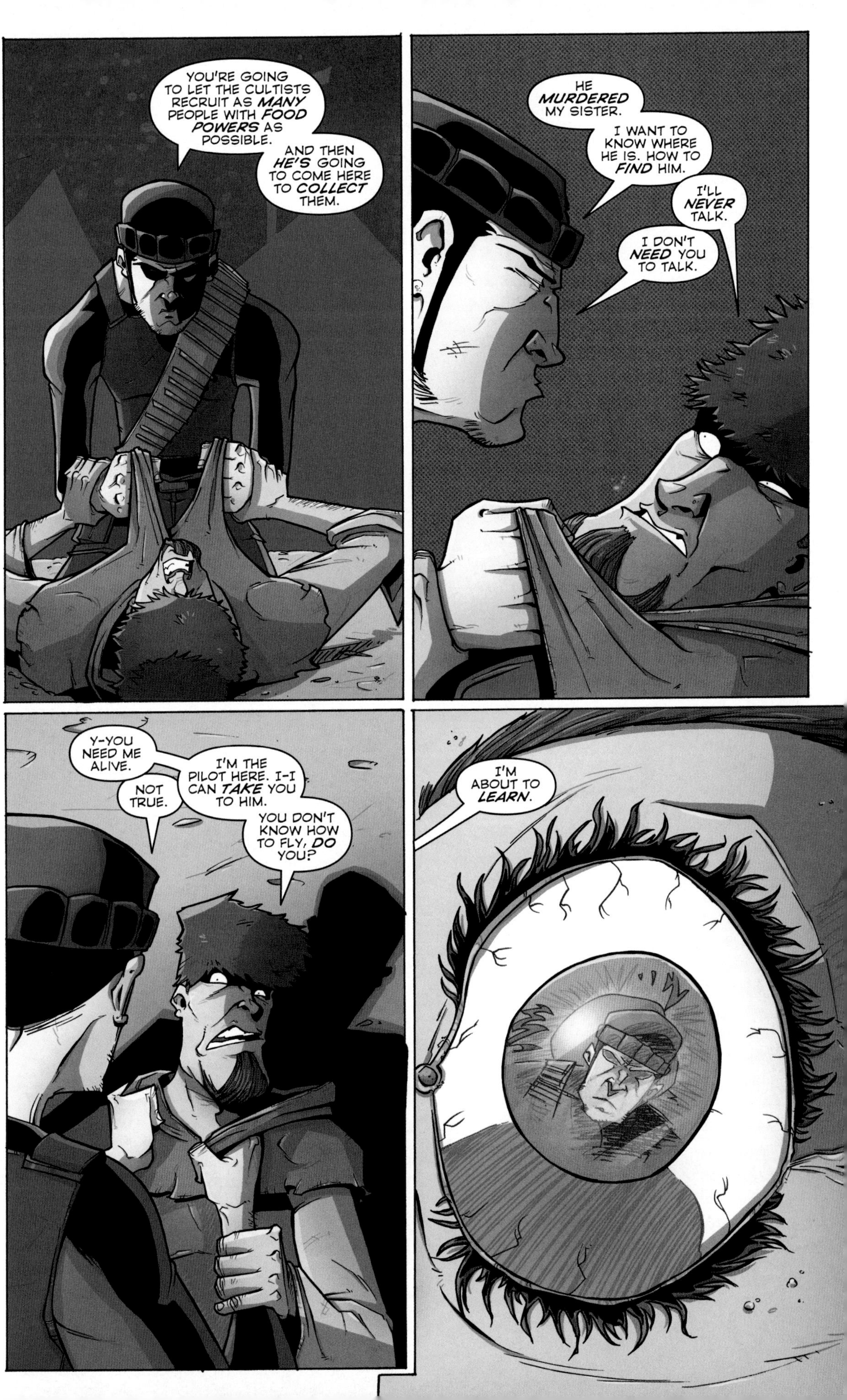
YOU'RE GOING TO LET THE CULTISTS RECRUIT AS MANY PEOPLE WITH FOOD POWERS AS POSSIBLE.
AND THEN HE'S GOING TO COME HERE TO COLLECT THEM.
HE MURDERED MY SISTER.
I WANT TO KNOW WHERE HE IS. HOW TO FIND HIM.
I'LL NEVER TALK.
I DON'T NEED YOU TO TALK.
Y-YOU NEED ME ALIVE.
NOT TRUE.
I'M THE PILOT HERE. I-I CAN TAKE YOU TO HIM.
YOU DON'T KNOW HOW TO FLY, DO YOU?
I'M ABOUT TO LEARN.

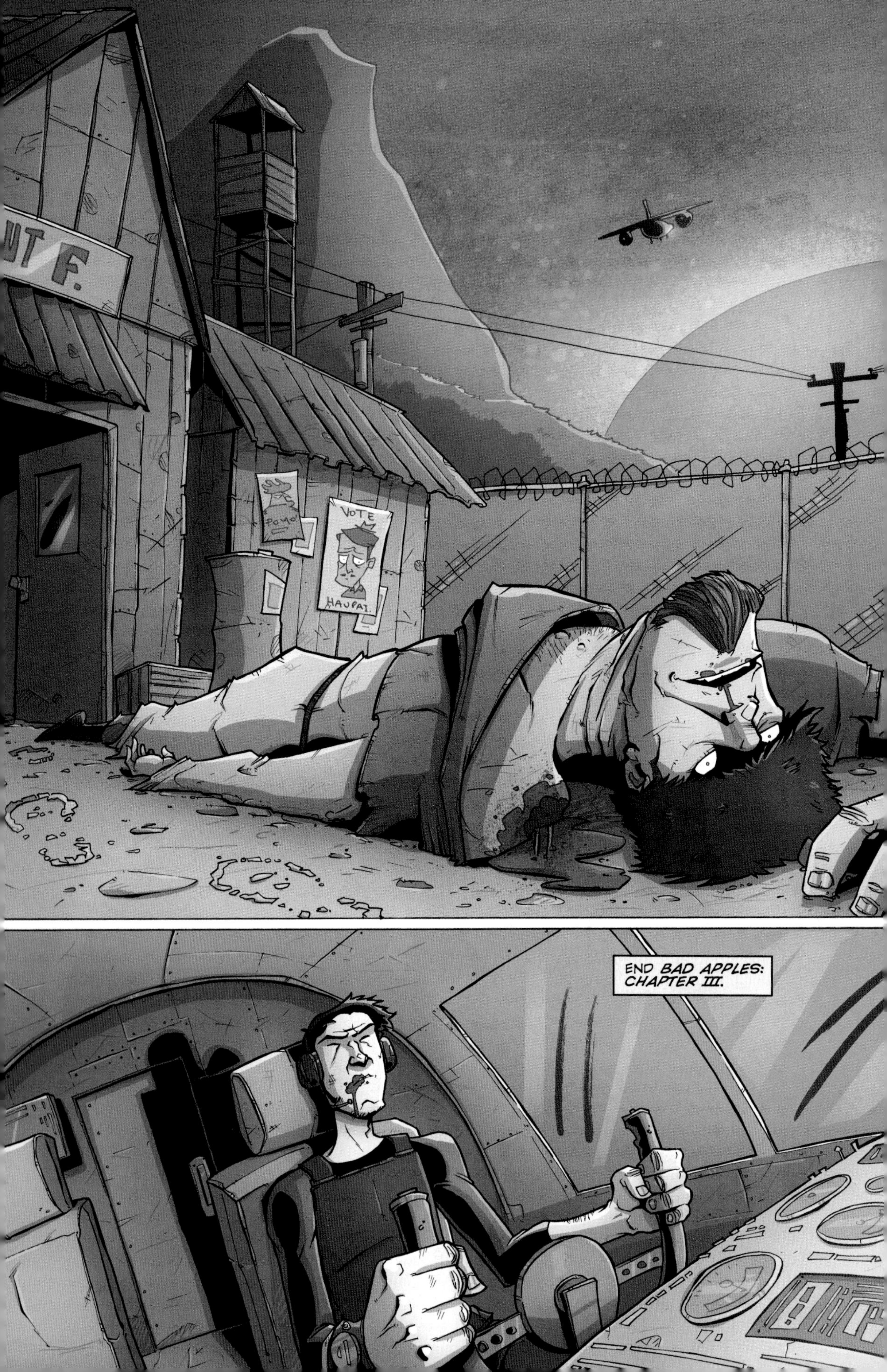
UT F.
VOTE
HAUPAI.
END BAD APPLES: CHAPTER III.

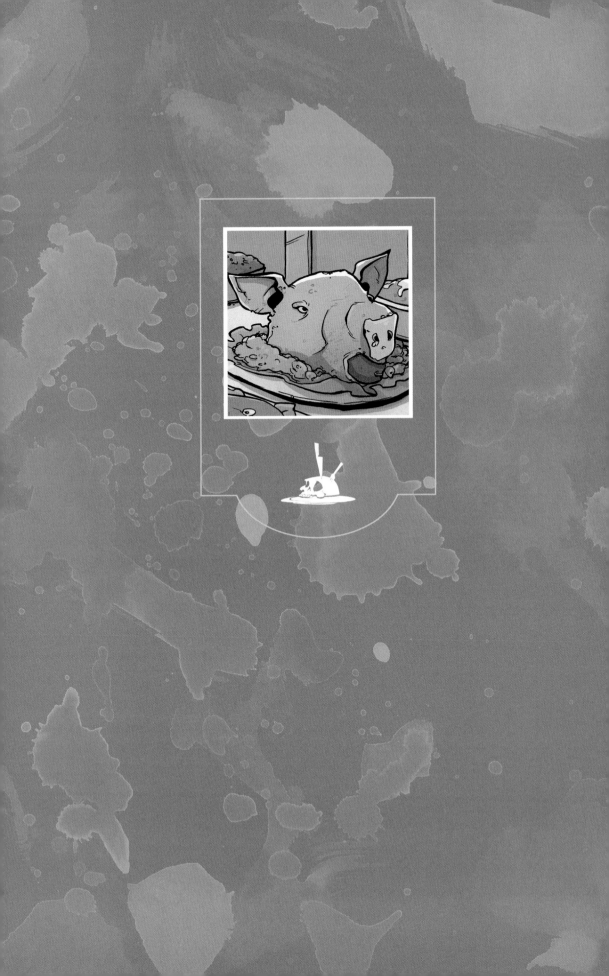

Chapter 4

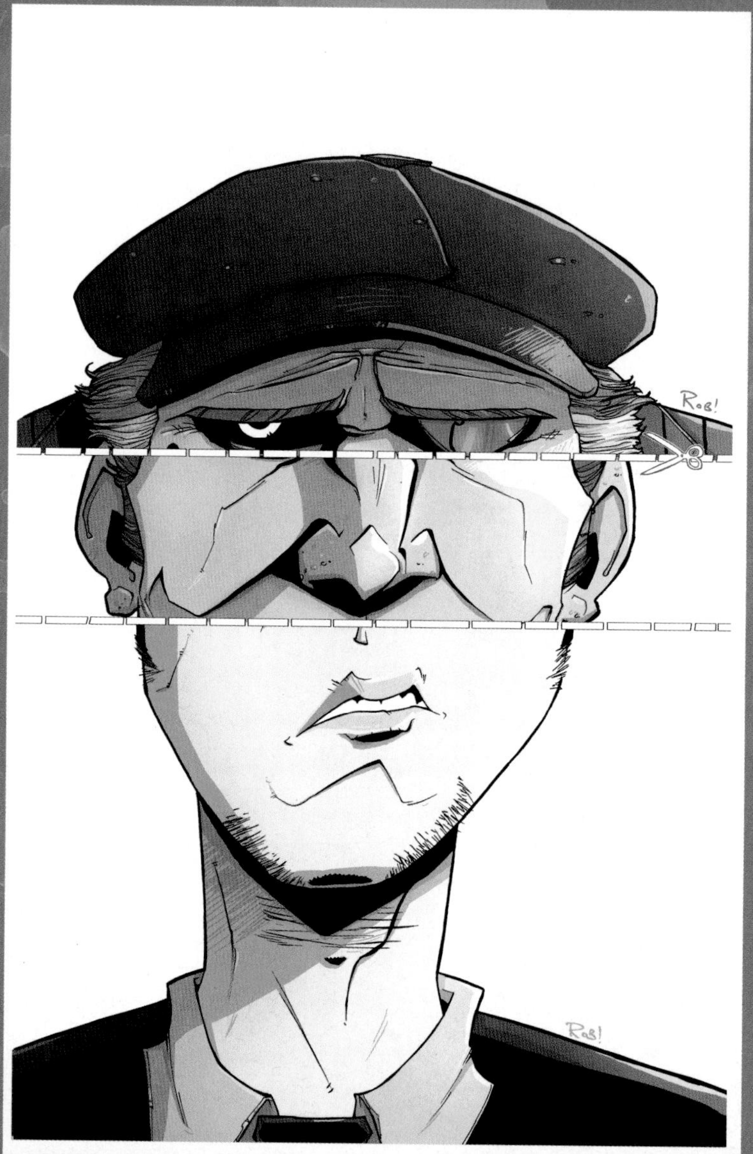
ROB!
ROB!

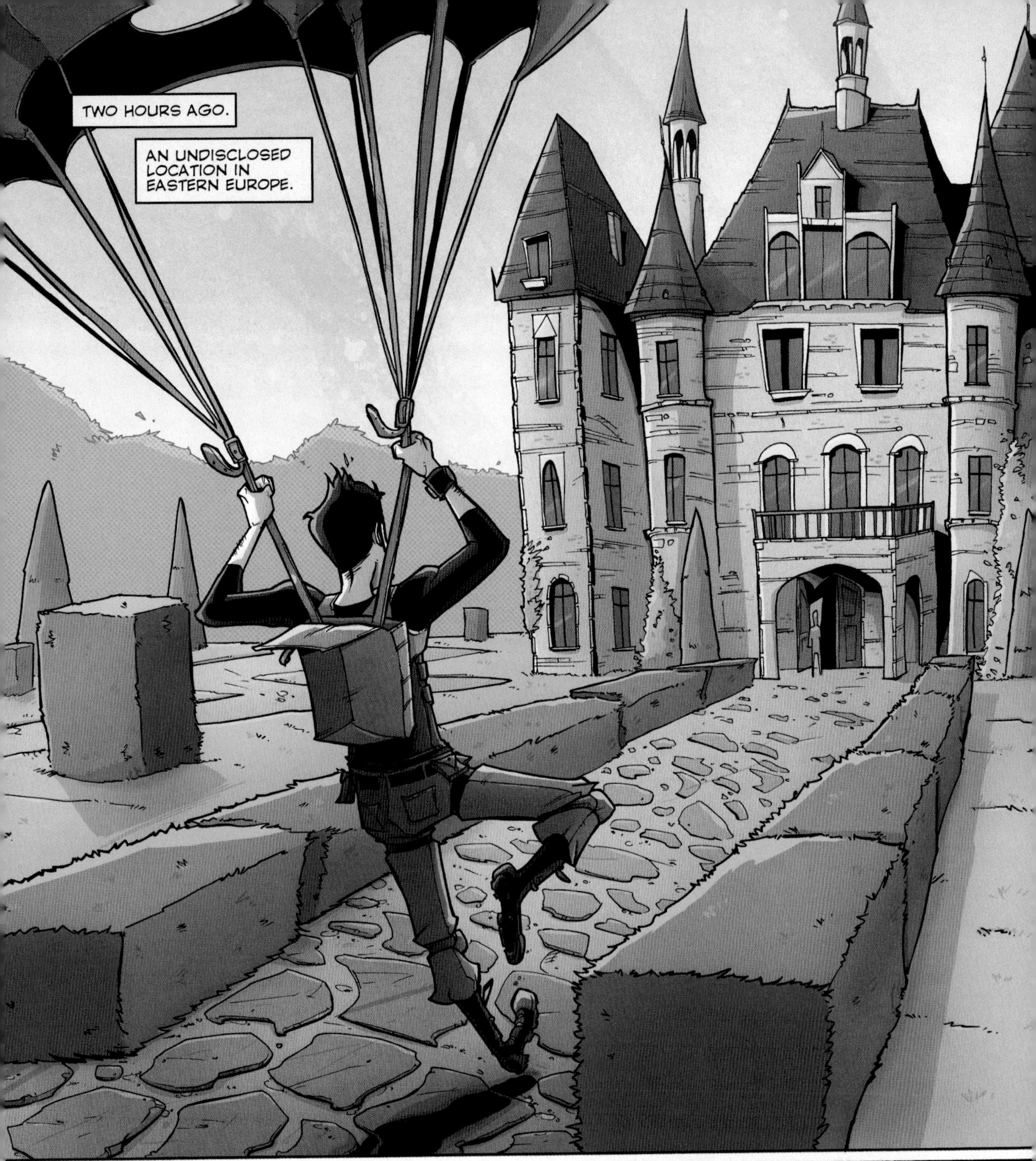
TWO HOURS AGO.
AN UNDISCLOSED LOCATION IN EASTERN EUROPE.

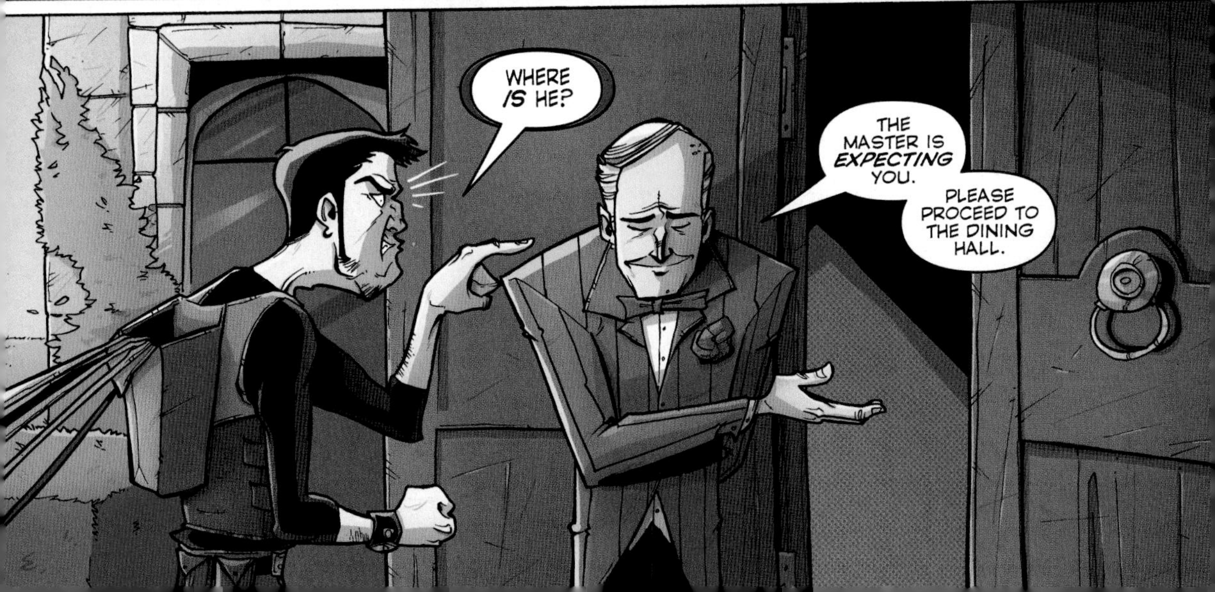
WHERE *IS* HE?
THE MASTER IS *EXPECTING* YOU.
PLEASE PROCEED TO THE DINING HALL.

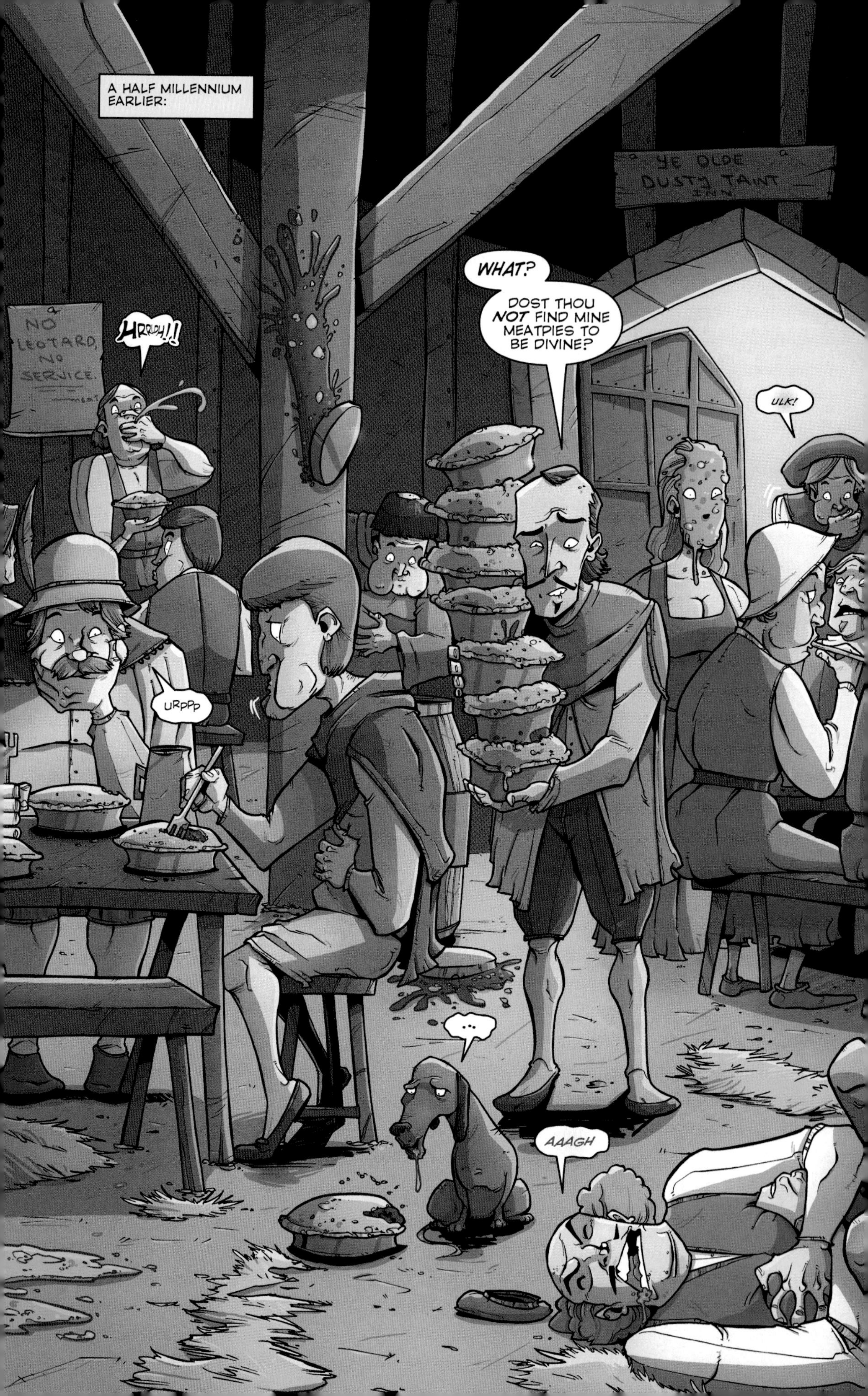
A HALF MILLENNIUM EARLIER:
YE OLDE DUSTY TAINT INN
NO LEOTARD, NO SERVICE.
HRRUGH!!
WHAT?
DOST THOU NOT FIND MINE MEATPIES TO BE DIVINE?
ULK!
URPPP
...
AAAGH

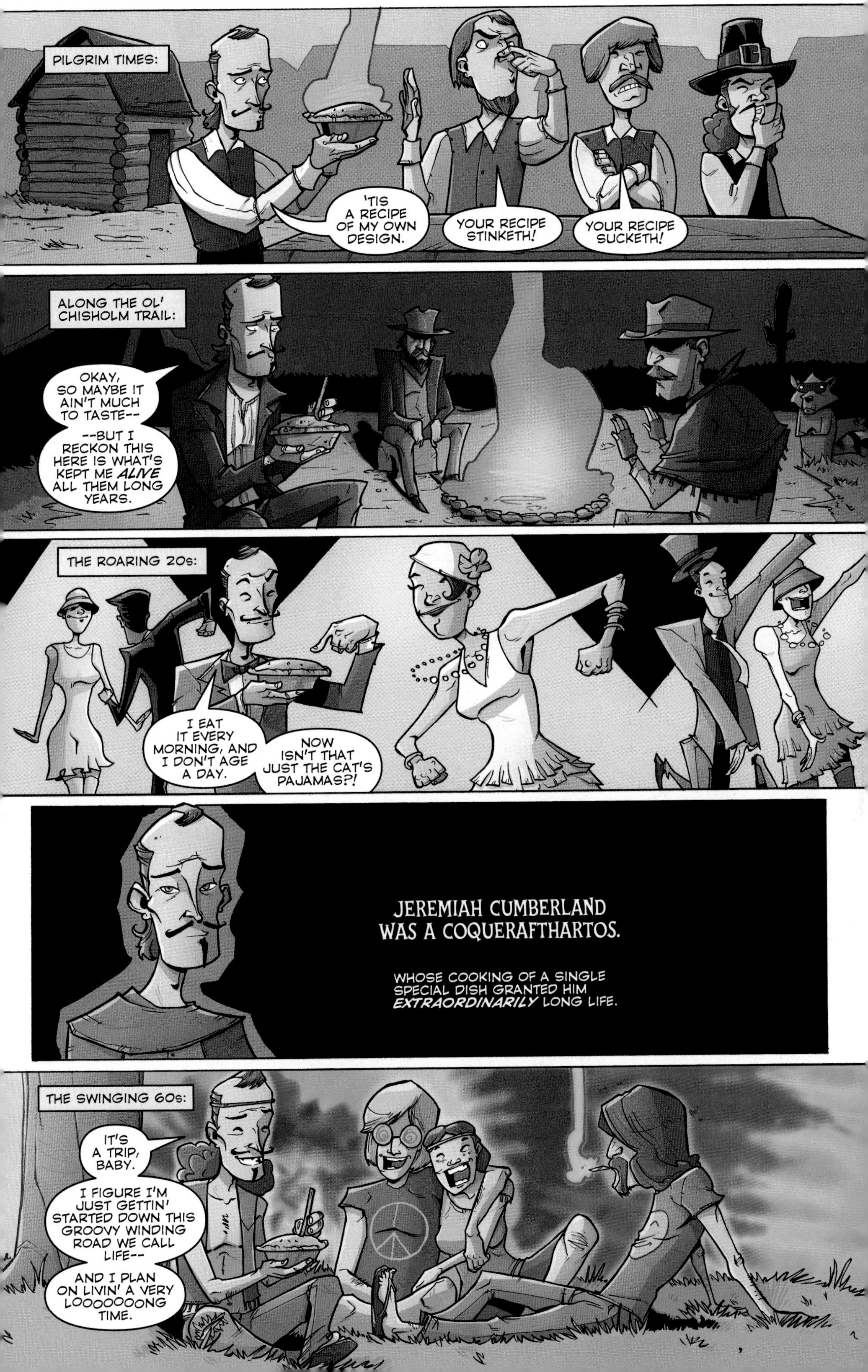
PILGRIM TIMES:
'TIS A RECIPE OF MY OWN DESIGN.
YOUR RECIPE STINKETH!
YOUR RECIPE SUCKETH!
ALONG THE OL' CHISHOLM TRAIL:
OKAY, SO MAYBE IT AIN'T MUCH TO TASTE--
--BUT I RECKON THIS HERE IS WHAT'S KEPT ME *ALIVE* ALL THEM LONG YEARS.
THE ROARING 20s:
I EAT IT EVERY MORNING, AND I DON'T AGE A DAY.
NOW ISN'T THAT JUST THE CAT'S PAJAMAS?!
JEREMIAH CUMBERLAND WAS A COQUERAFTHARTOS.
WHOSE COOKING OF A SINGLE SPECIAL DISH GRANTED HIM *EXTRAORDINARILY* LONG LIFE.
THE SWINGING 60s:
IT'S A TRIP, BABY.
I FIGURE I'M JUST GETTIN' STARTED DOWN THIS GROOVY WINDING ROAD WE CALL LIFE--
AND I PLAN ON LIVIN' A VERY LOOOOOOONG TIME.

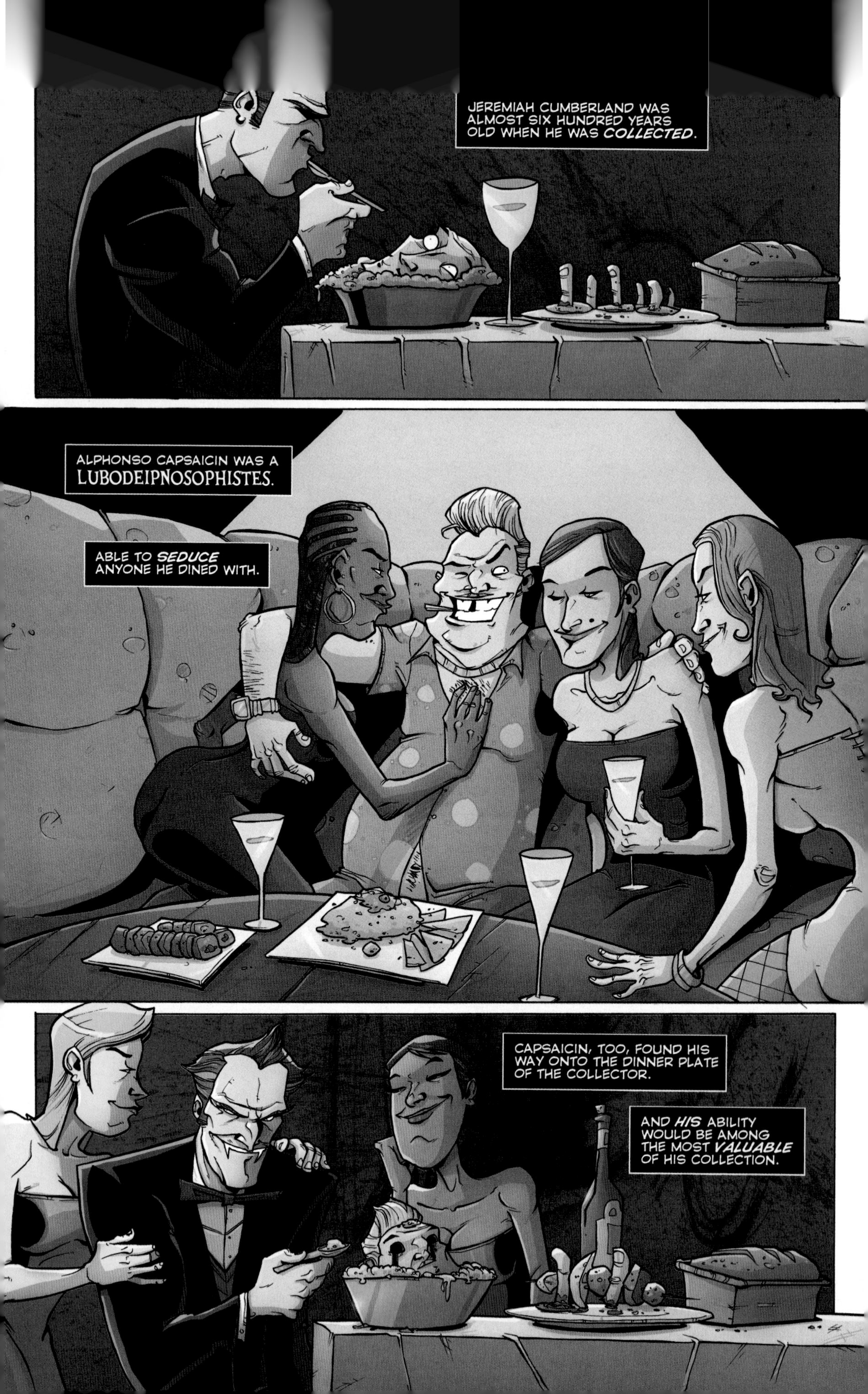
JEREMIAH CUMBERLAND WAS ALMOST SIX HUNDRED YEARS OLD WHEN HE WAS *COLLECTED*.
ALPHONSO CAPSAICIN WAS A LUBODEIPNOSOPHISTES.
ABLE TO *SEDUCE* ANYONE HE DINED WITH.
CAPSAICIN, TOO, FOUND HIS WAY ONTO THE DINNER PLATE OF THE COLLECTOR.
AND *HIS* ABILITY WOULD BE AMONG THE MOST *VALUABLE* OF HIS COLLECTION.

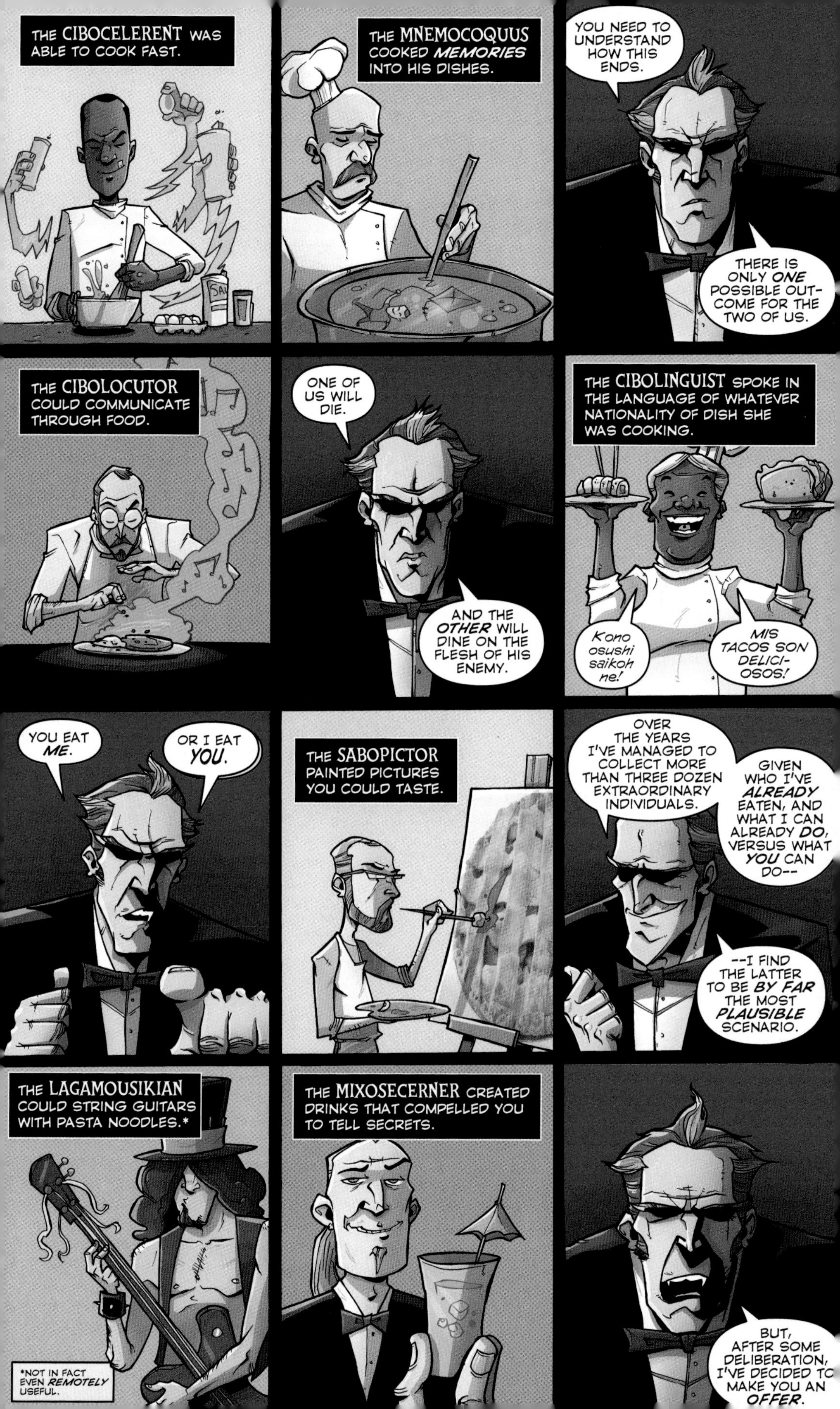

THE CIBOCELERENT WAS ABLE TO COOK FAST.
THE MNEMOCOQUUS COOKED *MEMORIES* INTO HIS DISHES.
YOU NEED TO UNDERSTAND HOW THIS ENDS.
THERE IS ONLY *ONE* POSSIBLE OUT-COME FOR THE TWO OF US.
THE CIBOLOCUTOR COULD COMMUNICATE THROUGH FOOD.
ONE OF US WILL DIE.
AND THE *OTHER* WILL DINE ON THE FLESH OF HIS ENEMY.
THE CIBOLINGUIST SPOKE IN THE LANGUAGE OF WHATEVER NATIONALITY OF DISH SHE WAS COOKING.
Kono osushi saikoh ne!
MIS TACOS SON DELICI-OSOS!
YOU EAT *ME*.
OR I EAT *YOU*.
THE SABOPICTOR PAINTED PICTURES YOU COULD TASTE.
OVER THE YEARS I'VE MANAGED TO COLLECT MORE THAN THREE DOZEN EXTRAORDINARY INDIVIDUALS.
GIVEN WHO I'VE *ALREADY* EATEN, AND WHAT I CAN ALREADY *DO*, VERSUS WHAT *YOU* CAN DO--
--I FIND THE LATTER TO BE *BY FAR* THE MOST *PLAUSIBLE* SCENARIO.
THE LAGAMOUSIKIAN COULD STRING GUITARS WITH PASTA NOODLES.*
*NOT IN FACT EVEN *REMOTELY* USEFUL.
THE MIXOSECERNER CREATED DRINKS THAT COMPELLED YOU TO TELL SECRETS.
BUT, AFTER SOME DELIBERATION, I'VE DECIDED TO MAKE YOU AN *OFFER*.

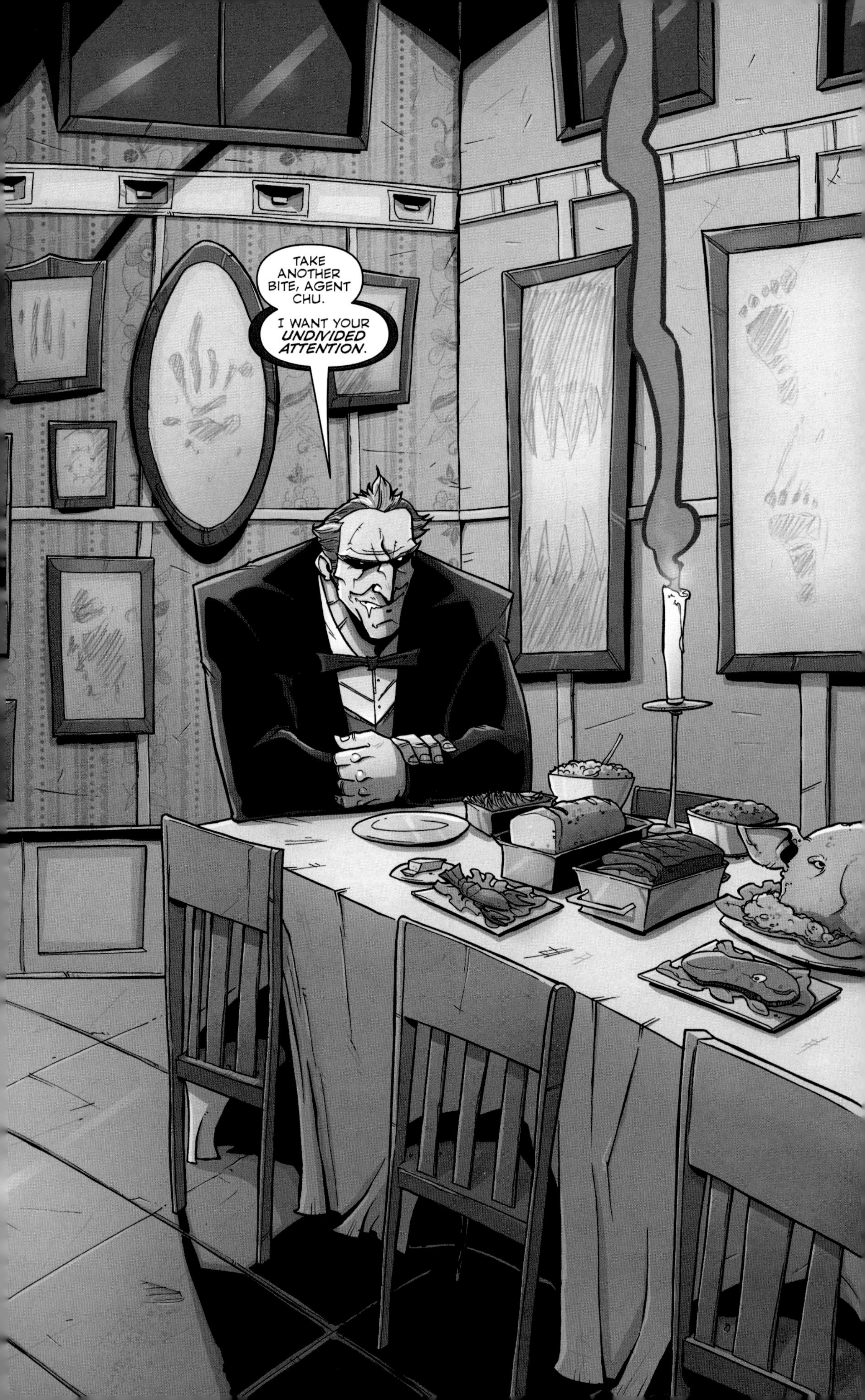
TAKE ANOTHER BITE, AGENT CHU.
I WANT YOUR *UNDIVIDED ATTENTION*.

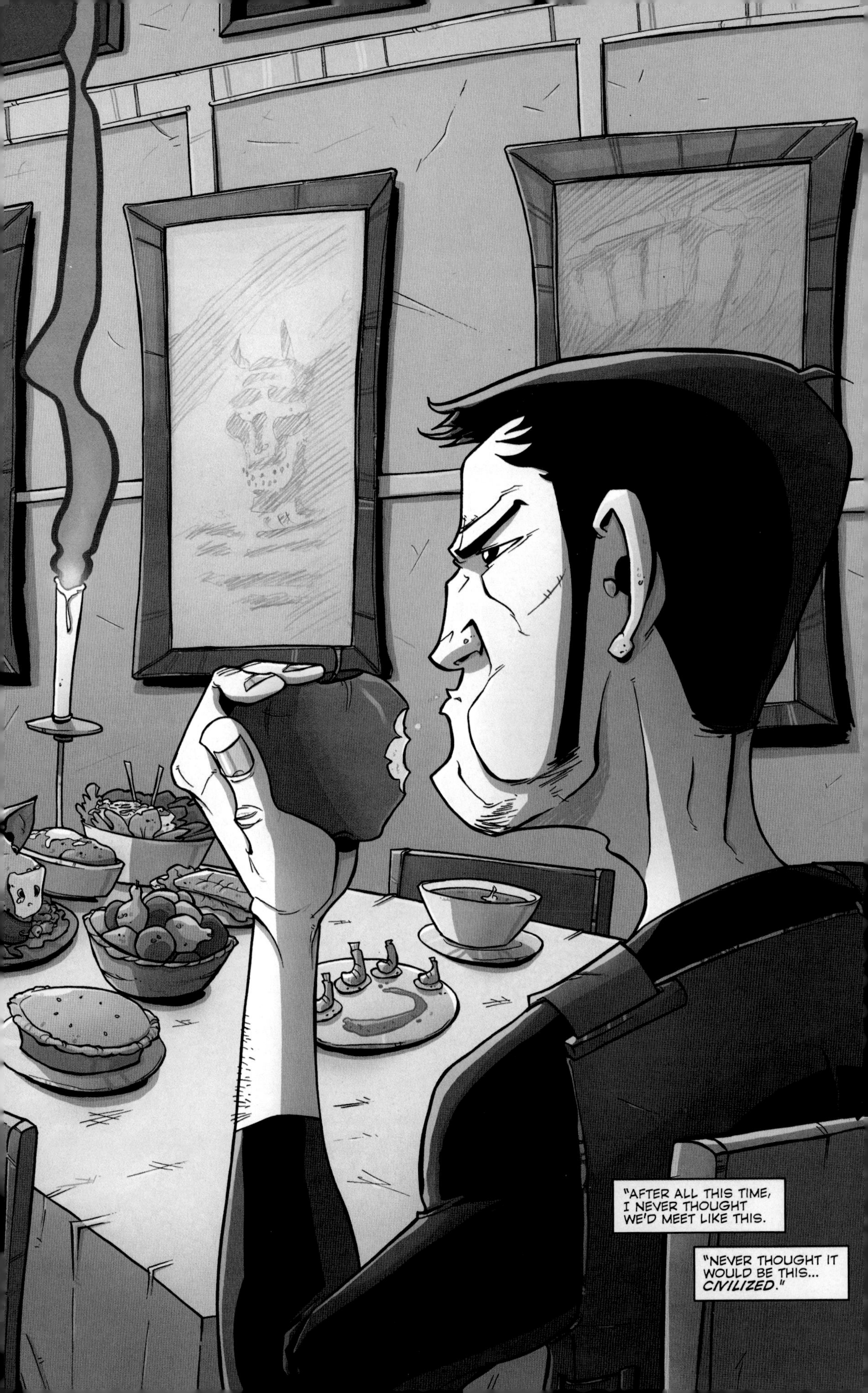
"AFTER ALL THIS TIME, I NEVER THOUGHT WE'D MEET LIKE THIS.
"NEVER THOUGHT IT WOULD BE THIS... *CIVILIZED*."

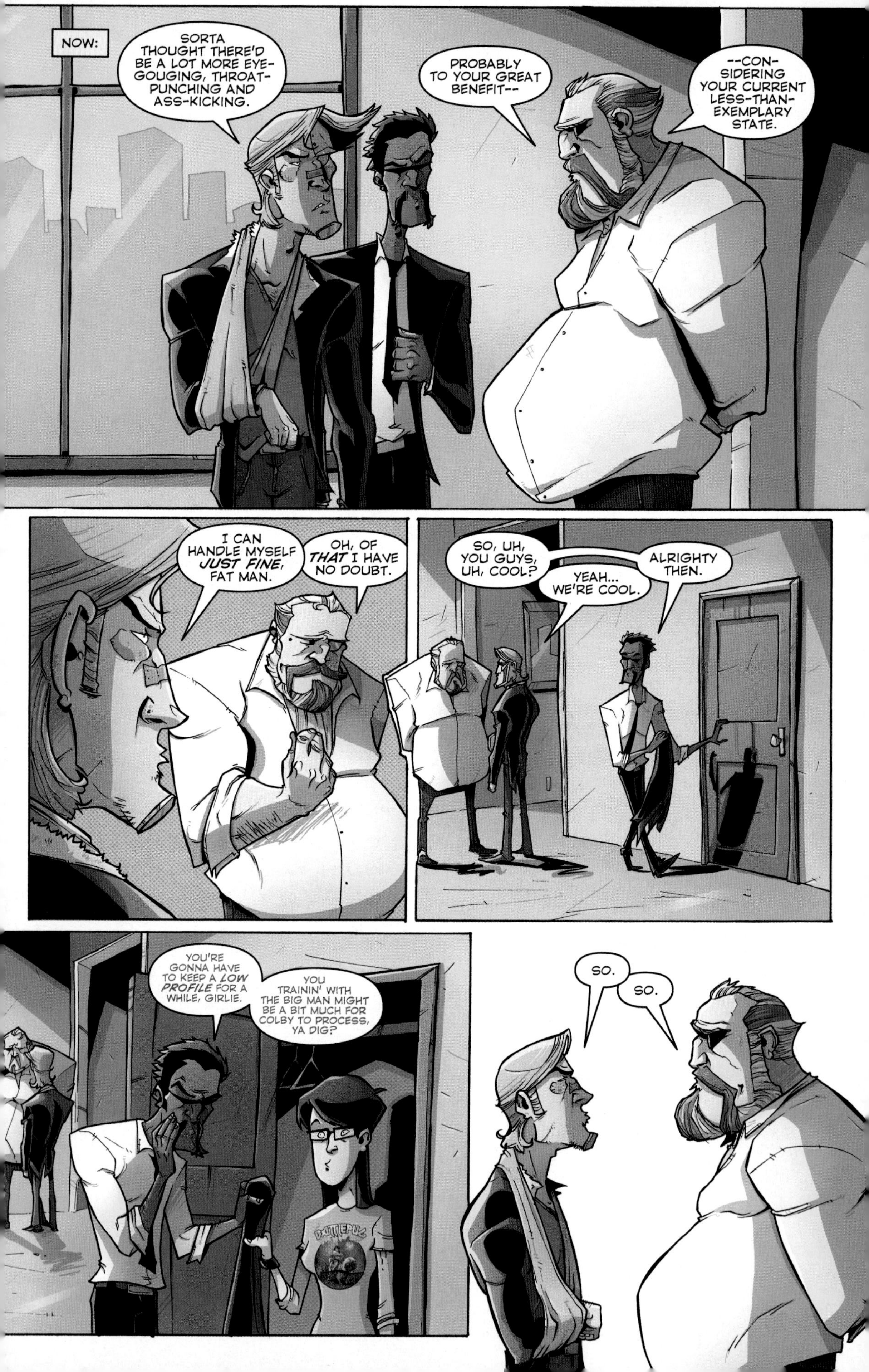
NOW:
SORTA THOUGHT THERE'D BE A LOT MORE EYE-GOUGING, THROAT-PUNCHING AND ASS-KICKING.
PROBABLY TO YOUR GREAT BENEFIT--
--CON-SIDERING YOUR CURRENT LESS-THAN-EXEMPLARY STATE.
I CAN HANDLE MYSELF JUST FINE, FAT MAN.
OH, OF THAT I HAVE NO DOUBT.
SO, UH, YOU GUYS, UH, COOL?
YEAH... WE'RE COOL.
ALRIGHTY THEN.
YOU'RE GONNA HAVE TO KEEP A LOW PROFILE FOR A WHILE, GIRLIE.
YOU TRAININ' WITH THE BIG MAN MIGHT BE A BIT MUCH FOR COLBY TO PROCESS, YA DIG?
SO.
SO.

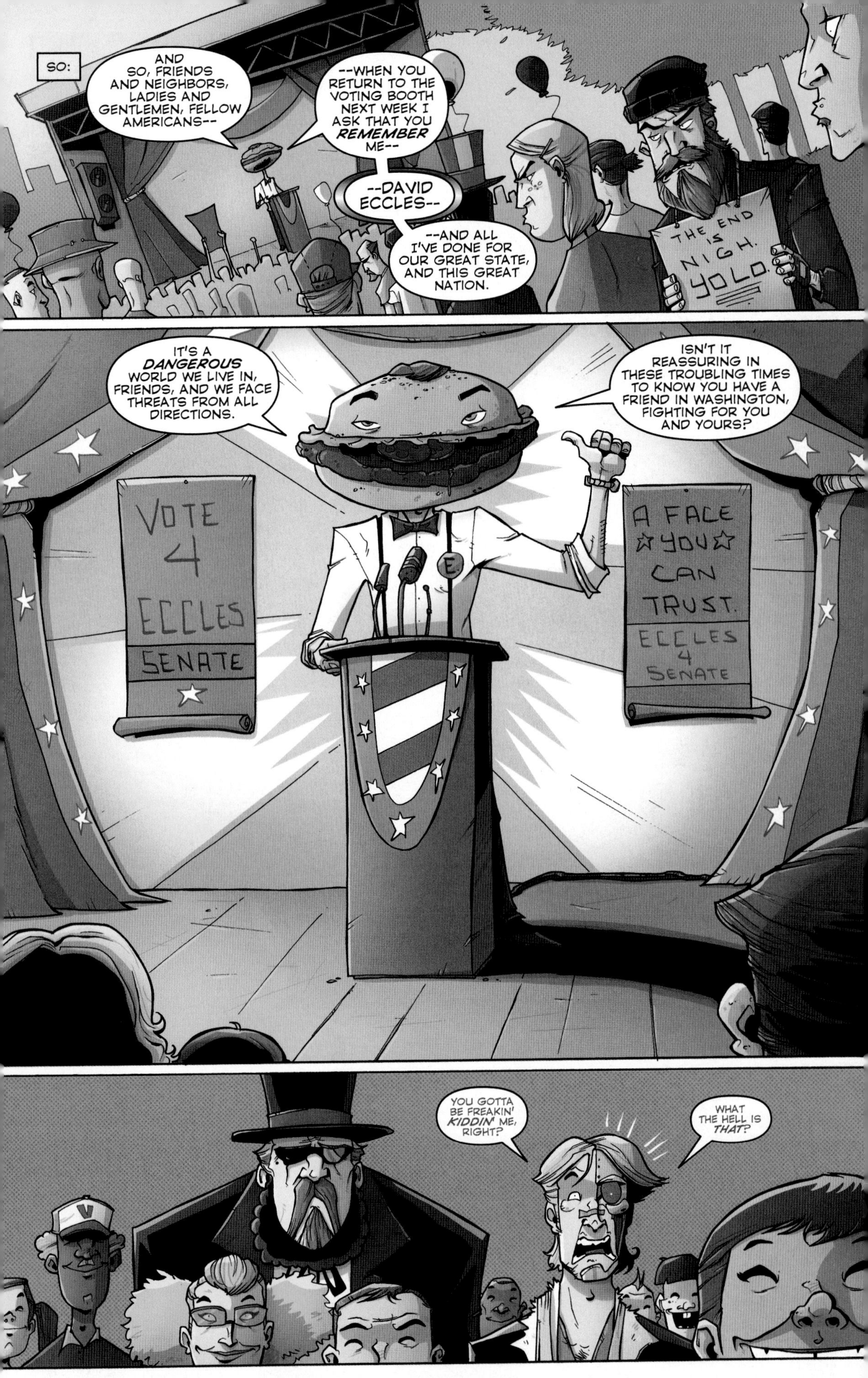
SO:
AND SO, FRIENDS AND NEIGHBORS, LADIES AND GENTLEMEN, FELLOW AMERICANS--
--WHEN YOU RETURN TO THE VOTING BOOTH NEXT WEEK I ASK THAT YOU *REMEMBER* ME--
--DAVID ECCLES--
--AND ALL I'VE DONE FOR OUR GREAT STATE, AND THIS GREAT NATION.
THE END IS NIGH. YOLO.
IT'S A *DANGEROUS* WORLD WE LIVE IN, FRIENDS, AND WE FACE THREATS FROM ALL DIRECTIONS.
ISN'T IT REASSURING IN THESE TROUBLING TIMES TO KNOW YOU HAVE A FRIEND IN WASHINGTON, FIGHTING FOR YOU AND YOURS?
VOTE 4 ECCLES SENATE
A FACE YOU CAN TRUST. ECCLES 4 SENATE
YOU GOTTA BE FREAKIN' *KIDDIN'* ME, RIGHT?
WHAT THE HELL IS *THAT*?

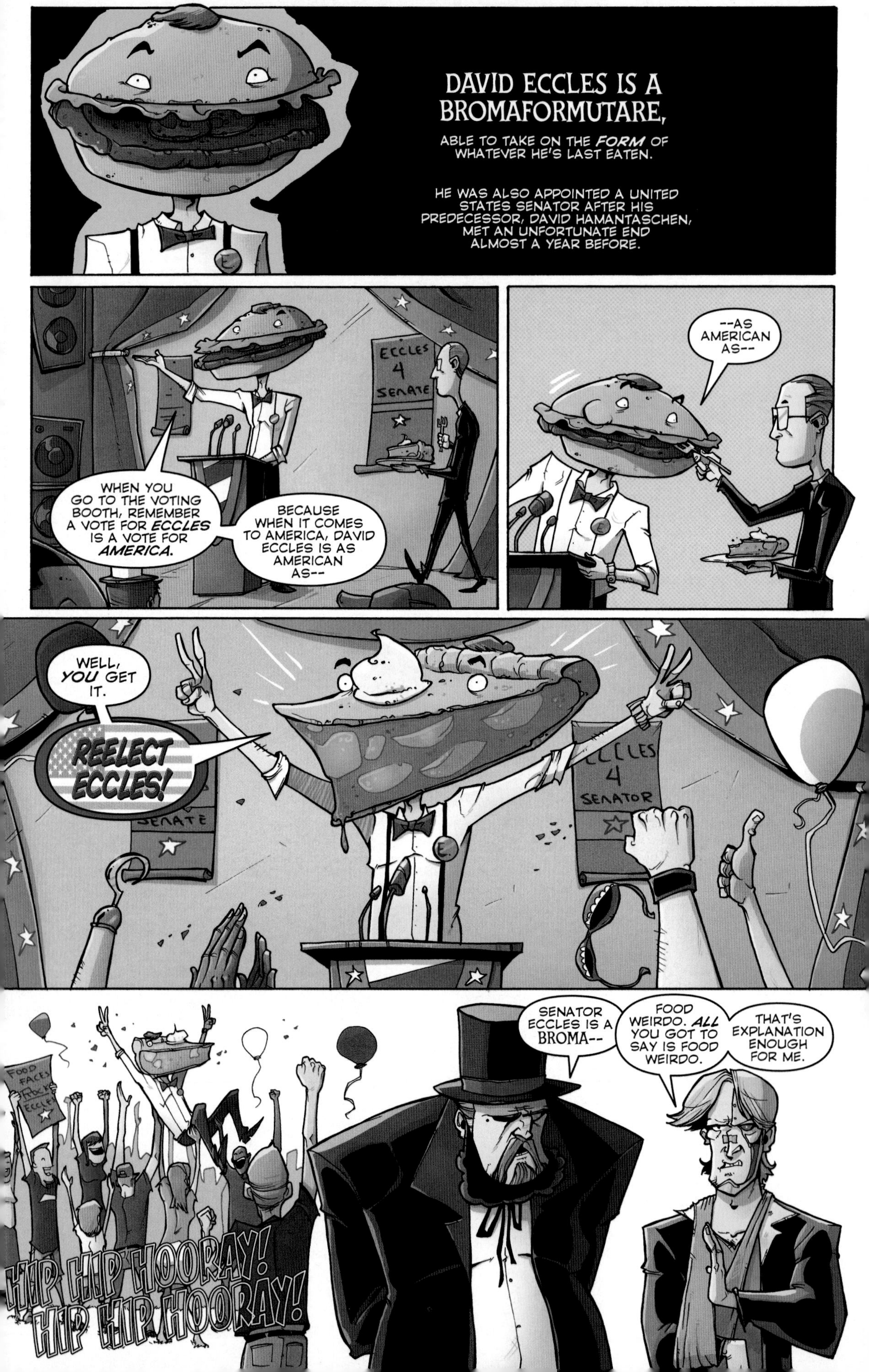
DAVID ECCLES IS A BROMAFORMUTARE,
ABLE TO TAKE ON THE *FORM* OF WHATEVER HE'S LAST EATEN.
HE WAS ALSO APPOINTED A UNITED STATES SENATOR AFTER HIS PREDECESSOR, DAVID HAMANTASCHEN, MET AN UNFORTUNATE END ALMOST A YEAR BEFORE.
ECCLES 4 SENATE
WHEN YOU GO TO THE VOTING BOOTH, REMEMBER A VOTE FOR *ECCLES* IS A VOTE FOR *AMERICA.*
BECAUSE WHEN IT COMES TO AMERICA, DAVID ECCLES IS AS AMERICAN AS--
--AS AMERICAN AS--
WELL, *YOU* GET IT.
REELECT ECCLES!
ECCLES 4 SENATOR
SENATE
FOOD FACES ROCK ECCLES
SENATOR ECCLES IS A BROMA--
FOOD WEIRDO. *ALL* YOU GOT TO SAY IS FOOD WEIRDO.
THAT'S EXPLANATION ENOUGH FOR ME.
HIP HIP HOORAY! HIP HIP HOORAY!

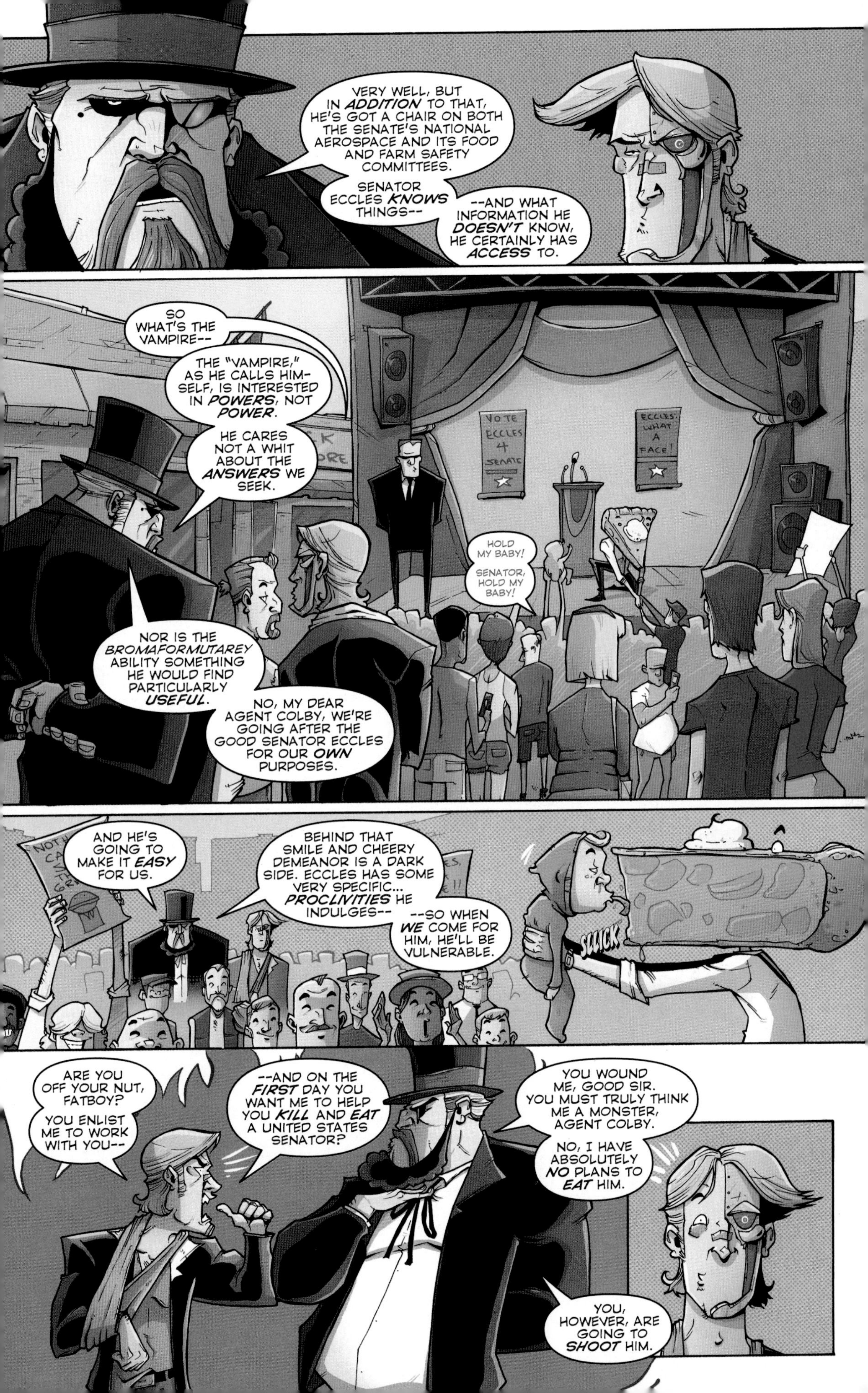
VERY WELL, BUT IN ADDITION TO THAT, HE'S GOT A CHAIR ON BOTH THE SENATE'S NATIONAL AEROSPACE AND ITS FOOD AND FARM SAFETY COMMITTEES.
SENATOR ECCLES KNOWS THINGS--
--AND WHAT INFORMATION HE DOESN'T KNOW, HE CERTAINLY HAS ACCESS TO.
SO WHAT'S THE VAMPIRE--
THE "VAMPIRE," AS HE CALLS HIMSELF, IS INTERESTED IN POWERS, NOT POWER.
HE CARES NOT A WHIT ABOUT THE ANSWERS WE SEEK.
VOTE ECCLES 4 SENATE
ECCLES: WHAT A FACE!
HOLD MY BABY!
SENATOR, HOLD MY BABY!
NOR IS THE BROMAFORMUTAREY ABILITY SOMETHING HE WOULD FIND PARTICULARLY USEFUL.
NO, MY DEAR AGENT COLBY, WE'RE GOING AFTER THE GOOD SENATOR ECCLES FOR OUR OWN PURPOSES.
AND HE'S GOING TO MAKE IT EASY FOR US.
BEHIND THAT SMILE AND CHEERY DEMEANOR IS A DARK SIDE. ECCLES HAS SOME VERY SPECIFIC... PROCLIVITIES HE INDULGES--
--SO WHEN WE COME FOR HIM, HE'LL BE VULNERABLE.
SLLICK
ARE YOU OFF YOUR NUT, FATBOY?
YOU ENLIST ME TO WORK WITH YOU--
--AND ON THE FIRST DAY YOU WANT ME TO HELP YOU KILL AND EAT A UNITED STATES SENATOR?
YOU WOUND ME, GOOD SIR. YOU MUST TRULY THINK ME A MONSTER, AGENT COLBY.
NO, I HAVE ABSOLUTELY NO PLANS TO EAT HIM.
YOU, HOWEVER, ARE GOING TO SHOOT HIM.

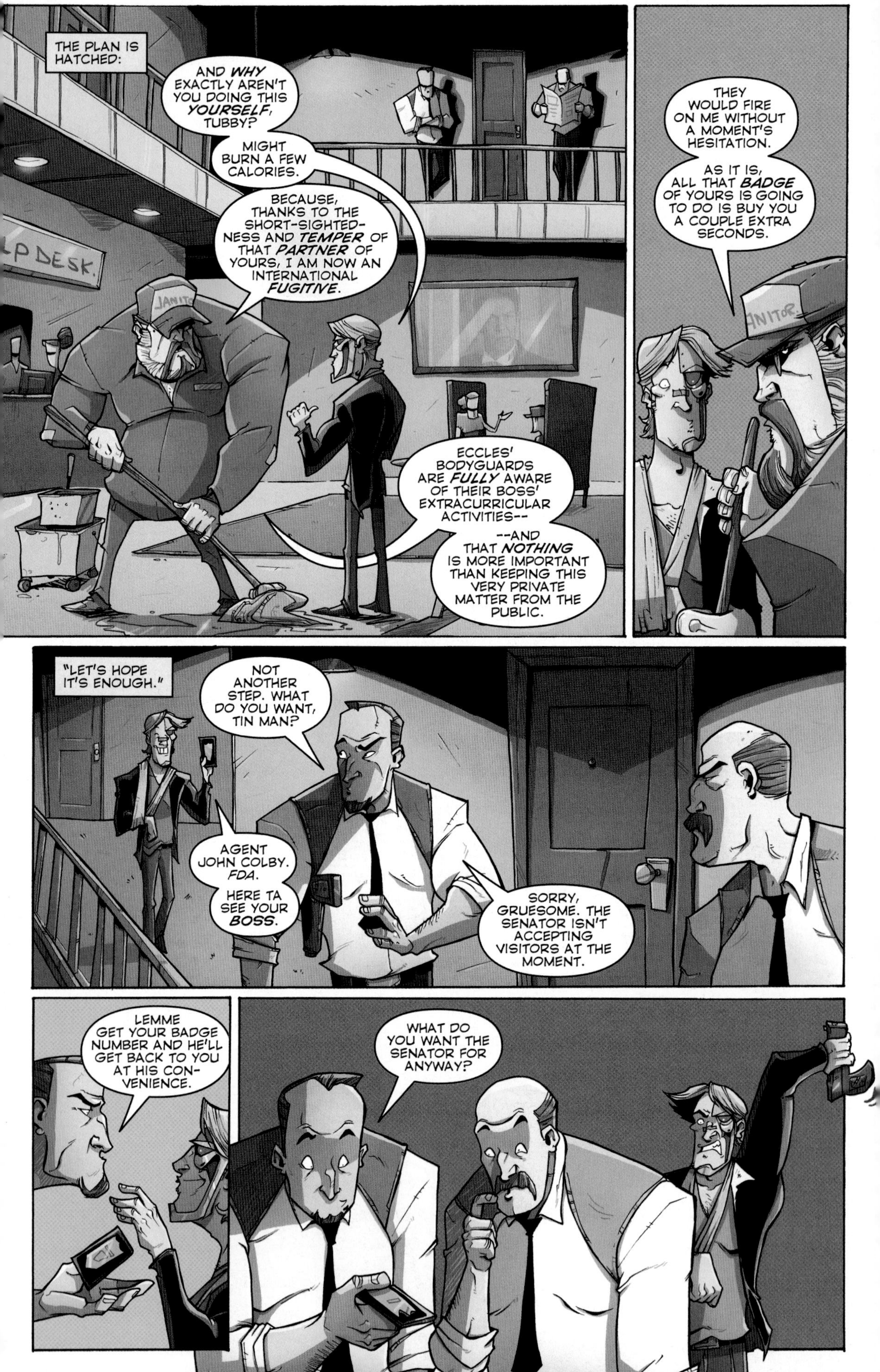

THE PLAN IS HATCHED:
AND WHY EXACTLY AREN'T YOU DOING THIS YOURSELF, TUBBY?
MIGHT BURN A FEW CALORIES.
BECAUSE, THANKS TO THE SHORT-SIGHTED-NESS AND TEMPER OF THAT PARTNER OF YOURS, I AM NOW AN INTERNATIONAL FUGITIVE.
ECCLES' BODYGUARDS ARE FULLY AWARE OF THEIR BOSS' EXTRACURRICULAR ACTIVITIES--
--AND THAT NOTHING IS MORE IMPORTANT THAN KEEPING THIS VERY PRIVATE MATTER FROM THE PUBLIC.
THEY WOULD FIRE ON ME WITHOUT A MOMENT'S HESITATION.
AS IT IS, ALL THAT BADGE OF YOURS IS GOING TO DO IS BUY YOU A COUPLE EXTRA SECONDS.
"LET'S HOPE IT'S ENOUGH."
NOT ANOTHER STEP. WHAT DO YOU WANT, TIN MAN?
AGENT JOHN COLBY. FDA.
HERE TA SEE YOUR BOSS.
SORRY, GRUESOME. THE SENATOR ISN'T ACCEPTING VISITORS AT THE MOMENT.
LEMME GET YOUR BADGE NUMBER AND HE'LL GET BACK TO YOU AT HIS CON-VENIENCE.
WHAT DO YOU WANT THE SENATOR FOR ANYWAY?

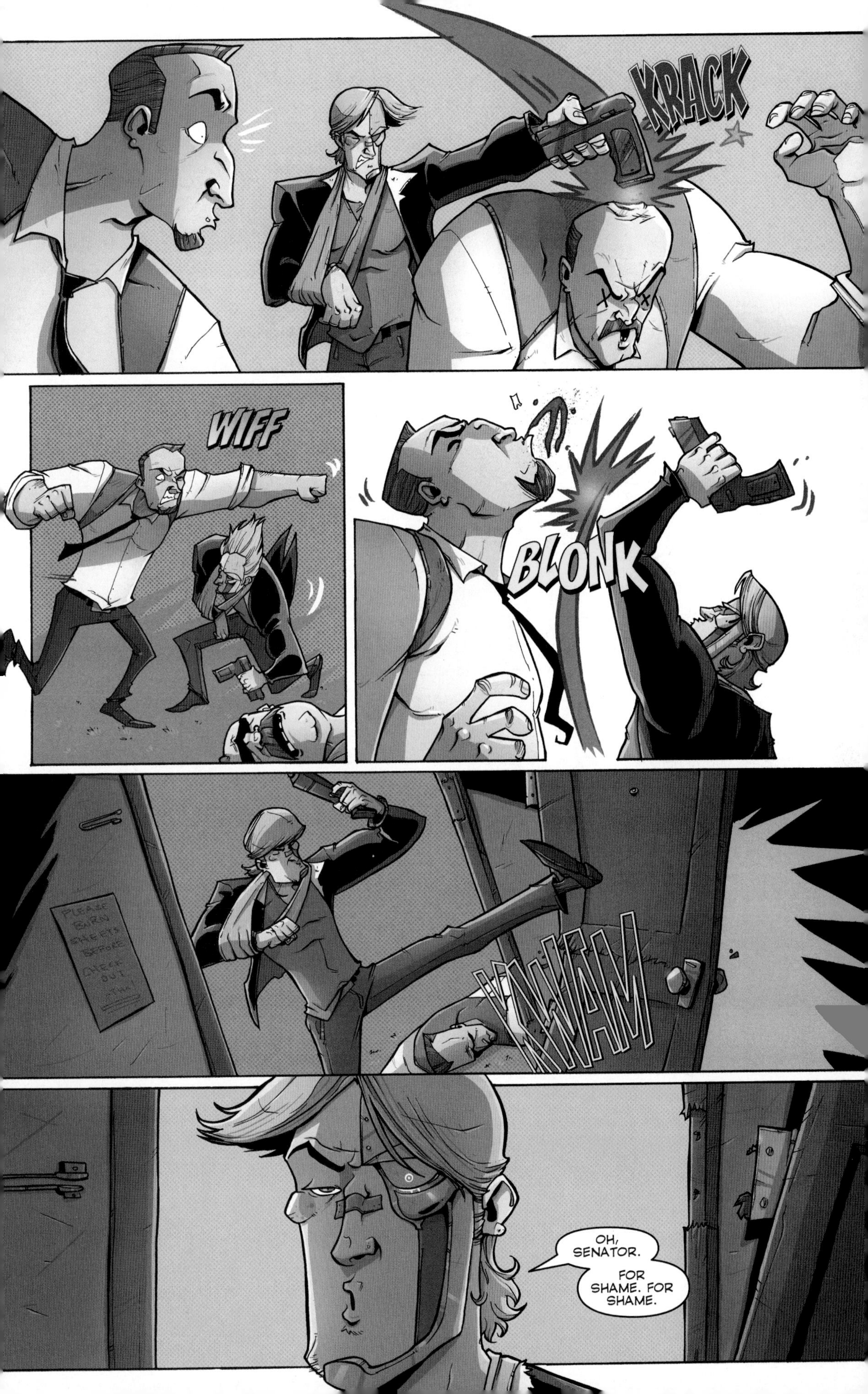
KRACK
WIFF
BLONK
PLEASE BURN SHEETS BEFORE CHECK OUT
KWAM
OH, SENATOR.
FOR SHAME. FOR SHAME.

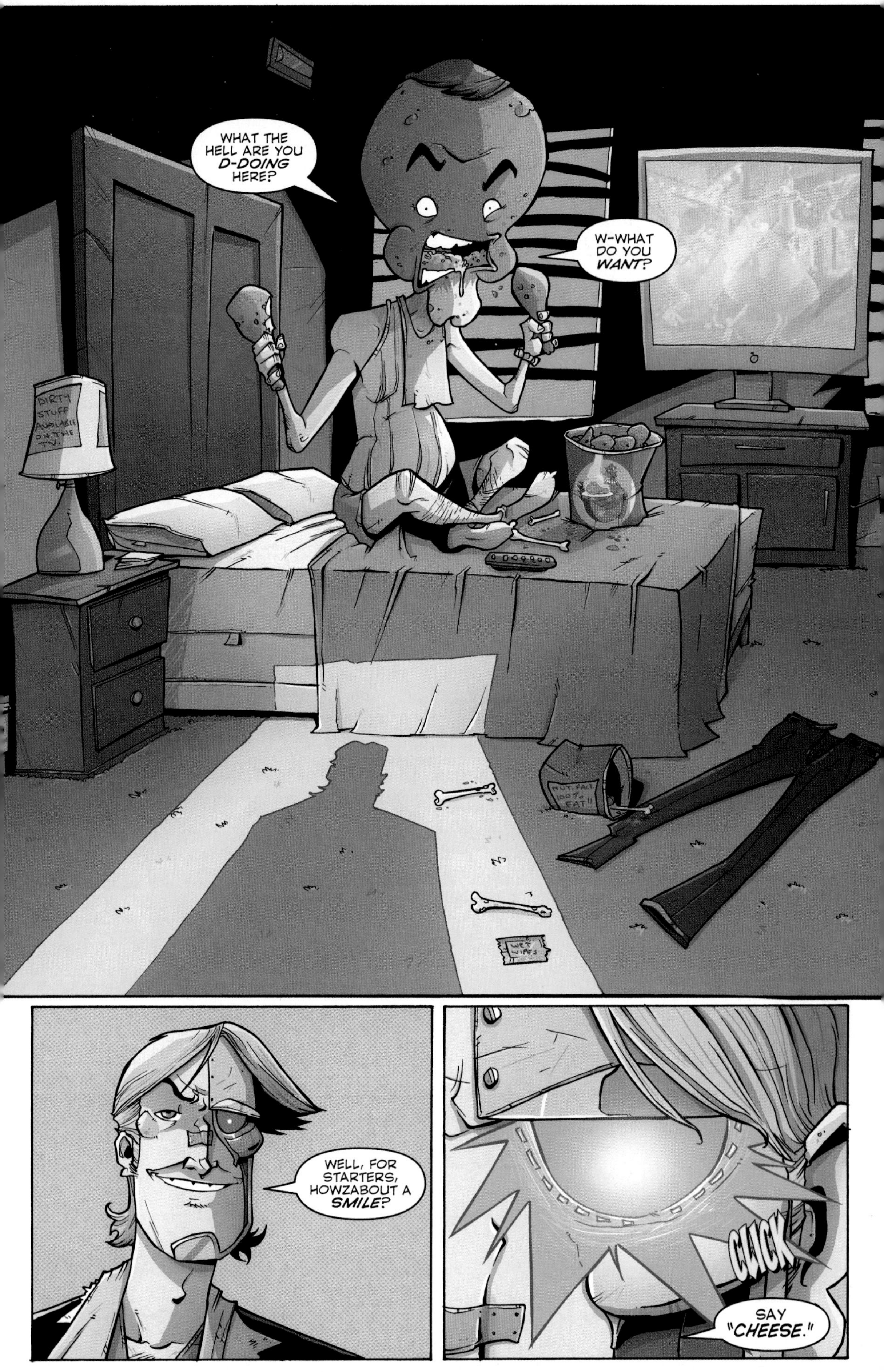
WHAT THE HELL ARE YOU D-DOING HERE?
W-WHAT DO YOU WANT?
DIRTY STUFF AVAILABLE ON THE TV.
NUT. FACT 100% FAT!!
WET WIPES
WELL, FOR STARTERS, HOWZABOUT A SMILE?
CLICK
SAY "CHEESE."

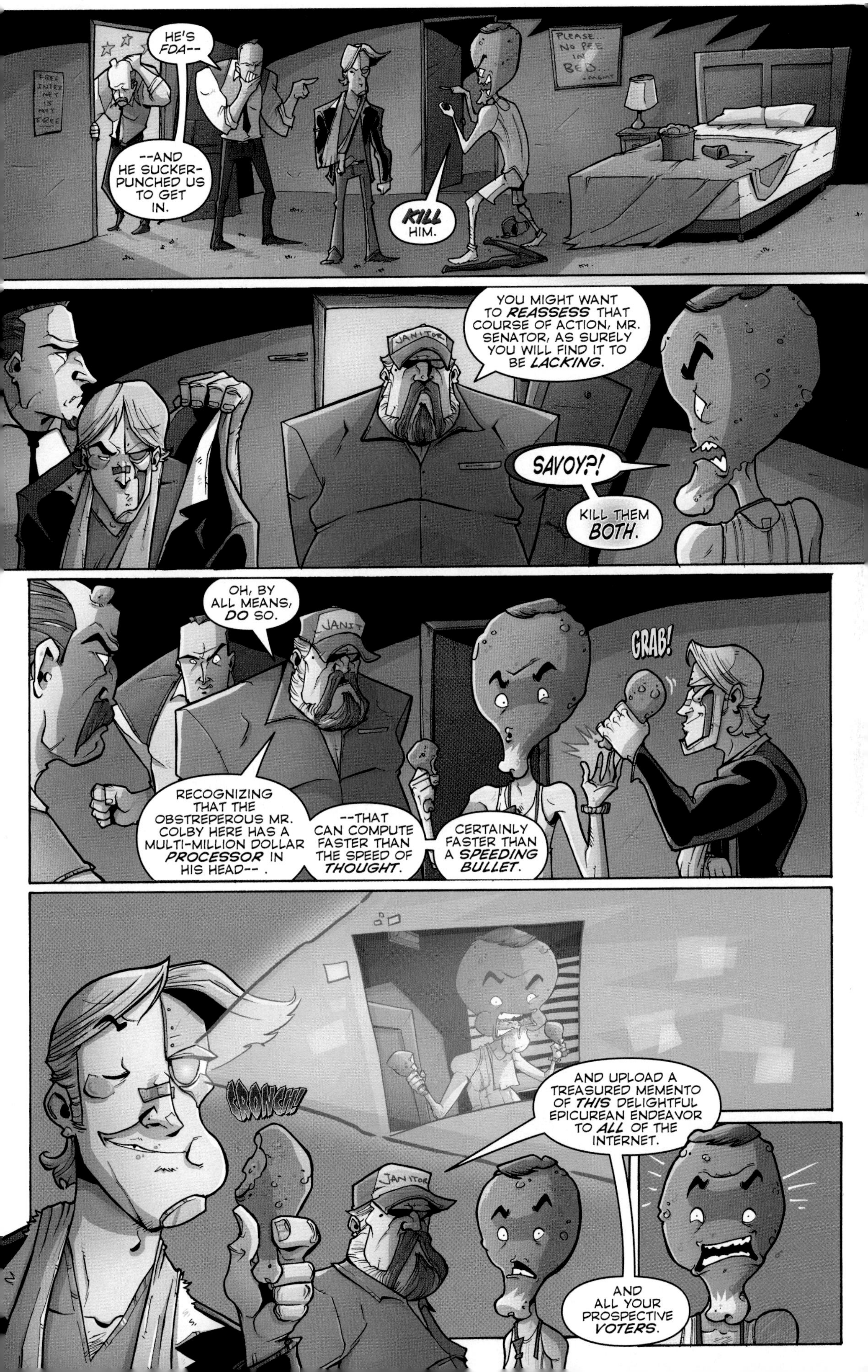
FREE INTERNET IS NOT FREE
PLEASE... NO PEE IN BED... -MGMT
HE'S FDA--
--AND HE SUCKER-PUNCHED US TO GET IN.
KILL HIM.
JANITOR
YOU MIGHT WANT TO REASSESS THAT COURSE OF ACTION, MR. SENATOR, AS SURELY YOU WILL FIND IT TO BE LACKING.
SAVOY?!
KILL THEM BOTH.
OH, BY ALL MEANS, DO SO.
GRAB!
RECOGNIZING THAT THE OBSTREPEROUS MR. COLBY HERE HAS A MULTI-MILLION DOLLAR PROCESSOR IN HIS HEAD-- .
--THAT CAN COMPUTE FASTER THAN THE SPEED OF THOUGHT.
CERTAINLY FASTER THAN A SPEEDING BULLET.
CRONCH!
JANITOR
AND UPLOAD A TREASURED MEMENTO OF THIS DELIGHTFUL EPICUREAN ENDEAVOR TO ALL OF THE INTERNET.
AND ALL YOUR PROSPECTIVE VOTERS.

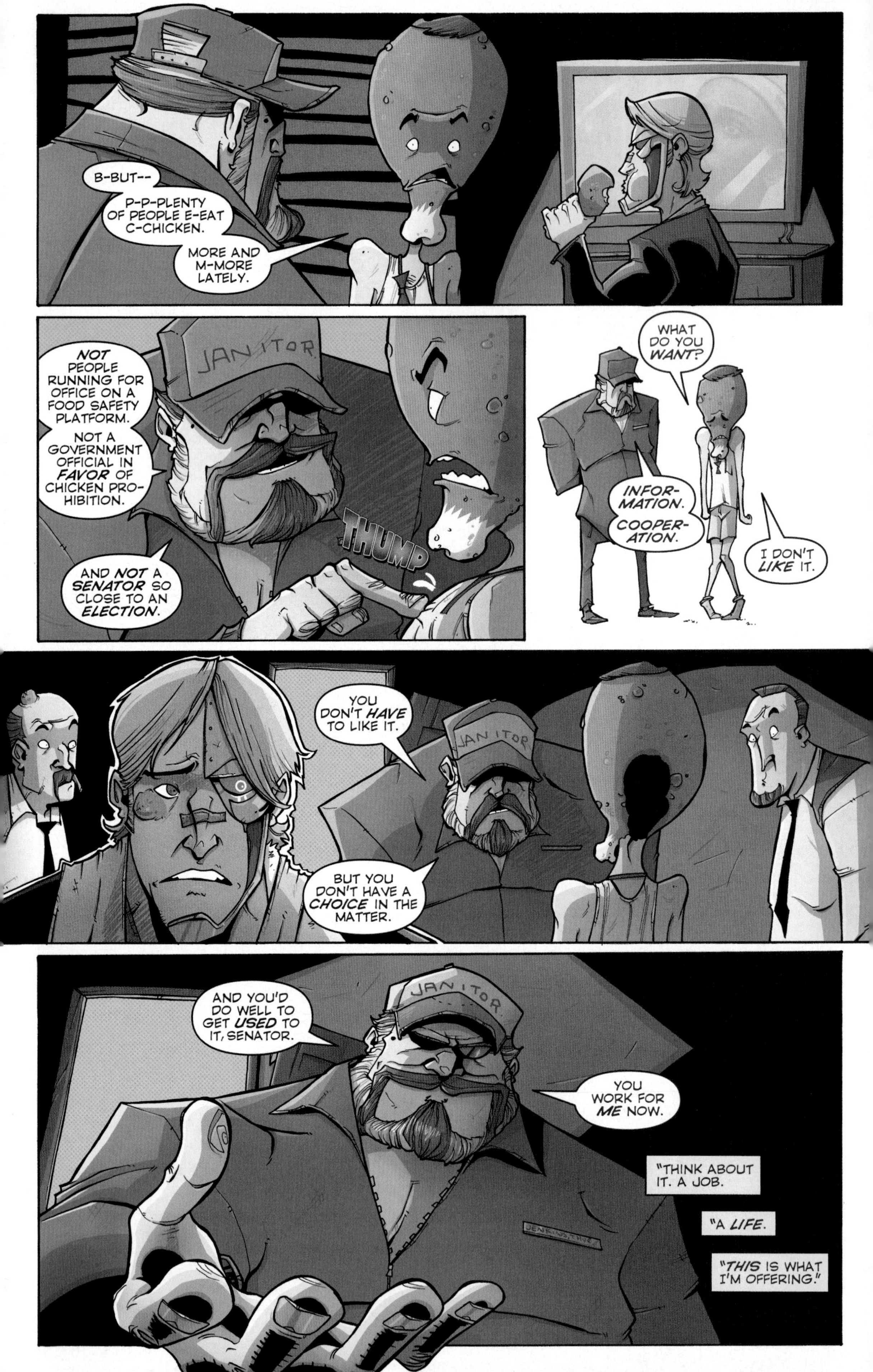
B-BUT--
P-P-PLENTY OF PEOPLE E-EAT C-CHICKEN.
MORE AND M-MORE LATELY.
NOT PEOPLE RUNNING FOR OFFICE ON A FOOD SAFETY PLATFORM.
NOT A GOVERNMENT OFFICIAL IN *FAVOR* OF CHICKEN PROHIBITION.
AND *NOT* A *SENATOR* SO CLOSE TO AN *ELECTION*.
THUMP
JANITOR
WHAT DO YOU *WANT?*
INFORMATION.
COOPERATION.
I DON'T *LIKE* IT.
YOU DON'T *HAVE* TO LIKE IT.
BUT YOU DON'T HAVE A *CHOICE* IN THE MATTER.
AND YOU'D DO WELL TO GET *USED* TO IT, SENATOR.
YOU WORK FOR *ME* NOW.
"THINK ABOUT IT. A JOB.
"A *LIFE*.
"*THIS* IS WHAT I'M OFFERING."

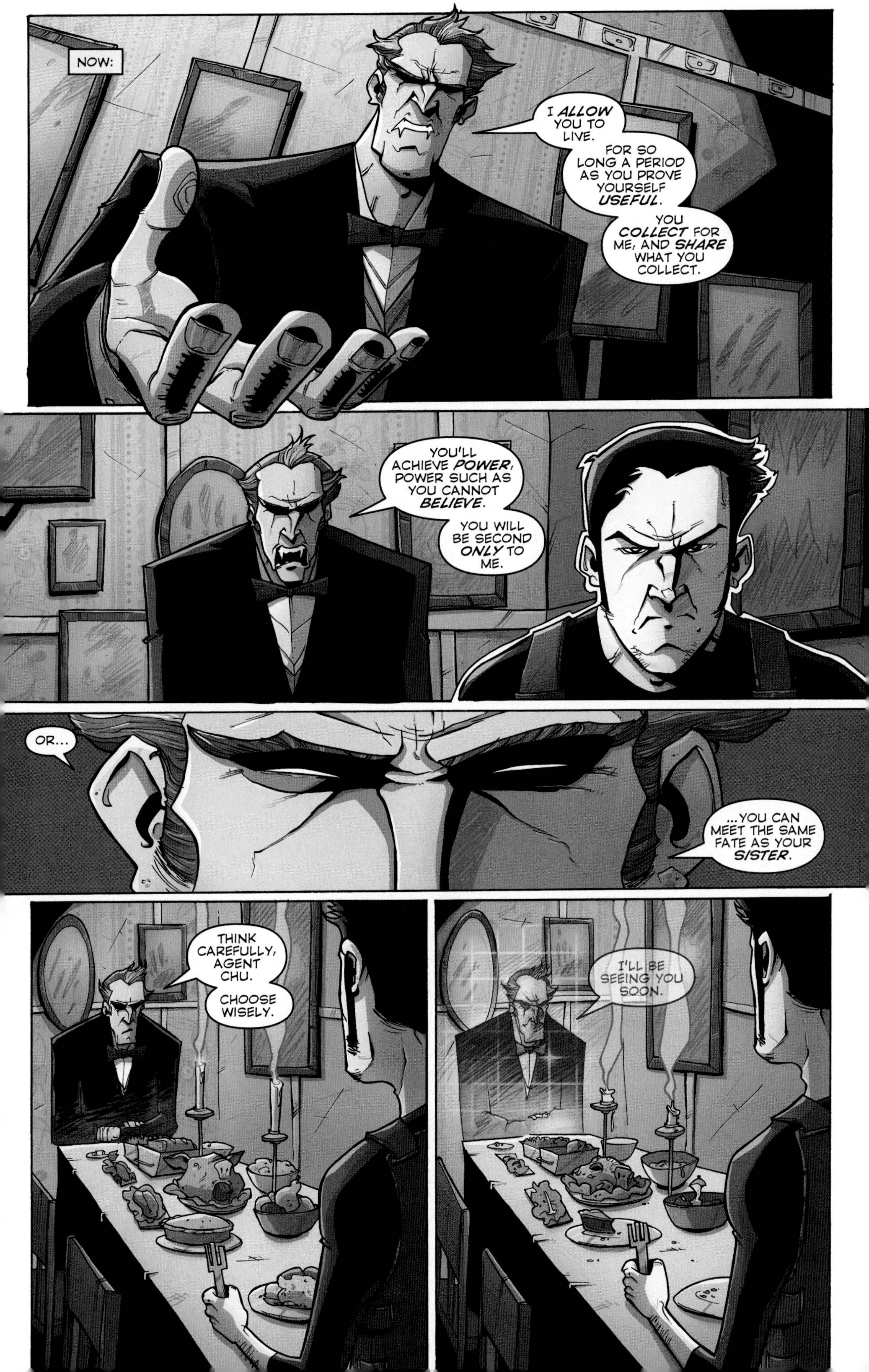
NOW:
I ALLOW YOU TO LIVE.
FOR SO LONG A PERIOD AS YOU PROVE YOURSELF USEFUL.
YOU COLLECT FOR ME, AND SHARE WHAT YOU COLLECT.
YOU'LL ACHIEVE POWER, POWER SUCH AS YOU CANNOT BELIEVE.
YOU WILL BE SECOND ONLY TO ME.
OR...
...YOU CAN MEET THE SAME FATE AS YOUR SISTER.
THINK CAREFULLY, AGENT CHU.
CHOOSE WISELY.
I'LL BE SEEING YOU SOON.

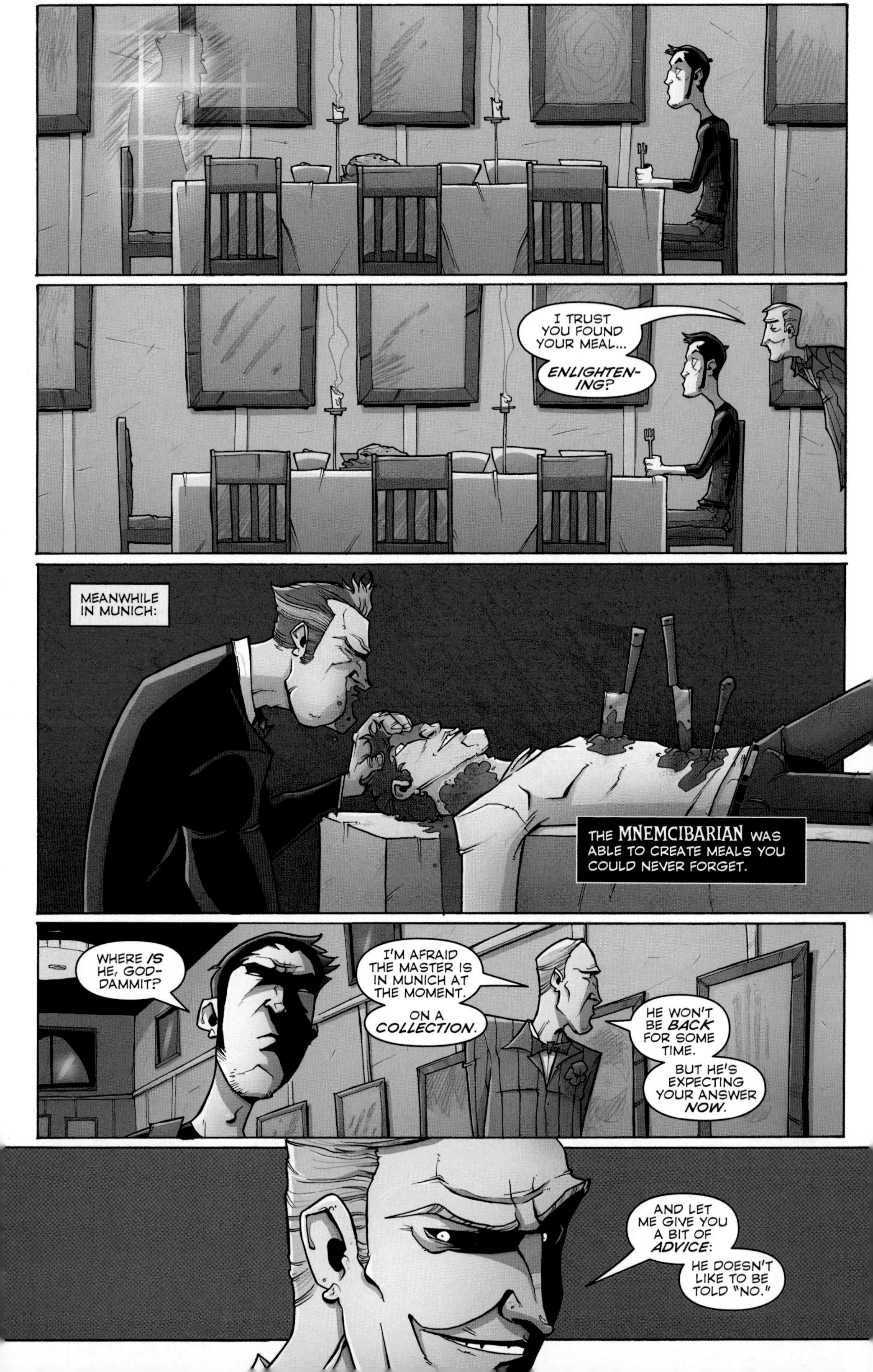
I TRUST YOU FOUND YOUR MEAL...
ENLIGHTEN-ING?
MEANWHILE IN MUNICH:
THE MNEMCIBARIAN WAS ABLE TO CREATE MEALS YOU COULD NEVER FORGET.
WHERE IS HE, GOD-DAMMIT?
I'M AFRAID THE MASTER IS IN MUNICH AT THE MOMENT.
ON A COLLECTION.
HE WON'T BE BACK FOR SOME TIME.
BUT HE'S EXPECTING YOUR ANSWER NOW.
AND LET ME GIVE YOU A BIT OF ADVICE:
HE DOESN'T LIKE TO BE TOLD "NO."

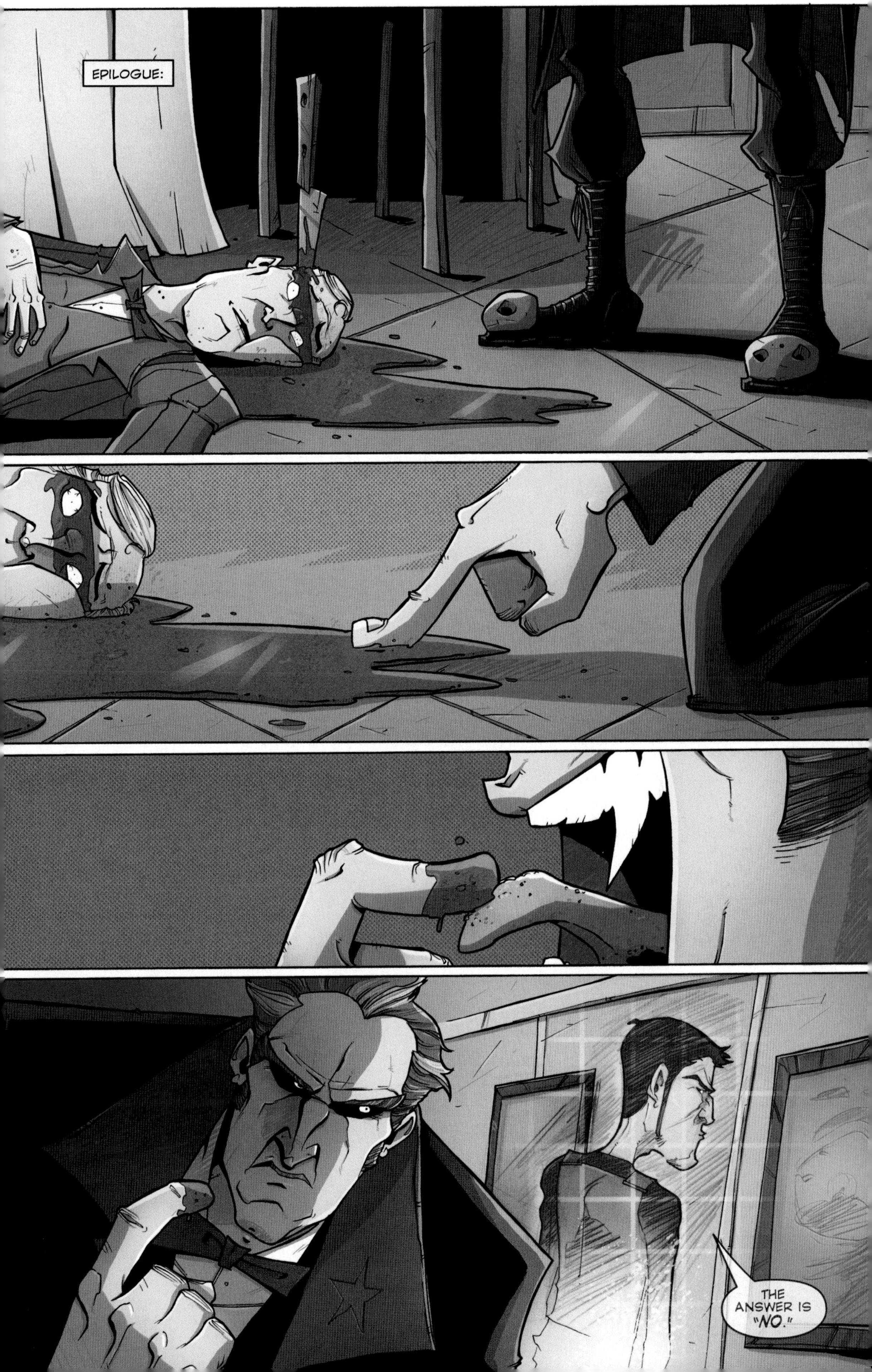
EPILOGUE:
THE ANSWER IS "NO."

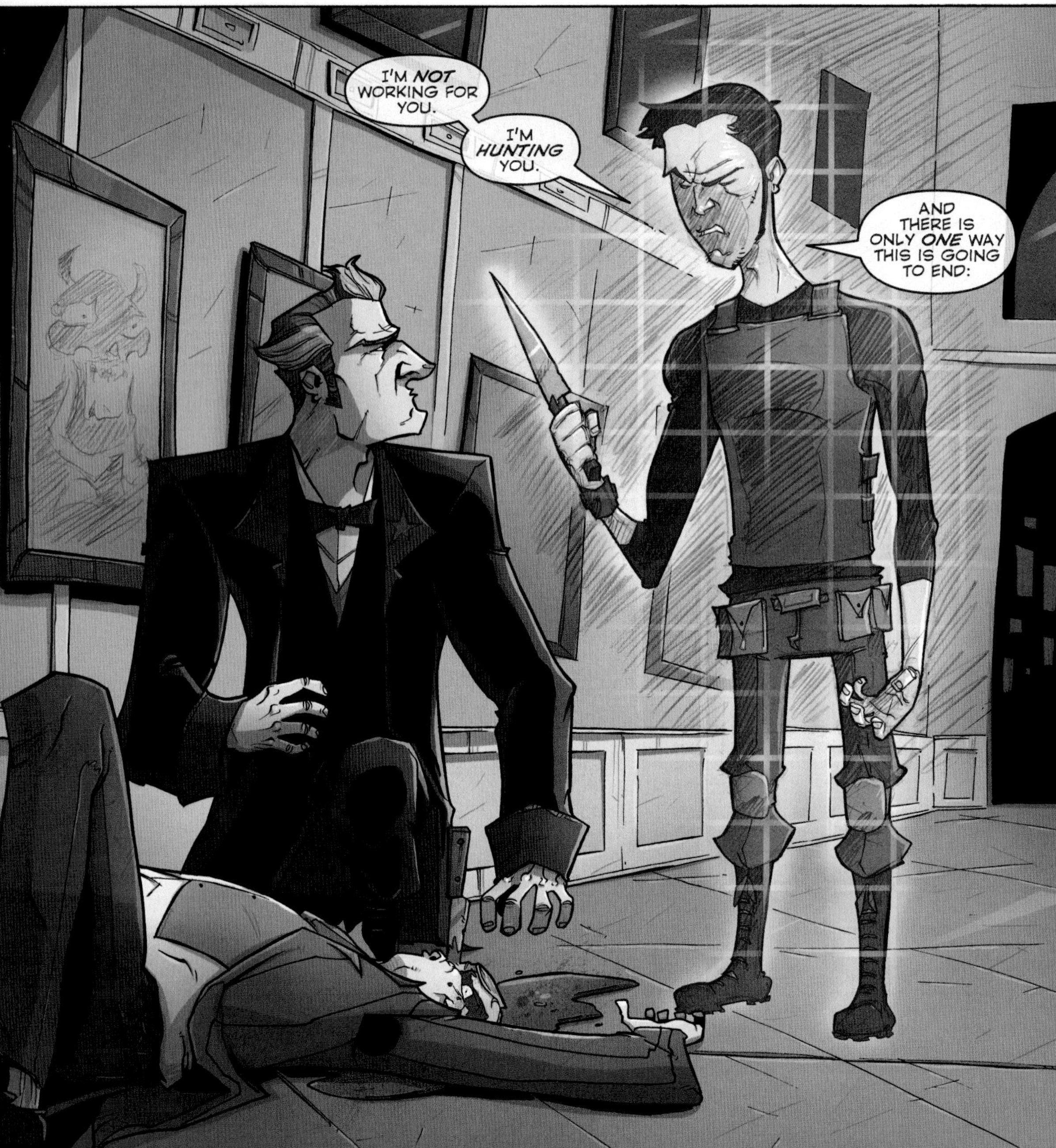

I'M *NOT* WORKING FOR YOU.
I'M *HUNTING* YOU.
AND THERE IS ONLY *ONE* WAY THIS IS GOING TO END:

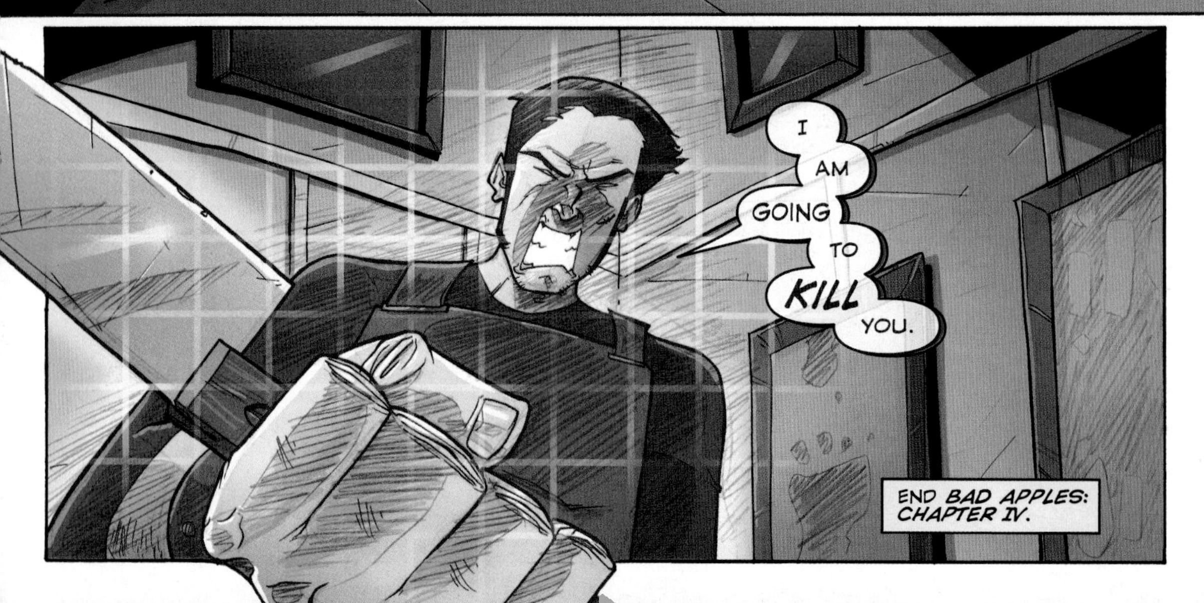

I AM GOING TO ***KILL*** YOU.
END *BAD APPLES: CHAPTER IV.*

Chapter 5

THOU
SHALT
NOT
RoB!

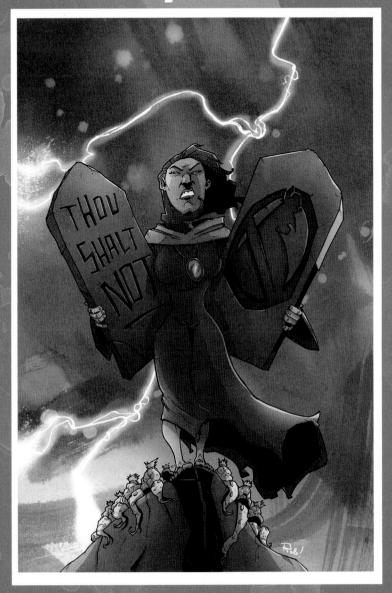

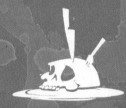

LAYMAN · GUILLORY · CHEW
DESTROY SAVOY
VOLUME 35

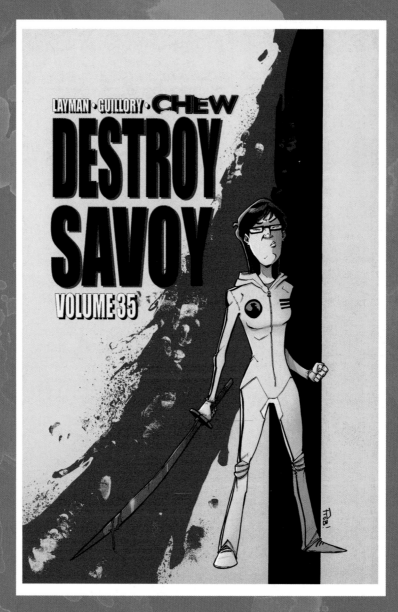

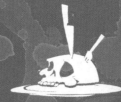

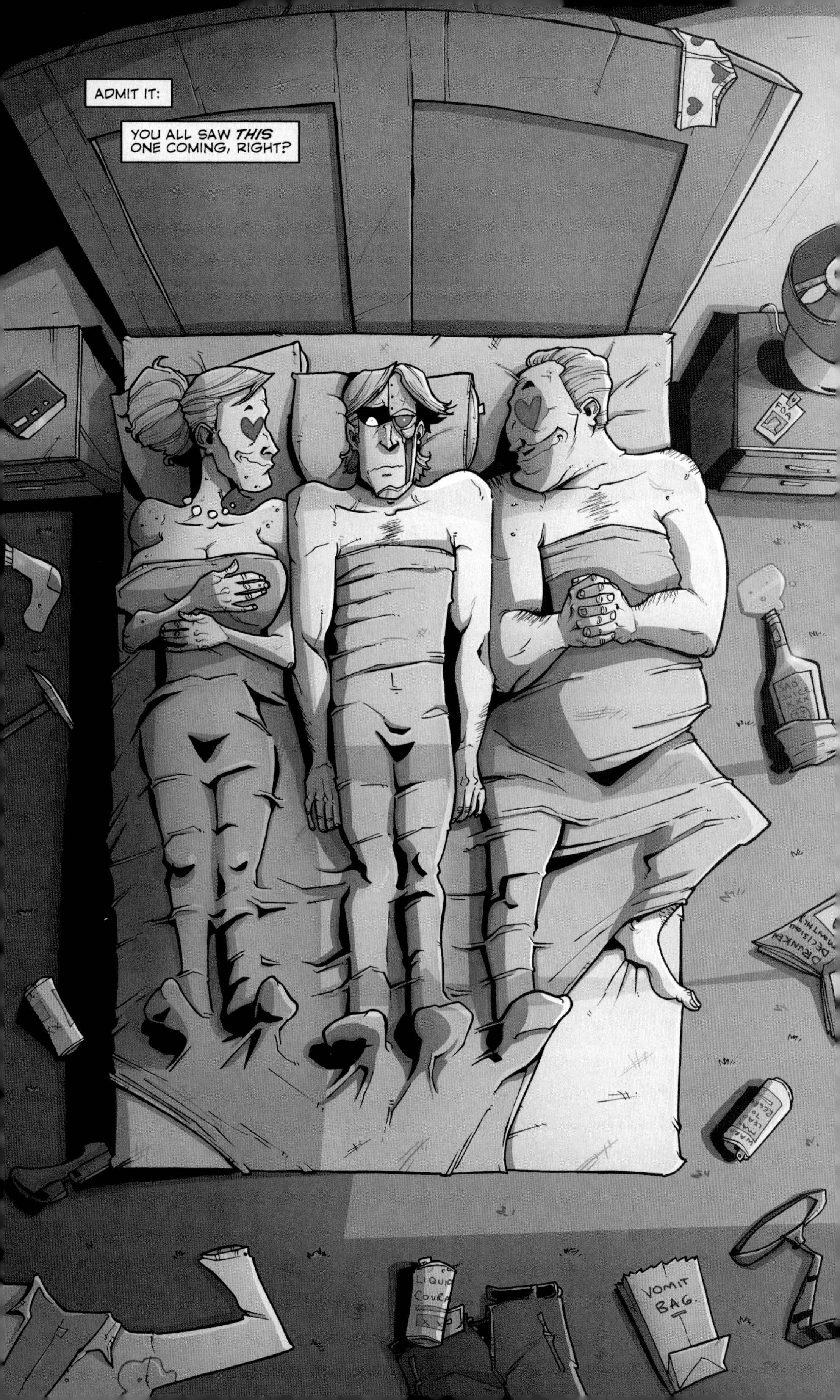
ADMIT IT:
YOU ALL SAW *THIS* ONE COMING, RIGHT?
SAD JUICE XXX
VOMIT BAG.

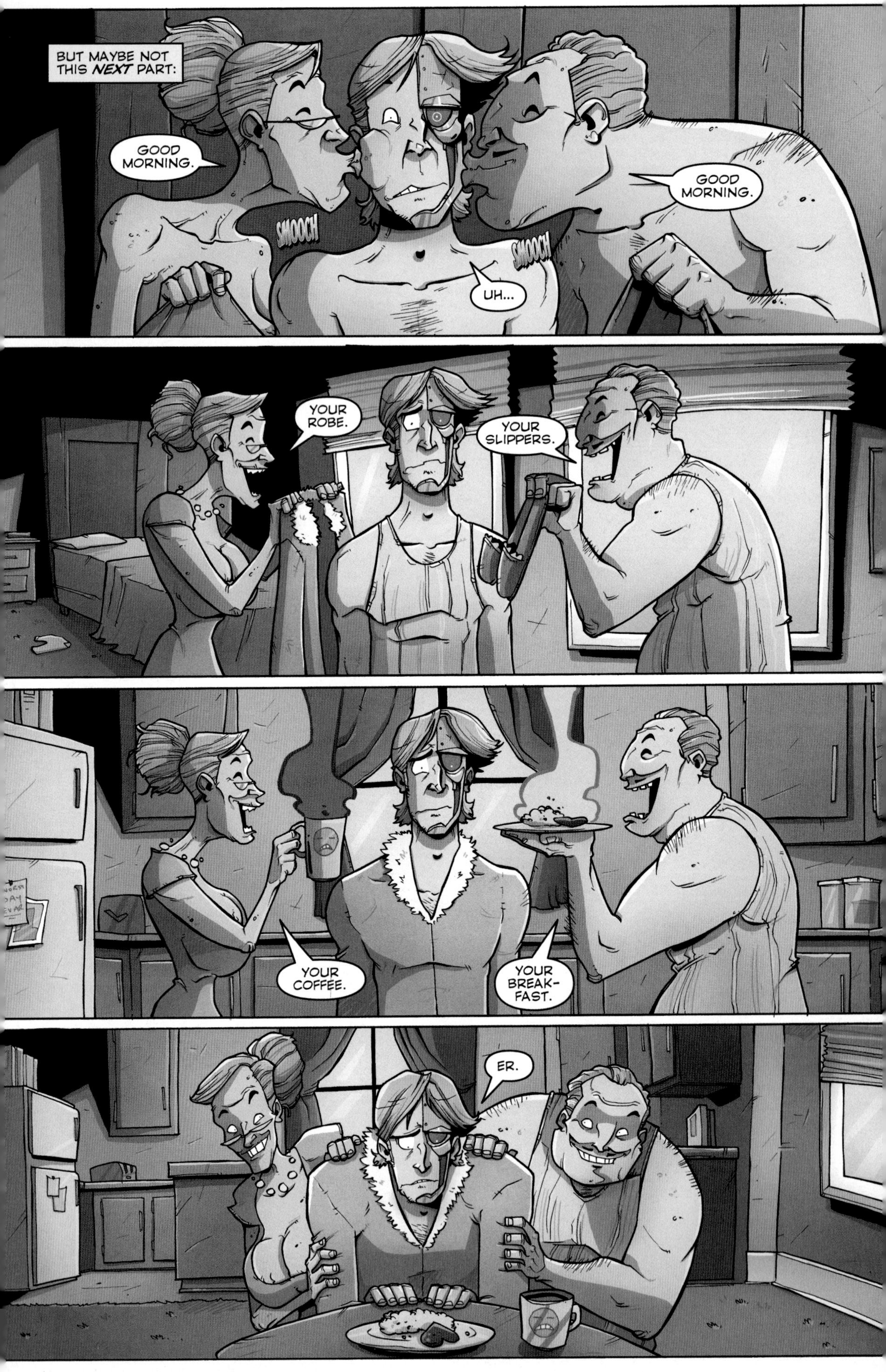
BUT MAYBE NOT THIS *NEXT* PART:
GOOD MORNING.
SMOOCH
GOOD MORNING.
SMOOCH
UH...
YOUR ROBE.
YOUR SLIPPERS.
YOUR COFFEE.
YOUR BREAK-FAST.
ER.

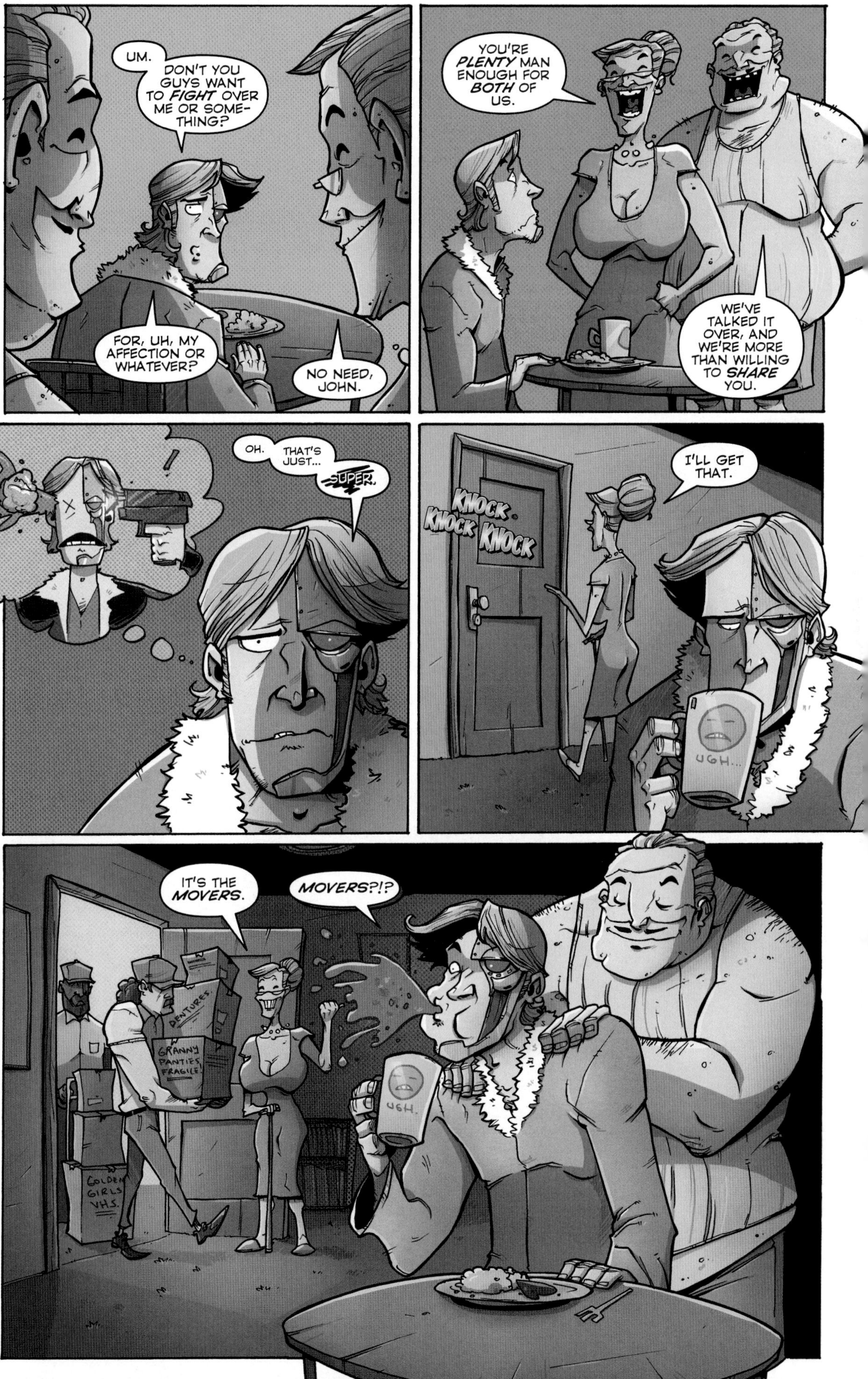
UM.
DON'T YOU GUYS WANT TO FIGHT OVER ME OR SOMETHING?
FOR, UH, MY AFFECTION OR WHATEVER?
NO NEED, JOHN.
YOU'RE PLENTY MAN ENOUGH FOR BOTH OF US.
WE'VE TALKED IT OVER, AND WE'RE MORE THAN WILLING TO SHARE YOU.
OH.
THAT'S JUST...
SUPER.
KNOCK. KNOCK KNOCK
I'LL GET THAT.
UGH...
IT'S THE MOVERS.
MOVERS?!?
DENTURES
GRANNY PANTIES FRAGILE
GOLDEN GIRLS VHS.
UGH.

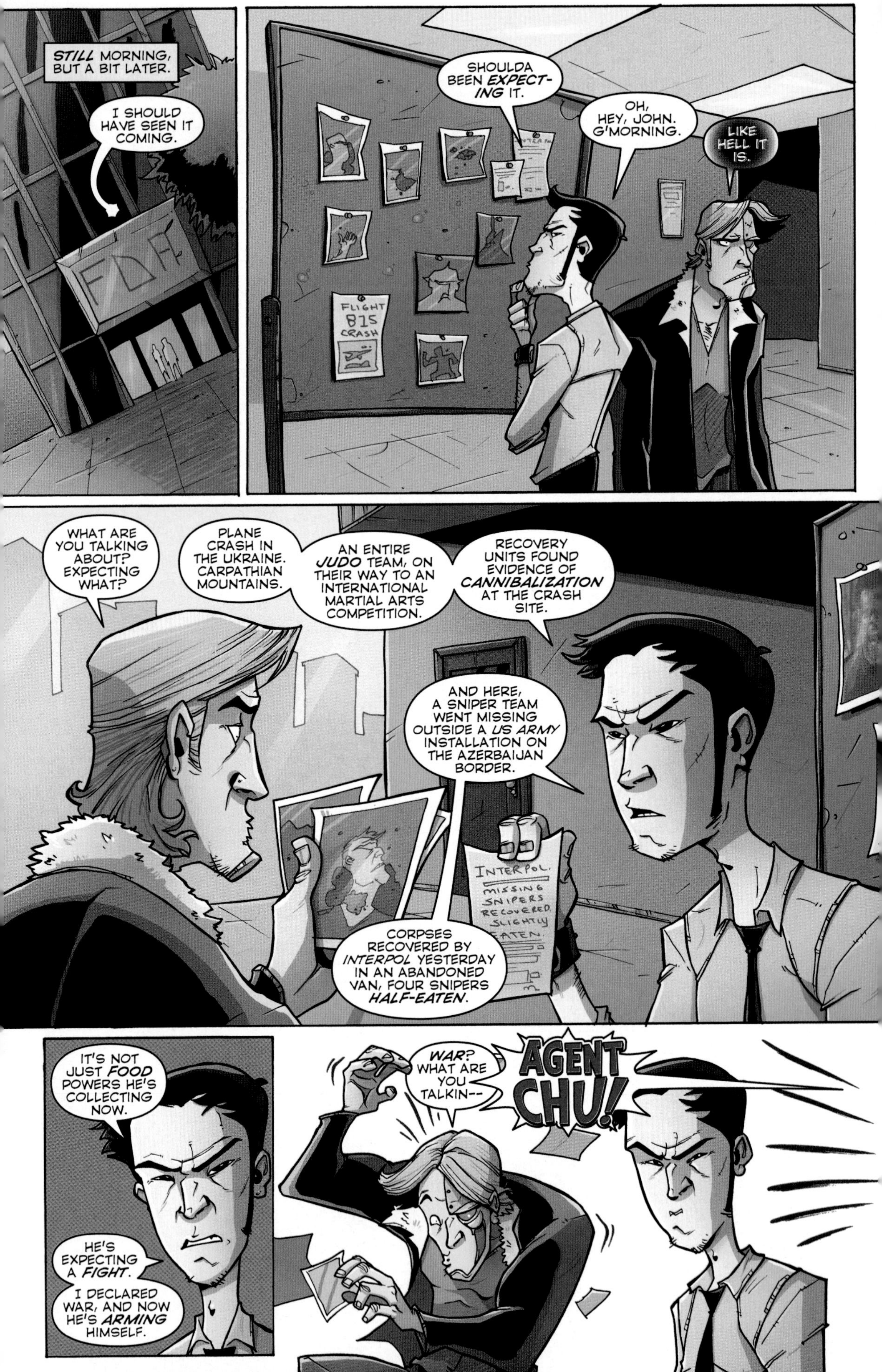
STILL MORNING, BUT A BIT LATER.
I SHOULD HAVE SEEN IT COMING.
FDA
SHOULDA BEEN EXPECTING IT.
OH, HEY, JOHN. G'MORNING.
LIKE HELL IT IS.
FLIGHT 815 CRASH
WHAT ARE YOU TALKING ABOUT? EXPECTING WHAT?
PLANE CRASH IN THE UKRAINE. CARPATHIAN MOUNTAINS.
AN ENTIRE JUDO TEAM, ON THEIR WAY TO AN INTERNATIONAL MARTIAL ARTS COMPETITION.
RECOVERY UNITS FOUND EVIDENCE OF CANNIBALIZATION AT THE CRASH SITE.
AND HERE, A SNIPER TEAM WENT MISSING OUTSIDE A US ARMY INSTALLATION ON THE AZERBAIJAN BORDER.
INTERPOL. MISSING SNIPERS RECOVERED. SLIGHTLY EATEN.
CORPSES RECOVERED BY INTERPOL YESTERDAY IN AN ABANDONED VAN, FOUR SNIPERS HALF-EATEN.
IT'S NOT JUST FOOD POWERS HE'S COLLECTING NOW.
HE'S EXPECTING A FIGHT.
I DECLARED WAR, AND NOW HE'S ARMING HIMSELF.
WAR? WHAT ARE YOU TALKIN--
AGENT CHU!

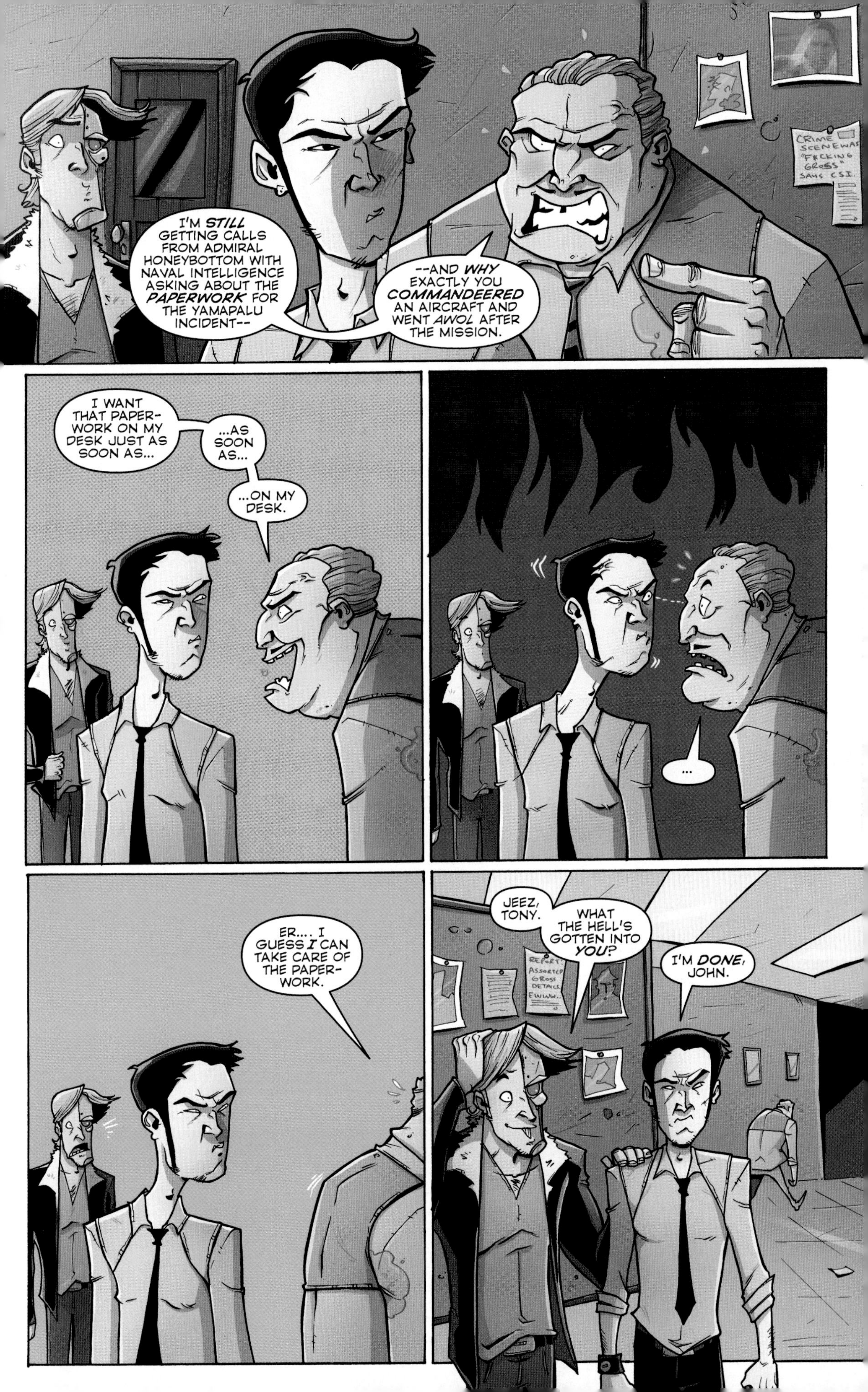
CRIME SCENE WAS "F*CKING GROSS" SAYS CSI.
I'M STILL GETTING CALLS FROM ADMIRAL HONEYBOTTOM WITH NAVAL INTELLIGENCE ASKING ABOUT THE PAPERWORK FOR THE YAMAPALU INCIDENT--
--AND WHY EXACTLY YOU COMMANDEERED AN AIRCRAFT AND WENT AWOL AFTER THE MISSION.
I WANT THAT PAPER-WORK ON MY DESK JUST AS SOON AS...
...AS SOON AS...
...ON MY DESK.
...
ER.... I GUESS I CAN TAKE CARE OF THE PAPER-WORK.
REPORT: ASSORTED GROSS DETAILS. EWWW.
JEEZ, TONY.
WHAT THE HELL'S GOTTEN INTO YOU?
I'M DONE, JOHN.

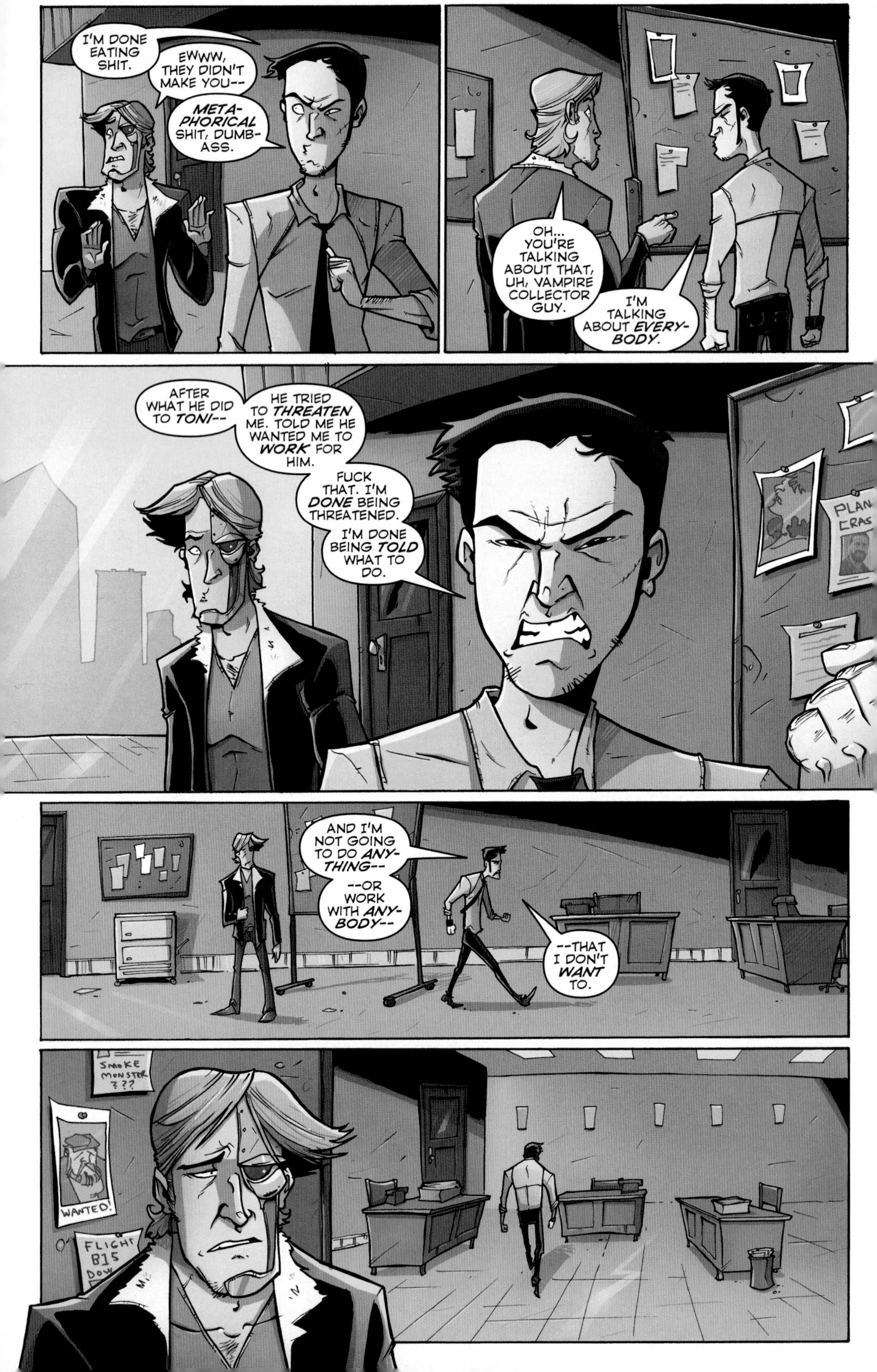

I'M DONE EATING SHIT.
EWWW, THEY DIDN'T MAKE YOU--
METAPHORICAL SHIT, DUMB-ASS.
OH... YOU'RE TALKING ABOUT THAT, UH, VAMPIRE COLLECTOR GUY.
I'M TALKING ABOUT *EVERYBODY*.
AFTER WHAT HE DID TO *TONI*--
HE TRIED TO *THREATEN* ME. TOLD ME HE WANTED ME TO *WORK* FOR HIM.
FUCK THAT. I'M *DONE* BEING THREATENED.
I'M DONE BEING *TOLD* WHAT TO DO.
AND I'M NOT GOING TO DO *ANYTHING*--
--OR WORK WITH *ANYBODY*--
--THAT I DON'T *WANT* TO.
SMOKE MONSTER ???
WANTED!
FLIGHT 815 DOW

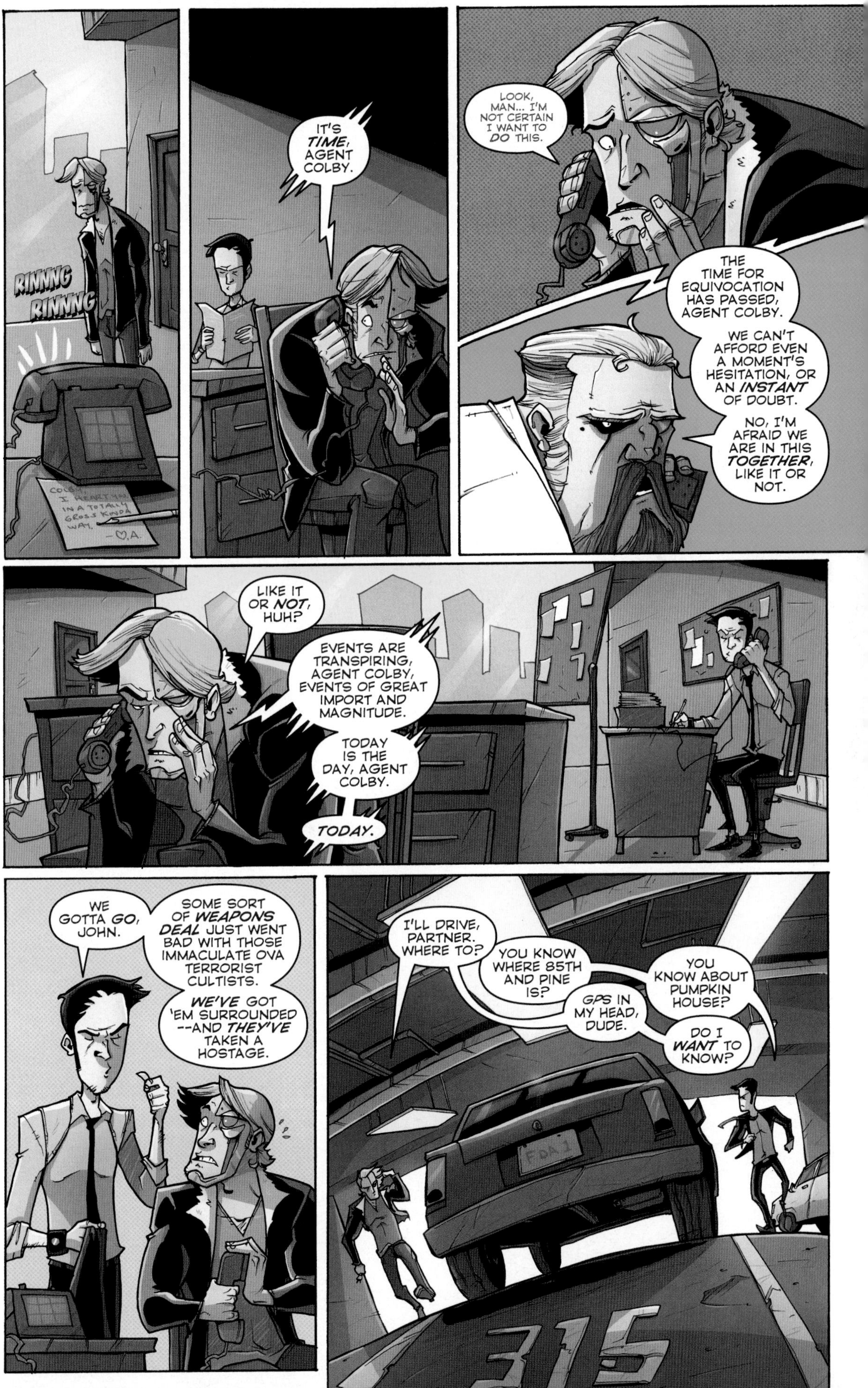
RINNNG
RINNNG
COLBY, I HEART YOU IN A TOTALLY GROSS KINDA WAY. —♡.A.
IT'S *TIME*, AGENT COLBY.
LOOK, MAN... I'M NOT CERTAIN I WANT TO *DO* THIS.
THE TIME FOR EQUIVOCATION HAS PASSED, AGENT COLBY.
WE CAN'T AFFORD EVEN A MOMENT'S HESITATION, OR AN *INSTANT* OF DOUBT.
NO, I'M AFRAID WE ARE IN THIS *TOGETHER*, LIKE IT OR NOT.
LIKE IT OR *NOT*, HUH?
EVENTS ARE TRANSPIRING, AGENT COLBY, EVENTS OF GREAT IMPORT AND MAGNITUDE.
TODAY IS THE DAY, AGENT COLBY.
TODAY.
WE GOTTA *GO*, JOHN.
SOME SORT OF ***WEAPONS DEAL*** JUST WENT BAD WITH THOSE IMMACULATE OVA TERRORIST CULTISTS.
WE'VE GOT 'EM SURROUNDED --AND ***THEY'VE*** TAKEN A HOSTAGE.
I'LL DRIVE, PARTNER. WHERE TO?
YOU KNOW WHERE 85TH AND PINE IS?
GPS IN MY HEAD, DUDE.
YOU KNOW ABOUT PUMPKIN HOUSE?
DO I *WANT* TO KNOW?
FDA 1
315

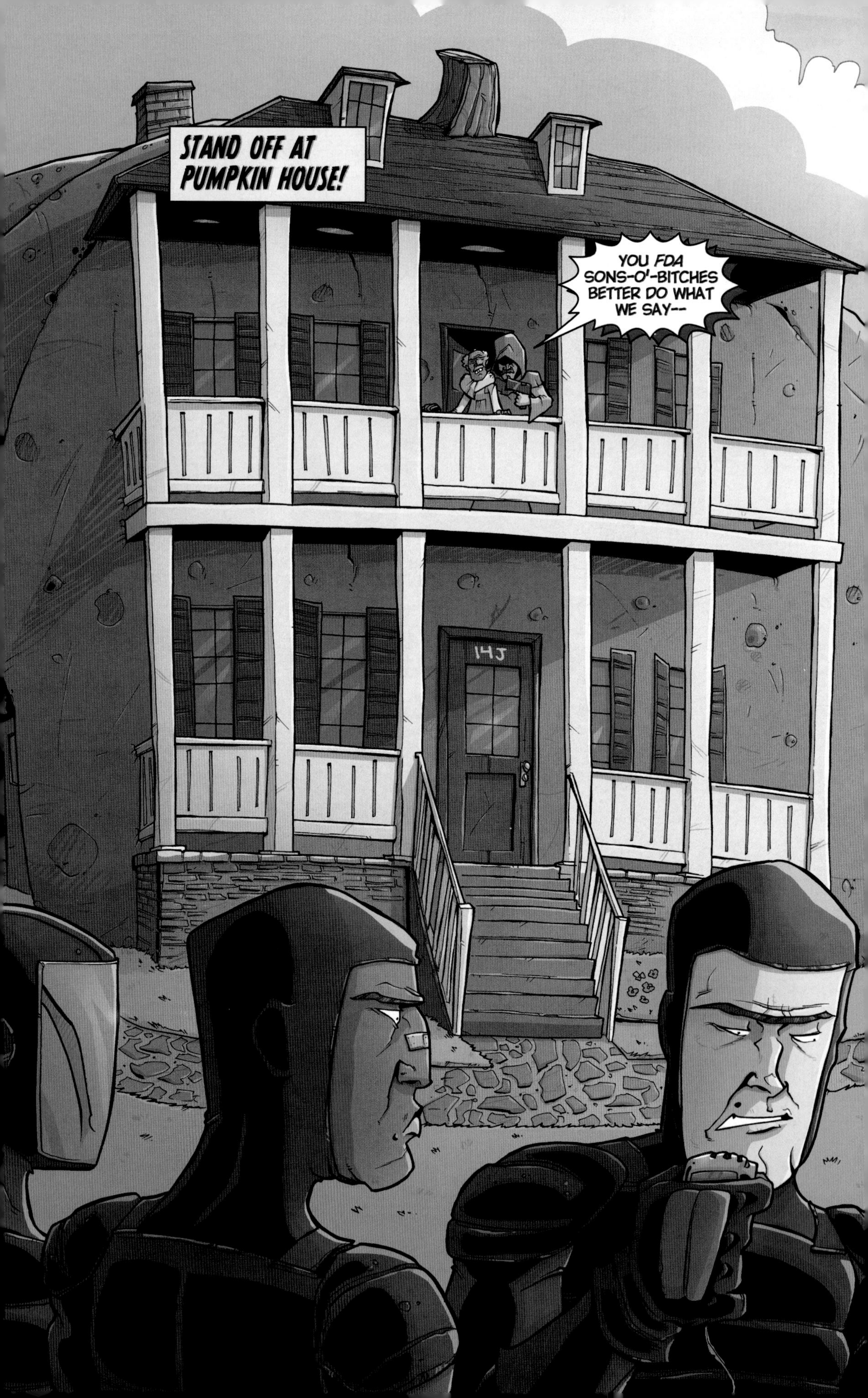
STAND OFF AT PUMPKIN HOUSE!
YOU *FDA* SONS-O'-BITCHES BETTER DO WHAT WE SAY--
14J

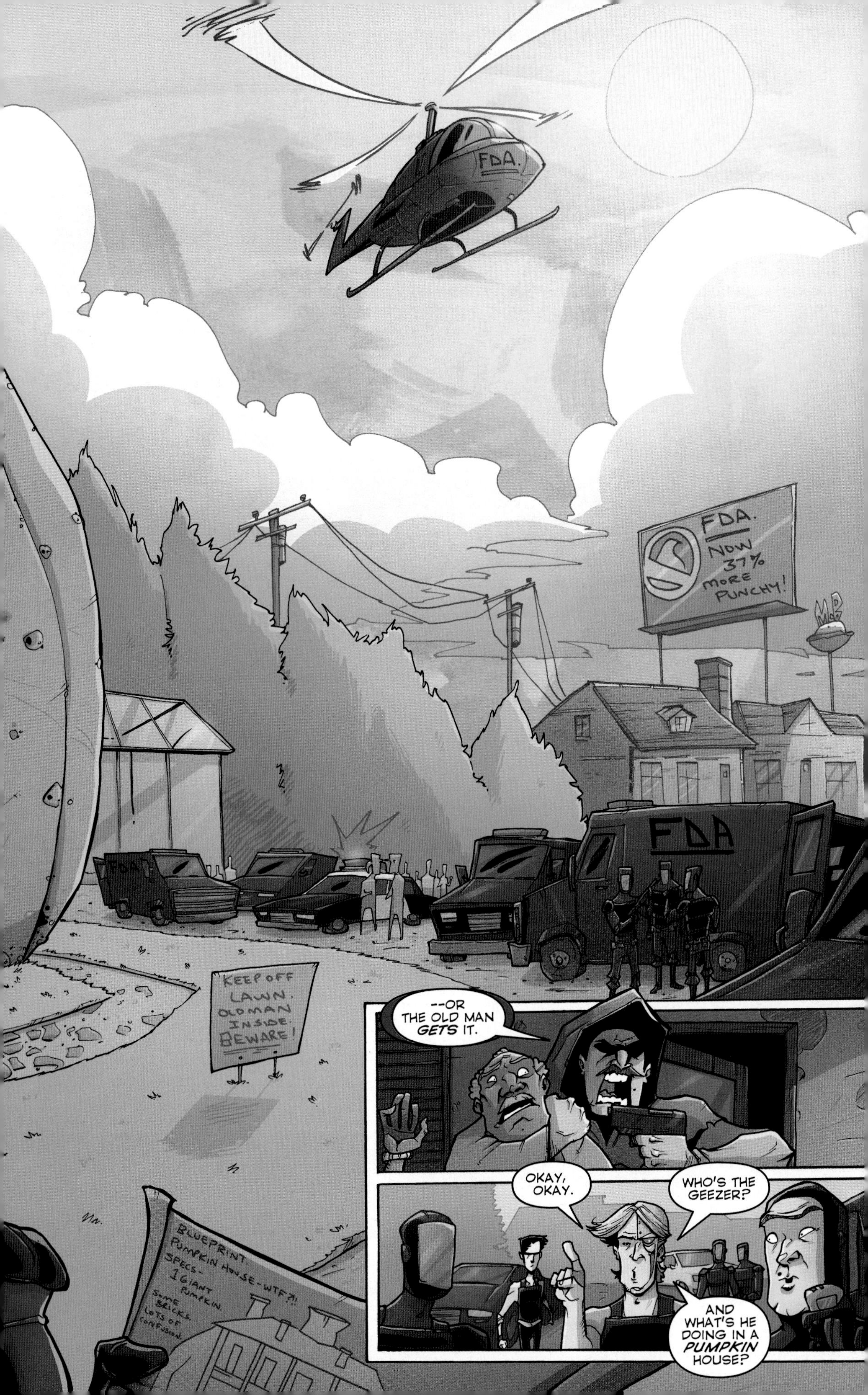
FDA.
FDA.
NOW 37% MORE PUNCHY!
FDA
KEEP OFF LAWN. OLD MAN INSIDE. BEWARE!
--OR THE OLD MAN *GETS* IT.
OKAY, OKAY.
WHO'S THE GEEZER?
AND WHAT'S HE DOING IN A *PUMPKIN* HOUSE?
BLUEPRINT. PUMPKIN HOUSE-WTF?!
SPECS- 1 GIANT PUMPKIN.
SOME BRICKS. LOTS OF CONFUSION.

DONALD BARLEY IS A HORTAMAGNATROPH--

--WHOSE SKILLS IN THE GARDEN ALLOW HIM TO GROW FRUITS AND VEGETABLES OF *ENORMOUS* SIZES.

BARLEY HAD A LONG AND WILDLY SUCCESSFUL CAREER IN AGRICULTURE--

--WITH ONE OF THE LARGEST AND MOST LUCRATIVE FARMS IN THE ENTIRE WESTERN HEMISPHERE.

THREE YEARS AGO, BARLEY HAD AMASSED A LARGE ENOUGH FORTUNE THAT HE WAS ABLE TO RETIRE, AND HE PLANNED TO LIVE OUT THE REST OF HIS DAYS IN A MULTITUDE OF HOMES--

--ALL OF WHICH HE GREW HIMSELF.

OCCASIONALLY, HE WOULD SUPPLEMENT HIS RETIREMENT INCOME BY SELLING *SEEDS*.

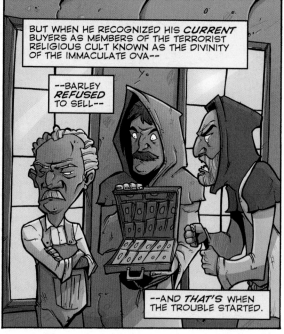

BUT WHEN HE RECOGNIZED HIS *CURRENT* BUYERS AS MEMBERS OF THE TERRORIST RELIGIOUS CULT KNOWN AS THE DIVINITY OF THE IMMACULATE OVA--

--BARLEY *REFUSED* TO SELL--

--AND *THAT'S* WHEN THE TROUBLE STARTED.

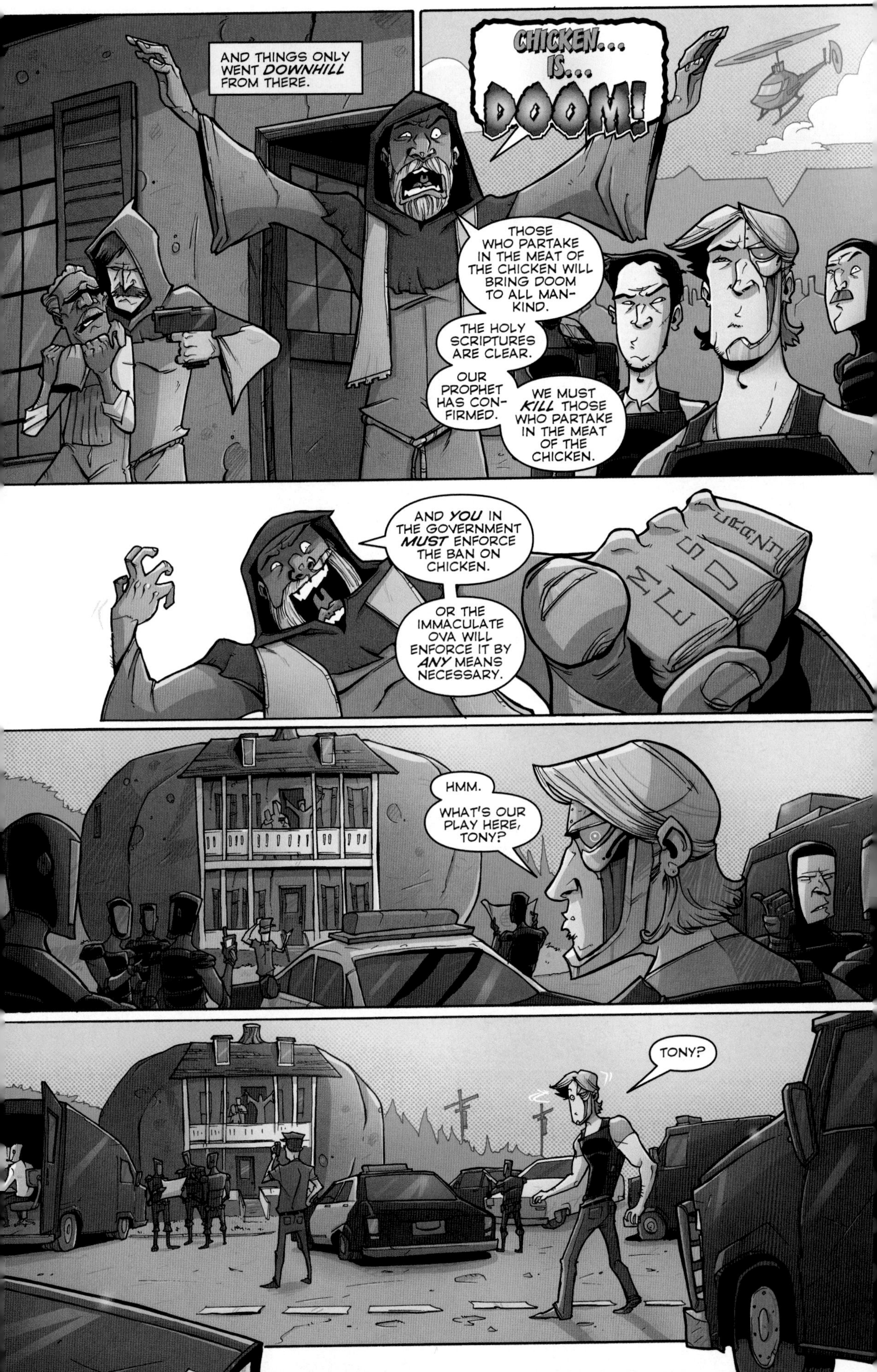
AND THINGS ONLY WENT DOWNHILL FROM THERE.
CHICKEN... IS... DOOM!
THOSE WHO PARTAKE IN THE MEAT OF THE CHICKEN WILL BRING DOOM TO ALL MAN-KIND.
THE HOLY SCRIPTURES ARE CLEAR.
OUR PROPHET HAS CON-FIRMED.
WE MUST KILL THOSE WHO PARTAKE IN THE MEAT OF THE CHICKEN.
AND YOU IN THE GOVERNMENT MUST ENFORCE THE BAN ON CHICKEN.
OR THE IMMACULATE OVA WILL ENFORCE IT BY ANY MEANS NECESSARY.
HMM.
WHAT'S OUR PLAY HERE, TONY?
TONY?

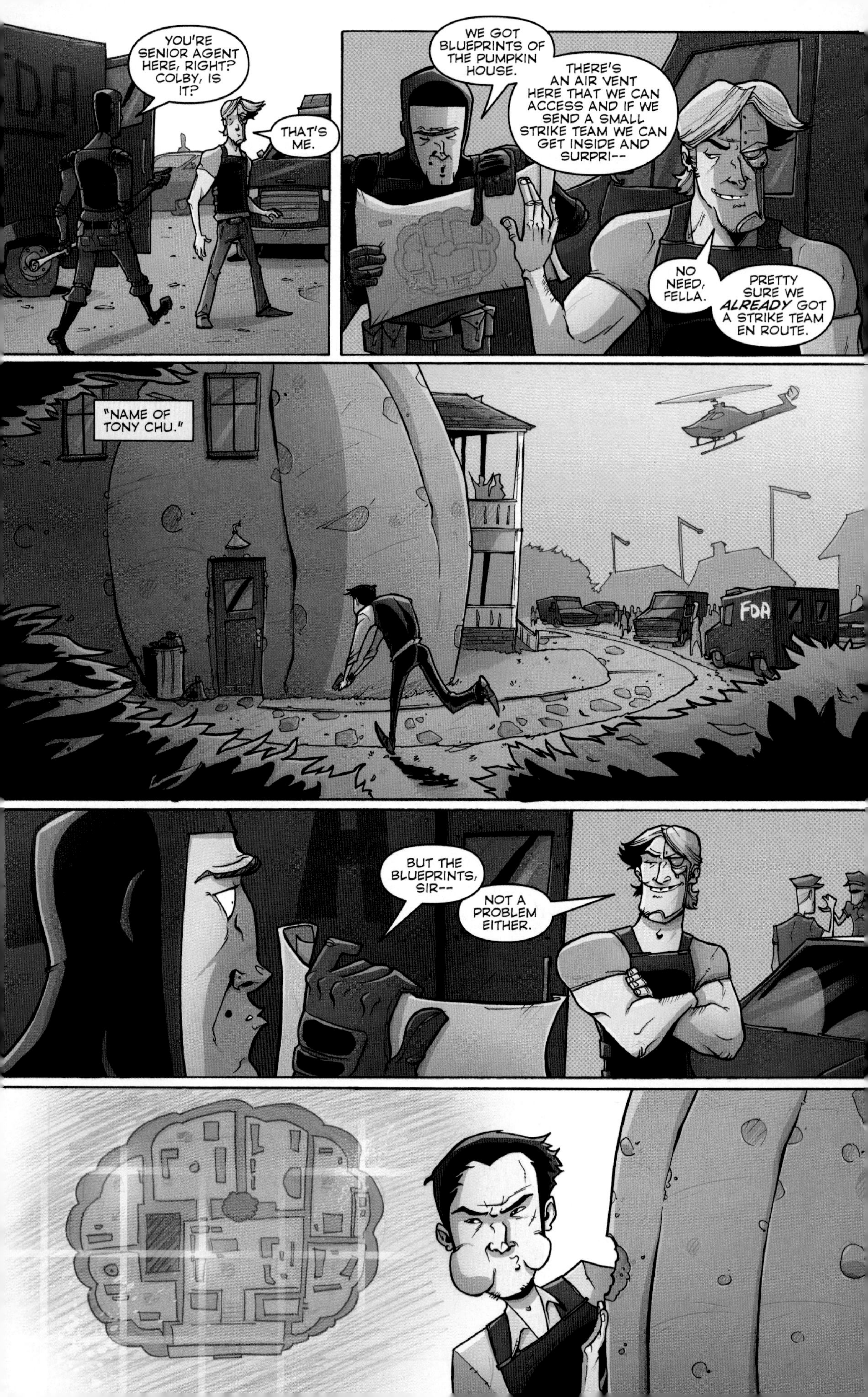
YOU'RE SENIOR AGENT HERE, RIGHT? COLBY, IS IT?
THAT'S ME.
WE GOT BLUEPRINTS OF THE PUMPKIN HOUSE.
THERE'S AN AIR VENT HERE THAT WE CAN ACCESS AND IF WE SEND A SMALL STRIKE TEAM WE CAN GET INSIDE AND SURPRI--
NO NEED, FELLA.
PRETTY SURE WE *ALREADY* GOT A STRIKE TEAM EN ROUTE.
"NAME OF TONY CHU."
FDA
BUT THE BLUEPRINTS, SIR--
NOT A PROBLEM EITHER.

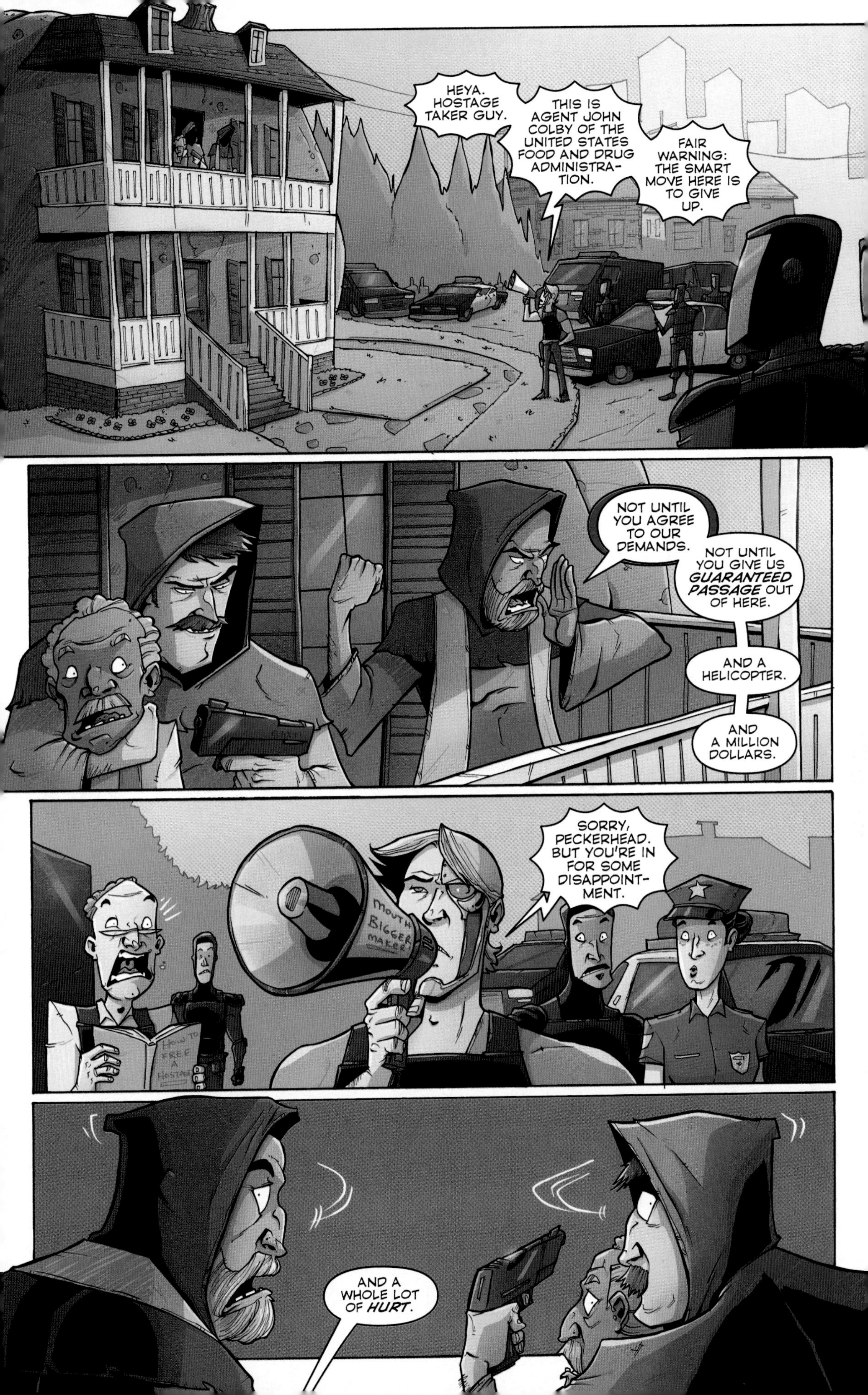
HEYA. HOSTAGE TAKER GUY.
THIS IS AGENT JOHN COLBY OF THE UNITED STATES FOOD AND DRUG ADMINISTRA-TION.
FAIR WARNING: THE SMART MOVE HERE IS TO GIVE UP.
NOT UNTIL YOU AGREE TO OUR DEMANDS.
NOT UNTIL YOU GIVE US GUARANTEED PASSAGE OUT OF HERE.
AND A HELICOPTER.
AND A MILLION DOLLARS.
MOUTH BIGGER MAKER
HOW TO FREE A HOSTAGE
SORRY, PECKERHEAD. BUT YOU'RE IN FOR SOME DISAPPOINT-MENT.
AND A WHOLE LOT OF HURT.

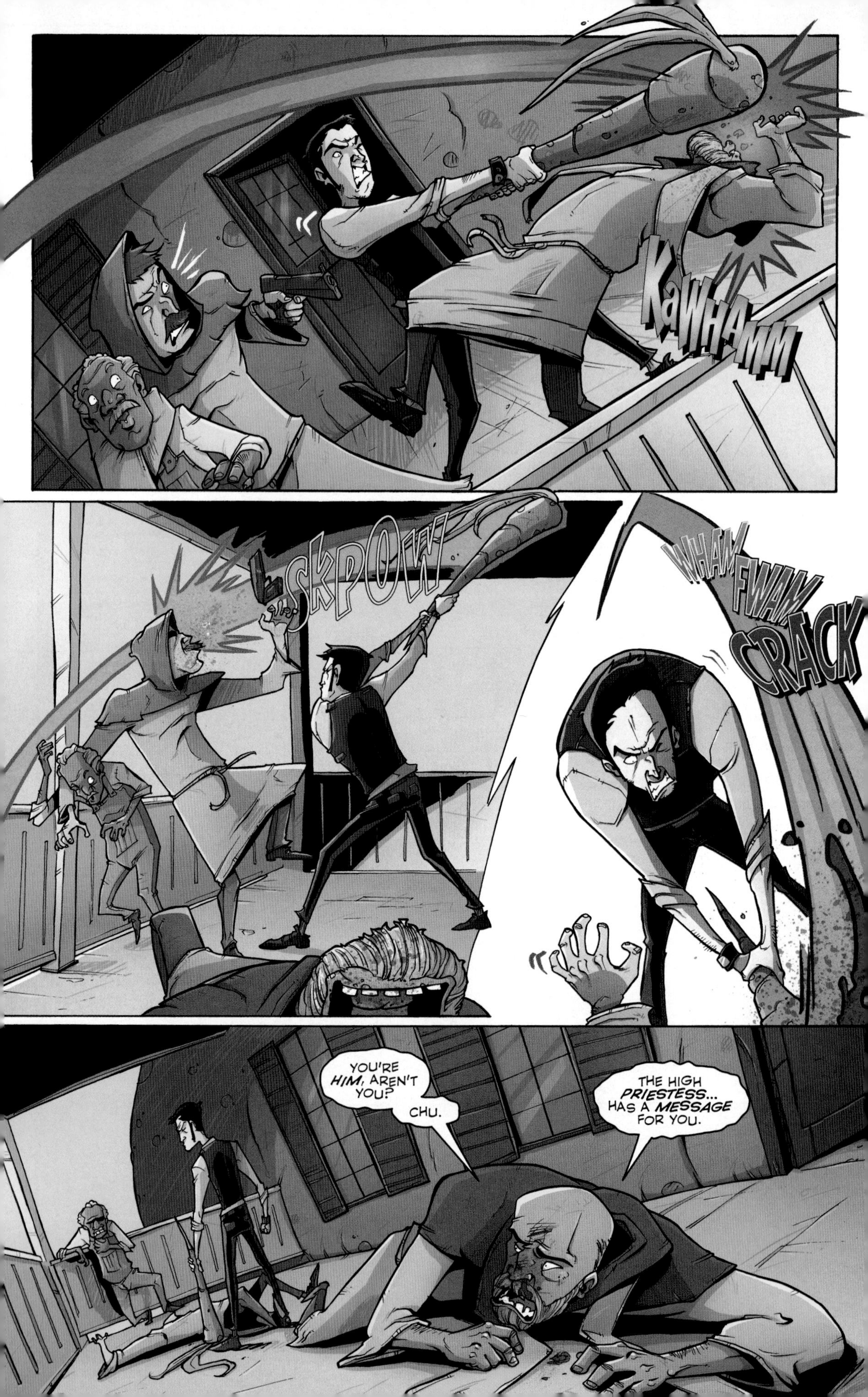
KaWHAMM
SKPOW
WHAM
FWAM
CRACK
YOU'RE *HIM*, AREN'T YOU?
CHU.
THE HIGH *PRIESTESS*... HAS A *MESSAGE* FOR YOU.

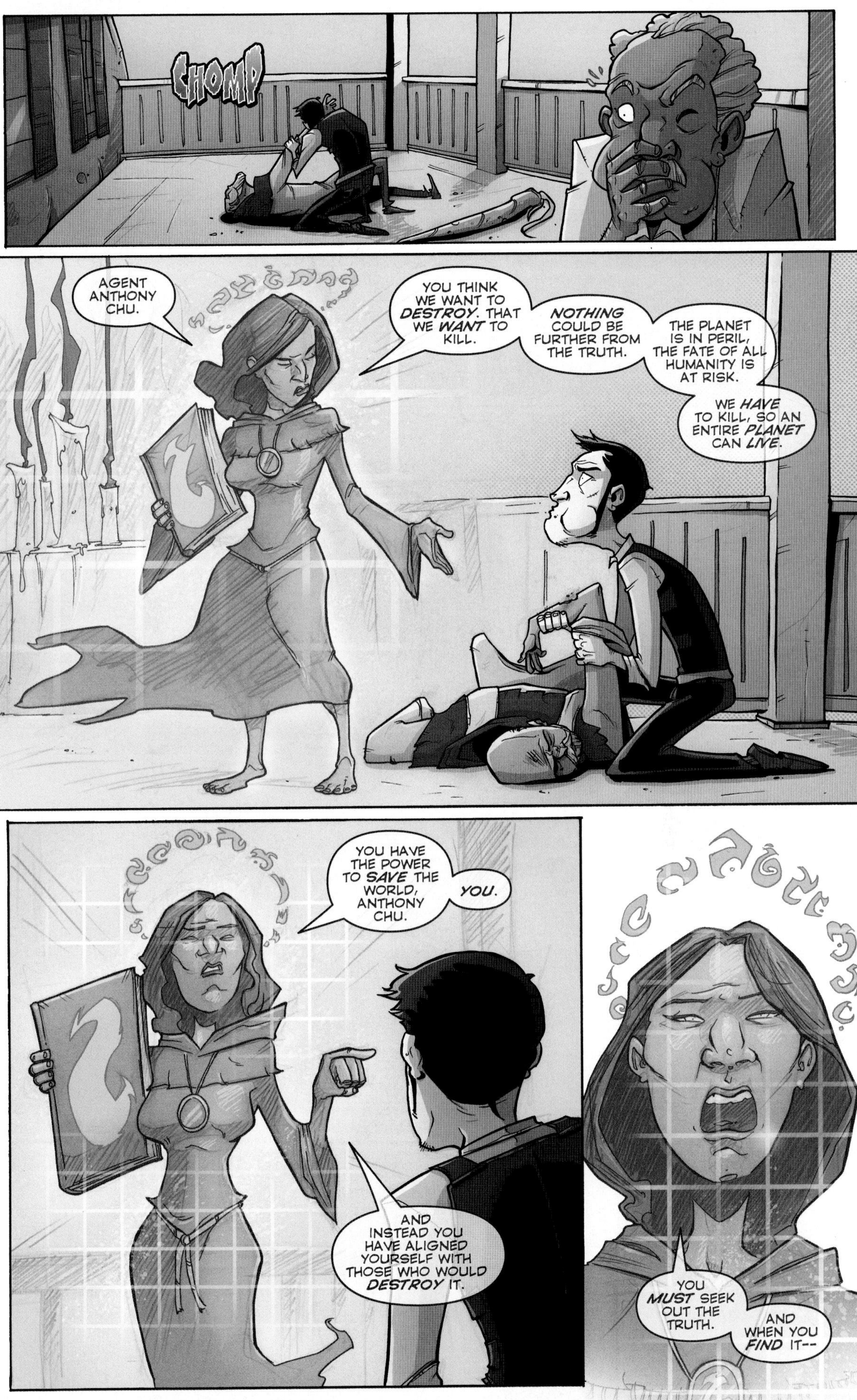

CHOMP
AGENT ANTHONY CHU.
YOU THINK WE WANT TO DESTROY. THAT WE WANT TO KILL.
NOTHING COULD BE FURTHER FROM THE TRUTH.
THE PLANET IS IN PERIL, THE FATE OF ALL HUMANITY IS AT RISK.
WE HAVE TO KILL, SO AN ENTIRE PLANET CAN LIVE.
YOU HAVE THE POWER TO SAVE THE WORLD, ANTHONY CHU.
YOU.
AND INSTEAD YOU HAVE ALIGNED YOURSELF WITH THOSE WHO WOULD DESTROY IT.
YOU MUST SEEK OUT THE TRUTH.
AND WHEN YOU FIND IT--

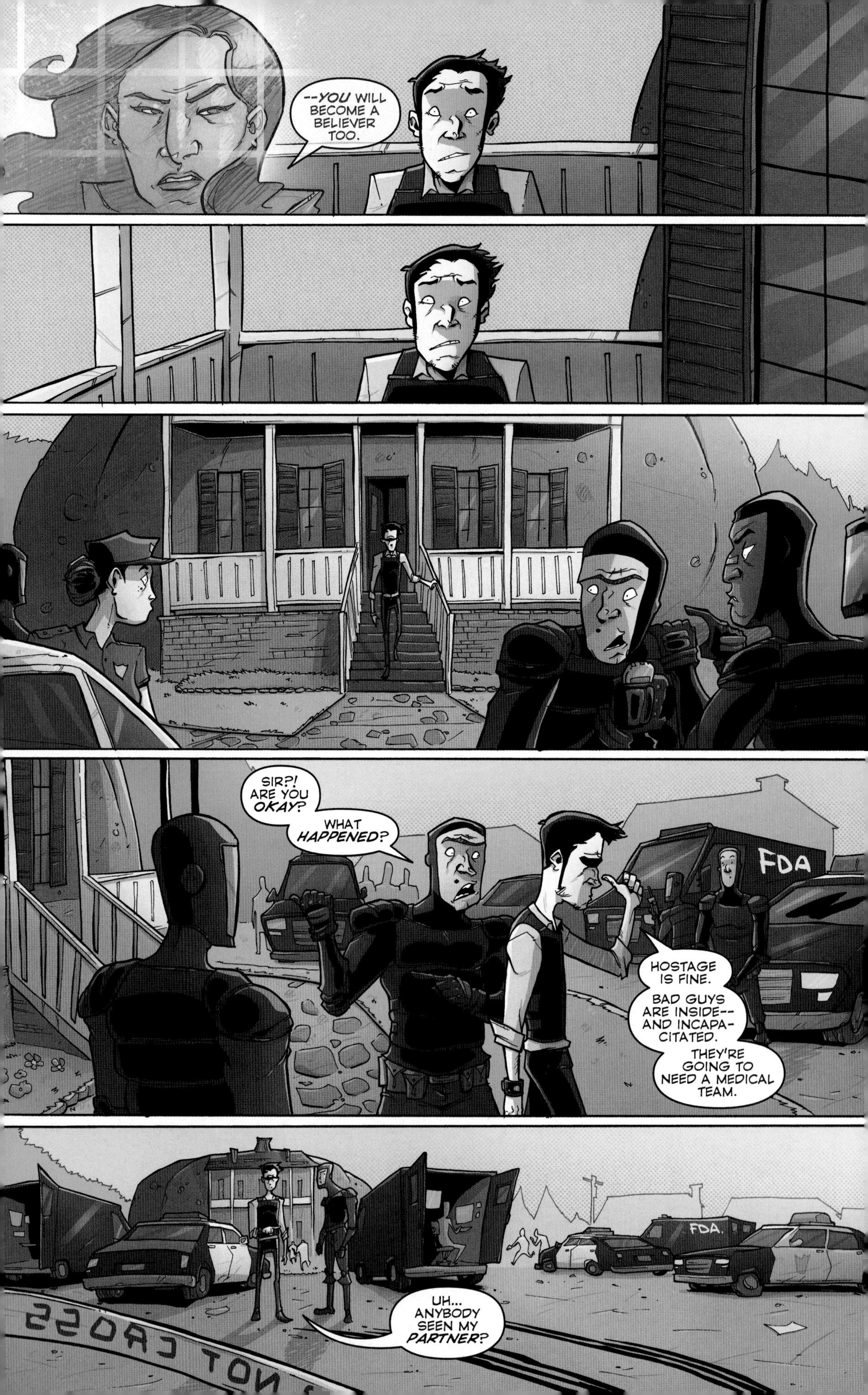
--YOU WILL BECOME A BELIEVER TOO.
SIR?! ARE YOU OKAY?
WHAT HAPPENED?
HOSTAGE IS FINE.
BAD GUYS ARE INSIDE-- AND INCAPACITATED.
THEY'RE GOING TO NEED A MEDICAL TEAM.
FDA
FDA.
NOT CROSS
UH... ANYBODY SEEN MY PARTNER?

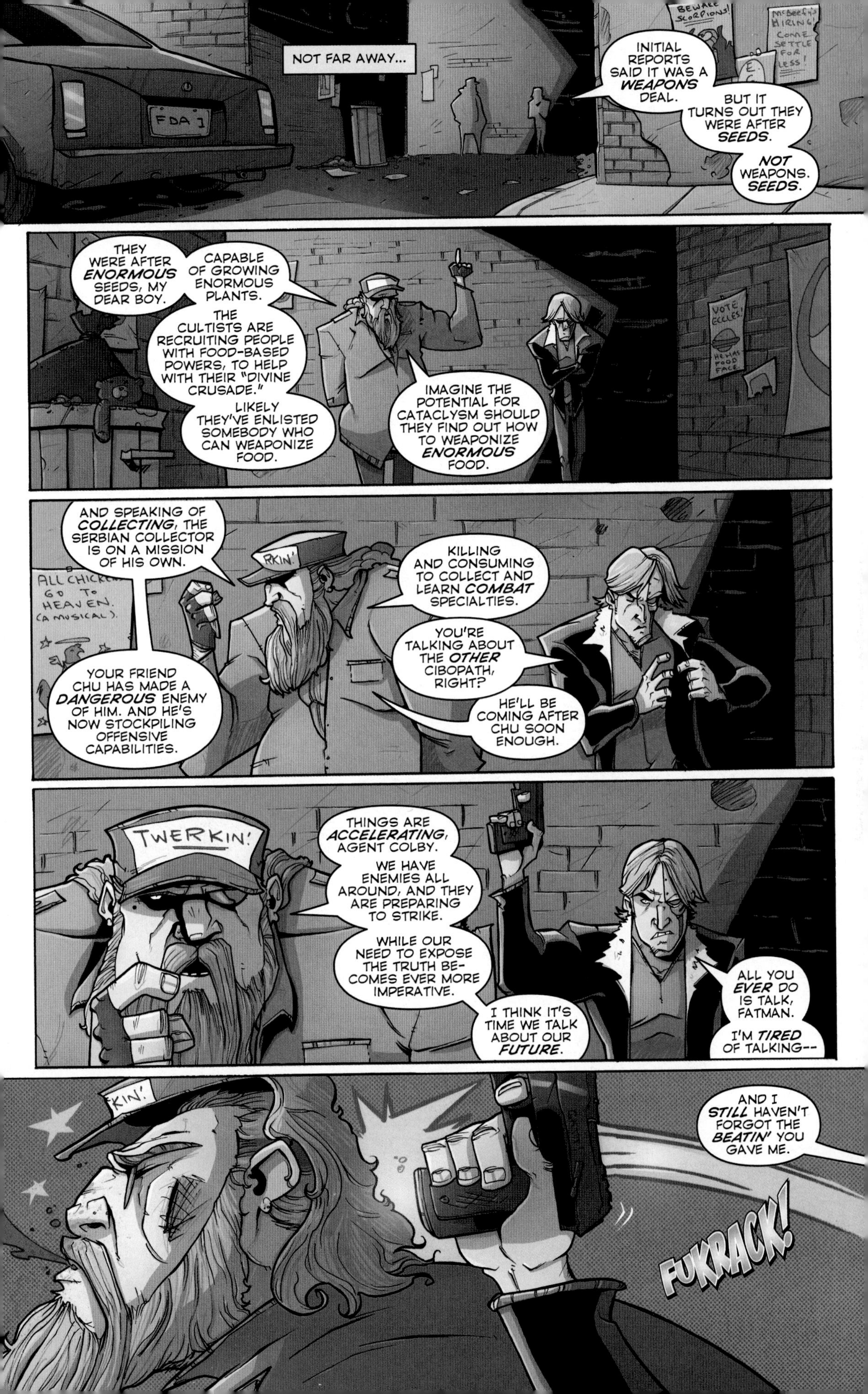

NOT FAR AWAY...
FDA 1
BEWARE SCORPIONS!
McBeefy's HIRING! COME SETTLE FOR LESS!
INITIAL REPORTS SAID IT WAS A WEAPONS DEAL.
BUT IT TURNS OUT THEY WERE AFTER SEEDS.
NOT WEAPONS. SEEDS.
THEY WERE AFTER ENORMOUS SEEDS, MY DEAR BOY.
CAPABLE OF GROWING ENORMOUS PLANTS.
THE CULTISTS ARE RECRUITING PEOPLE WITH FOOD-BASED POWERS, TO HELP WITH THEIR "DIVINE CRUSADE."
LIKELY THEY'VE ENLISTED SOMEBODY WHO CAN WEAPONIZE FOOD.
IMAGINE THE POTENTIAL FOR CATACLYSM SHOULD THEY FIND OUT HOW TO WEAPONIZE ENORMOUS FOOD.
VOTE ECCLES! HE HAS FOOD FACE.
AND SPEAKING OF COLLECTING, THE SERBIAN COLLECTOR IS ON A MISSION OF HIS OWN.
ALL CHICKEN GO TO HEAVEN. (A MUSICAL).
KILLING AND CONSUMING TO COLLECT AND LEARN COMBAT SPECIALTIES.
YOUR FRIEND CHU HAS MADE A DANGEROUS ENEMY OF HIM. AND HE'S NOW STOCKPILING OFFENSIVE CAPABILITIES.
YOU'RE TALKING ABOUT THE OTHER CIBOPATH, RIGHT?
HE'LL BE COMING AFTER CHU SOON ENOUGH.
TWERKIN'
THINGS ARE ACCELERATING, AGENT COLBY.
WE HAVE ENEMIES ALL AROUND, AND THEY ARE PREPARING TO STRIKE.
WHILE OUR NEED TO EXPOSE THE TRUTH BECOMES EVER MORE IMPERATIVE.
I THINK IT'S TIME WE TALK ABOUT OUR FUTURE.
ALL YOU EVER DO IS TALK, FATMAN.
I'M TIRED OF TALKING--
AND I STILL HAVEN'T FORGOT THE BEATIN' YOU GAVE ME.
FUKRACK!

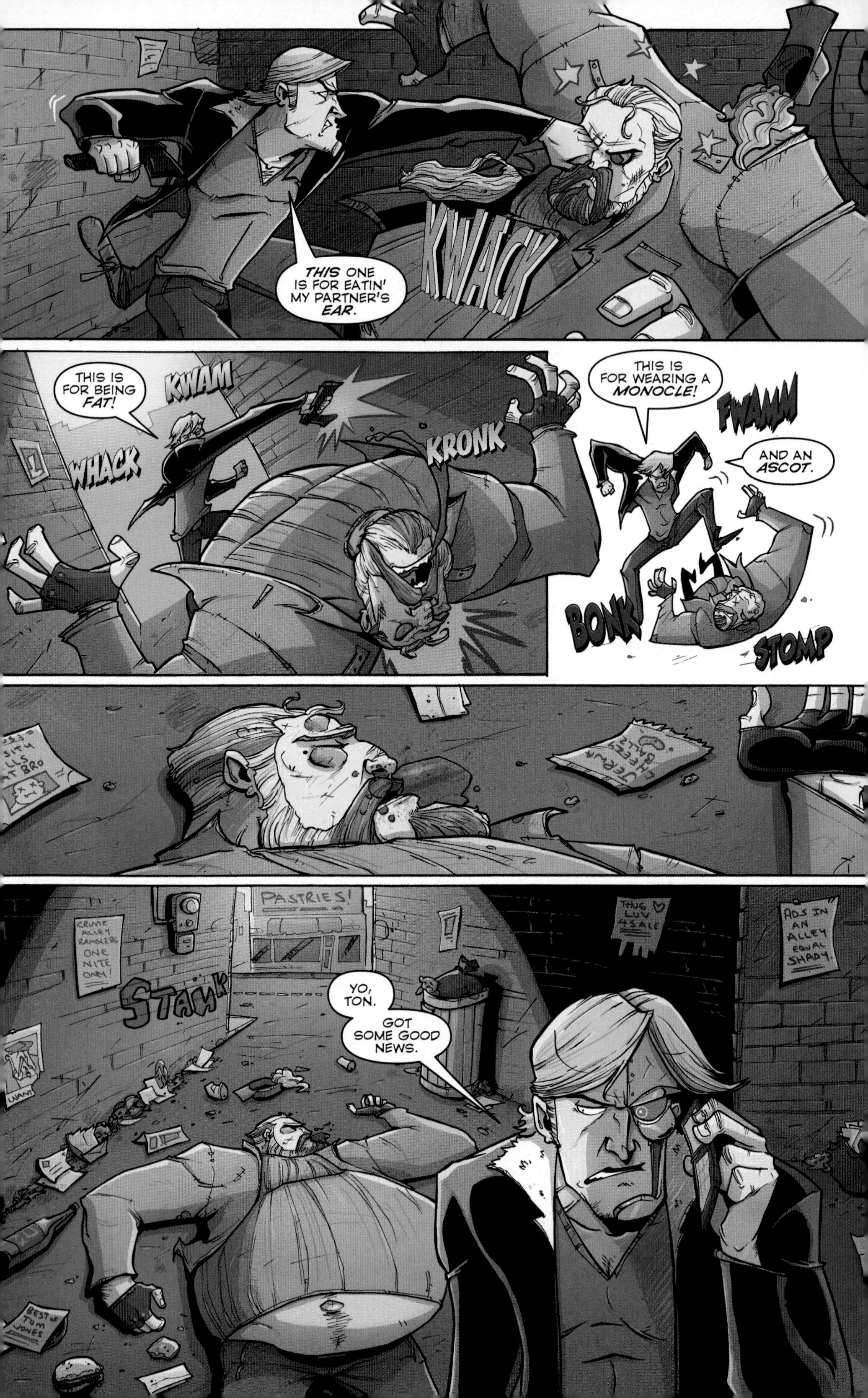
THIS ONE IS FOR EATIN' MY PARTNER'S EAR.
KWACK
THIS IS FOR BEING FAT!
KWAM
WHACK
KRONK
THIS IS FOR WEARING A MONOCLE!
FWAMM
AND AN ASCOT.
BONK
STOMP
CRIME ALLEY RAMBLERS ONE NITE ONLY!
PASTRIES!
THUG LUV 4 SALE
ADS IN AN ALLEY EQUAL SHADY
STANK
YO, TON.
GOT SOME GOOD NEWS.
BEST OF TOM JONES

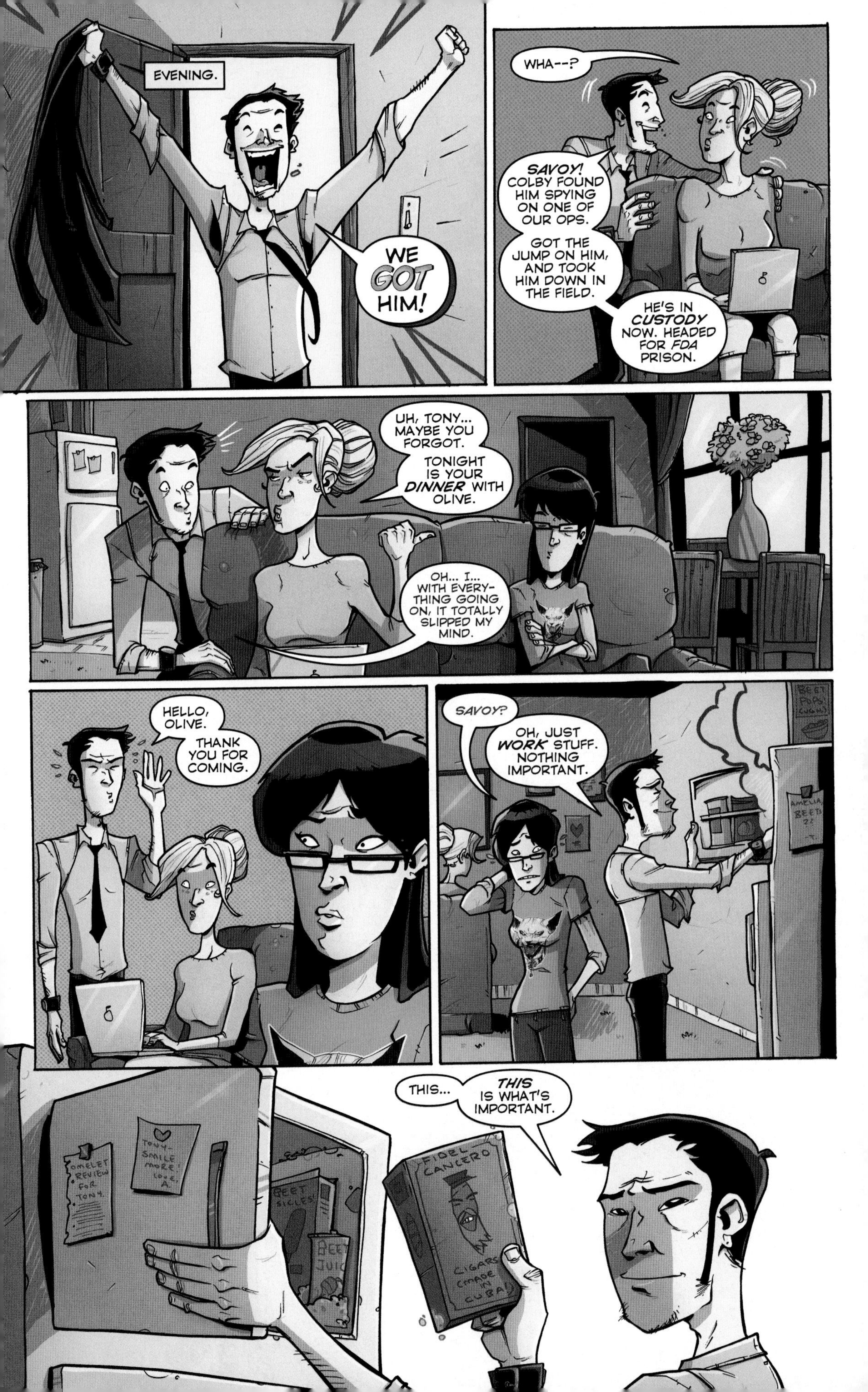

EVENING.
WE GOT HIM!
WHA--?
SAVOY! COLBY FOUND HIM SPYING ON ONE OF OUR OPS.
GOT THE JUMP ON HIM, AND TOOK HIM DOWN IN THE FIELD.
HE'S IN CUSTODY NOW. HEADED FOR FDA PRISON.
UH, TONY... MAYBE YOU FORGOT.
TONIGHT IS YOUR DINNER WITH OLIVE.
OH... I... WITH EVERY-THING GOING ON, IT TOTALLY SLIPPED MY MIND.
HELLO, OLIVE.
THANK YOU FOR COMING.
SAVOY?
OH, JUST WORK STUFF. NOTHING IMPORTANT.
THIS...
THIS IS WHAT'S IMPORTANT.
OMELET REVIEW FOR TONY.
TONY- SMILE MORE! LOVE, A.
FIDEL CANCERO
CIGARS (MADE IN CUBA)

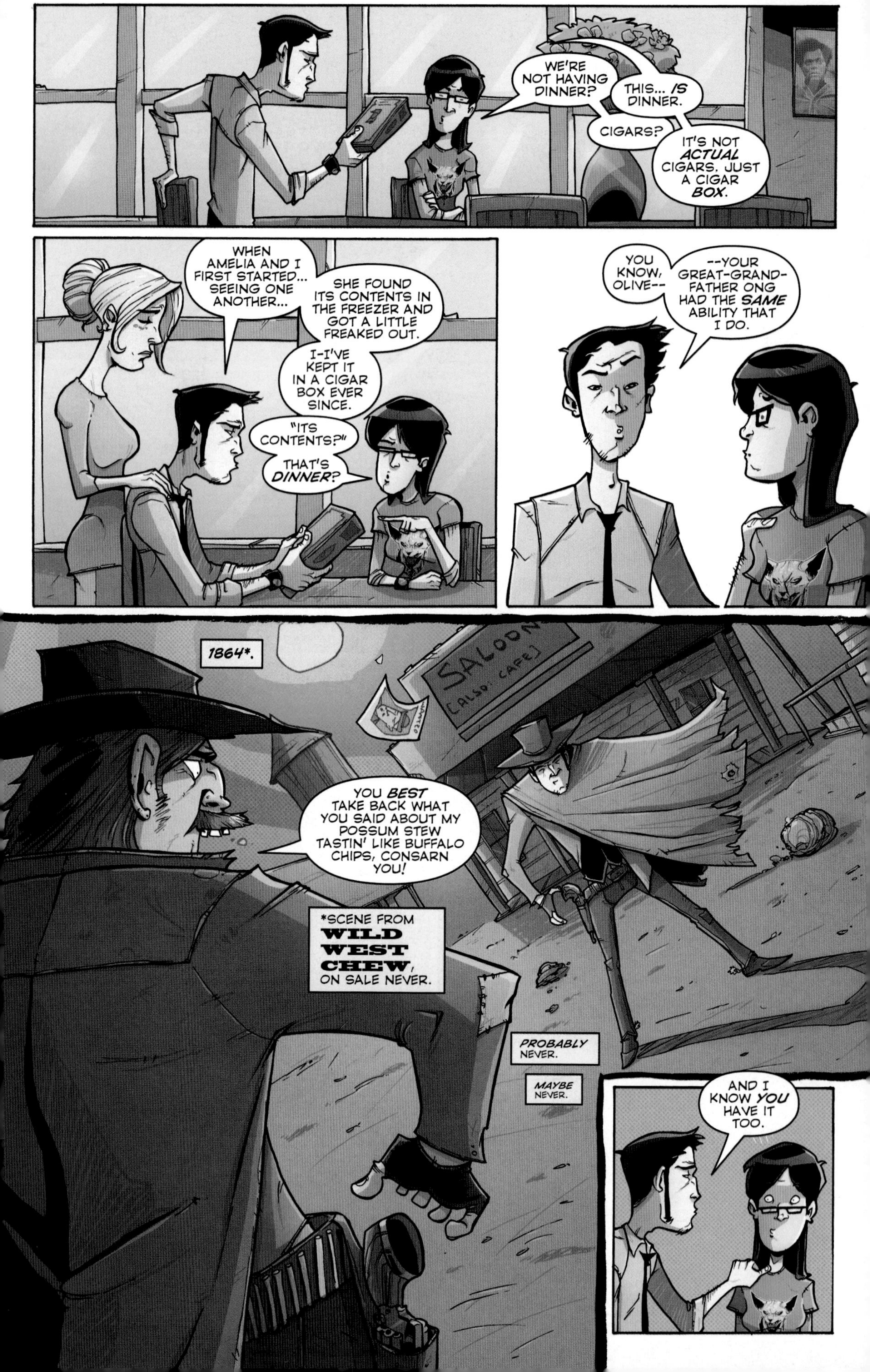
WE'RE NOT HAVING DINNER?
THIS... IS DINNER.
CIGARS?
IT'S NOT ACTUAL CIGARS. JUST A CIGAR BOX.
WHEN AMELIA AND I FIRST STARTED... SEEING ONE ANOTHER...
SHE FOUND ITS CONTENTS IN THE FREEZER AND GOT A LITTLE FREAKED OUT.
I-I'VE KEPT IT IN A CIGAR BOX EVER SINCE.
"ITS CONTENTS?"
THAT'S DINNER?
YOU KNOW, OLIVE--
--YOUR GREAT-GRAND-FATHER ONG HAD THE SAME ABILITY THAT I DO.
1864*.
SALOON (ALSO: CAFE)
YOU BEST TAKE BACK WHAT YOU SAID ABOUT MY POSSUM STEW TASTIN' LIKE BUFFALO CHIPS, CONSARN YOU!
*SCENE FROM WILD WEST CHEW, ON SALE NEVER.
PROBABLY NEVER.
MAYBE NEVER.
AND I KNOW YOU HAVE IT TOO.

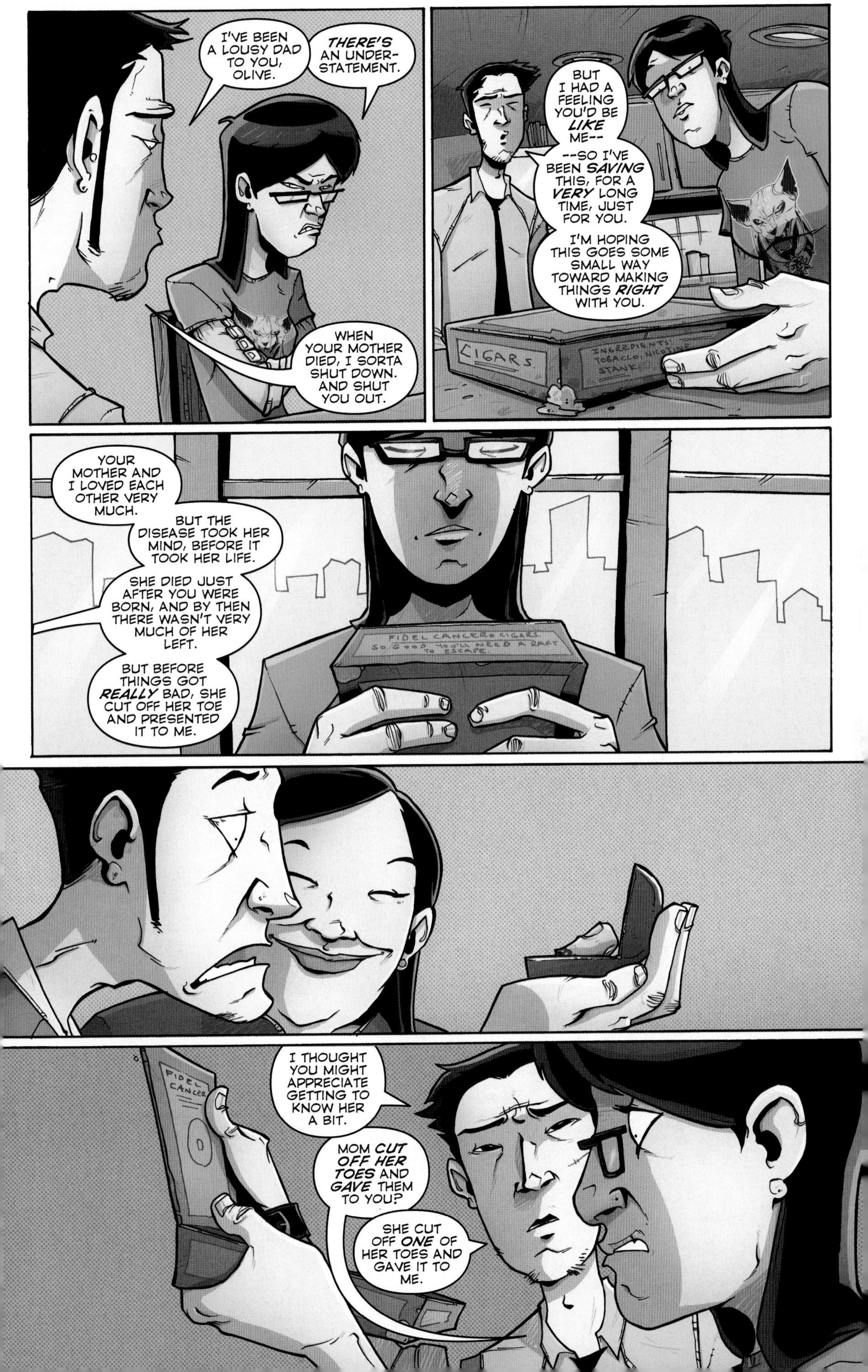
I'VE BEEN A LOUSY DAD TO YOU, OLIVE.
THERE'S AN UNDER-STATEMENT.
WHEN YOUR MOTHER DIED, I SORTA SHUT DOWN. AND SHUT YOU OUT.
BUT I HAD A FEELING YOU'D BE LIKE ME--
--SO I'VE BEEN SAVING THIS, FOR A VERY LONG TIME, JUST FOR YOU.
I'M HOPING THIS GOES SOME SMALL WAY TOWARD MAKING THINGS RIGHT WITH YOU.
CIGARS.
YOUR MOTHER AND I LOVED EACH OTHER VERY MUCH.
BUT THE DISEASE TOOK HER MIND, BEFORE IT TOOK HER LIFE.
SHE DIED JUST AFTER YOU WERE BORN, AND BY THEN THERE WASN'T VERY MUCH OF HER LEFT.
BUT BEFORE THINGS GOT REALLY BAD, SHE CUT OFF HER TOE AND PRESENTED IT TO ME.
FIDEL CANCERO CIGARS
I THOUGHT YOU MIGHT APPRECIATE GETTING TO KNOW HER A BIT.
MOM CUT OFF HER TOES AND GAVE THEM TO YOU?
SHE CUT OFF ONE OF HER TOES AND GAVE IT TO ME.

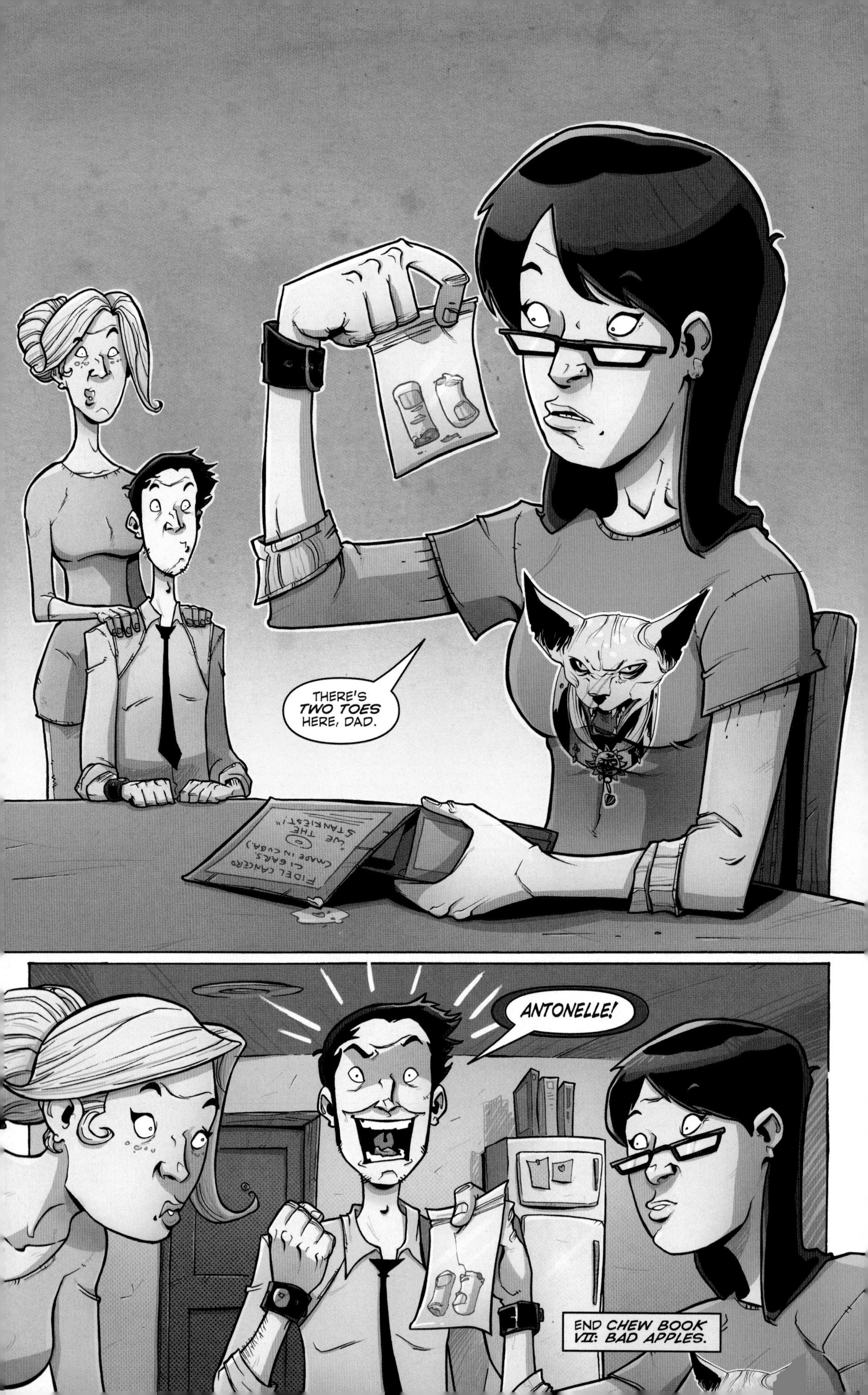
THERE'S TWO TOES HERE, DAD.
FIDEL CANCERO CIGARS. (MADE IN CUBA.)
"WE THE STANKIEST!"
ANTONELLE!
END CHEW BOOK VII: BAD APPLES.

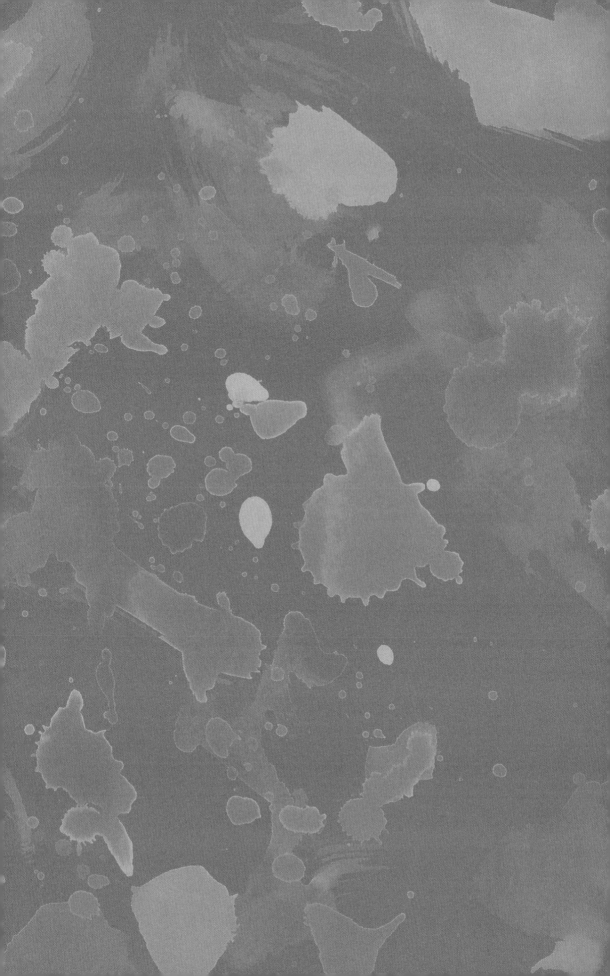

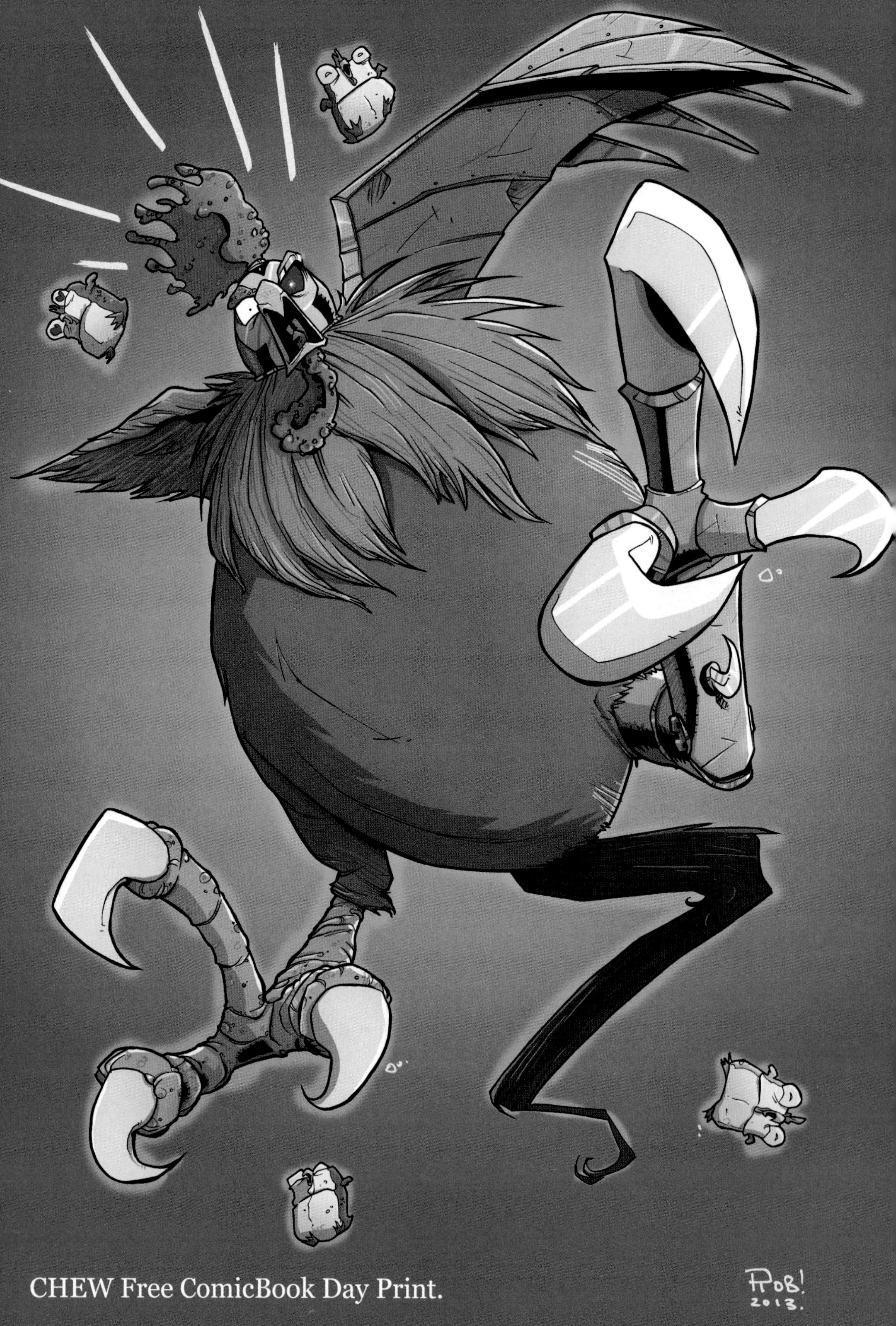
ROB!
2013.

CHEW Free ComicBook Day Print.

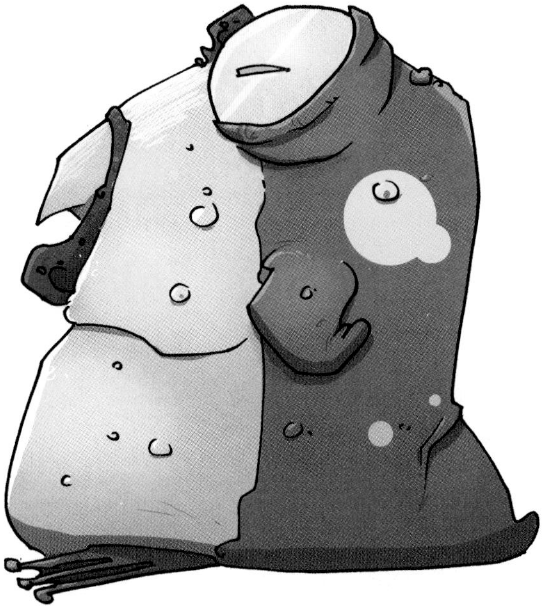

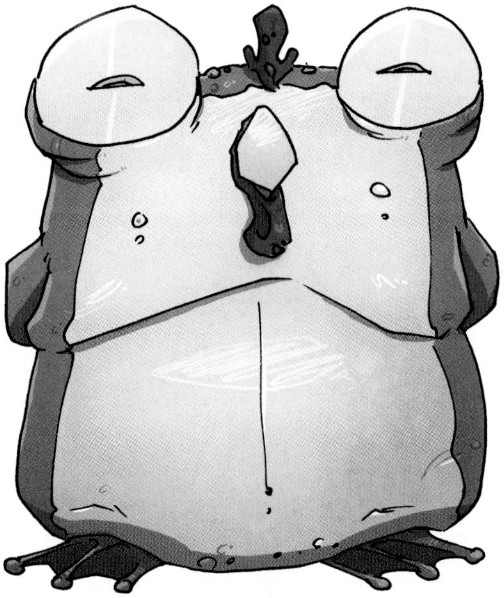

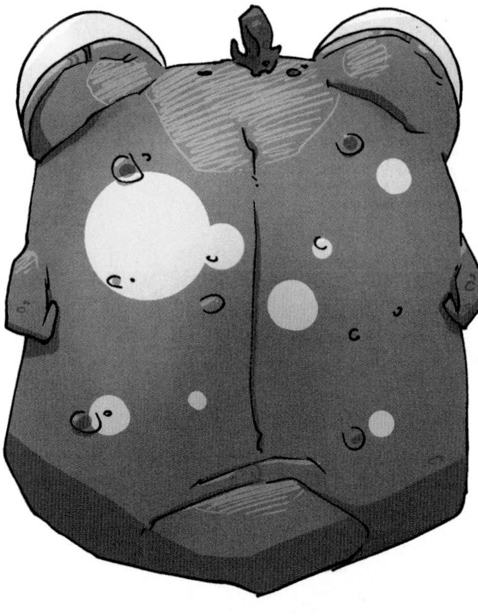

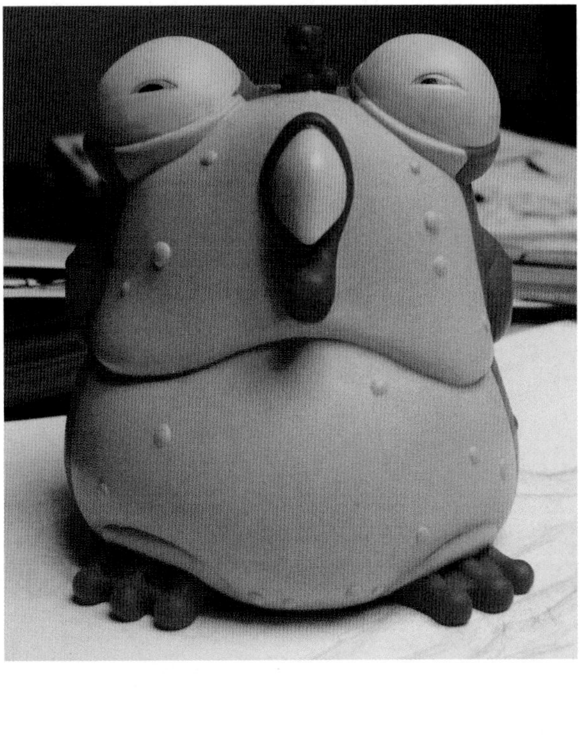

Concept drawings for a CHOG Vinyl figure.
Final Vinyl Product by Skelton Crew Studio.
(www.skeltoncrewstudio.com)

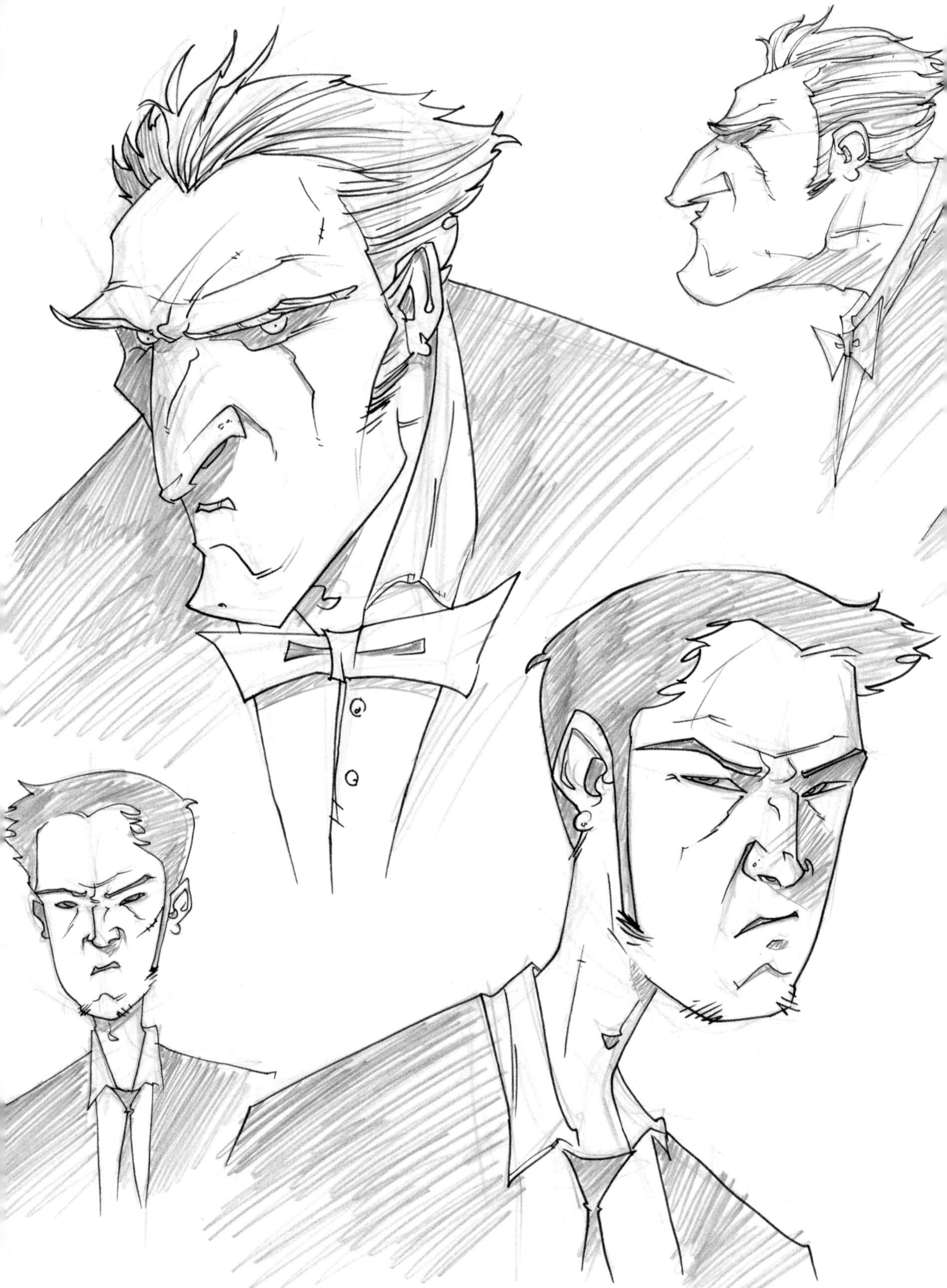

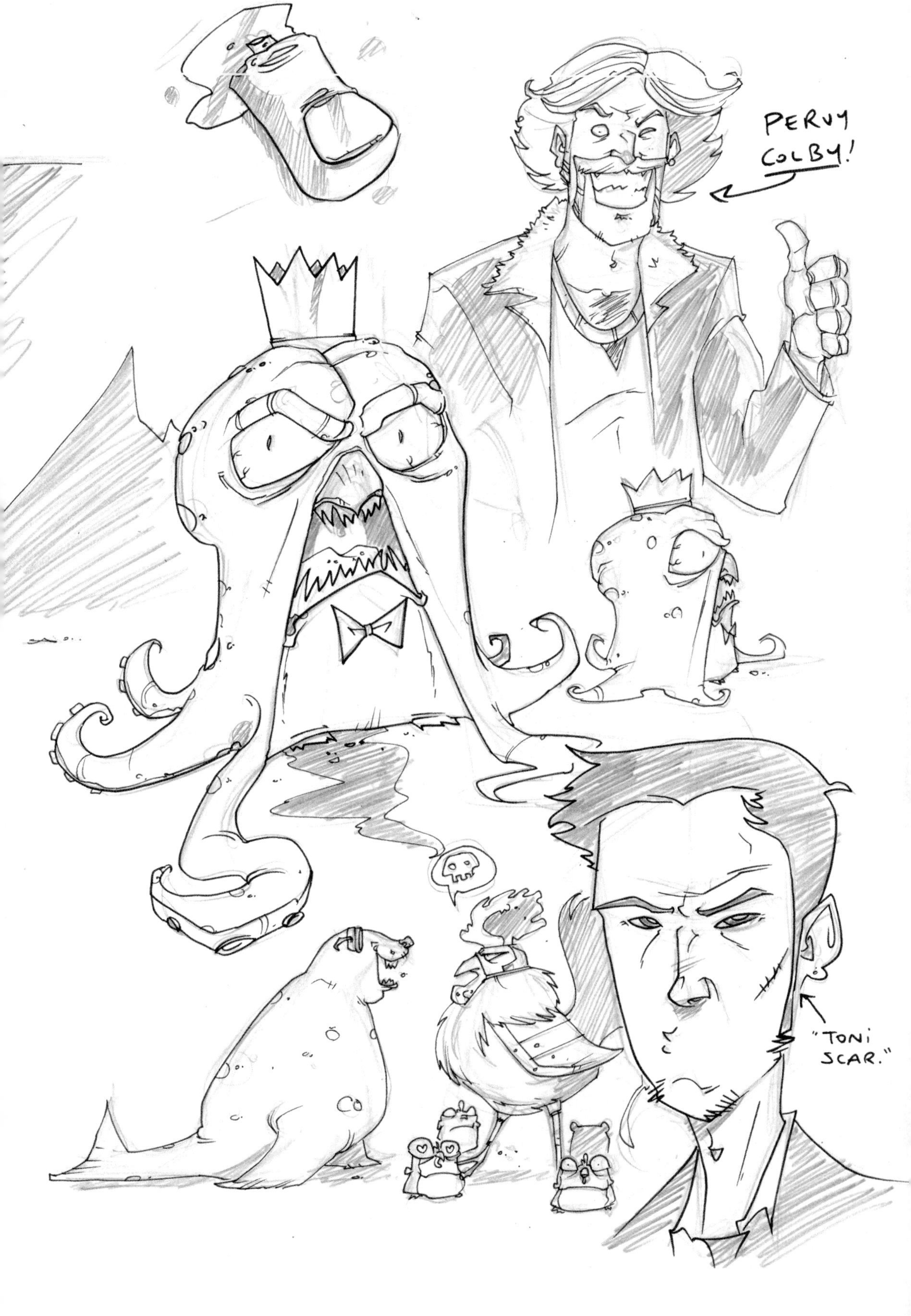
PERVY COLBY!
"TONI SCAR."

Random Sketchbook page.

#34 “unmixed” Tony cover

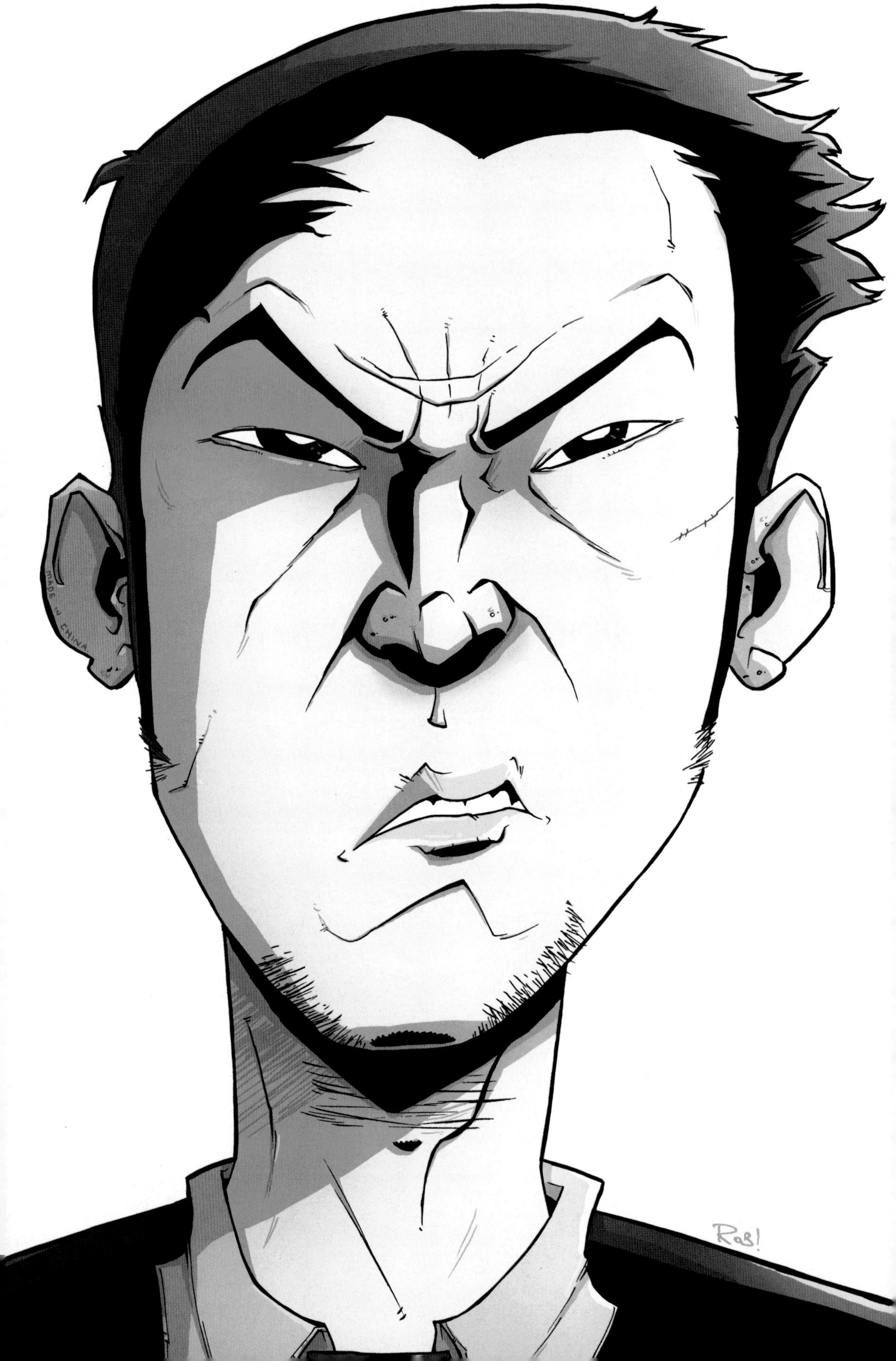

#34 "unmixed" Savoy cover

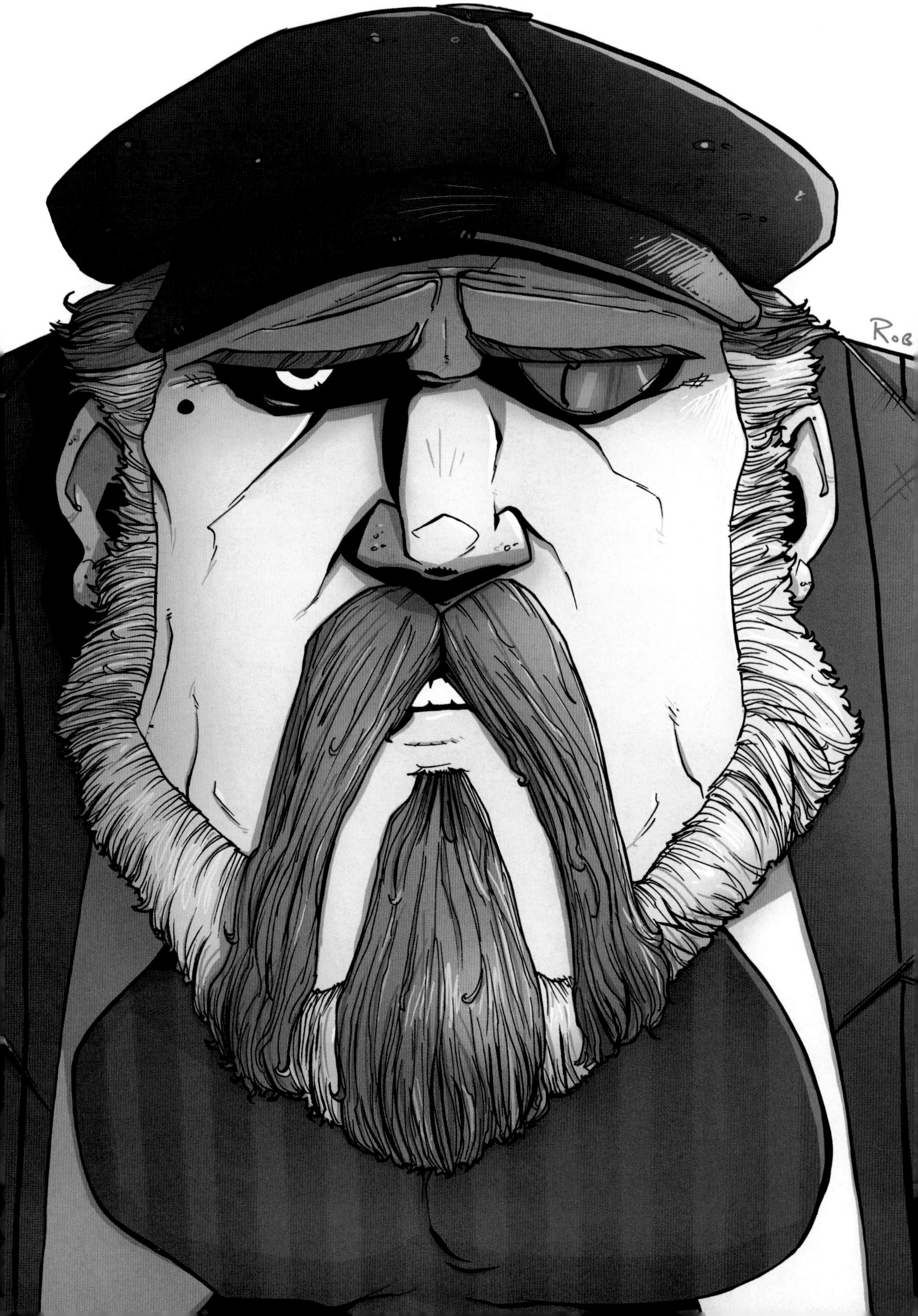

#34 "unmixed" Vampire cover

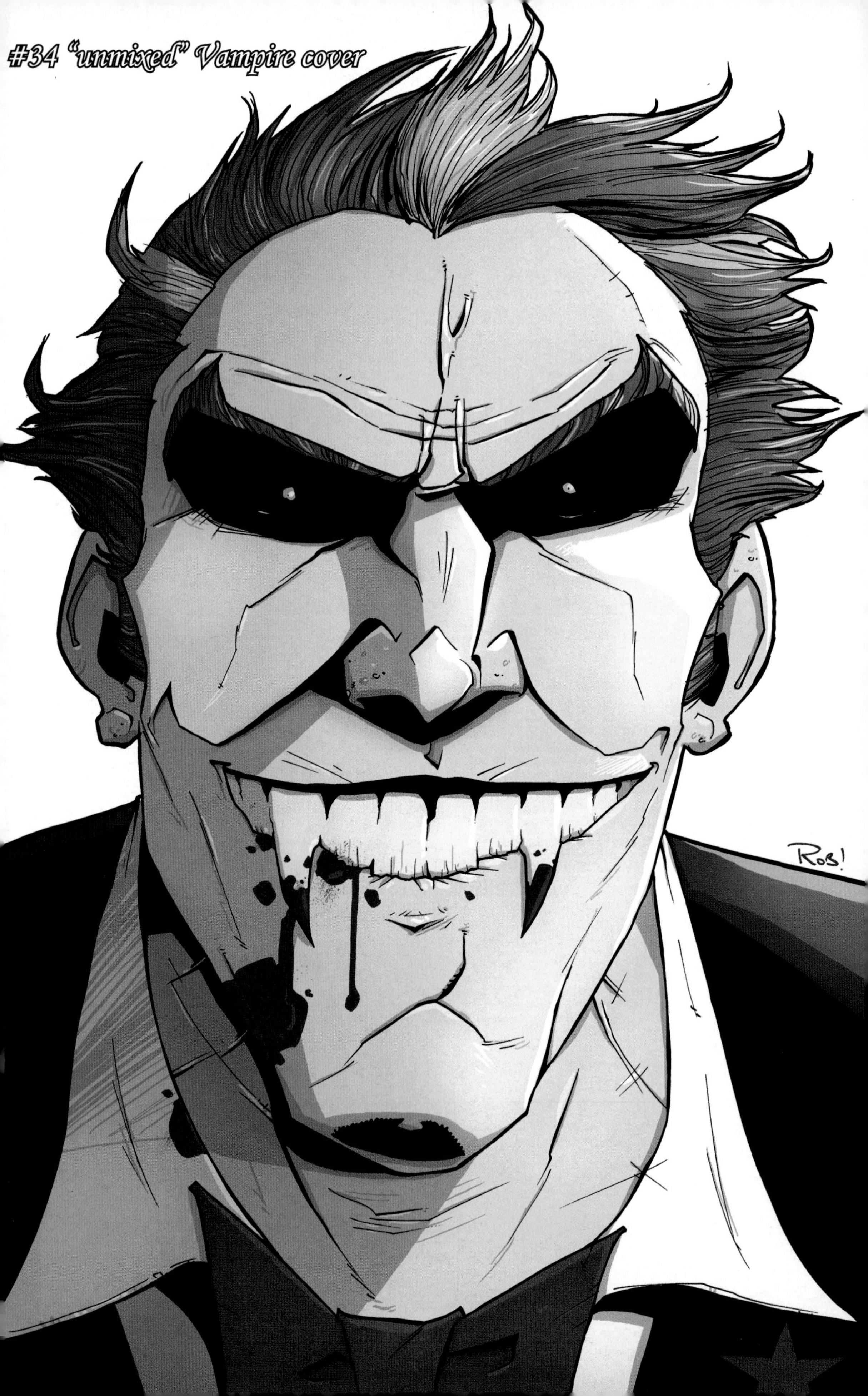
ROB!

Chew/Mars Attacks cover

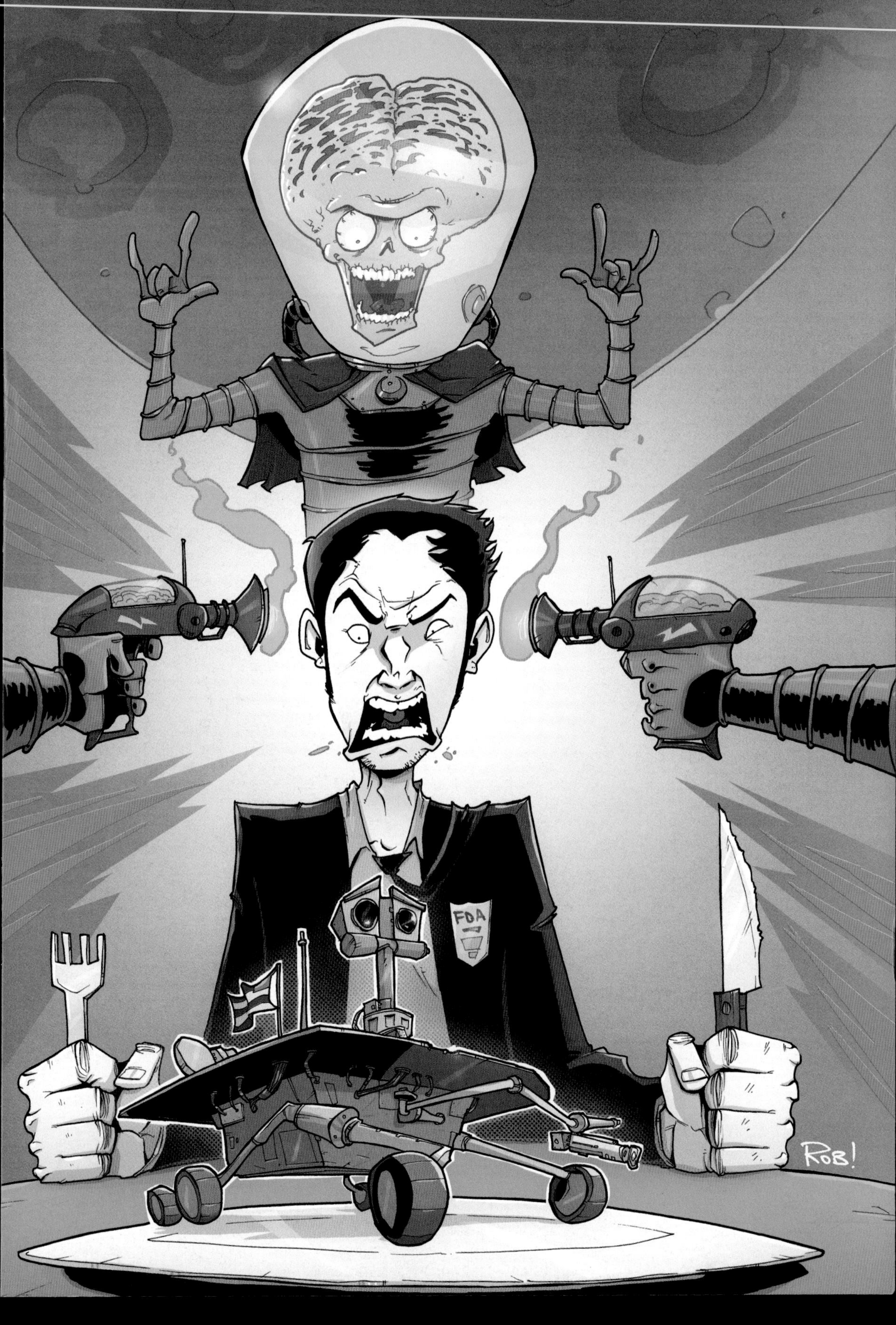

FDA
ROB!

JOHN LAYMAN

Poor Old Layman. So much sadness in his life.

Layman has three cats, Rufus, Ash and Ruby. They bring him much sadness.

*And yet, Layman persists. He does so at **Laymanlegoproject.tumblr.com**. He does so for you.*

ROB GUILLORY

Rob Guillory is based in Lafayette, Louisiana. He has a wife, a two-year-old manchild and several needy cats. He likes naps, but doesn't get to take them often. It kinda sucks, too. Because he has this nifty futon in his studio.

***RobGuillory.com** and **RobGuilloryStore.com** are his sites.*

ChewComic.com
For Original Art Sales, please visit
RobGuilloryStore.com.